PENGUIN BOOKS

DRAGONLANCE® PRELUDES
Volume 3
BROTHERS MAJERE

Known as the Man in Black, Kevin Stein has a degree in English and has studied in England and America. When he's not writing, Kevin enjoys dancing, the company of friends, and Chicago in the springtime.

PRELUDES

VOLUME THREE

Brothers Majere

Kevin Stein

Cover Art
JEFF EASLEY

Interior Illustrations
TOM BAXA

PENGUIN BOOKS
in association with TSR, Inc.

PENGUIN BOOKS

Published by the Penguin Group
27 Wrights Lane, London W8 5TZ, England
Viking Penguin Inc., 40 West 23rd Street, New York, New York 10010. USA
Penguin Books Australia Ltd, Ringwood, Victoria, Australia
Penguin Books Canada Ltd, 2801 John Street, Markham, Ontario, Canada L3R 1B4
Penguin Books (NZ) Ltd, 182–190 Wairau Road, Auckland 10, New Zealand

Penguin Books Ltd, Registered Offices: Harmondsworth, Middlesex, England

First published in the USA by TSR, Inc. 1990
Distributed to the book trade in the USA by Random House, Inc. and in Canada by
Random House of Canada Ltd
Distributed to the toy and hobby trade by regional distributors
Published in Penguin Books 1990
1 3 5 7 9 10 8 6 4 2

Printed and bound in Great Britain by
Cox & Wyman Ltd, Reading

I was about to dedicate this book to Rett, when suddenly . . . .

Map of

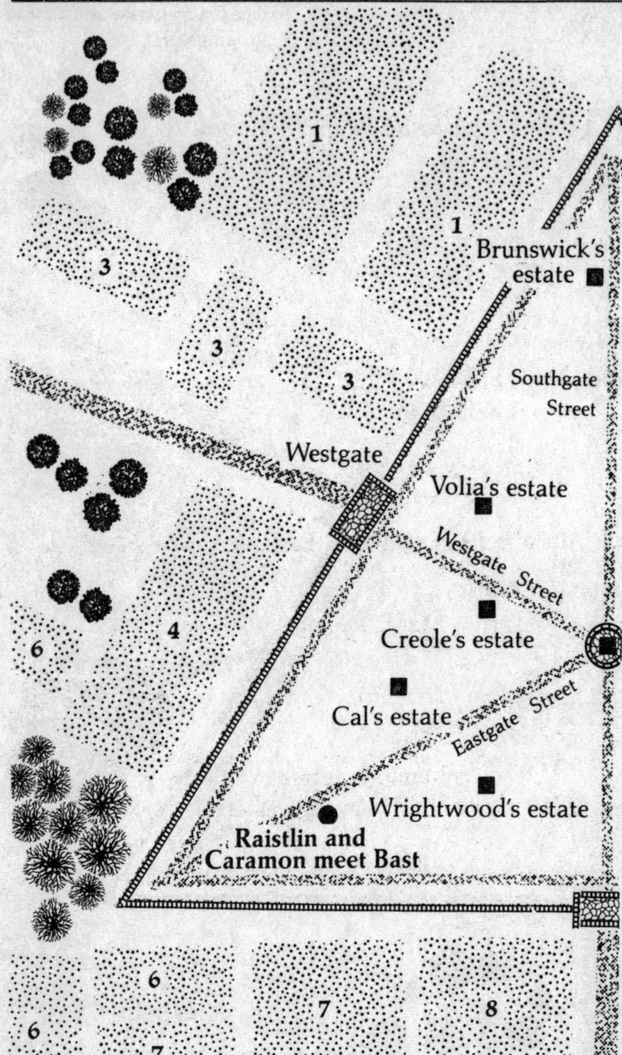
1
1
3
3
3
Brunswick's estate
Southgate Street
Westgate
Volia's estate
Westgate Street
4
6
Creole's estate
Cal's estate
Eastgate Street
Wrightwood's estate
Raistlin and Caramon meet Bast
6
6
7
7
8

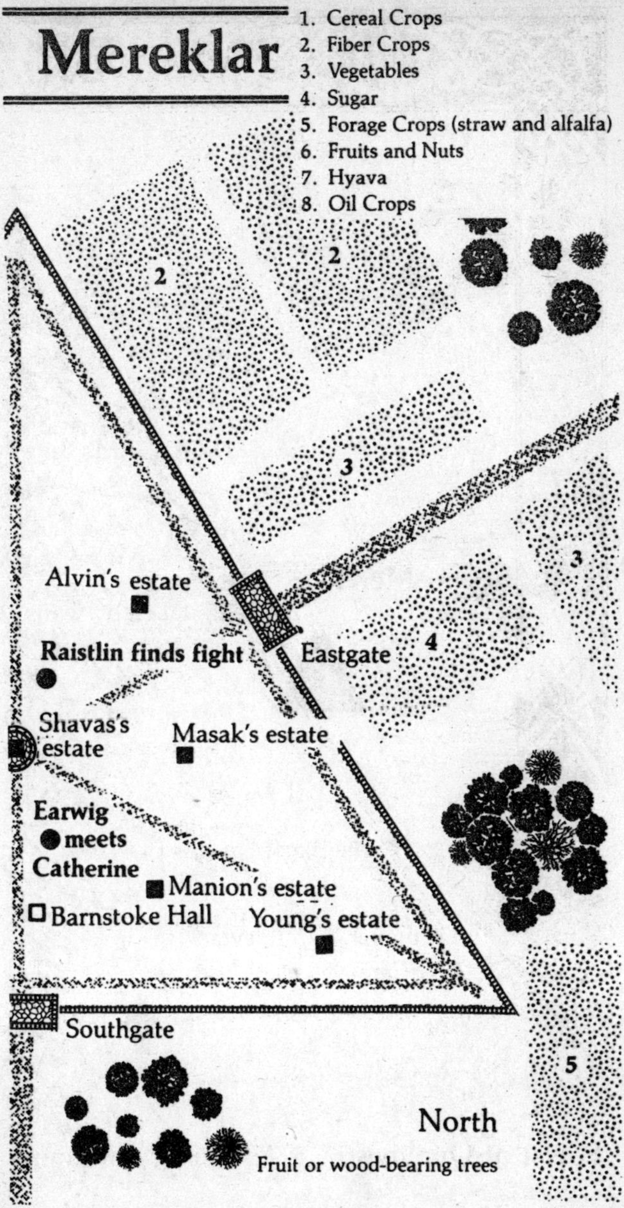

Mereklar

1. Cereal Crops
2. Fiber Crops
3. Vegetables
4. Sugar
5. Forage Crops (straw and alfalfa)
6. Fruits and Nuts
7. Hyava
8. Oil Crops

2

2

3

3

4

Alvin's estate

Raistlin finds fight

Eastgate

Shavas's estate

Masak's estate

Earwig meets Catherine

Manion's estate

Barnstoke Hall

Young's estate

Southgate

5

North

Fruit or wood-bearing trees

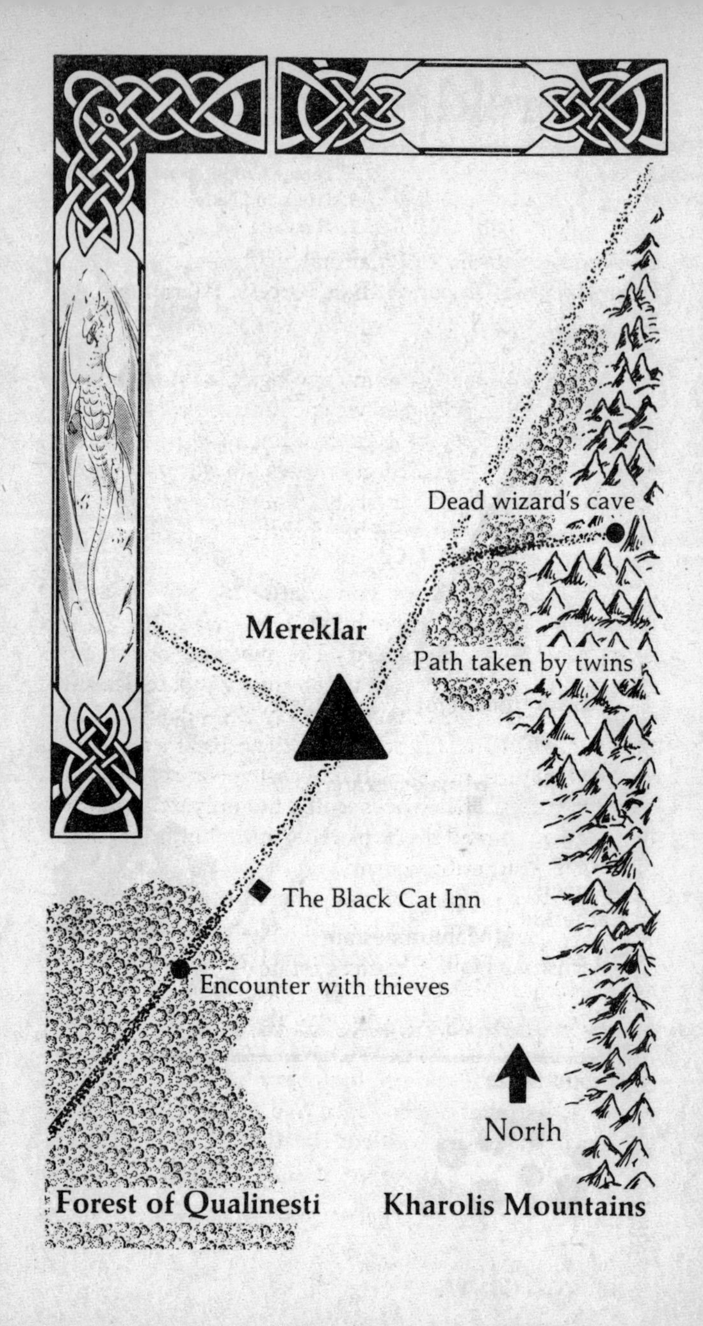
Dead wizard's cave
Mereklar
Path taken by twins
The Black Cat Inn
Encounter with thieves
North
Forest of Qualinesti
Kharolis Mountains

To Bertram, Library of Palanthas
From Dalamar, Tower of High Sorcery, Palanthas

Greetings,

First, sir, allow me to offer my apologies for startling you and the young scribe when we encountered each other in the great library. I am so accustomed to traveling the paths of sorcery that I forget others are not used to my sudden appearances. I trust that the young scribe is, by now, fully recovered from his unfortunate tumble down the stairs.

My messenger (I hope you are not too put off by its rather ghastly appearance) holds in its "hand" the manuscript which you requested. The material of which I spoke—i.e., a collection of notations written by Raistlin Majere himself concerning his early life—cannot, I am afraid, be delivered to the library. In accordance with his secretive nature, the Shalafi had cast spells of confusion over his books. These spells would not only make it difficult for you to read the books, Bertram, but might actually cause you serious harm.

I have taken it upon myself, therefore, to rewrite the account. All information is complete and accurate to detail as far as I was able to determine from Raistlin's notes and Caramon Majere's memory. I searched for the kender, Earwig Lockpicker, who was also a companion during several adventures, but I was unable to find him. (Needless to say, I did not look very hard!)

The material is divided into two parts. The first and shorter of the pieces is titled "Raistlin and the Knight of

Solamnia."[1] This piece is important in that it provides us with information on the kender, Earwig, and how he came to join up with the twins. The story concerns the Shalafi's encounter with a stiff-necked knight, whose pride very nearly gets them all killed. (Considering our current good relations with the knights, you might think twice before publishing this story in Solamnia.)

The second story, which I have titled "Brothers Majere," is interesting for a number of reasons, particularly for the account of the mysterious and fascinating personage met by the twins. As you know, there has been considerable discussion among the scholars of the land concerning this "demi-god." Is he real, or is he merely a creature of legend and myth? I remember discussing the subject with Raistlin, and I wondered at the time at the Shalifi's knowing smile. True to form, he never told me that he knew, firsthand, the truth about "Bast."

That Raistlin was interested in Bast himself is best indicated by the fact that he went out of his way to collect other tales concerning the dark-skinned "thief." These can be forwarded to you when I have time to break the spells guarding them.

Next, about your request for information regarding the chronological order of the stories in your collection, I offer you the following for your records. (The information is based both on my notes and on discussions with Caramon Majere.)

After the separation of the Companions at the Inn of the Last Home, Raistlin and Caramon left immediately on their journey to the Tower of High Sorcery. Raistlin took the test, with results that have now become legend.[2]

The twins then wandered in the magical Wayreth Forest for perhaps as long as a month before being allowed

---

[1] DRAGON® Magazine, Issue #154

[2] "The Test of the Twins," short story, DRAGONLANCE® Tales Trilogy, Volume 1

to leave. It is during this period of time that popular myth would have us believe Raistlin encountered the strange woman who would, unbeknowst to the Shalafi, bear him a child.[3] (By the way, in regard to this rumor, I can give you no information. The stories about this liaison did not begin to circulate until several years *after* Raistlin's death. I find nothing in his notes pertaining to such a liaison.)

Upon escaping Wayreth Forest, the twins returned to Solace, where Raistlin spent several months seeking a cure for his malady. He studied and became expert in the sciences of alchemy and herbal lore and gained greatly in knowledge that would serve him all of his life. Unfortunately, his efforts failed to improve his health. Funds running low, the brothers were forced to leave Solace to seek their fortunes.

Caramon recalls that they intended to cross New Sea, but he is unclear as to why they were traveling to such wild and dangerous lands. Perhaps he himself did not know. Marginal notes in one of the Shalafi's alchemy texts indicate that Raistlin may have been continuing his search for some magical life-giving elixir.

During this time, Raistlin was also hunting for a true cleric. I venture to speculate that he was not seeking one out of a high-minded search for truth, but—again—in hopes that he would find someone to heal him. (It is, however, interesting to note that, four years later, when he meets Goldmoon, he tells her that her healing powers will not help him. What happened to him in that intervening time period to teach him this harsh lesson? Perhaps, in further explorations through his texts, we will discover the answer.)

---

[3] "Raistlin's Daughter," short story, DRAGONLANCE Tales Trilogy, Volume 3

Undoubtedly it is due to his bitter disappointment in being unable to find a true cleric that he continues to ferret out and expose charlatans. One of these is the infamous fraud of Larnish (mentioned briefly in this volume). It is shortly after this encounter that Raistlin and Caramon met the Knight of Solamnia and rid Death's Keep of its curse. Continuing on their way to New Sea, they enter Mereklar.

This adventure is not the end of the brothers' journeyings. They would travel another four years before the outbreak of the War of the Lance. My teaching, as well as the work involved in being Head of the Order of Black Robes, leaves me little time to pursue my research but, hopefully, at some later date, I will be able to decipher the remainder of the Shalafi's notes. Like you, Bertram, I must admit that I find the subject fascinating.

My Shalafi was undoubtedly the most skilled and powerful wizard who has ever lived. I am pleased that you are setting down the true facts concerning his life. It is my profound hope that future generations will remember and honor the tragedy and ultimate triumph of Raistlin Majere.

I hope that this is helpful to you. I trust the messenger will deliver it to you safely. (If he leaves any slime on the parchment, you may remove it with a solution of lemon water and vinegar.)

Please extend my greetings and respect to Astinus.

Prologue

The boy looked up from his play to see two strangers, standing at the crossroads, reading the sign. Keeping his eyes on them, the boy continued what he was doing—sailing a makeshift boat in a puddle. But when the larger and stronger of the two men—a warrior, by the number of weapons he carried—ripped the parchment off the post, the boy left the boat to sink slowly into the muddy water. Hidden by a scraggly shrub, the boy crept close to listen.

"Hey, Raist, look at this!" yelled the big man to the other, who stood only a few feet away.

The boy stared at this second man with intense interest. The child had never seen a mage before, he'd only heard about them in tales. He had no trouble recognizing a wizard, however, by his outlandish robes—their color red as blood—the mysterious pouches and feathered amulets that hung from the mage's simple rope belt, and a black wooden staff on which he leaned when he walked.

"Stop bellowing! I'm not deaf. What have you found?" the mage spoke irritably.

"It says . . . here, you read it." The warrior handed over the notice. He watched as the mage studied it. "Well, what do you think? Unless, of course, it's outdated."

"This posting is recent. The parchment's not even weatherworn yet."

"Oh, yeah. So maybe this is what we're looking for, huh?"

"Fee negotiable." The mage frowned. "Still, that's better than nothing. The reward we earned for ending the curse of Death's Keep is nearly gone. We'll never be able to cross New Sea unless we have the means to hire a boat." He rolled up the parchment and thrust it in the sleeves of his robes.

The warrior sighed. "Another night sleeping on the ground?"

"We need to carefully conserve what little money we have."

"I guess. I could sure use a mug of ale, though."

"I've no doubt," said the mage sourly.

"You ever heard of this Mereklar place?" asked the warrior after a pause.

"No, have you?"

"Nope."

The mage looked from the signpost to the road it indicated. The road was muddy and overgrown with grass and weeds.

"It doesn't look as if many people have heard of it. I—"

"Whew! Here you are! Finally!"

The boy heard someone gasping in relief. Peering around the hedge, he saw a person, smaller in stature than the other two, pumping up the road as fast as his orange-stockinged legs would carry him.

A kender! recognized the boy and immediately clasped fast in his hand all his worldly possessions, which consisted of a half-eaten apple that had been lunch and a small, broken knife used for whittling boats.

Perhaps the branches of the bush rustled when the boy moved, because he was astonished and alarmed to see the mage suddenly turn his head and cast a piercing glance into the shrubs that concealed him. The boy froze. He'd never seen a face like that, not even in a dream. The mage's skin had a gold cast to it, and his eyes were golden, the pupils shaped like hourglasses.

Fortunately for the boy, the kender began to talk again.

"I thought I'd never catch up with you two! You left me behind by mistake. Why didn't you guys tell me you were taking off in the middle of the night? If I hadn't woken up and seen you two sneaking past my door, carrying your packs, I never would have known which way you were going! As it was, I had to take a moment to gather up all my things and then I had a dreadful time keeping up and once I lost you, but I have a special device that I use for finding my way and it showed me which path you took. Do you want to see it?" The kender began to fumble through innumerable pouches, spilling out various articles and objects into the street. "It's in here, somewhere. . . ."

The warrior exchanged a long-suffering glance with the mage. "Uh, no, that's all right, Earmite—"

"Earwig!" corrected the kender indignantly.

"Uh, yeah. Sorry. Earwig Nosepicker, isn't it?"

"Lockpicker!" The kender jabbed the forked stick he was carrying into the ground for emphasis. "Lockpicker. A highly honored name among—"

"Come, Caramon," said the mage in a voice that would have chilled boiling water. "We must be going."

"Where are we headed?" asked the kender, cheerfully falling into step.

The mage came to a halt and fixed the kender with his strange eyes.

"*We* aren't headed anywhere."

The boy thought that anyone but a kender would have curled up and sunk into the ground under the mage's baleful stare. But the kender just gazed up at him solemnly.

"Oh, but you need me, Raistlin. You really do. Wasn't I a help to you in solving the mystery of Death's Keep? I was. You said so yourself. I gave you the clue that made you think the maiden was the reason for the curse. And Caramon never would have found his favorite dagger if it hadn't been for me—"

"I never would have lost it, if it hadn't been for you," muttered the warrior.

"And then Tasslehoff told me— You remember my cousin, Tasslehoff Burrfoot? Anyway, he told me that you always took him with you on your adventures and that he was always getting you out of trouble and since he's not around you should take me to do the same thing. And I can tell you lots of interesting stories, like the one about Dizzy Longtongue and the minotaur—"

"Enough!" The mage pulled his cowl farther down over his head, as if the cloth could shut out the monologue.

"Ah, let him come along, Raist," said the warrior. "It'd be company for us. You know we get bored, just talking to each other."

"I know I get bored just talking to you, my brother. But I do not think the situation will be alleviated by taking on a kender!"

The mage started off down the road, leaning heavily on his staff and walking slowly, as if he had just been through a recent illness.

"What did he say?" the kender asked, coming to walk beside the warrior.

"I'm not sure," said the warrior, shaking his head. "But I don't think it was a compliment."

"Oh, well," said the kender, twirling his forked stick in the air until it made a shrill, whistling sound. "I'm not much used to compliments anyway. Where did you say we were going?"

"Mereklar."

"Mereklar. Never heard of it," stated the kender happily.

The boy saw the three well on their way before he ran to an old, dilapidated inn that huddled in the woods near the crossroads. A man sat at a table, an untasted drink in his hand.

The boy went up to the man and told what he had seen.

"A warrior, a mage, and a kender. All three heading for Mereklar. And now that I've done what you wanted, where's my money?" the child demanded boldly. "You promised."

The man asked a few questions, wanting to know what color robes the mage was wearing and if the warrior appeared to be very old and battle-hardened.

"No," said the boy, considering. "He's only about the age of my big brother. Twenty or so if he's a day. But his weapons seemed well used. I don't think you'll pick him off so easily."

The man fished a steel piece from his pocket and tossed it on the table. Rising from his seat with unusual haste, considering he'd been sitting in the inn for three days—ever since he'd posted the sign—the man ran out into the woods and was soon lost to sight in the shadows.

Chapter 1

Raistlin awoke from deep slumber to the sound of pipes—a haunting, eerie sound that reminded him of a time of everlasting pain, a time of torture and torment. Propping himself up on weak elbows from his red, tattered sleeping roll, he stared into the embers of the fire.

The dying coals only served to remind Raistlin of his ill health. How long had it been since he took the test? How much time had passed since the wizards in the Tower of High Sorcery had demanded this sacrifice in return for his magic? Months. Only months. Yet it seemed to him that he'd been suffering like this all his life.

Lying back down, Raistlin lifted his hands up in front

of his face, examining the bones, veins, and sinews, barely discernible in the dimly lit grove. The firelight gave his flesh an unearthly reddish tinge, reflecting off his golden skin—the gold skin he had earned in his gambit for personal power, gold skin he had earned fighting for his life.

Smiling grimly, Raistlin clenched his hand into a fist. He'd won. He'd been victorious. He had defeated them all.

But his moment of triumph was short-lived. He began to cough uncontrollably, the spasms shaking and convulsing him like a battered puppet.

The pipes played on while Raistlin managed to catch his breath. He fumbled at his waist to find a small burlap bag filled with herbs. Holding this over his nose and mouth, he breathed the sickly sweet scent of crushed leaves and boiled twigs. The spasms eased, and Raistlin dared let himself hope that this time he'd found a cure. He refused to believe he would be this feeble all of his life.

The herbs left a bitter taste on his lips. He stashed the pungent bag away in a purse under his cloth belt, which was a darker red than the rest of his robes from constant use and wear. He didn't look for the blood that was beginning to slowly dry on the medicine pouch. He knew it would be there.

Breathing slowly, Raistlin forced himself to relax. His eyes closed. He imagined the many and varied lines of power running through his life—the glowing, golden weave of threads of his magic, his mind, his soul. He held his life in his hands. He was the master of his own destiny.

Raistlin listened to the pipes again. They did not play the eerie, unnatural music he thought he had heard upon waking—the music of the dark elf, the music he dreamed about in his worst nightmares since his indoctrination into the higher orders of sorcery. Instead it was the shrill, lively music of an inconsiderate kender.

Throwing off the heavy blankets piled on top of him, Raistlin shivered in the cold evening air. He clutched his staff with hands eager to feel the smooth wood once again safely in their grip, and pulled himself upright.

"*Shirak*," Raistlin said softly.

Power flowed from his spirit into the staff, mingling with the magic already housed in the black-wood symbol of the mage's victory. A soft white light beamed from the crystal clutched in a dragon's claw atop the staff.

As soon as the light flooded the grove, the music stopped abruptly. Earwig looked up in surprise to see the red-hooded figure of the magician looming over him.

"Oh, hi, Raistlin!" The kender grinned.

"Earwig," said the mage softly, "I'm trying to sleep."

"Well, of course, you are, Raistlin," answered the kender. "It's the middle of the night."

"But I can't sleep, Earwig, because of the noise."

"What noise?" The kender looked around the campsite with interest.

Raistlin reached out his gold-skinned hand and snatched the pipe from Earwig's grasp. He held it up in front of the kender's nose.

"Oh," said Earwig meekly. "That noise."

Raistlin tucked the pipes into the sleeve of his robes, turned, and started back to his bed.

"I can play you a lullaby," suggested Earwig, leaping to his feet and trotting along behind the mage. "If you give me back my pipes, that is. Or I could sing one for you—"

Raistlin turned and stared at the kender. The firelight flickered in the hourglass eyes.

"Or maybe not," said Earwig, slightly daunted.

But a kender never stayed daunted for long. "It's really

boring around here," he added, keeping up with the mage. "I thought being on night watch would be fun, and it was for a while, because I kept expecting something to jump out of the woods and attack us since Caramon said that was why we had to keep watch, but nothing has jumped out and attacked us and it's really getting boring."

"Dulak," Raistlin whispered, starting to cough again. The light from the globe dimmed and died. The mage sank down onto his sleeping mat, his tired legs barely supporting him.

"Here, Raistlin, let me help you," offered Earwig, spreading out the blankets. The kender stood, gazing down at the mage hopefully. "Would you make the staff light up again, Raistlin?"

The mage hunched his thin body beneath the heavy quilt.

"Could I have my pipes back?"

Raistlin closed his eyes.

Earwig heaved a gusty sigh, his gaze going to the sleeve of the mage's robes into which he'd seen his pipes disappear.

"Good night, Raistlin. I hope you feel better in the morning."

The mage felt a small hand pat his arm solicitously. The kender trotted away, small feet making little noise in the dew-wet grass.

Just as Raistlin was finally drifting off to sleep, he heard, once again, the shrill sound of the pipes.

* * * * *

Caramon awoke hours before the dawn, just in time for his watch. The companions had agreed to set two guards, Earwig taking the first watch, Caramon the second. Caramon preferred to take the last watch of the night, known as "the dead man's watch" because it was a time when there was the greatest possibility of trouble.

"Earwig, turn in," said Caramon, only to find his order had already been obeyed.

The kender lay fast asleep, a set of pipes clutched tightly in his hand.

Caramon shook his head. What could you expect from a kender? By nature, kender were not afraid of anything, living or dead. It was extremely difficult, therefore, to impress upon a kender the need to set a guard on the campsite.

Not that the warrior believed they were in any danger; the lands around them were peaceful and calm. But Caramon could no more have gone to his rest without setting a watch then he could have gone for a day without eating. It was one reason—at least so he had told his brother—that they needed Earwig to accompany them on their journey.

The warrior settled himself beneath a tree. He enjoyed this time of night. He liked to see the moons and stars fade into morning's first light. The constellations turned and wheeled and faced each other—the platinum dragon Paladine, the five-headed dragon Takhisis, between them the god Gilean, the symbol of balance. Few others on Krynn believed in these ancient gods anymore, or even remembered the names of their constellations. Caramon had learned them from his brother. Sometimes the warrior wondered if Raistlin believed in the despised gods. If he did, he never mentioned it or worshipped them openly. Probably a good thing, Caramon reflected. This day and age, that type of faith could get you killed.

Caramon connected the bright points, his imagination drawing lines and curves, forming the stars into symbols of good and evil. He found the twins' namesake—the god Majere, called the Single Rose by the elves (according to his friend, Tanis), the Mantis by the Knights of Solamnia (according to Sturm). The constellation lay deep in the pool of darkness overhead. Caramon knew from Raistlin that it was supposed to grant stability of thought, peace of mind. The heavens did give him a feeling of stability, of lasting equilibrium in the world. No matter what happened, the constellations would always be there.

Giving the stars a salute, Caramon heaved himself to his feet. Time to work. Moving silently, careful not to awake his sleeping brother, Caramon piled his weapons at his feet and began giving each a cursory examination. There were three swords, all aged and battle worn. One was a bastard sword, also called a hand-and-a-half sword, because it could be used with either one or two hands. The hilt was dirty, blackened with blood. The cross-guard—a simple, unadorned metal bar running across the hilt where it met the four-foot blade—was notched and cut from parrying the attacks of countless opponents.

The other swords were smaller: an old, worn broadsword with a counterweight at the bottom and a main-gauche—a one and a half foot long parrying dagger with a large basket hilt and wide blade. These were the arms of a skilled warrior, of one who never sacrificed his honor to win a confrontation. They were old and trusted friends.

Caramon's other weapons were the spoils of war, the gifts of the dead. One, two, or even three dagger blades jutted out from hilts carved into the likenesses of demons and dragons. There was a double-edged stiletto, its blade curved like a snake, and several small throwing weapons such as darts and hand-axes. Other weapons included a brass cestus, punch-daggers, ring blades. All these had been taken from enemies who no longer needed them.

Taking out a whetstone and cloth, the warrior began

cleaning his weapons. Deciding to do his swords first, he sharpened them with the stone, wiping them down with a cloth he wet from the waterskin. He lifted the blades, inspecting them by Solinari's silver light, holding each one up to his eye to make sure the blade was straight, bending it with his bare hands when it didn't meet with his satisfaction. He looked for cracks or dents that meant the sword had to be thrown away lest it break in the middle of a battle. There were none. Caramon, an expert at all forms of personal combat, never allowed his tools to wear, knowing full well that preventive maintenance could save his life.

He put away his gear, sheathing the swords, or strapping them back onto his huge, muscular form. His arms could bend the thickest bars, lift the heaviest weight, move the largest obstacle. Veins stood out against the definition of muscles as firm as iron plates. The thinning leather thongs that held in place Caramon's unadorned metal hauberk creaked when he breathed deeply, and the thick armored greaves he wore barely covered his lower legs. Strong and powerful, Caramon was born to fight, even as his brother was born to magic. It was difficult for most people to believe the two were twins.

The sky was clear, the stars shone brightly, with no hint of clouds.

"Tomorrow should be a fine day," Caramon said to himself, stretching. He scratched his neck with his left hand while rubbing his face with his right. He was cold.

Earwig had let the fire die down until nothing was left but smoldering embers.

Sighing heavily, muttering imprecations on the head of the careless kender, Caramon began to walk the perimeter of the grove, searching for fallen limbs and sticks. Raistlin would need the warmth of a fire when he awoke. He would require flames to heat the herb mixture on which he relied to ease his cough.

Caramon was disappointed to find the immediate area devoid of any useful wood. Giving a backward glance at his brother still shrouded in his coverings, the warrior traveled deeper into the forest, hoping to spot some fuel without having to move too far from his companions.

He had been away from the camp fifteen minutes when he heard a strange sound back near the grove. At first, he thought it was the movement of some forest predator, but then he heard other movement—stealthy, furtive.

Caramon dodged behind a huge oak, quietly drawing the large bastard sword and the smaller, heavy main-gauche. Listening carefully, the warrior thought he could hear whispered signals being passed—signals of caution, signals to strike as one. He edged his way back to the clearing. The forest provided excellent cover, the same cover his opponents had used to hide their presence earlier.

"Five of the bastards," Caramon counted to himself as he crouched in the shadow of another oak tree.

He heard again the sounds of their movements, learned their methods as he stalked them, listening for the whistles of the commander, the replies of his followers.

He considered sheathing his parrying dagger and using a throwing weapon, perhaps a dart or knife, to remove the intruders one by one. But as he neared the edge of the clearing, he lost all thought of strategy.

Solinari and Lunitari lit the scene in the grove, the silver and red light mixing to give double shadows that moved and swayed as the intruders did.

Three men holding war spears stood over Raistlin's sleeping roll. Two others stood beside Earwig.

"These fools will never reach Mereklar," said one, the

tallest of the three, wearing a black hood over his head. Raising his spear, he plunged it into Raistlin's body.

Bursting from the woods, roaring in outrage, Caramon dashed forward. He struck down one of the thieves standing over Earwig with the bastard sword as he stabbed the other through the stomach with the main-gauche. He left his parrying dagger in the thief's body and gripped his sword in both hands. Blood pounded in his ears, drowning out all other sounds as he raced after the remaining three bandits.

One raised his spear to parry, but Caramon's down-stroke shattered the haft and sank deep into his enemy, who died with a look of surprise on his face. But the blow cost Caramon.

The second leaped to stab the big warrior in the back, and the big man could not turn in time to block the attack. It didn't matter. His brother was dead, his life was over anyway. Sobbing, Caramon saw, out of the corner of his eye, the blade's flashing descent—

It halted in midair. The thug went stiff as a corpse.

Caramon stared, amazed, nearly dropping his sword. Then he heard softly chanted words coming from the edge of the forest and saw Raistlin emerge from the shadows. Caramon reached out an unsteady, trembling hand toward his brother.

"Raist?" he whispered.

Raistlin stopped him with a glance.

"What's the matter, Caramon? You look as if you'd seen a ghost."

Caramon let his hand sink back to his side. "I thought for a minute I had, Raist! I thought you were dead!" The big man could barely talk for his relief.

The mage's face, shadowed by his red hood, showed no hint of emotion.

"Small thanks to you I wasn't!" He walked over to look with cold curiosity at the remaining attacker. The thief's limbs were stiffened by sorcery. He was unable to move, unable to overcome the irresistible will of magic.

"I went to get wood," mumbled Caramon, shamefacedly. "I honestly didn't think there was any danger. I haven't heard word of thieves around these parts. And the fire was out and I knew you'd be chilled to the bone, and then there's that stuff you drink—"

"Never mind!" Raistlin impatiently cut short his brother's explanations. "No harm was done. You know what a light sleeper I am. I heard them coming from some distance away." The mage paused, carefully scrutinizing their prisoner. "A bit unusual for professional thieves, don't you think, Caramon?"

"Yeah, as a matter of fact," said the warrior, scratching his head. "They did seem sort of clumsy."

"A pity the leader escaped."

"Did he?" Caramon growled and glanced around.

"The man with the black hood. He ran off the moment you burst into the grove. I think a conversation with him might have been quite interesting. Did you hear his words before he struck what he thought was my limp and unresisting form?"

Caramon thought back, past blood and fear and grief, and heard in his memory, "These fools will never reach Mereklar!"

"I'll be damned," said the big warrior, stunned, the implication dawning on him.

"Yes, my brother. Not thieves, but hired killers."

"I could go after him."

"You would never find him. He is on home ground, and we are not. Let's have a look at what we've captured. *Shirak*!"

The magical light of the staff gleamed. Raistlin held it close to the assassin while his brother grasped the greasy, leather helmet the man wore and yanked it off him. The face that stared back at them had been frozen by Raistlin's spell just at the time he was prepared to strike down Caramon. The killer's mouth was twisted in a grin of bloodlust. He had obviously been enjoying the idea of knifing a man in the back.

"I'm going to lift the spell. Hold onto him," Raistlin instructed.

Caramon grabbed the man, encircling the scrawny neck with his huge arm, a dagger held to the assassin's throat.

At a movement of Raistlin's gold-skinned hand, the man's body jerked. Finding himself free of the enchantment, the attacker attempted briefly to get away. Caramon tightened his grip slightly, the dagger pricking the killer's skin.

"I won't run!" the man whined, going limp. "Just don't let him do no more of that magic on me!"

"I won't . . . if you answer a few questions," said Raistlin in his soft, whispering voice.

"Sure, I'll tell you anything! Just don't do that magic stuff again!"

"Who hired you to kill us?"

"I dunno. A fella in a black hood. I never saw his face."

"His name?"

"I dunno. He didn't tell us."

"Where did you meet him?"

"In an inn near Mereklar. The Black Cat. Last night. He said he had a job for us. He said we was just goin' to rob you! He didn't say nothing about killin'!"

"You're lying," said Raistlin coolly. "You were hired to murder us in our sleep."

"No! I swear! I was—"

"I'm tired of listening to his babbling. Shut him up, Caramon."

"Permanently?" suggested Caramon, his hand engulfing the assassin's throat.

Raistlin appeared to consider the matter. The thief kept silent, his face now twisted into an expression of terror.

"No, I have another use for him. Hold him tight."

Raistlin pulled the hood back from over his head. The twin moons' shimmering light reflected into his eyes—the eyes with the pupils of hourglasses, the eyes that saw everything decay, wither, and die. It glistened off the golden skin and the prematurely white hair that looked ghastly on a young man of twenty-one. Slowly, Raistlin approached the thief.

The man screamed and struggled desperately in Caramon's tight grip.

Reaching out one gold-skinned hand, Raistlin placed five fingers on the thief's forehead. The man writhed beneath the mage's touch and began to howl.

"Shut up," Caramon grunted, "and listen to my brother!"

"When you see the man in the black hood, you will tell him that my brother and I are coming to Mereklar and that we will not rest until we have found him. Do you understand that?"

"Yes! Yes!" cried the man pitifully.

"And now I put this curse upon you. The next time you take a life in cold blood, the ghost of the murdered man will rise up and follow you. By day it will dog your steps. By night it will hound your dreams. You will do anything to try to rid yourself of it, but to no avail. The ghost will drive you to madness and, finally, at the end, it will cause you to turn your foul knife on yourself."

Raistlin removed his hand. "Let him go, Caramon."

The big man released the assassin, who fell to his knees. He remained crouched on the ground, glancing furtively at the brothers. Caramon made a threatening gesture with his dagger, and the man leaped to his feet and dashed, panic-stricken, into the forest. For long minutes after, they could hear him crashing into trees and blundering into bushes.

"That was a horrible curse," said Caramon, awed. "I didn't know you could cast those kind of spells on people."

"I can't," said Raistlin, then began to cough, doubling over with the spasms that racked his thin body.

He held out his arm to his brother, who gently took it and guided the mage back to his blankets.

"You mean . . . there's not really a curse on him?" asked Caramon, confused. He assisted his twin to lie down.

"Oh, there is a curse on him," said Raistlin, when he could speak again. "But I didn't cast it." The mage's thin lips parted in a slight smile. "He will do that himself. Don't just stand there gaping at me! I'm chilled to the bone. Go gather more wood. I will keep the staff lighted until you have built the fire."

Caramon shook his head, not understanding.

Going to pick up the wood he had dropped during his attack on the killers, the warrior almost fell over Earwig's sleeping roll. In the excitement, he had forgotten the kender. Caramon remembered the assassins standing over Earwig, their spears held high. Kneeling down, the warrior put his hand on the small, blanket-covered form.

"Earwig?" Caramon said worriedly.

From the depths of the blanket came a yawning sound, a stretching motion, and eventually a head popped out of the top. Looking around in sleepy confusion in the brightening early morning light, the sound-sleeping kender saw the hacked and bloodied corpses lying on the ground, broken weapons scattered about, the grass torn and churned by trampling feet.

Earwig's mouth dropped open. His eyes bulged. He looked from Raistlin to Caramon wildly and back again. The kender threw back his head and began to wail.

"It's all right, Earwig," said Caramon soothingly. "Don't cry. You're safe. The killers are gone."

"I know!" cried Earwig, flinging himself on the ground and kicking his feet in the sod. "Don't rub it in!"

"What?" demanded the warrior, startled. "What's the matter, then?"

"How could you, Caramon?" sobbed Earwig. "I thought we were friends! A fight—and you let me sleep through the whole thing!"

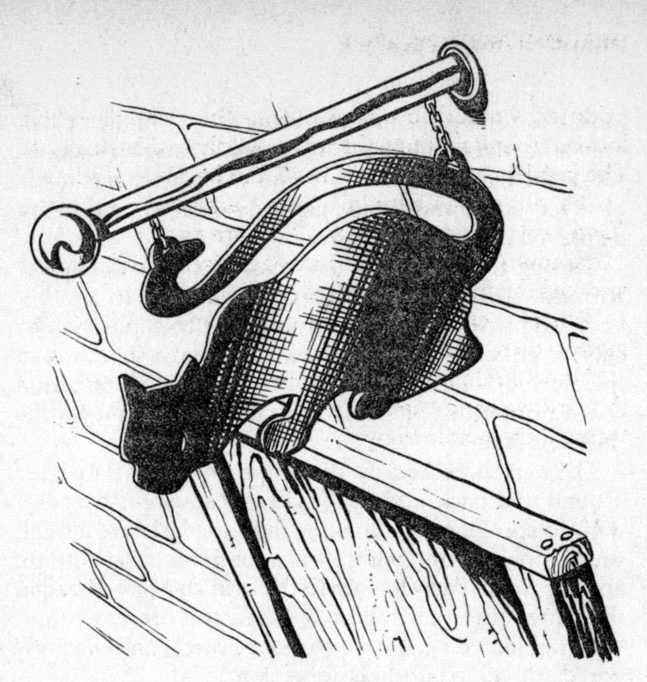

Chapter 2

DAWN BROKE, AND CARAMON'S OPTIMISTIC PREDICTION proved correct: it was, indeed, a fine day. The temperature rose to a comfortable level, warm enough for walking, but still cool enough to be pleasant. The sun, bright in a sky that was clear of clouds, clear of chaos, shone down upon the companions.

The dead bodies of the would-be assassins still lay in the clearing. Earwig, to make up for having missed last night's action, was occupied in searching the bodies, "looking for some clue to tell us who these people were," as he put it. In one of the thieves' pockets he found a broach made from strands of gold woven together to look like rope. Opening the broach by a hidden catch only a kender would have discovered, Earwig found inside a collection of miniature musical instruments made of silver, bone, and ebony, perfectly detailed, waiting to be played by a tiny orchestra.

Closing the medallion and tossing it onto a blanket with the other "treasure," Earwig went over to another body and saw three rings on the dead brigand's hands, each of gold and glittering with diamonds, sparkling in the morning's light. But what caught Earwig's attention was a mysterious twist of wire that had fallen from the thief's pocket.

The kender picked up the looped metal that twisted around and back into itself with no apparent purpose, with no specific form. Shaking the wire, he heard a small sound come from within—a sound of glass rattling against metal. He held it up to the light and saw a bead in the center of the coils. Earwig gazed at it for many minutes, fascinated by this mysterious object, until he grew bored and added it to his collection.

The kender went from body to body, collecting gold and diamonds and other precious things, holding them in his hand, feeling their weight and shape, only to toss them aside, forgotten, as he reached down to pick up an old writing quill with a bright silver tip, a piece of purple glass, and a wood carving of an eagle, no bigger than the middle of his palm. Worth and values set by other races mean nothing to kender. Curiosity makes them desire anything that enchants their eye, regardless of what they already hold in their hands.

"Well, did you find anything?" Caramon asked.

"That's it," said Earwig proudly, pointing at the blanket. "Well, aren't you going to look at it?" he asked, noting Caramon's hesitation.

"I guess so," said the big man heavily, starting to kneel down. "But it shivers my skin to paw through possessions of the dead."

"Why? You took their weapons."

"That's different."

"How? I don't understand—"

"It just is! All right?" Caramon glared at the kender.

"You are too squeamish, Brother," said Raistlin in his soft voice, coming up to stand behind them. "Move over. You're blocking the light. I have no superstitious fear of a dead man's personal belongings."

The mage bent down. His slender, delicate hands ran lightly over the objects scattered before him. Some he lifted and inspected with an expert eye. Earwig watched eagerly.

"Those are the biggest diamonds I've ever seen. Did you ever see any that big, Raistlin?"

"Glass," remarked the mage, tossing the ring aside in contempt.

Earwig appeared slightly crestfallen, but cheered up again. "That golden chain is quite heavy, isn't it, Raistlin?"

"It should be. It's lead. What's this?"

The mage lifted a silver charm between thumb and forefinger. Holding it in his palm, he exhibited it to his brother. Caramon, looking at it, made a face.

"Ugh! Who would wear that?"

"I would!" said Earwig, staring at the trinket longingly.

The charm was shaped into the likeness of a cat's skull, with tiny rubies in the eye sockets.

"Which one was wearing this?" Raistlin asked.

Earwig thought. "None of them. I found it in the grass, over there." He pointed near Raistlin's neatly rolled-up blankets.

"The leader," grunted Caramon.

"Yes," Raistlin agreed, staring at the charm. A shudder

passed through his body, his hand trembled. "It is evil, Caramon. A thing of darkness. And it is old. Its time stretches back before the Cataclysm."

"Get rid of it!" said the warrior tersely.

"No, I—" Raistlin hesitated, then turned to Earwig. "Would you truly like to wear this?"

"Oh, yes!" sighed the kender. "Wow! A 'thing of darkness'!"

"Raist—" began Caramon, but his brother shot him a swift, warning glance, and the big man hushed.

Threading the skull on a silver chain that was among the loot, the mage slipped it over the kender's neck. Raistlin murmured soft words, touched the metal chain with his fingers. Earwig, his face bright with pleasure, stared at his new necklace in awe.

Raistlin rose and stretched his thin body, then began to cough in the chill morning air. Turning, he made his way back to the fire. Caramon followed.

"What do we do with that stuff?"

"Leave it. There is nothing of value."

Glancing back, Caramon saw Earwig happily stuffing as much of the treasure as he could into his packs and pouches.

"You've made the kender a target, Raistlin," said the big man.

The mage knelt by the fire, his thin body huddling near for warmth. "Not a target, brother," he corrected coolly. "Bait."

"Either way, he's in danger. Whoever wore that might be looking for it. He'll know the kender was a witness to his crime. What were those words you said over the necklace? Some sort of protective spell?"

Raistlin snorted. "Don't be a fool, Caramon. It was a simple cantrip, one that will prevent the kender from removing the necklace. As for the danger, he's in less danger than either you or I would be, wearing that charm.

No one takes kender seriously. They'll assume he found it and put it on for a lark. We must watch for those who might take an unusual interest in it."

"I don't like it, Raist," persisted Caramon with unusual stubbornness.

"I didn't like being nearly murdered in my sleep!" his twin snapped. He rose to his feet, leaning on the magical staff. "Come along. It's time we were going. I want to get there before dark."

"There? Where? Mereklar?" Caramon scattered the coals of the fire with his booted foot and tossed water on them.

"No. The Inn of the Black Cat."

* * * * *

Caramon never ceased to be amazed by his brother. Ever since the infamous test required of every mage who aspired to enter the higher realms of magic—the test that could prove lethal—Raistlin's health had been shattered. His body was thin, barely skin and bones. He coughed persistently. Sometimes Caramon wondered fearfully if his brother would be able to draw another breath. Plagued by terrible dreams, Raistlin tossed and turned and often screamed aloud in his sleep. Some mornings, he was barely able to crawl from his bed.

Yet this morning, the young mage seemed unusually well. He walked with a brisk step, barely leaning on his staff. He had eaten—for him—a good breakfast consisting of bread and fruit. He had not needed to drink the herbal tea that soothed his cough nor breathe the fumes of the bag. His eyes were bright, glittering in the morning light.

"It's this mystery," Caramon said to himself. "He

thrives on intrigue. I'm glad Raist is handling it. Me—I'd rather face an army of goblins. I hate skulking about."

The warrior heaved a sigh. He spent the day walking with his broadsword in hand, sending piercing, darting glances into the woods, expecting another ambush at any moment.

Caramon's other companion was also enjoying himself. Earwig skipped down the path, twirling in the air the kender's favorite weapon—the hoopak. A walking stick with a sling fitted to the yoke at the top, Earwig's hoopak was unusual in that the top could be removed, turning the staff into a blowgun. It fired small, sharp, barbed darts that the kender carried in the inner right sleeve of his traveling outfit.

Earwig was, in fact, extremely fond of weapons of all sorts and prided himself on his collection. An unusual throwing knife with five blades curving out in separate directions was his pride and joy. He also carried another invention of his own—eggshells filled with special powders and liquids that could be released on impact. Besides these, he owned many other weapons, but usually forgot or absentmindedly exchanged them for other, more exciting, objects.

Earwig had been with the twins only a short time, but he was willing to follow them as they began new adventures. He was fascinated by the magician with the strange eyes and shining golden skin and was happy to be with someone so interesting and unique. The kender did feel sorry for Raistlin, however. The mage was so gloomy. Earwig took it upon himself, therefore, to regale the mage with tales of fantastic adventures in other parts of Krynn or stories he had heard from friends and relatives, trying to cheer Raistlin from the continual melancholy that surrounded him as heavily as his red robes.

The mage would simply ignore him or, if Raistlin was in a particularly bad mood, he would attempt to sweep

Earwig out his way with his staff.

When this happened, Earwig would skip over to talk with Caramon, who was always interested in stories and had a few wild tales of his own that even the kender had difficulty believing.

Today, Earwig noted that Raistlin seemed unusually cheerful. The kender was determined to keep the conjurer in a good mood, so he began telling one of his favorite jokes.

"Hey, Raistlin," he began, "have you ever heard of Dizzy Longtongue, the kender who could throw his hoopak with such skill and accuracy he could make it return to his hand? Well, one day a minotaur made a bet with the kender that he couldn't throw his staff around the girth of a forest, and Dizzy said, 'I'll bet you the gold in my pocket against the ring in your nose that I can make my hoopak come back to me from around the forest.' The minotaur accepted and said that if he didn't make it, he would have Dizzy for dessert with dinner. Dizzy naturally agreed."

Earwig paused, waiting for some reaction from Raistlin. But the mage, occasionally coughing, kept his hooded gaze on the road.

The kender, shrugging, continued. "Dizzy took a hundred pace running start before he let go of his hoopak with a mighty zing!" Earwig imitated Dizzy's magnificent throw, arcing his hoopak over his head without letting go, the sling-thong making an appropriate buzz. "Dizzy and the minotaur waited for hours, listening for the sound of the returning hoopak. After a day had passed, the minotaur said, 'Well, my lad, it looks like I'm having you for afters,' and Dizzy said—"

"Look, Caramon." Raistlin raised the staff and pointed. "An inn."

"No, I don't think that's what Dizzy said." Earwig scratched his head. " 'Look, Caramon, an inn,' just doesn't make sense, does it? Actually, what Dizzy said was—"

"I can't see the sign." Caramon peered through the trees.

"No, no, no!" Earwig cried, exasperated. "That wasn't it, at all! And, if you must know, there's a black cat on the sign. Now, if you'll be quiet, I'll tell you what Dizzy said to the minotaur who was about to eat him for dinner. He said—"

"Dinner," said Raistlin softly. "I believe we should stop here for dinner and a night's rest, my brother. Don't you agree? It's what you were wanting, after all."

"Sure, Raist," Caramon said without enthusiasm, eyeing the inn darkly. He thrust the broadsword back in its sheathe, but kept it loose in the scabbard.

Earwig, seeing these preparations, opened his eyes wide. "Oh, Caramon! Do you think there's going to be trouble?"

The big man grunted. Raistlin, turning to Earwig with a smile, reached out his hand and arranged the kender's necklace so that it was clearly visible on his small breast.

"Thanks, Raistlin," said the kender, charmed. He couldn't remember the mage being so attentive. He must like my jokes, he concluded inwardly. Aloud, he continued, "Dizzy said to the minotaur—"

But Raistlin and Caramon had both walked away.

The inn, a huge, two-story house next to the road, stood outside the edge of the forest. Its walls were white stucco with brown woodwork, obviously old but not falling to ruin, with darkly stained crossworks decorating the sills around the windows and ledges. Each pane of glass was clean and clear, and the setting orange sun reflected blindingly from the upper-story windows, catching the last rays before they were trapped in the forest's paths and tangles of brush and tree.

His joke forgotten in his excitement, Earwig raced ahead to the tavern, constantly looking behind him, begging the two men to hurry. Caramon was more than willing to increase his pace, but Raistlin suddenly seemed to have more and more difficulty walking. He leaned on the staff heavily, his back bent as if carrying some unseen weight on his shoulders, his feet slipping.

Was this sudden weakness real or feigned? Caramon wondered uneasily, aiding his brother's faltering steps. With Raistlin, he never knew.

The three eventually reached the open fence of simple wooden posts that surrounded the inn. Caramon stared inside a large glass window, its panes held rigid by vertical and horizontal strips of wood, their simple, decorative carving hiding their practical use. The tavern appeared warm and friendly, and though the sun was just setting, many of the patrons were already sitting down with mugs of ale and goblets of wine.

Above their heads, a sign swung in the breeze with a muted screech, much like the call of a small cat. The illustration on the board was a depiction of a black cat, standing proudly with its head up and tail curved over its back.

"Interesting," murmured Raistlin.

"It's a cat," said Caramon.

"Yes, a black one. Black cats are the favored familiar of the evil wizards of the black robes. Generally any depiction of a black cat is derogatory, portraying the animal as evil as its master. The cat in this picture seems protective, benevolent. Interesting."

Caramon made no comment, but opened the huge wooden door that had been reinforced with iron bars and a large iron lock. Inside, the inn was as hot as a furnace. A huge fire in the center of the building burned brightly. The night air was turning cold, and the blaze was a welcome sensation to the companions. The big warrior stretched his muscles, extending his huge arms at his sides, arching his back, flexing his legs.

Earwig, curious to see what was going on, ran through the great archway that separated the dining room and drinking hall from the main entrance hall. Raistlin moved hurriedly to the fire. Leaning the staff against his shoulder, he held out both hands directly in front of the blaze, his gold skin reflecting dully in the light.

Caramon looked once at his brother, to make certain he was all right, then the big man tried to spot Earwig in the gathering crowd of people. It was hopeless; the kender had disappeared. Caramon sighed, wondering how they were going to protect Earwig when half the time they couldn't even find him. The warrior didn't know what to expect—evil men in black hoods leaping out at them from under a table, perhaps. He cast his sharp-eyed gaze around the crowd. No one looked particularly dangerous. But long experience in inns told the warrior something was wrong here. Everyone was too . . . quiet.

Caramon walked over to the worn desk that ran most of the length of the left side of the room. He waited patiently for a few minutes, glancing back at his brother, still standing in front of the fire. Raistlin had not moved. He didn't even seem to be breathing. Caramon looked back into the eating hall, listening for the sounds of hasty oaths and shattering pottery that usually heralded Earwig's introduction into a crowd. But he heard nothing. The warrior began to drum his fingers against a large, leather-bound book sitting on the desk, its pages opened to reveal the names of patrons currently staying at the inn.

Caramon waited ten minutes without anybody coming to the desk. The warrior began to grow irritated. He had heard his twin begin to cough hoarsely, and he feared that Raistlin's deficient strength might give out completely. Caramon started to move away from the desk to help his brother to a chair when a middle-aged man wearing a clean apron came out of the eating area.

The man's head was bowed, as if he were thinking of something and was not fully aware of his surroundings. He walked to the rear of the desk, took a candle from a drawer, lit it, and went into a dark room behind the reception area without paying any heed to the huge warrior standing in the main hall.

Caramon, who had mutely watched the entrance and exit of the man, was almost ready to shout with frustration when the fellow came out again from the now-lit room. He jumped at the sight of the weli-armed man and then gazed at the fighter morosely.

"We want a room," Caramon demanded. "A room with three beds and"—looking back to Raistlin—"it's got to have a fireplace."

Caramon glared into the man's brown eyes, daring him to say they didn't have anything like that available. But the innkeeper simply slid the guest book in front of the fighter, handed him a quill, and said, "Sign here, please."

Caramon looked again at his brother, and this time the innkeeper followed the big man's gaze.

"A wizard!" said the man, shocked out of his preoccupation.

"Yeah. So?" said Caramon. "I'm his brother."

"I'm sorry, sir. No offense. It's just . . . we don't see many wizards in these parts."

Probably because they're all murdered in the woods, Caramon thought but didn't say. He took the quill and signed his name, adding a quick sketch of a rose with a shining star in the center of the blossom—his personal picture for the old, forgotten god, Majere, whom his late father had taken for his surname.

Caramon turned the book around for the other man to inspect, but instead of looking down, the innkeeper just said, "My name's Yost. If you have any problems, please talk to me." Handing Caramon a key, Yost pointed up the stairs. "Third room to the right." He left the desk and quickly returned to the eating hall, his gaze darting to Raistlin.

Caramon frowned. He'd never been in an inn so curious. He looked at the key, which was attached to a small leather fob with the number 221 engraved on it. Shaking his head, the warrior walked over to his brother and started to put his arm around Raistlin's thin shoulders to help him to their room.

"Shhh!" The mage held up a warning finger. "Sit down!" he hissed out of the corner of his mouth.

Puzzled, Caramon began, "When you're ready, we can go up to our room. It's got a fireplace and—"

"Yes, yes, I heard," Raistlin snapped, cutting his brother off with a sweeping motion of one golden hand.

Caramon, shrugging, turned to obey and nearly fell over Earwig, who was coming out of the dining hall.

"Don't bother going in," said the kender. "It's dull as a tomb in there. No one's laughing or singing or anything. Hey, why do they say that, Caramon? 'Dull as a tomb'? I'd think a tomb could be pretty lively—"

Raistlin snarled in irritation, then began to cough. The spasms seemed almost to be trying to tear him apart. He leaned on his staff, relying on its strength to hold him up until he could breathe easier again. This time, Caramon knew his brother wasn't faking.

"Take me to my room," gasped Raistlin, holding out his arm for the warrior.

Caramon gently helped his twin up the flight of stairs

to the room on the second floor. Passing a small, open window, he saw that it was night. The two moons gracefully rose in the eastern sky, the silver and red crescents fuller now than they had been a few days ago.

When the twins reached room 221, Raistlin began to shake, coughing violently, his breath leaving his body and refusing to return. Caramon quickly opened the door and led his brother to a bed near the fireplace. There was a small stack of wood in the grate.

Moving quickly, Caramon began building a fire.

"Stop," Raistlin ordered Caramon in a choked voice. "Go downstairs and fetch some boiling water. Quickly!" he added when he saw his brother hesitate, not willing to leave the mage alone with his pain.

Caramon ran out of the room and down the stairs to do as he was bid.

Raistlin sat, leaning forward over the floor, holding his staff in straining hands, watching stars sparkle and glimmer before him. Lack of air and muscle spasms caused his eyes to play tricks on him. Fumbling at the herbal bag, he held it to his mouth and breathed. He looked again deep within himself, deep within the dark where the stars truly shone in his own night sky, where the sun shone in the same sphere. He still ruled, his goals firm, his desires unwavering.

Hearing Caramon pounding back up the stairs, Raistlin stood the staff against the bed and began to take out the medicine he needed for his drink. Caramon carried a pot of water, curling steam rising from the top, in his hand. Raistlin motioned him over to the bed and held out a small bag filled with the leaves that suppressed the mage's sickness, if only for a while.

Caramon hastily poured water into a cup, poking his finger into the scalding water, hoping to create the mixture before his brother started coughing again.

Raistlin, watching, said breathily, "Remember, Caramon, shaken, not stirred."

The bitter smell of the tea filled the room. The twins' mother had always said, "The worse medicine tastes, the better it works." Caramon was surprised this stuff didn't raise the dead.

Raistlin drank it and finally closed his eyes. Drawing a deep breath, he leaned back against the headboard.

"This is a strange place, Raist," muttered Caramon. "I don't like it. It's too quiet."

The mage took another deep breath. "Yes. But it's not a den of assassins and thieves as I'd expected. Did you see the people, my brother? Peasants, simple working folk, middle-aged farmers."

"Yeah," said Caramon, running his fingers through his hair. "But it's like Earwig said. Everyone sitting around talking in low voices. No singing or laughing. Maybe there's a war," he added hopefully. He'd like that. Plain and simple. Good old bashing the other's guy's brains out.

"No, I don't think so. I was eavesdropping on the conversations in the other room before you came blundering over and distracted me."

"Sorry. I thought you were sick. I didn't know—"

Raistlin went on softly, as if he hadn't heard the interruption, as if talking to himself. "The people are terrified, Caramon."

"Yeah? What of? Assassins?"

"No. Their cats have disappeared."

Chapter 3

The twins descended the stairs from their room on the second floor, Raistlin leaning on both his brother and the staff, the black wood resounding hollowly. Moving around the huge open fire in the main hall, they went to the dining room. But before Caramon could enter, Raistlin stopped him, drawing his hood back to expose one ear.

The fighter recognized this signal—a sign the twins had developed over the years—and quickly ducked back around the corner of the doorway before any of the patrons could notice him. He cocked his ear, listening, hoping to discover what his brother found so interesting.

Voices wafted like mist from the room.

"'Tis the work of evil, I say!"

"Aye, it's true!"

"I've lived eighty years," interjected an old man, "and I've seen nothing like it! Always we've taken care of the cats, as the legend says. And now they've left us! Doom will fall on our heads!"

"Probably the work of some foul wizard."

"Never did trust them."

"Yeah! Burn 'em all up, I say! Like in the old days."

"What do you think will happen to Mereklar, then, old man?"

"Mereklar? I fear for the world!"

"I heard there're no cats at all left in the city," stated a man, wearing a farmer's smock and broad-brimmed hat. "Is that true?"

"There are a few left, a hundred or so, perhaps," said the old man.

"A hundred where there used to be a thousand," added another.

"And their numbers dwindle daily."

Everyone began to talk at once, adding rumors they'd heard. They were beginning to work themselves into a frenzy.

Caramon came out from his hiding place to join his brother. He plucked Raistlin's sleeve.

"I think we've wandered into an asylum," he whispered loudly. "These people are crazy! To get this worked up over a bunch of cats!"

"Hush, Caramon. You should take this matter seriously. I would guess that this has much to do with the job we are seeking."

"We're being hired to look for lost cats?" Caramon began to laugh, his booming baritone roaring through the inn. Everyone fell silent, glaring at the brothers with baleful looks.

"Remember, Caramon!" Raistlin closed his thin-fingered hand over his brother's thick arm. "Someone tried to kill us over it, as well."

Caramon's laugh sobered quickly. The two entered the room. Their presence was not welcome. They were outsiders, intruding on a fear they could not understand. No one said a word, no one bade them sit down.

"Hey! Raistlin! Caramon! Over here!" Earwig's shrill voice split the sullen silence.

The twins walked to the back of the room. The inn's patrons cast furtive glances at the mage, and there was whispering and shaking of heads and glowering scowls. Raistlin ignored them all with a disdainful air and a slight sneering curl of his lips.

Caramon helped his brother sit down and get as comfortable as possible on the hard, wooden bench. The warrior beckoned to one of the barmaids, who—after a nod from Yost—came over to the table.

Caramon sniffed at the air and wrinkled his nose, not liking much what he smelled cooking.

"Rabbit stew," said the woman. "Take it or leave it."

"I'll take it," said Caramon, thinking regretfully of Otik's spiced potatoes at the Inn of the Last Home. He looked at his brother. Raistlin covered his mouth with a cloth and shook his head.

"My brother will have some white wine. Do you want something, Earwig?"

"Oh, no, thanks, Caramon. I ate already. You see, there was this plate of stew, just sitting there. My mother always said it was a sin to waste food. 'People in Solamnia are starving,' she'd say. So, to help the starving people in Solamnia, I ate the stew. Although just how that helps them I'm not certain. Do you know, Caramon?"

Caramon didn't. The barmaid hurried off and returned shortly with a plate of food and a mug of ale, which she slapped down in front of Caramon, and a goblet of wine for Raistlin.

Caramon plunged into his dinner with gusto, slurping and chewing and shoveling rapidly. Earwig observed him in round-eyed admiration. Raistlin was watching with disgust when suddenly the mage's attention focused on Caramon's half-empty plate.

"Let me see that!" he said, snatching it away.

"Hey! I wasn't finished! I—"

"You are now," said Raistlin coldly, scrapping the rest of the food onto the floor.

"What is it? Show me!" Earwig scrambled around to sit beside the mage.

"It's a poem," said Raistlin, gazing at the surface of the plate with interest.

"A poem!" Caramon growled. "You ruined my dinner for a poem!"

Raistlin read it to himself, then handed it over to his brother.

It is written, the land will know five ages,
but the last shall not come if darkness
succeeds, coming through the gate.
Darkness sends its agents, stealthy
and black, to find the gate, to
be there when the time arrives.
The cats alive are the turning
stone, they decide the fate,
darkness or light, in the
city that stands before
the first gods.

"Well?" said Raistlin.

"Cats, again," answered Caramon, handing the plate back.

"Yes," Raistlin murmured, "cats again."

"Do you understand it?"

"Not entirely. Up to now, there have been four ages—the Age of Dreams, the Age of Light, the Age of Might, and the Age of Darkness, which we are in now. A new age coming . . ."

"But not 'if darkness succeeds,' " said Caramon, reading the plate upside down.

"Yes. And 'the cats alive are the turning stone.' Interesting, my brother. Very interesting." Raistlin placed the plate carefully down on the table, his lips pressed together in thought.

"Wait a minute!" said Earwig. "I just remembered something."

Leaping up, he ran across to another table, grabbed hold of an empty plate, and brought it to the mage. "Look! Another poem! I found it when I'd finished my dinner."

He plunked the plate down in front of Caramon, and, seeing the fighter absorbed in reading it, appropriated his mug of ale.

It is written,
the Lord of Cats
will come, aiding his
dominion, leading only
for them, following no other,
the agents for one and three.
The cats alive are the turning stone,
they decide the fate, darkness or light,
in the city that stands before the first gods.

" 'The city that stands before the first gods.' " Raistlin repeated, taking the plate from Caramon and reading it again and again. He was always interested in stories and rumors of the first gods, the gods he truly believed still existed. "In all our travels, my brother, we've never come across anything like this! Perhaps here I'll find the answers I seek!"

"Uh, Raist!" Caramon said warningly.

The other patrons had fallen deathly silent and were staring at the brothers and the kender with dark and angry expressions. A few were rising to their feet.

"What do you strangers think you're doing? Mocking the prophecy?" demanded one, his hand clenched into a fist.

"We're just reading it, that's all," began Caramon, face flushing. "Is that a crime?"

"It could be. And you won't like the punishment."

Caramon rose to his feet. He was one against twenty, but the big warrior was undaunted by the odds. He could see, out of the corner of his eye, his brother's hand glide swiftly to the pouch Raistlin carried at his side—a pouch whose contents were as magical and mysterious as the man who used them.

"A fight?" asked Earwig, jumping up and down. The kender grabbed his hoopak. "Is there going to be a barroom brawl? I've never been in a barroom brawl before! Boy, Cousin Tas was right about you guys!"

"There's no fighting in my establishment," cried a stern voice. "Come now, Hamish and you, too, Bartoc, settle down."

The innkeeper placed himself between Caramon and the crowd, making placating gestures with his hands. The men calmed down, resuming their seats and their gloomy conversation. Caramon, slowly and warily, returned to the table.

"I'm sorry, sirs," Yost said to the twins. "We're not usually this unfriendly, but there are some bad things happening in Mereklar."

"What happened to the barroom brawl?" Earwig demanded.

"Shut up." Caramon grabbed the kender and stuffed him into his seat.

"Bad things—such as the cats disappearing?" asked Raistlin.

Yost stared at the mage in awe. "How did you know, sir?"

Raistlin shrugged.

"But then, you're a wizard, after all," continued the innkeeper with a sidelong glance. "I guess you know a lot of things the rest of us don't."

"And that's why everyone's ready to leap down our throats?" asked Caramon, pointing over his shoulder with his right thumb at the others in the inn.

"It's just that our cats mean as much to us as his word of honor means to a Knight of Solomnia."

Thinking back to his friend Sturm, Caramon was impressed. The Knights of Solomnia would willingly die to uphold their honor.

"Sit down, sir—"

"Yost. Everyone just calls me Yost."

"Sit down . . . um, Yost," said Raistlin in his soft voice, "and tell us about the cats."

Nervously, glancing back again at the other patrons, Yost took a seat opposite Earwig.

Caramon reached for his ale, only to discover that the kender had finished it.

"I'll have the girl bring you something else to drink," Yost said.

Caramon looked at his brother, who shook his head, reminding the warrior of the depleted state of their funds. The warrior heaved a sigh, "No, thanks. I'm not thirsty."

Smiling, the innkeeper gestured at the barmaid. "On the house," he said. "Maggie, bring us glasses and my own private stock."

The barmaid returned, bearing a dust-covered brown bottle that Caramon recognized as distilled spirits. Yost poured a glass for himself and one for the warrior. Raistlin declined.

"You want some?" Yost asked the kender. "It'll curl your hair."

"It will?" Earwig asked, gazing at the mixture in wonder. The kender ran a hand over his topknot of hair, his pride and joy. "Uh, I guess not, then. I like my hair the way it is."

Yost continued, "In Mereklar and the area around the city, we believe that our cats will one day save the world."

Caramon sniffed at the drink he had just been offered and gingerly took a small sip. He grimaced at the taste, then his eyes widened with delight at the pleasant burning sensation warming his insides. He belched and took a larger gulp.

"How?" asked Raistlin, glancing at his brother and frowning.

"Nobody knows for sure, but we all believe it will happen. Our heritage is based on it." Yost rolled the liquor on his tongue and swallowed. "That's why cats are always welcome in any home in Mereklar. It's against the law to harm a cat, punishable by death. Not that anyone would." The innkeeper gazed around sadly. "I used to have thirty or so here, myself. They'd be walking around, jumping on your shoulder, curling up in your lap. The choicest bits on everyone's plates were theirs. The sound of their purring was so soothing-like. And now"—he shook his head—"they're gone."

"And you've no idea where?" Raistlin persisted.

"No, sir. We've looked. And there's not a trace of 'em.

Another drink, friend?" Yost held up the bottle. "I can see you enjoy this."

"I do!" said Caramon, tears in his eyes and a huskiness in his throat. "What's it called?"

"Dwarf spirits. Hard to come by these days, since the dwarfs have closed up Thorbardin." Yost turned to Raistlin. "You seem unusually interested in our business, wizard. May I ask why?"

"Show him the paper, Caramon."

"Huh? Oh, yeah." Fumbling beneath his leather harness, the warrior brought out the parchment they'd found at the crossroads and exhibited it to Yost.

"Ah, yes! The council voted to offer a reward to anyone who could find our cats—"

"It doesn't say so," Caramon pointed out.

"No, well." Yost flushed, embarrassed. "We know that to the world outside, our love for our cats seems kind of strange. We didn't figure outsiders would understand until they got here."

"If they got here," murmured Raistlin, with an unpleasant smile.

Yost glanced at the mage sharply. Not certain if he had heard him correctly or not, he decided to ignore the statement.

"The idea of the reward came from the city's Councillor, Lady Shavas. If you're interested in the job, she's the one you should talk to."

"We intend to do so," said Raistlin, glaring at Caramon, who was helping himself to another drink of the potent brew.

Earwig yawned. "Are you going to tell us any more stories? What about this Lord of the Cats? Do you know him?"

"Ah, that." Yost stared into his drink. He appeared

highly uncomfortable. "The Lord of Cats is the king of the cats, the deity who tells them what to do." Pausing, taking a small swallow, he went on, "The only thing is, though, the stories aren't clear as to whether he'll help the world or destroy it."

"So you believe in the Lord of the Cats?" Caramon asked.

"We believe in his existence," Yost said, glancing around nervously as if he feared he was being watched. "We just don't know what motivates him."

Caramon reached for the bottle. Raistlin's hand shot out and closed over his brother's wrist.

"Where's the gate of which the prophecy speaks?" the mage asked.

"We don't know much about the prophecy, I'm afraid," said Yost. "It was found long ago, right after the Cataclysm. Maybe if we did, we'd know what was going on. Still, if you're interested, I've heard that Lady Shavas has books that tell about the Lord of the Cats and the prophecy and some of these other things. They're written in the your language—the language of magic, though there hasn't been a mage in these parts for over a hundred years. One was never wanted, if you get my meaning."

The bartender stood up and prepared to leave, taking his bottle with him, much to Caramon's disappointment.

"You look done in. Why don't you go back to your rooms?" suggested Yost pointedly.

"Thank you for your concern," returned Raistlin. "But we're not tired."

"Suit yourself." Yost shrugged and left.

Earwig was, in fact, fast asleep, his head pillowed on his arms. Caramon, probably as a result of the liquor, was glassy-eyed, staring rapturously at nothing. Reaching across the table, Raistlin grabbed him by the arm and shook him.

"Uh?" said the big man, blinking.

"Sober up, you fool! I need you. I don't trust that man. Look, he's talking to someone in the corner. I want—"

Raistlin saw, out of the corner of his eye, the line. A faint, though definitive, illumination was rising from the floor—a stream of white light running the length of the room, flowing north. He felt power, power that was as old as the world, power that ran through Ansalon, over the oceans, and beyond, extending to unobserved, inconceivable realms. Only those who walked on shadowy planes could know of such realms. Or one who had made contact with another who walked there.

Shuddering, Raistlin closed his eyes. When he opened them and looked again, all he saw was the floor—solid, dark with age, wet with spilled ale.

"What is it, Raist?" said Caramon, his voice slightly slurred. "What's the matter? What's down there?"

Caramon hadn't seen it. Raistlin rubbed his eyes. Was it his sickness, playing tricks on him again? Wine on his fingers made his eyes sting and water. He peered through the doorway at the side of the room to the fireplace in the main hall. There was the line again, an eerie white light, about a handspan wide. He turned his head, looked at it directly. The line disappeared.

"Raist, are you all right?"

"It must be a trick of my eyes," Raistlin muttered to himself, though he knew, since he had felt the power, that it wasn't.

But with the power came fear—horrible, debilitating fear. He didn't want to meet *him* again. He wasn't ready. The mage studied the ceiling, the beams, supports, and struts made from thick wooden bars that formed an archway overhead. Whenever he looked somewhere else, the line became visible—soft light rising from the floor. Sought directly, it vanished.

Raistlin grabbed his staff and quickly stood up, knocking over a bench.

"Barroom brawl?" Earwig's head jerked up. He blinked sleepily.

"Hush," said Caramon.

"What's Raistlin doing?" whispered the kender.

"I don't know," Caramon shot back. "But when he's like this, you better leave him alone."

What have I seen? What could it be? Do I even really see it? The mage moved to the south wall of the large eating hall. He looked out the back window and stared up into the sky. The glow appeared on the soft green grass lit silver and red in the light of the two moons. Raistlin kept his eyes open so long that they began to tear. The line grew brighter.

Returning to the table, Raistlin thrust his fingers into his glass of wine and wiped them across his eyes, the alcohol making them water again. The line became clear to his blurred vision—a band of power leading north. Raistlin faced the north window and saw that the stream flowed from the floor, through the wall, and out into the grass—a steady flowing river of white light. The mage sat down heavily on his bench.

"Hey, Raistlin," Earwig cried, jumping to his feet. "You're crying!"

"Raist—"

"Shut up, Caramon."

Sweeping the staff over the kender's head, causing Earwig to duck or be decapitated, the mage pointed downward.

"What do you see, kender?"

Earwig, startled by the question, followed the length of the staff with his large brown eyes. The pale blue orb at its top hovered inches from the floor.

"Uh, I see wood and a few dust bunnies. Isn't that a funny name? Dust bunnies? I guess it's because they look like little rabbits—"

"Look at me," ordered the mage.

"Sure." The kender looked up obediently.

Raistlin put his fingers in his glass and flicked wine straight into Earwig's wide-open eyes.

"Ouch! Hey, what are you doing?" Earwig cried in pain. He rubbed his hands against his eyes, trying to clear them of the spirits.

"Now what do you see?" Raistlin asked again.

The kender, squinting, tears running down his cheeks, peered around blearily. "Oh, wow! The room's gone all blurry. Everyone's sort of swelled up! Thanks, Raistlin. This is fun!"

"I mean on the floor," said Raistlin, exasperated.

"I can't see the floor," the kender said. "It's nothing but a dark lump."

Raistlin smiled.

"What is it, Raist?" asked Caramon, tensing, knowing by the expression on his brother's face that something remarkable had occurred.

"Hey, Caramon, what do you see?" Earwig cried gleefully. Grabbing the glass, the kender tossed wine in the warrior's face.

"A dead kender!" Caramon shouted, spluttering. "What do you think you're doing?" he demanded, collaring Earwig.

"Peace, my brother," Raistlin said, holding up the palm of his right hand. Caramon let go of the kender, pushing him roughly into the seat.

"By the way," the mage continued mildly, "what *do* you see, Caramon?"

"Not a damn thing!" the warrior muttered, wiping his streaming eyes with the backs of his hands.

"Nothing on the floor?"

"What's this about the floor? You keep staring at it, Raist. It's just a floor, all right?"

"Yes, just a floor. Caramon, go find that bartender. What's his name . . . Yost."

"Sure, Raist." Caramon's eyes lit up. "Do you want me to bring him back?"

"No, just ask him a question. Which direction is Mereklar from here?"

"Oh." Caramon shrugged. "All right."

"I'll come with you," offered Earwig, growing bored now that the stinging and burning had faded from his eyes.

The two left. Raistlin fell limply back into his seat. He felt drained, suddenly completely bereft of energy. The line was magic, visible to his eyes only. But what did it mean? Why was it there? And why this tiny, icy sliver of fear? . . .

* * * * *

Caramon found Yost and the bottle of dwarven spirits. Earwig watched and listened to them for a while but soon grew restless. He didn't want to go back into the eating room. He'd been there already.

"I guess I'll go out for a walk," he said to Caramon.

"Uh, sure, Earwax. Go ahead." The big warrior nodded. His voice sounded fuzzy.

"Earwig! Oh, never mind!"

Hoopak in hand, the kender skipped through the inn's front door and ran smack into three men, standing in the moonlight.

"Excuse me," said Earwig politely.

The men were tall, muscular, and wore black leather clothing that reeked with age. Wide straps crossed their bodies, holding bags and glittering, bladed weapons.

"Hello, little one. Do you mind if we ask you a question?" the man standing in the middle of the three asked in a smooth, rich voice. The ruddy glow from the firelight illuminated his face, and the kender was fascinated to see that the man's skin was as black as the night around them.

"No, please do!" Earwig urged.

The man's blue eyes shone deep red in the firelight. Deftly, with a graceful and fluid movement, he caught hold of one of the kender's small hands that was sliding into one of the man's own pouches.

"I'd keep that hand to myself, if I were you," advised the black-skinned man.

"I'm sorry," said Earwig, staring at his hand as though it had leaped from his body and was now acting on its own. "I can't think how it came to be there."

"No harm done. My friends and I"—the man indicated the two other men standing next to him—"were wondering where you got that magnificent necklace?" He pointed to the silver cat's skull that hung around the kender's neck.

"What necklace?" Earwig said, confused. Truth to tell, he'd forgotten all about it. "Oh, this?" He glanced down, saw it, and held the charm out for the men to admire. "It's an heirloom, been in my family for days."

"That's too bad," said the black-skinned man. His eyes gleamed as red as the ruby eyes in the charm's skull. "We were hoping that you might remember where you got it, so that we could get one for ourselves."

"Well, I can't, but you can have this one," offered Earwig, who loved giving presents. He tried to unfasten the chain. It wouldn't give. "That's odd. Uh, well, I'm sorry, sir. I guess you can't have it."

"Yes, we're sorry, too," the leader said in a soft voice. He leaned down, nearer Earwig, and the kender saw that the man's red-glowing eyes were slightly slanted. "Take your time. Think about where you got it. We have all night."

"Well, I don't!" Earwig snapped. He was beginning to tire of the conversation. Besides, there was no telling what trouble Caramon was getting himself into without the kender around to keep an eye on him. Earwig moved to push past the three men, but they blocked his way. One of them put a rough hand on the kender's arm.

"We can drag the information out of you and your guts along with it!"

"Could you really do that?" Earwig asked, thinking things might be getting interesting again. "Drag out my guts? How? Through my mouth? Wouldn't it be sort of messy—"

The man growled, his grip on Earwig's arm tightened painfully.

"Wait!" the black-skinned man ordered. "You're positive, kender, that you can't think how you came by the necklace?"

Back to the necklace again. Earwig jerked his arm free. Now he was beginning to get irritated.

"No, I can't! Really! Now, if you'll excuse me, I must be getting back."

The kender took a step toward the three men, giving every indication that if they didn't move, he was going to walk through them. The leader stared down at him. The red eyes flashed. Suddenly, with a fluid and graceful bow, he glided to one side of the door. His henchmen stepped back, out of the kender's way.

"If you remember how you came by the necklace, please tell us," whispered the smooth voice as the kender walked past him.

When Earwig turned to reply, he saw, to his amazement, that the men were gone.

* * * * *

Sitting alone, Raistlin was seized with a coughing fit. His breath refused to enter his lungs. He felt himself begin to lose consciousness. His head swayed slightly and he looked down into his cup, where he saw the remainder of his medicine, the leaves sticking to the bottom. Reaching out with a skeletal hand, he clutched at the passing barmaid.

"Hot water!" he gasped.

Maggie stared at the hand clasping her apron, the hand colored gold and as thin as death.

"Are you ill, sir? Can I help?"

"Water!" Raistlin snarled.

The woman, half-afraid, rushed to fill the order.

Raistlin slumped over, his head buried in his arms. Motes of light danced before his eyes, as he had seen at an illusionist's show once—dancing, spinning, sparkling, changing color, shape, form, but always illusory, always unreal, no matter how strongly he willed it to be different. He thought of how often he wanted things to be different, to change because he desired them to change. He thought of how many times he'd been disappointed.

Why couldn't he have been given the physical strength to match his mental strength? Why couldn't he be handsome and winning and make people love him? Why had he been forced to sacrifice so much for so little?

"So little now," Raistlin said to himself. "But I will gain more as time goes by. Par-Salian promised that my strength would someday shape the world!"

He fumbled at his side for the bag of herbs. Who knew but what this might cure him? He had thought he was feeling stronger. But his weak hand would not obey his command, and it occurred to Raistlin that he required Caramon's help.

I don't need him, the mage thought with dull defiance. The lights in the room dimmed with the darkness covering his eyesight. Listening to himself, he realized how childish he sounded. His lips twisted in a bitter smile. Very well, I need him now. But there will come a time when I won't!

The barmaid brought him his water, setting the pitcher down quickly, wanting to leave, wanting to stay. Maggie didn't like the mage with the gold skin and wizard's staff and the terrifying eyes that stripped away the soul. She didn't like him, yet she was fascinated by him. He was so frail, so weak, yet—somehow—so strong.

"I'll pour the water for you, sir, shall I?" she asked in almost a whisper.

Gasping, almost unable to lift his head, Raistlin nodded and clutched the cup with both hands. He drank deeply, his tongue numbed, the lack of sensation caused by his faintness removing any discomfort from the heat. He emptied the cup and let out a long, steady breath. The mage leaned against the back wall of the tavern, his eyes closed to the world.

Caramon found him thus when he returned. The warrior slid quietly into the booth, thinking his brother asleep.

"Caramon?" Raistlin asked without opening his eyes.

"Yeah, it's me. You want to go upstairs now?" The warrior's words were slurred, and his breath reeked of the foul-smelling liquor.

"In a moment. Which way is Mereklar from here?"

"North. Almost due north."

North. Without opening his eyes, Raistlin could see the white line running north, leading him, guiding him.

Impaling him.

Chapter 4

RAISTLIN KNEW HE WAS DREAMING, AND THE DREAM terrified him—he'd dreamed it many times before—but he couldn't force himself to wake. Something inside him, stronger than his own will, demanded that he give in.

The young mage left his bed, went to the door, stepped through the door, opened the door, closed the door, and walked into the gray mist that shrouded the hallway of the inn. Looking back, he could not see Caramon but he could see Caramon breathing peacefully in his sleep.

The mage took to the stairs that led down to the main hall. In his hand was the Staff of Magius, though he didn't remember taking it with him.

He needed light. The way was terrifyingly dark except for the white line that flowed beneath him with power and for the golden thread that connected him with another. "*Shirak*," he whispered.

The line guided him, directing his steps. He wandered the hallways and pathways of the inn and the surrounding areas, which were covered by gray mists that moved and roiled with unseen life. Ahead lay the one he sought, the one who had the answers to so many of his questions, the lifebringer and the destroyer.

Fantastic winged beasts—red, black, green, and blue—flew across his path, disturbed from their dreams by his wanderings, the staff's light waking them. The beasts gazed at him with hate-filled, hungry eyes. They wanted to destroy him, but could not. Not now, not this day.

Raistlin entered a room. Its four walls were solid, but the ceiling and floor lacked substance. A small table stood in front of him. He took one of the two drinks upon it and gulped it down. The liquid brought cold, soothing relief—a taste of fruit and spirit. He waited for the other to arrive.

A shadowy figure clad in long, black robes, dimly seen, dimly recognized, appeared.

"You are he?" Raistlin asked. His voice sounded strange. He didn't recognize it as his own. He saw the golden thread run glistening from himself to the other.

"Of course. You don't remember?" asked the other, as he always did.

"And the price?" Raistlin inquired, as he always did.

"You have already paid a part. The rest will be paid later," answered the other, as he always answered.

Only this time, there was a difference. The conversation did not end. The room did not vanish. Raistlin was able to ask the one question previously forbidden to him.

"And my reward?"

"Follow the line, as others are."

"Others?"

"You are watched even now."

"Who can see me here?"

"A man, though not a man."

"Does he wish me good or evil?"

"It depends on what you wish him."

Raistlin left the four walls with the ceiling and floor that didn't matter, the winged beasts flying from his path. The line led him back to the inn and the safety of his bed. The golden thread flowed backward, shimmering, trailing off into darkness.

Chapter 5

The city of Mereklar stood in the middle of a triangle shaped by three huge stone walls, each towering thirty feet high. The stone was pure, unblemished, without seams, cracks, or holes. But the white stone walls that faced outward were etched with symbols, signs, and pictures, each depicting some era of the world. Some of the legends were easily discernible—the Greystone of Gargath, the Hammer of Kharas, Huma and the Silver Dragon. Others had been lost to the memory of human, elf, or dwarf. All were depicted with a skill none now could rival or hope to attain.

When the stories came to an end, the walls were left

blank, as if waiting for the original artisan to return and place another piece of history upon them. Those who lived in Mereklar believed that when the outer walls were filled with stories, the world would end and another would be reborn in its place.

Unlike the outer walls, the inner walls of the city held no symbols. The ancient stone could not be cracked by any tool or weapon known to the hands of Krynn. It was a mystery to the citizens how anyone came to build the walls. In fact, the very origin of Mereklar was as much a mystery to the current inhabitants of the city as it was to their ancestors.

Their legends claimed that Mereklar was created by the first gods of good for purposes unknown. Following the Cataclysm, its first inhabitants had come down from the hills and mountains surrounding it, fleeing the chaos in the world, to find the city already built, as if awaiting their arrival. The people moved in and had, from that time until the present, been safe from any outside interference. Even the oldest of Mereklar's families, who had lived there for hundreds of years, knew nothing of the city's origins. The world changed, people changed, but Mereklar, City of the White Stone, remained the same.

There were ten noble families of Mereklar, and each lived in a large, opulent estate whose great white spires could be seen rising high above the streets. The ten great families were the first negotiators and coordinators, supervising the fields of grain, orchards of fruit, and pastures for animals, making the city grow and thrive. They maintained their positions with wisdom and foresight, intelligence and flexibility.

Each of the ten great homes had its own park, lush, green, filled with trees and flowers that remained in full bloom the year round. Small streams running through the city created ponds where members of the noble families would occasionally gather for parties or walk alone to relieve the romantic, melancholy needs of a somber heart. The houses themselves were four-storied and four-sided, as were almost all the houses in Mereklar.

The city was prosperous and self-sufficient. Everyone living in Mereklar accepted the legends and prophecies found in ancient tomes left in unused libraries and engraved on the outer protecting walls. That cats would save the world, they had no doubt. All doors were left open. Small paws made hardly a sound as they went from home to home, receiving food and warmth and comfort. The cats were always loved, always revered. They congregated in the parks, sunning themselves lazily, or wandered the streets, rubbing against the legs of a passerby.

Perhaps Lord Alfred Brunswick, Minister of Agriculture, was contemplating this very history of Mereklar, or perhaps he was pondering the absence of the cats. The servants wondered what he was doing, locked up alone in his study, all day and long into the night. His wife wondered as well.

"I never see you anymore, dear," she complained daily. "I know you're worried about the cats, but there's nothing you can do—"

At this point in the conversation, Lord Brunswick always got up and left the room, returning to his study and locking the door.

The study was a large, round room, filled with the books of the lord's ancestors, each telling a different tale of Mereklar. In the center of the room stood a triangular table, as long on each side as a man is tall, surrounded by ten chairs—one for each of the ministers of Mereklar. On the table was a perfect model of the city, exact in every detail. Each tree was in place, every river and stream flowed in the proper direction, even the carvings on the outside walls were duplicated with unprecedented skill. Like the city, the model's origins were a mystery. It had been here when the lord's ancestors moved into the estate.

Surrounding the model were the lands Lord Brunswick controlled—the lands of fruit and grain and corn. The servants had seen him studying at the model, determining when an orchard should be abandoned or expanded, a prairie burned or left to stand. His wife had watched him record notes in books and scrolls. That was before he had taken to locking the door to his study.

"Dinnertime, my lord," said one of the servants, knocking gently on the door.

Each night, the Brunswick family sat around a white, glass-topped table, father and mother sitting at the far ends, the youngest children sitting to the right, and the two older daughters at the left. The meal always began with thanking the cats, protectors of the lands and world, for their kindness. These last few weeks, however, that custom had been abandoned.

"No," Lord Brunswick had said abruptly one evening when his wife had begun to recite the words. "Cats will not be mentioned in this house again."

His wife and children knew, of course, why he was upset. Their cats had been among the first to disappear. And so the Brunswicks said nothing of cats, but talked of other things at dinner. Matters that were not likely to worry Lord Brunswick.

"How were things in the Council today, dear?" his wife asked, dishing up the soup.

"The usual," Lord Brunswick replied shortly.

"Daddy," his eldest daughter began, "you know that the Festival of the Eye is in two weeks."

Lord Brunswick glanced at his daughter sharply but

said nothing.

The girl drew a breath, gathering her courage. "When may I buy my new dress for the ball, Papa?"

"You're not going," said the minister.

"Oh, but you said I might! Only a month before, didn't he, Mama?" the daughter cried.

"Yes, dear. You promised," said Lady Brunswick, looking at her husband strangely. "Don't you remember?"

"Did I?" said Lord Brunswick vaguely. Suddenly he snapped, "Festival of the Eye! I don't have time for such foolishness."

Lady Brunswick shook her head. To her tearful daughter, she said quietly, "We'll discuss this later."

The dinner proceeded in silence. After dessert, the girls excused themselves from the table, going back up to their rooms.

"What's the matter, my dear?" Lady Brunswick turned to her husband, her face lined with concern. "You always enjoy the Festival of the Eye. Surely, even with these dreadful problems, you can relax and participate in it. After all, it occurs only once a year."

"Why must you always bother me with trivial matters?" the lord exploded.

His wife gazed at him, shocked. "In twenty years of our marriage, you've never raised your voice to me," she cried, her eyes filling with tears.

"I'm going to take a walk for some peace and quiet!"

Night had fallen. This was the same night, in an inn a short distance from the city, that a kender argued with a strange, black-skinned man; a mage gasped for breath; and a warrior shared a bottle of dwarven spirits with an innkeeper. The minister left his estate through the back doors of his house and began to walk his gardens, strolling with his left arm held stiffly behind his back, in the manner of a proper gentleman. The few cats left in Mereklar, who had wandered into the yard, scattered at his approach.

Glancing behind to see that he was not being followed, Lord Brunswick continued walking until he reached the edge of his land. Here stood a tall ceramic urn, one of many that lined the Brunswick property. The lord leaned against it casually. Waiting a few moments to assure himself that he was alone, the minister pushed slightly with his shoulder. The urn slid aside, revealing a hidden passageway into the ground.

Searching the area one last time, the minister stepped down onto the stairway, which began to glow with a strange, eerie light. Reaching out, he tugged on a lever that jutted from the wall. The urn moved back over the entrance, concealing it.

* * * * *

Lord Alvin, Minister of Property, finished his dinner at the same time as Lord Brunswick. Compared to the opulent meal the Minister of Agriculture had eaten, Lord Alvin's fare was simple, served on stone crockery in the kitchen of his home. He ate alone, preparing his food himself, without the aid of servants. The lord lived alone on his huge estate, hiring only a groundskeeper to maintain the gardens and trees. Lord Alvin was a misanthrope, a miser.

Going back to his study, Lord Alvin sat down stiffly in his chair. He glanced without interest over a book—a list of lands and their owners. When the chimes on his waterclock struck for the eighth time, he rose to his feet and made his way to the cellar beneath his house.

The wine cellar was a large room, storing hundreds of bottles of spirits, each vintage held in its own separate storage rack. Wine had been stored here for years, growing more and more valuable each day.

The lord walked down the flight of wooden stairs. Taking an oil lamp from its holder, he lit it with a match and continued on to the very back of the cellar. The minister moved heedlessly through the maze of racks, not caring that he jarred them. When a bottle fell to the floor and smashed, he didn't even glance around.

Far in the back, where the oldest bottles were stored, Lord Alvin came to a particularly ancient-looking rack. Running his fingers along the top, the minister reached out and pulled on a red bottle. The rack moved back with a subdued grinding sound, sliding into the wall. The lord stepped inside a tunnel that opened up behind the rack, his footsteps echoing hollowly in chill corridors.

* * * * *

That night, throughout the white-walled city of Mereklar, seven other noble lords were walking seven other dark and different paths, all leading to the same place.

Chapter 6

The local patrons of the Inn of the Black Cat stayed up far into the night, discussing the ominous portent of their missing cats, unwilling to let their fears take control of their dreams. Eventually, however, sleep overpowered them and they left for their homes. Only one man remained in the eating hall.

He'd been there all night, sitting alone, holding the same drink he had ordered at the beginning of the evening. No one spoke to him, he spoke to no one. Finally, Yost approached him.

"I'm closing up now. Either rent a room for the night, or leave."

The man rose to his feet. "You lock the front door, do you? No one can go out . . . or come in?"

"Not without waking me, they can't," Yost snorted. "Think I'd let people just stroll in or out without making certain they'd paid?"

The man nodded and laid down a steel piece, more than enough for what he had not drunk. He unhitched his plain brown horse from a post at the rear of the inn, and rode off into the quiet night.

He traveled swiftly through the fields and lands, avoiding hedgerows and muddy streams. The horse's harness brought music with every motion of the animal's long powerful legs, each stretch and toss of its head. Moving at a steady gallop, horse and rider traveled north.

Mereklar slept quietly under the brilliance of the two moons. Solinari's light rained down, showering the towers with silver, brightening the dimmest corners with heavenly light. Lunitari's glow spread over the city like a blanket, peaceful and content, throwing red shadows limned with shimmering silver.

The rider galloped up to the town gates and showed the guards an emblem he carried in his hand. Gold flashed in the moonlight. The guards let him pass. Without stopping, the man raced on to his destination.

On a small hill in the very center of the city stood a house unlike any other house in Mereklar. A rectangular shape, the house had a steepled roof, with two turrets rising from the front and back, and was built from yellow-brown stone instead of the pure white stone of Mereklar. Dark wood, weathered from wind and rain, held up the walls. Vines and ivy reached up to grasp the roof. Stained glass windows, shining with myriad colors, were lit from inside, creating strange, shifting patterns that seemed alive.

The rider dismounted and lashed his horse to one of the many trees that surrounded the strange house. He hurried up a path made of crushed white stones that shifted under his feet. Reaching the massive oaken door, apparently cut from a single living tree, he extended his hand to touch the doorknob—a piece of metal forged in the shape of a menacing cat.

The man withdrew his hand quickly. The iron of the handle was cold with the chill night air. Reaching out again, grasping the knob with a steady hand, he pushed slightly. The door did not open. Looking around the house for some sign of life, craning his neck to peer into the colored windows, the rider tried again. This time, the door opened easily at his touch. He had heard nothing. He drew his hand back, fear creeping up his spine.

Walking inside, the rider glanced around uneasily, listening again for any sign of life. There seemed to be none, yet someone—or something—had opened the door. He walked to the far end of the wood-paneled foyer and entered the main waiting room. A plush chair should have been warm, soft, and comforting. But when he sat in it, he felt unwanted, an intruder. He sighed pensively, crossing his legs and looking around nervously, uncertain when his hostess would arrive, uncertain if there was someone else in the dark, expansive home with him.

The only sounds he heard were his heart beating in time with an unseen clock—its water dripping down at regular, measured intervals—and the sighing of the wind through an open window. He had the eerie impression that the house was alive with blood and breath. The man started to get up and pace the floor, but changed his mind at the last moment. It was as if he feared disturbing the house.

He couldn't gauge the number of minutes that passed. Time seemed to have lost all meaning. The man was beginning to get angry. He'd been told to hasten. At the far end of the room was another door, a duplicate to the one the rider had first entered. He grasped the handle and twisted it down, hearing the latch click loudly in the silence of the house.

The door opened into another room, similar in size to the first, lit by a solitary fireplace at the far end. Looking in, he could dimly see bookcases filled with hundreds of books, hinting at the knowledge of ages past. Suits of armor reflected with steel-tinted light, each holding a weapon—a two-handed sword, a halberd, a pike.

"What news do you bring?" a rich voice asked in a tone sensual and feminine.

The man almost jumped back out of the doorway, his hand going to the dagger he kept in his belt. Squinting, he could see the lone robed figure of a woman sitting near him at the end of the table. A black cowl edged in white was thrown over her head. He could have sworn she had not been there when he opened the door.

"The three came to the Inn of the Black Cat, my lady," the man replied in a low voice. "They discovered the prophecies and asked questions. They asked the way to Mereklar."

The woman was silent a moment, thoughtful, brooding. "When will they arrive?" she asked at last.

"Tomorrow, my lady." The man discovered that he was still clutching his knife.

"You have done well," the woman said, ending the conversation.

He bowed respectfully. Closing the door as quietly as possible so as not to disturb his hostess, the man walked swiftly and thankfully out of the house. Mounting his nervous horse, he rode away into the city, eager to return to the comfort of his own home, where the rooms did not abhor his presence.

The lady in the black cowl had lived in the house atop the only hill in Mereklar all of her life. She felt comfortable in its rooms and hallways, the lights from outside creating patterns through the stained glass as mysterious as the lights shining from within.

After her agent had left, she rose gracefully in a single, fluid motion from her chair and walked confidently through the darkness of the study to a door in the east wall. The unseen waterclock that still ticked away the hours was the only sound in the house. The lady made no noise as she glided through a door into a side hall. Here she came to another door, set at the end of the corridor. She entered an arboretum, moved along a narrow path to the huge glass door facing the outside, then left the garden, closing the door behind her. The cowl of her robes was pulled low, hiding her face from the faces of the moons.

With sure and steady strides in the moonlit darkness, she quickly traversed one of the gardens surrounding her home. Coming to an old tree, dead and brown and pitted, she pushed away bramble with her foot, revealing an entrance leading into the ground—a passage devoid of light. She walked with even steps into the darkness.

Traveling untold distances, finding her way through mazes, paths, and passageways that went in all directions, she finally reached her destination—a cavern of stone flattened at the end opposite the entrance. Torches flickered in sconces, a stage for dancing shadows. In the center of the hall stood a rounded semicircle of stone holding a slab of rock so large it would require hundreds of men to move it. Standing around this altar were nine people, each wearing robes of state and service.

"You are late, Shavas," Lord Alvin said as he turned to face the entrance.

"Yes," said the woman in the doorway, stepping into the room, torchlight shadows staining her gown.

The ministers looked at each other, then at the woman.

"What news do you bring us?" asked another when it was obvious the woman was not going to offer an excuse.

The lord who spoke was a short man, stoop-shouldered, a gold medallion shaped like a sunburst weighing down his thin frame. He was dressed in a dark blue coat lined with gold-braided trim. Gold buttons ran down the front of his shirt, partially hidden by a dark blue vest.

"The three men are coming to the city's aid."

"And they will solve the mystery of the disappearing cats?" the short man asked again.

"They will try," corrected Shavas, the hood of her robes still hiding her face.

"We don't want panic," remarked a stern-faced, gray-haired woman. "We're close to that now."

"There's no choice," Lord Alvin spoke shortly. "You must hire these men, Shavas."

"I concur," said Lord Brunswick.

The consenting murmurs of the others filled the room, their united voices muffled in the underground cavern.

"What you mean is that you want me to do what is needed to repair your blunder," Shavas said. She flashed them a scornful glance, turned, and walked from the room. Her right hand gripped tightly a large fire opal she wore around her neck, holding onto it as if she were holding onto her very life.

* * * * *

That same night, someone else at the inn noticed the rider's hasty departure with interest. A black shape, almost invisible in the darkness, bounded down the same path the rider had taken. Moonlight glinted red in its eyes.

Chapter 7

Caramon awoke the next morning with a pound-ing in his head that his metal-working friend, Flint Fireforge, would have envied. The steady hammer blows, falling with excruciating regularity, made him wince with pain. The delicate sounds of chirping birds were like the clash of spears, and the shuffling noises of the other patrons at the inn created a wave of agony.

Slowly drawing the sheets back from his head, exposing only his sleep-matted hair and bloodshot, half-closed eyes, the fighter glanced around the room, wincing again as a shaft of light struck him full in the face.

"A cruel blow!" he muttered.

Quickly pulling the sheets back over his head, Caramon lifted the bedspread from the side—avoiding another bright onslaught—and peered across the room to his brother. Still asleep, Raistlin appeared to be in pain—his back was arched slightly, his hands were curled into claws. But he breathed easily. Caramon sighed in relief.

The warrior glanced over to Earwig's bed, hoping that the kender—with his shrill voice—was also still asleep. He was, if the steady rise and fall of his blankets was any indication.

"Good," said Caramon to himself. "I'll go downstairs and use my tried-and-true remedy for overindulgence."

The warrior eased himself out of bed, his head bent against the morning's light.

"Good morning, Caramon!" Earwig shrilled cheerfully, his voice piercing Caramon's skull. The warrior fell over the bed as if toppled by a mighty blow.

He couldn't remember the last time he'd felt so miserable. Thinking of Flint reminded him of one of the old dwarf's many sayings, "A fighter's greatest enemy is himself." He had never understood what that meant until now. He wondered, too, if Flint had been referring to that terrible stuff—dwarf spirits—that had been the warrior's downfall.

"Earwig," Caramon began, speaking softly through clenched teeth, his hands slowly clamping his head to ease the pressure. "If you don't shut up, I'm going to have to kill you."

"What?" Earwig shouted, his voice just as loud as before. "What did you say? I couldn't hear you. Would you repeat that, please?"

In answer, Caramon grabbed a pillow with his left hand, walked over to the kender, and bagged Earwig's head with the pillowcase.

"Is this a game? What do I do now?" cried the kender, highly excited.

"Just sit there," growled Caramon, "till I tell you to move."

"All right. Say, this is fun." Earwig, pillowcase over his head, composed himself to wait for whatever wonderful part of the game was going to come next.

Caramon walked out of the room.

Going to the well outside, he brought up a bucket of cold water and immersed his head in it. Sputtering, he shook himself like a dog, wiping his face on his shirt sleeves.

Returning indoors, still rubbing himself dry, Caramon went into the eating hall, where breakfast was being served. The smell of eggs, bacon, and hot muffins helped ease the unrelenting pain in his head and reminded him that he hadn't eaten since dinner last night—and that had been interrupted.

It's a good thing I never get sick when I drink, he thought to himself with pride.

The room was practically empty. The few sullen patrons seated there glanced at the big man, scowled, and glanced away.

Caramon ignored them. Going to the table he had occupied last night, he plopped his body down with such force that he almost fell over on the bench. Righting himself, the warrior sat very still until the queasiness left him.

"Well, almost never," he amended.

"What can I get for you this morning?" It was Yost, the innkeeper, a slight smile stealing across his face.

"A drink. Two-thirds grain, one part juice, one part cooking spice, and a green vegetable stalk, something absolutely tasteless. And plenty of pepper," Caramon added.

"Ah," said Yost, "a seasoned warrior. The Old Fighter's Favorite. And I bet you'll be wanting some breakfast as well. Maggie!"—his yell caused Caramon to groan aloud—"bring something to eat for the gentleman here."

Caramon drank three Old Fighter's Favorites, gulping the first two down quickly. The heavy taste of pepper drowned out the horrible taste of the brew. He stirred each one with a vegetable stalk absentmindedly as he poked at his food with a fork, unsure if he could stomach anything.

By the fourth dose of cure, however, Caramon's appetite came back. He ate slowly at first, building momentum. Eventually, he felt more like himself, and he sat back against the wall, leaning the bench backward, his shoulders propping him up. The other patrons had gone, the fighter was the only one in the tavern.

Yost came over to stand by Caramon and glanced about with a gloomy air. "If this trouble doesn't end soon, I'll be ruined. The Festival of the Eye is coming up. A lot of people from Mereklar come to my inn to celebrate. But they won't this year. Maggie, clear the table."

Maggie hustled over and began picking up plates and stacking them on a wooden tray. Caramon noted that she was an unusually pretty, red-cheeked girl with a buxom figure and straw-colored hair worn tied up with a yellow ribbon. He seemed to dimly recall that she had smiled at him last night.

"Here, that's too heavy for you," he said, taking the tray from her.

"Oh, no, sir. This is my job," said Maggie, flushing deeply and trying to take the tray back.

During the friendly wrestling match that ensued, Caramon managed to kiss a rosy cheek. Maggie slapped him playfully, and the tray filled with dishes nearly ended up on the floor.

"Which way to the kitchen?" asked Caramon, who had emerged as the victor.

"It's over here, sir." Blushing furiously, Maggie led the

way. Caramon followed, carrying the tray, and a morose Yost brought up the rear.

The kitchen was large and spotlessly clean. Numerous pots and pans hung from hooks nailed into the white-washed walls.

"Any more for breakfast?" asked the cook, a small, thin, dark-haired woman.

"No," said Yost gloomily.

The cook began to make ready for the luncheon guests. Maggie motioned Caramon to one of the sinks. Quickly taking the plates from the tray he carried, she plunged them into the soapy water.

"Well, Master Innkeeper," Caramon began, talking to Yost but looking Maggie boldly in the eye, causing her to blush again and nearly drop a cup. "If it makes you feel better, my brother and I are going to Mereklar to try to earn that reward."

"Oh, are you, really?" Maggie turned, her motion sending a spray of bubbles over Caramon. "Lord! I'm sorry, sir!"

Grabbing a towel, she tried to dry the warrior's expansive chest. Caramon caught hold of her hand and held it fast. The girl's eyes were brown, with long lashes. Her hair was the color of the leaves of the vallenwood trees in autumn. She didn't even come up to his shoulder. Caramon's heart beat fast. He bent down to steal another kiss, but Maggie—with a sidelong glance at her employer—pulled away and began to wash dishes at a furious pace.

Yost nodded. "I figured as much. That mage asking all those questions. He really your brother?"

"My twin brother," said Caramon proudly. "He took the Test in the Tower of High Sorcery when he was only twenty. The youngest ever. And he passed. Though it cost him . . . cost both of us," the warrior added, but only to himself, beneath his breath.

Maggie heard, however, and gave him a warm and sympathetic glance. "He's real sick, your brother," she said in a soft voice.

"Yeah. I worry about him a lot. But," Caramon spoke hastily, seeing Yost's face grow longer, "he's stronger than he seems. If anyone can solve this mystery of yours about the cats, Raistlin can. He got all the brains, you see, and I got the muscle," the big man said cheerfully.

"Why would you bother with us?" Yost asked, staring at Caramon suspiciously.

"We're low on funds. We can use the job. Though, of course, more personal reasons have come up." He winked at Maggie, who smiled demurely.

"And what, if I may ask," Yost continued, "would a mage want with money? I thought they could conjure it out of thin air or something."

"They don't do that. It's just a myth, like touching a frog and getting warts," Caramon said loftily, showing off his vast knowledge of magic.

"Toad," the cook corrected quietly under her breath, without looking up from her work, sifting flour into a large bowl.

Caramon glanced at her in astonishment.

"You get warts from a toad," she repeated. "And we don't need any magic-users around here."

"There's never been one," agreed Yost, "and we've got along fine so far. It seems odd, you know." His voice hardened. "Our cats disappearing and your brother coming into town about the same time."

"From what I've heard, your cats began disappearing weeks ago. My brother and I weren't anywhere near—" Caramon began hotly.

"There was a wizard lived here once," Maggie interposed quickly. "Remember, Yost? That crazy old hermit who had a cave in the mountains?"

"Oh, him," said the innkeeper, remembering, "I'd almost forgotten about him. He never bothered us. Word was that he died, scared to death by spooks or something like that."

"Nobody knows for sure," added the cook ominously, concentrating on her pie crusts.

"Well, it doesn't matter." Yost frowned, dismissed the subject. "I was just wondering why a wizard would want to help us, that's all."

"My brother has his own reasons," Caramon said curtly. "He's done a lot of things just to help others, like expose that phoney cleric at Larnish."

"Larnish!" the cook exclaimed. She dropped a bag of flour on the table in front of her, sending a small, spectral cloud of white into the air.

"You've heard of it?" Caramon asked.

"I had people there," the cook answered.

The warrior waited, but she said nothing more.

"Well, I say it bodes no good! Mages! Huh!" muttered Yost, and walked out of the kitchen.

"Here, I can dry those for you," said Caramon, grabbing a dishtowel and sidling up beside Maggie.

"Oh, no, sir! This is woman's work! Besides, you might break—"

Maggie stopped, noting that Caramon was drying the plates swiftly, deftly.

"My mother was sick a lot," said Caramon quietly, by way of explanation. "My brother and I got used to fending for ourselves. Raist always washed and I dried. It was fun. We enjoyed it. We used to talk . . ." His voice died as the warrior remembered happier times.

But Maggie was smiling at him, a smile that lit the room more brightly than the sun shining through the window.

* * * * *

Returning to his room, Caramon found Raistlin and Earwig finishing breakfast.

"I don't think much of that game, Caramon," said Earwig severely.

"Huh?" The big warrior looked blank.

"Never mind," snapped Raistlin. "Where've you been?"

"Oh, just visiting. Finding out a few things. Can I help you pack, Raistlin?" Caramon walked over to his brother, who was poking his fork at a small piece of bread and assorted pieces of fruit.

"I'm already packed." Raistlin seemed unusually distant, withdrawn. His face had a gray tinge, and there were dark circles beneath his eyes.

"Bad night?" asked Caramon.

"The dream again," Raistlin answered briefly. He looked away from his brother to stare out the window.

"I'm packed, too!" Earwig stuffed a huge piece of a corncake into his mouth. Syrup dripped down his chin and back onto the plate in front of him. Still chewing, he gulped milk from a mug.

"Earwig, go outside," ordered Caramon.

"I'm not done!"

"You're done. Raist, I think I should—"

"That is an excellent suggestion. Wait outside with him, my brother."

"But—"

"Go!" the mage commanded, thin hands clenching into fists. He stared out the window.

"Sure, Raist. We'll wait for you downstairs. Come when you're ready."

Caramon grabbed his pack and his brother's and left the room. Taking a last gulp from his mug, Earwig followed.

Raistlin heard the door close behind them. The sun, warm and encouraging, shone through the window, causing the mage's skin to glow with an inner golden light that seemed healthy in comparison with the sickly tinge it had acquired the night before. He reached over and touched the Staff of Magius with his hand, finding comfort in the feel of the wood.

"Why can't I remember? And why am I maddened by a half-dream I can't recall? It was important. Something important—"

"Excuse me, sir," came a timid voice, taut with fear.

Raistlin turned swiftly. He had not heard the door open. "What do you want?" he asked dourly, seeing a thin, dark-haired woman standing in the doorway.

The woman blanched at his harsh tone, but, gathering her courage, she took a trembling step forward into the room.

"Pardon, sir, but I was talking to your brother, and he said you was the one brought about the downfall of the cleric of Larnish?"

The mage's eyes narrowed. Was this some religious fanatic, about to berate him? "He was a fraud and a charlatan. A third-rate illusionist," Raistlin whispered. Turning to face the woman, he pulled back his hood.

The woman saw hourglass eyes sunken into golden skin, reflecting in the morning light. The sight was alarming, but she held her ground.

"He stole money from innocent people in the name of his false gods," Raistlin continued. "He ruined countless lives. Yes, I was responsible for his downfall. I repeat again, woman, what do you want of me?"

"I've . . . I've just come to thank ye, and give ye this," the cook said. She crept nearer the mage, holding something in her hand. "My boy, sir. He was one of them that was took in. He's back home with me now, sir, and doing well."

The woman dropped her gift in the mage's lap.

"It's a good-fortune charm," the woman said shyly.

Raistlin lifted it. The amulet sparkled and glimmered, shining and glittering as it spun slowly on its chain. It was ancient, the jewels in it valuable. He recognized it as a treasured possession, one that could have been sold to ease poverty, but was kept in remembrance of loved ones long dead.

"I must get back to my work now," said the cook, backing up. "I just wanted to tha—"

Raistlin reached out a skeletal hand and took hold of the woman's arm. She cringed, shrinking backward.

"Thank you, mistress," he said softly. "This is a wondrous charm you have given me. I shall cherish it always."

The woman's thin face brightened with pleasure. Bending down, she timidly kissed his hand, shuddering slightly at the feel of the too-warm skin. The mage let loose of her arm, and she fled out the door.

Alone again, Raistlin tried to recapture the dream, but it wouldn't be caught. Sighing, he stuffed the charm into one of his pouches, and—leaning on the staff—pulled himself to his feet. He took one final look out the window and saw, shimmering along the grass, the strange white line leading north, leading to Mereklar.

Raistlin walked outside the inn. The staff's golden claw shone in the sunlight, the pale blue orb it held seemed to absorb the dawn, transforming the light into its own.

"Where's Caramon?" the mage asked Earwig, who was sitting hunched over on the packs.

"He told me to stay here and wait for him, but it's getting awfully boring. Can't we go now?"

"Where—" began Raistlin again.

"Oh, he went around the side of the building about a minute ago." The kender pointed.

Raistlin looked at the packs that had obviously been rifled and wondered just how much of their possessions had made their way into Earwig's pouches. Caramon was such a fool sometimes.

The mage, face set into grim lines, stalked around to the back of the inn. He found his brother and one of the barmaids embracing, the warrior's huge body enfolding the girl's smaller one.

Raistlin stared silently. A slight breeze barely moved his robes, the only motion around his body. No breath could be heard, no sound passed from his lips. Emotions surged from a well he knew must be sealed forever if he was to achieve true power. He stood and watched, his chest burning, though a coolness was already rushing from within to extinguish the heat. Even with great effort of will, there was something that made him stand and watch until he could bear no more.

"Come, Caramon! We don't have time for another one of your little conquests!" Raistlin hissed.

He enjoyed watching them both jump, enjoyed seeing the girl flush red with shame, his brother red with embarrassment.

The mage turned around, digging the staff deep into the ground, and walked back to the front of the inn.

"I've got to go now," Caramon said, swallowing his passion.

"Sure," Maggie whispered, brushing her disheveled hair from her face. "Here. I want you to have this." She thrust something into the bosom of his shirt. "Just a charm. To remember me and to bring you good luck in your journeying."

"I'll never forget you!" Caramon vowed, as he had

vowed a hundred times before to a hundred women before, each time meaning it with all his heart and soul.

"Oh, get along with you!" said Maggie, giving him a playful shove. Sighing, she sank back against a tree, her eyes half-closed, watching the warrior run after the mage.

The companions started on their way, walking for a time in silence—the mage working off his ire, the warrior letting his twin cool down. Earwig, mercifully, had dashed up ahead "to check things out."

The road was empty, though there was evidence that a horse had galloped over it not many hours before. Its hooves had dug deep into the damp earth.

Raistlin studied the horse's hoofprints and wondered what urgency had driven a rider to press his animal so. There could be any number of reasons, but the mage felt suddenly, intuitively, that it had something to do with them. An uneasiness was growing in Raistlin. He had the distinct impression that, instead of walking toward Mereklar, they should be hastening away from it. He came to a stop.

"Caramon. What is that?" Raistlin pointed with the staff toward a spot in the mudddy road.

Caramon came back to look. "That track?" The warrior knelt down, brow furrowed in concentration. "I'm not sure, Raist," he said, rising to his feet, his face carefully expressionless. "I'm not a very good tracker. You'd have to get one of those Que-shu barbarians—"

"Caramon, what kind of animal made that track?"

The warrior looked uncomfortable. "Well, if I had to say—"

"You do."

"I guess . . . a cat."

"A cat?" Raistlin's eyes narrowed.

"A . . . big . . . cat." Caramon gulped.

"Thank you, my brother." Raistlin continued walking.

Caramon, falling in next to him, sighed in relief that his twin's ill humor was apparently over. The warrior drew a small ball of cloth out of his pocket. He put it to his nose, sniffing at it and smiled at the sweet, spicy smell. The ball was decorated with sequins that had been sewn onto it by loving hands. A long yellow ribbon—a hair ribbon—fluttered gaily from the top.

"What's that?" Raistlin asked coldly.

"A gift. It's supposed to bring good fortune!" Caramon held it up by the ribbon, spinning it in the morning's light, watching the sequins reflect a rainbow of fascinating colors.

The mage thrust his hand into his pouch, his fingers touching his own gift of the morning.

"You're a superstitious fool, brother!" Raistlin said with a sneer.

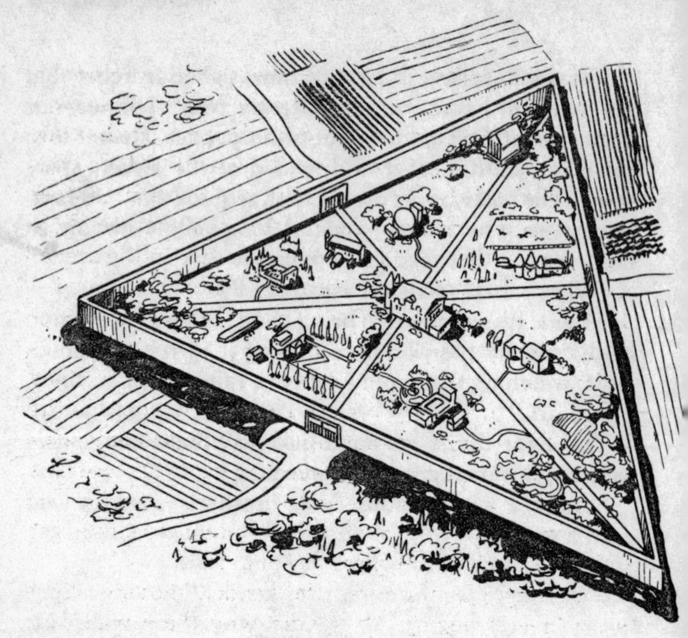

Chapter 8

It was night when they reached Mereklar. The city's white walls glowed eerily in the silver moonlight. The bas-reliefs on the walls— raised patterns of the history of Krynn expanded into huge shapes, actors forever frozen— threw strange, shifting shadows over the surrounding grounds.

Earwig was fascinated. He'd never, in all his travels, seen anything so marvelous. He loved stories, and this was like having every one he'd ever heard come real before his eyes. The kender ran his hands along the walls, walking slowly, gazing in wonder.

"There's Huma and the Silver Dragon," he said, pointing to the hero and his tragic love, each perfectly inscribed, every line, curve, and angle in exact proportions. "I don't recognize that one, though. Or that one either. That guy's a wizard, isn't he, Raistlin? Like you. Why, he *is* you! Look, Raistlin, you're fighting another wizard—a real, real old wizard. And that warrior there looks sort of like you, Caramon. The one in the arena, battling a minotaur. And"—Earwig's mouth dropped—"I'll swear that's Cousin Tas! There! Talking to a five-headed dragon! Look, Raistlin, look!"

"Nonsense!"

The mage gasped for breath. He barely glanced at the walls. His strength was failing fast. It always did, with the coming of night. He had been leaning on his brother's strong arm for the last few miles.

"Hurry up, Earwig!" snapped Caramon, anxious to get his brother to a place where he could rest.

"I'm coming," murmured the kender, moving along slowly, feet dragging. "I wonder why these walls are blank. . . . I know! I'll bet they're waiting—waiting for great deeds of the future to be recorded on them. Maybe"—he heaved an ecstatic sigh—"maybe I'll be up there someday!"

Each pass of his fingers over the slate sent thrilling chills down his arms and back. He could almost see himself, immortalized in stone, joining the rest of Krynn's famous and heroic.

"Earwig!" Caramon called irritably.

The kender paused, glancing back at the wall. The wizard certainly did resemble Raistlin. But how could the mage be here and be bacl in the past at the same time? He'd have to remember to ask.

"Kender!" Caramon shouted in a voice that meant no nonsense. "Get up here now, or we'll leave you behind!"

Earwig hurried to catch up. He might have a chance, in this wondrous city, to be a hero and have his picture on the wall. Imagining his adventures, he forgot all about asking Raistlin how he could be master of the past and the present.

"Wait a moment, Caramon!" Raistlin clutched his chest. "Let me . . . catch my breath."

"Sure, Raist."

Caramon stopped walking. Raistlin, gripping the staff to support himself, stood before the city walls. He wasn't coughing, however. Looking closer, the fighter saw that his brother was staring down at the ground, intently, concentrating. Raistlin's face could not be seen behind the red cowl, hiding from the silver moonlight.

Caramon experienced a feeling he often had around his brother, the sense that nobody in the entire world could ever intrude upon the young mage's thoughts, that no force in the world would ever shake Raistlin's ambition. Caramon found himself wondering, with a feeling of uneasiness, just what Raistlin's ambitions were.

Raistlin glanced up, turning to face his brother. Red moonlight filled the mage's hood, making his gold skin blaze with fire—a brazier of inner strength, indomitable, unquenchable. The hourglass eyes were filled with crimson, unscarred by the silver of the other moon. Caramon gaped, wondering if the apparition before him was truly his twin.

Raistlin smiled slightly, seeing his brother's obvious discomfort.

"Aren't we going in?" Earwig was looking at them anxiously.

Caramon suddenly wanted to shout, "No!" turn around, and walk straight back to the inn. He knew with the intuitive sense that made the brothers nearer twins on the inside than they were on the outside that Raistlin believed great danger lay ahead of them.

Great danger, but also great reward.

"Come on! You were the ones who told me to hurry!" Earwig urged, his shrill voice sounding too loud in the night stillness.

"Magic," Caramon muttered beneath his breath. "He'll risk his life for the magic!" And mine, too, the warrior added in silence.

Raistlin held out his left arm, sweeping it toward the open gate that led into Mereklar. His right hand clutched the Staff of Magius near the top, a black line in red and silver moonlight.

"Shall we enter, my brother?"

The huge gate leading into Mereklar was easily large enough to fit five horses riding comfortably abreast, with three more standing on each others' shoulders. It was raised and lowered by an unseen mechanism, hidden deep within the walls, out of sight. No chains or ropes were visible. Running grooves, one on either side, were used as guides to keep the barrier sliding smoothly. Though the city was old, the iron bars of the portcullis did not show any signs of age or wear. Metal plates, apparently for decorative use, embellished the bars. On each plate was inscribed the head of a cat.

The city wall was five feet thick, and perfectly smooth and unblemished. Even the slots cut into the sides of the portal and ceiling had no imperfections. Not the smallest chip scarred the surface of the stone near the grooves, where anyone who had ever seen a castle's gate knew that rock began to disintegrate most quickly at those high stress points.

The companions walked inside the open gate. Caramon gazed at the city's defenses with a soldier's eye. Earwig stared with wonder at the incredible size of the gate and wall. Raistlin saw only the line of power, shimmering at his feet, extending into the city.

"Halt!" cried a voice. A soldier stepped out of a guardhouse, gesturing for five of his men to follow. They had been sitting out of sight, comfortably reclining in chairs in the cool evening air. Now they ran up to the party, holding their glaives in both hands, their bodies moving with exaggerated swings to the left and right, balancing with the weight of their heavy weapons.

The twins and the kender came to a standstill. Caramon stood with his arms folded across his chest, the hilt of his sword jutting up over his back, the main-gauche sitting at his hip. Raistlin leaned heavily on the staff, his back bent with fatigue. Earwig stepped forward, politely extending his small hand.

"Hi! I really love your walls!"

Caramon caught hold of him and pulled him back. "I'll do the talking!"

The soldier who called for them to halt was a tall, thin man with large hands. Insignia on his simple blue uniform indicated that he was a sergeant.

"By law, we must question all strangers wanting to enter the city."

"Certainly, we understand, Sarge," Caramon said, smiling in a friendly manner.

"Your names?"

"Caramon Majere. Raistlin Majere," Caramon said, gesturing to his twin with a hand. "And this"—patting the kender on the shoulder—"is Earwig."

"Earwig. Surname?"

"Uh, just Earwig."

"No, it's not 'just Earwig'!" said the kender indignantly, ignoring the warrior's attempts to hush him. "My name is Earwig Lockpicker."

Caramon groaned softly.

"Lockpicker?" The sergeant glowered. "And just what might that name mean, I wonder?"

"Well, if you're interested, I'll tell you," offered Earwig brightly. "You see, when the kender first lived in Kendermore, my great-great-great-great-great-grandfather . . . I think. I mean, I know it was my grandfather, but I'm not sure if I put enough 'greats' in there. Maybe it was my great-great-great-great-great-*great*-grandfather who—"

"It is simply a name, officer, and has no meaning outside of tribal identification," Raistlin said, smoothly breaking into Earwig's recitation of his family tree. "It's quite common among kender."

"Common? It's not common—" cried Earwig, but Caramon managed to muffle the kender with a large hand over his mouth.

"You seem to know a lot about them, sir. Do you have many kender friends?" The sergeant turned suspicious eyes on the mage, who stood perfectly motionless behind his brother.

"Exactly two more than I'd like," answered Raistlin dryly. He suddenly began to cough and nearly fell.

Caramon sprang forward to assist him. "Look," said the big man angrily, "we've answered your questions, Sergeant. Now let us pass. Can't you see that my brother's ill?"

"I can see it. And I don't like it. We hear that there's plague beyond our walls," said the sergeant, his frown deepening. "I think you three had better just go back to wherever it is you came from."

"I do not have the plague." Raistlin was breathing easier. He stood up straight. "And we are going into the city." The mage slid his left hand into voluminous robes, gliding between the simple hooks that held it closed in the front.

"Even if we have to go through you," added Caramon grimly, standing to one side of his brother and drawing his sword.

"Stop them!" yelled the sergeant.

The soldiers halfheartedly lowered their weapons, threatening the companions with the broad blades of their glaives. None actually moved to stop the mage. None wanted to get that close.

"Come on!" cried Earwig, swinging his hoopak in the air until it whistled. "We'll take you all on!"

"Wait, Sergeant!" called a voice.

A man motioned from the shadows where he must have been standing the entire time. The sergeant, glancing at the companions balefully, walked over. The two conversed briefly, then the sergeant nodded. He returned, looking relieved, and the man melted back into the shadows.

"Please excuse my suspicion, gentlemen," said the sergeant, bowing. "These are troubled times. You are welcome in our city."

"We are?" said Caramon dubiously.

"Yes. Rooms have been arranged for you at Barnstoke Hall."

"How did anyone know we would be com—" Caramon began, but fell silent when he felt his brother's hand close over his arm.

The sergeant handed Caramon an ornate scrollcase. "Here. This is for you."

Caramon handed it to his twin, who hid it within his robes.

"Where might we find the home of Councillor Shavas?" inquired Raistlin.

"Councillor Shavas's house is in the exact center of town. Follow any of the main roads. They all lead right to it. The lodging-house, Barnstoke Hall, is on this road, just a short distance away."

Raistlin had begun to cough again. Caramon took his brother's arm.

"Thank you, Sergeant. We'll be going now," the warrior said. They walked slowly up the street, leaving the guards to stare after them, shaking their heads and muttering in low voices.

Absorbed in discussing the arrival of a wizard, the guards never noticed a dark form scale the white walls of Mereklar. The figure, dressed all in black, used no ropes or tools of any kind, but climbed the wall with ease, finding foot- and hand-holds in the carvings. Gliding over the top of the wall, he dropped down lightly onto the street below, landing silently on all fours. Keeping to the shadows, he slinked past the guards and crept down the street, keeping the companions in his sight.

"How the devil did anyone in Mereklar know we were coming?" Caramon demanded when his brother could breathe again.

"The man standing in the shadows," Raistlin whispered. "He was at the inn with us. Remember the horse's hoofprints on the road?"

"Was he?" Caramon glanced around, pausing. "Maybe I should go back and—"

"No, you shouldn't!" snapped Raistlin. "I'm growing weaker by the moment. Would you leave me to die in the gutter?"

"No, Raist. Of course not," said Caramon patiently, helping his brother through the quiet streets.

Every building was constructed of the same white stone as the walls, every street was a perfect white slate, smooth and even. It seemed to have all been carved from a single mountain of rock.

"Flint would love this place," muttered Caramon.

"Hey! Look at that!" Earwig cried, pointing.

Motes of light were swelling out of the ground like water bubbling up from moist soil. After a few moments, the lights began to rise into the air, hovering above the walks and streets, flooding them with a radiant glow that illuminated the way for late-night travelers.

The lights were wasted tonight, however. No one was about, a fact Caramon thought strange, considering that it was not yet late. He peered constantly down the shadowy alleys and glanced sharply into each dark doorway they passed. The sharp-eyed kender noticed the warrior's nervousness.

"Do you think someone's going to jump out at us, Caramon?" Earwig asked eagerly. "You owe me a fight, you know, since you let me sleep through the one in the—"

"Keep quiet, kender!" Raistlin snarled.

Caramon glanced around. "Raist," he said in a low voice, for his brother's ears alone, "someone tried to stop us from coming to Mereklar that night. Why haven't they tried again?"

The mage nodded his head wearily. "A good question, my brother. Look at it this way. That night, no one knew we were coming to Mereklar except the assassin. We may assume, I believe, that someone saw you remove the sign from the post at the crossroads. If we had died that night—" The mage coughed, struggled to draw breath.

"If we had died that night," he repeated, when he could talk, "no would have known or cared. But, when we reached the inn, we made no secret of our interest in this city. People knew we were coming. If anything had happened to us on the way, questions would have been asked. Curiosity aroused."

"That's true," said Caramon, regarding his brother with admiration. "So you think we're safe now?"

Raistlin looked down at the white line, shimmering at his feet. It was very bright. He could see it clearly. No need for wine in his eyes. "No, Caramon, I do not—"

Pain seized Raistlin. Agony ran through his body like fiery darts. The motes of light left the streets and came to dance in his vision. The mage doubled over, the pain twisting his body into grotesque forms, squeezing the breath from his lungs, cutting off even his bubbling cry of torment.

Raistlin collapsed, unconscious. The staff clattered to the street. Lifting his brother, who was like a rag puppet in the big man's arms, the warrior looked frantically around for aid.

"There's the inn!" cried Earwig. "But it's all dark!"

"These people must go to bed at sunset! Go get help!" Caramon ordered.

Dashing down the road, the kender reached the door to Barnstoke Hall and began pounding on it.

"Help! Fire! Thieves! Man overboard!" he yelled, adding any other rousing alarm he thought suitable.

Lights flared. Heads poked out of upstairs windows.

"What is it?" demanded a man in a pointed nightcap, coming out on a second-floor balcony.

"Open up!" shouted Caramon.

"It's past hours. I'm locked up for the night. Come back in the morning—"

Caramon's lips pressed together grimly. Getting a firm grip on the limp and seemingly lifeless body of his brother, the warrior kicked the door to the lodging-house. Wood splintered, but the door held. Caramon kicked it again. There was a tearing and rending sound as the door shattered beneath the blow. The man on the balcony shrieked in anger and disappeared inside.

Caramon stalked through the wreckage. Looking around, he found a sofa and gently laid his brother down. The scrollcase that Raistlin had placed in the sleeve of his robes clattered to the floor. Caramon paid no attention to it. His brother's face was pinched, the lips blue. Raistlin had ceased breathing.

"I'll call the guard!" The innkeeper came clattering down the stairs, shaking his fist. "You'll pay—"

Caramon glanced at him.

"Hot water! Quickly!" the warrior ordered.

The innkeeper swelled up with fury, then his gaze fell on the scrollcase. He turned pale.

"Well, what are you doing, standing around, you lout?" the proprietor shouted at a sleepy servant. "Didn't you hear the gentleman? Fetch hot water! And be quick about it!"

The servant raced out and returned with a pot of boiling water, originally used for the evening tea.

Caramon poured steaming water into a cup and shook the contents of one of Raistlin's pouches inside. The herbs and barks bubbled and snapped. Propping up his brother's lifeless form, Caramon held the concoction to Raistlin's lips. The fumes seeped into the mage's nose and mouth. Raistlin's breathing began again, though the mage remained unconscious.

Sighing heavily, wiping his sweaty forehead with the back of his right hand, Caramon gently lifted his brother.

"Your rooms are ready, sir," said the proprietor, bobbing up and down. "This way. I'll show you myself."

"Sorry about the door," Caramon grunted.

"Oh, think nothing of it," said the innkeeper airily, as if he replaced heavy wooden doors every day. "Will you be needing anything else? Food? Drink?"

The procession wound its way up the stairs. Earwig, forgotten in the excitement, started to follow, when he remembered something.

"Raistlin's staff! He left it in the street. I'm certain he'd want me to go get it!"

Turning, the kender dashed back outside. There was the staff, lying in the middle of the road. Earwig gazed down at it in awe. The crystal orb, held fast in the dragon's claw, was as dark and lifeless, it seemed, as its master.

"Maybe I can make it light up," said the kender, reaching out a trembling hand to take hold of the staff. Of all the interesting things that had happened to him in his life, this was going to be the most wonderful. Carrying a wizard's staff—

"Hey!" Earwig cried out angrily. "What the—?"

The kender looked up into the air and down at his feet. He glanced around in all directions.

The staff was gone.

"Oops," said Earwig Lockpicker.

Chapter 9

Caramon watched over Raistlin throughout the night, never moving from the mage's side, never taking his eyes from the steadily rising and falling rhythm of his brother's breathing. The fighter had witnessed Raistlin this sick only once before, when they were being pursued in a forest by the Cleric of Larnish's men. The mage had expended most of his energies fending off spear and arrow, creating a glowing shield that could not be penetrated by missiles, protecting the twins from attack until eventually they found safety in a hidden cave.

Caramon had gone out to cover their tracks from the pursuers, and when he came back, he saw his brother, leaning against a wall, head bent at an odd angle, eyes rolled back so that only the whites showed. A few moments later, however, Raistlin had recovered and acted as if nothing had happened. But Caramon knew that his brother had exhausted himself beyond even the endurance of his indomitable will.

This night, however, Raistlin was not recovering, though Caramon was sure he had acted in time, forcing the vapors of the herbs into the mage's lungs.

"Something's going on that I don't understand," the warrior muttered.

Looking at the still figure on the bed, Caramon gently brushed the long, white hair away from the mage's face, revealing a mask of metal that gave no clue to the thoughts and feelings behind it. Raistlin was still wrapped in his red robes, a crimson shroud that concealed the weakness of his body.

Caramon, sitting in a large, plush chair near the bed, allowed himself a moment to close his eyes and stretch his huge frame. He was tired, but he had no intention of falling asleep while his twin was in the grip of this strange malady.

Oil lamps hung in each of the four corners of the room, suspended from the ceiling on silver wires, creating steady illumination that covered everything in a white-yellow glow. Moving to the lamps, Caramon blew them out one by one until the room was dark.

Turning from the last, Caramon caught his breath as he looked back to the mage. Raistlin's body was covered in a faint blue glow, an aura that moved and flickered and danced around the gold of the magician's skin. Arcs of lightning cracked between and around the fingers of his hands.

"Raist!" Caramon whispered in awe. "What's going

on? Please, tell me! I've never seen anything like this before! I'm frightened! Raist! Please!"

But his brother couldn't answer.

"It's not real. It's a trick of my eyes because I'm sleepy." Caramon rubbed his eyes, but the glow remained.

Hurrying to the bed, the fighter imagined he saw the nimbus growing brighter at his approach. He reached out with an unsteady hand and touched Raistlin's arm. The lines around the mage's hands extended toward him, as if groping out blindly to feel another's presence.

Caramon quickly backed away, unwilling to commune with the power that surrounded the sorcerer's body.

* * * * *

"Well, I can do one of two things," said Earwig to himself, standing in the middle of the empty street. "I can go back to Raistlin and tell him I lost his staff. . . ."

The kender paused to consider this course of action. Raistlin would not be pleased. And while he would undoubtedly do something very interesting to the kender, Earwig wasn't certain that he really wanted to live the rest of his life as a slug.

"Or," said Earwig, "I could go out and find the staff and bring it to him and he'd be eternally grateful."

That sounded much better. Earwig returned to the inn, intending to collect his pouches and his hoopak from where he'd left them when he went to get the staff. However, one of the servants had been posted at the ruined front door to guard against unwelcome intruders. He immediately stopped the kender.

"But I'm with Caramon and Raistlin Majere! I'm Earwig Lockpicker!" said the kender importantly.

"Yes, he's one of them," the proprietor concurred, hastening back down the stairs. "Councillor Shavas says to make them all welcome and provide them with every comfort. But," he said, shaking a finger at the kender, "you're to stay in your room and not go wandering about the town! Come on. This way!"

And before the startled kender could protest, the proprietor had hustled him up the stairs, into a room, and shut and locked the door behind him.

"Well!" said Earwig, and sat down to consider the matter. "It's nice of them to be concerned about my rest, but they don't know that I have a very important mission to perform. I don't want to hurt their feelings, though, after all the trouble they've gone to, so I'll just wait until they're in bed and then slip out."

When the proprietor's footsteps had died away and everything was quiet, Earwig walked to the door. Leaning his hoopak against the doorframe, the kender removed a leather case the size of a human's hand. Inside was an assortment of wood-handled tools, each adorned with a metal tip bent at strange angles or cut into unusual shapes. Running his fingers caressingly over each, Earwig pulled out an instrument with a V-shaped end and inserted it into the lock. Working for a few minutes, slowly and unhurriedly, the kender heard a click come from within the mechanism. The door swung open.

"Cheap lock. They should get it replaced. I'll tell them in the morning."

Creeping out into the hall, he glanced around to see if anybody had awakened.

Nobody had.

Earwig replaced the tool in its pouch, and replaced the pouch back into his bags. He was about to proceed down the stairs when he remembered the large and unfriendly servant sitting at the front door.

"He's probably fallen asleep. I won't disturb him," said

the thoughtful kender as he turned and went the opposite direction.

A locked window didn't even require the use of his tools, much to Earwig's disappointment. Climbing out, he crawled down a trellis and landed on the street behind the inn.

Barnstoke Hall stood in the middle of a long block of houses and shops on Southgate Street, one of the three main roads, each several miles in length, that apparently led from the gates to the center of Mereklar. The building was very long, paneled with light-colored wood on the floor and walls, though the ceiling was left uncovered, revealing the white foundation used for every building in the city.

The lights of Mereklar lit the street brightly, whatever magic they used for fuel apparently inexhaustible. Earwig stared up at one of the magical lights, hovering far above his short reach. He thought about using the rope he had at his waist to ensnare one of the miniature suns, but decided to wait until later. Right now he had a very important mission—finding Raistlin's staff. The kender turned to the right, then stopped, looking behind him, craning his head. Changing his mind, he turned to the left, but suddenly looked behind him again.

"Mmmm," Earwig murmured. "Which way should I go? Let me think. If I were a wizard's staff, where would I be?"

The kender tried to imagine himself a staff, but found that distinctly unhelpful. Reaching behind into his backpack, Earwig withdrew a velvet pouch that rattled with a hollow sound. He opened the drawstrings, revealing a multitude of game pieces: glass dice, ivory chessmen, colored sticks—anything used for chance, fortune, or skill. Jamming his hand into the bag, the kender fished around inside for a while, spilling dice and knights everywhere. Eventually, he pulled out a small, square board, about a fingerspan to a side, with a metal arrow pinioned through the center. Leaving the dropped pieces on the street, Earwig sat down on the ground and set the spinner on the white stone road in front of him.

"Now let's see which way the staff went," he said, the index finger of his right hand going to the spinner.

Taking a deep breath, Earwig gave the spinner a whirl. The arrow stopped, pointing straight back into Barnstoke Hall.

"Pooh! You've made a mistake. It can't be in there!"

Earwig spun again, only to have the arrow point back at the inn.

"Are you broken?"

The kender gave the needle a wrench, bending it. Putting the spinner back on the ground, he flicked the arrow another time with his finger. It pointed directly into the heart of the city.

"What a coincidence. That's just where I wanted to go!" Earwig said happily, stuffing the spinner into one of the pockets in his scruffy, baggy trousers. He started walking north up Southgate Street, his hoopak in his hand.

* * * * *

Raistlin thrashed in his bed. His back arched, his face contorted horribly, a mask of gold found only in theatrical *grotesques*. His mouth opened wide to scream, but the agony ripped his body. He could utter no sound, the air stolen from his chest.

Lightning engulfed the mage, covering him with sheets of blue and white that threatened to sear his flesh. Caramon, standing as near to his brother as possible, was forced to shield his eyes against the brilliant glow. Love for his brother overcame his fear. He edged nearer and nearer to the bed, moving inches at a time.

Caramon could no longer look at his twin. The light had grown so intense that it penetrated his eyelids, causing him to see flashes and phantoms, yellow images that floated across his vision. But still he moved forward, determined to give what help he could. Reaching out, he caught hold of Raistlin's hand.

The pain started at the front of Caramon's body, licked around his sides, and scored his back with harsh, blue-lightning claws. Every nerve was aflame, burning so that his flesh lost all sensation, numbed beyond feeling. Shafts of fire speared his lungs and stung his heart till he thought it would burst from the strain.

He lost his balance and fell to one knee, but he held fast to his brother's stiff hand.

And then, suddenly, the blinding light was gone. Caramon was plunged into darkness. He felt Raistlin's hand close firmly over his.

"It is over, my brother," the mage said, his breath coming quick and labored.

* * * * *

Earwig walked for hours, taking in the sights of Mereklar and remembering, occasionally, to search for the staff. He had never been in a city that was so quiet. Nobody else was in the streets. Not a sound could be heard, not even the calls of cats he had so eagerly expected. Earwig felt as if the city belonged to him—a vast, enclosed town whose magical lights burned brightly for him, the only wanderer.

He paused, looking around, finding himself at another intersection.

"Which way should I go this time?" he said aloud, then snapped his mouth shut quickly. He hadn't meant to disturb the silence.

A cat appeared, glanced at him tentatively, then darted off into the night. After a few moments, more cats ran into the middle of the road.

"Hi!" Earwig said, starting forward, but the cats scattered in all directions. The kender watched them with fascination.

"Wow! And to think there used to be thousands of cats around here! I wonder where these were going? I'll find out."

Shrugging and digging deep in his pocket, Earwig brought out the spinner again, flicking it with his finger. The arrow pointed backward, toward the inn.

"Stupid thing!" the kender muttered, placing the game piece back in his pocket.

He turned in the direction opposite the one the spinner had indicated—an alley that sloped slightly downward, a narrow corridor without light.

"That looks interesting. If I were a staff or a cat, I think I'd definitely be down there."

The kender walked into the alley. He started to whistle a favorite marching tune, but stopped, thinking better of it. After all, he didn't want to disturb anybody who might be asleep.

The walls of the passage looked gray and rough, the normally white, near-sparkling stone hidden from the light. Earwig had the feeling that there was something different about this place, but he couldn't decide what it was.

Noise. That was it. This part of the city was awake!

The kender heard the sounds of people singing and laughing. His sharp eyes could now detect the red of a fire's glow somewhere to the left of an open square—an area he could not see clearly yet.

Earwig reached the end of the alley and looked around

in amazement, stopping so suddenly that he almost fell over. He had entered an arcade filled with small storefronts and shops. His gaze darted from place to place, each dark and deserted store calling him to come forward, to come inside and see what it had to offer.

One shop was filled with brightly colored gems and jewelry that gleamed in the moonlight. Another sold cloth, dyed with beautiful patterns, and another offered weapons. Earwig danced forward into the middle of the marketplace, wondering where he should look first.

The sound of a scream and shatters of pottery made Earwig jump and glance around. He saw the source of the red glow—firelight streamed out the window of an inn. He heard another scream, coming from the same place.

"This is one fight I won't miss!" cried the kender in excitement, and peered inside a dirty window to see what the commotion was about.

Twenty men were seated at tables and booths in the room. They were all dressed in black armor of a type that looked familiar to the kender, though he couldn't recall why. Flagons of ale and beer sloshed over onto the floor as they talked, their voices muffled by the window. Barmaids walked between the patrons, nimbly avoiding groping hands.

The bartender, a large, unpleasant-looking man, cleaned glasses with a dirty towel behind the bar. Earwig could see that every one of the men carried weapons—knives and swords, some sheathed, others laid across tables, exposed and ready for trouble.

Standing higher on his toes, Earwig saw one of the barmaids, a girl of about twenty with dark, straight hair and attractive features, bend down to pick up a broken mug. One of the men, dressed in better clothes than the rest, hit her with the flat of his sword. He sent her stumbling into the window frame, causing the other men in the room to howl with laughter. Struggling to stand, the barmaid looked out the window. She and the curious kender made eye contact. The woman fell backward, a look of surprise on her face. Earwig continued watching with interest.

The barmaid walked warily up to the man who had hit her. "I think you've had enough, my lord. You better go back to your home."

"I'll have another!" was the slurred reply. "You can't throw me out!"

"Catherine," called the bartender, glowering. "Go wake the stableboy. Send him for Councillor Shavas."

At the sound of the name, the man appeared to reconsider. Grumbling, he pushed a chair back noisily and headed for the door, his steps unsteady. The wooden door banged open. Scratching his stomach with his right hand and the back of his neck with his left, the man looked around the alley and saw Earwig.

A street light shone full on the kender. The man, staring at Earwig's neck, lurched forward.

"Where'd you get that?" he demanded hoarsely, staggering down the short flight of stairs that led from the inn. "Itsh mine!"

Earwig, startled, put his hand to the cat's-skull necklace and frowned. He didn't like this man.

"You drunken sot!" the kender taunted, getting a firm grip on his hoopak. "I wouldn't tell you if it were day or night. I wouldn't tell you if your pants were unlaced, which, by the way, they are. I wouldn't—"

The man reached down, caught hold of the kender by the shirt, and pulled a dagger from his own belt.

"I kill your kind, vermin!"

"What with? Your stinking breath?"

Using all his strength, Earwig brought his hoopak up

between the man's legs, striking him in the groin. The man doubled over in pain, clutching himself. The hoopak fell a second time, this time on the man's head, knocking him unconscious.

"Oh, dear, now you've done it!" said a voice.

Earwig saw the barmaid standing in the doorway. She sounded worried, but he saw that she was trying hard not to laugh.

"You better go!" she said softly, hurrying down the stairs. "He's an important man in this town. There might be trouble."

"You mean from those guys in there? I can handle them!" said Earwig stoutly.

"No, not them. Just go, quickly. And . . . thank you," she whispered in a rich voice, soft and pleasant. Leaning over, she kissed the kender swiftly on the cheek. Then, hearing shouts inside, she waved at him and hurried back up the stairs, closing the door behind her.

Earwig stood in the alley, his hand pressed against his cheek, a look of rapture on his face.

"Wow! No wonder Caramon likes kissing girls. That's even more fun than picking a lock!"

* * * * *

Caramon stood over his brother, staring at him anxiously. "Are you sure you're all right? What happened, Raist? What was that?"

"I don't know," the mage said weakly. "I'm not certain. Be silent, Caramon. Let me think."

For some reason, his mind was pulling him back to their childhood. Raistlin had the vague feeling that something like this had happened to him before. Long ago.

He recalled brightly colored clothes and music and eating too many sweets . . . cookies . . . He seemed to smell fresh-baked cookies . . .

The Festival of the Eye!

Raistlin sat up quickly, causing his head to grow light and his sight dim. He fell over sideways on the bed, closing his eyes, reaching for the staff as he often did when weakness came upon him. When he touched the black wood, a huge sphere of lightning appeared, surrounding his arm, lighting the room with blue flame.

Caramon cried out in alarm, but the room grew dark again as the last vestiges of magic expended itself, released and channeled into the labyrinths of power within the staff.

Raistlin sat up. A bitter smile twisted his lips as he recalled his youth—a time when he was a target for contempt.

The Festival of the Eye. Once a year, the children were allowed to pretend they were adults. He'd worn the robes of a wizard, crudely sewn by the impatient and clumsy hands of his older half-sister, Kitiara. She had outfitted Caramon as a warrior, complete with wooden shield and sword, then took the twins from door to door, begging for the special cookies that were made in honor of that night. It had been the brothers' last festival together with their sister. Kit had left them soon after, to make her own way in the world.

That night, when they were returning home to gloat over their treasures in private, Raistlin had suddenly become ill, pain clenching his stomach and sides. His brother and half-sister had been forced to carry him. When he spat to remove a bitter taste in his mouth, a small gout of blue flame had shot out. He could still recall the looks of alarm he'd seen on the faces of his siblings.

The next morning, Raistlin was fine. The sickness had

never occurred again, and neither the brothers nor their sister had ever told anyone else what had happened.

Raistlin thought that now he was beginning to understand.

"Hand me my pack," he ordered his brother.

Mystified, Caramon obeyed.

The mage rummaged in it. Pulling out a small book, he flipped through the pages. Caramon, peering over his brother's shoulder, saw nothing but rows and columns of numbers printed on the yellowing pages. Phases and positions of the moons were also indicated.

Some of the dates had large circles around some of the numbers, when pictures of the two moons created a single dot on the page. Raistlin continued to leaf through the book, stopping when he reached the middle. Opening the book wide, making the binding crack in complaint, he laid it down on the bed in front of him. After a moment of silent calculation, he closed it and tossed it into his pack.

"What?" asked Caramon.

"The Festival of the Eye," said Raistlin. "Remember? A long time ago, when we were little?"

Caramon's eyes crinkled in thought. Suddenly, his mouth sagged. "I'll be damned," he murmured, staring at his brother. "What does it mean? It's just a holiday, that's all."

"To most of *you*, it is," Raistlin said, somewhat bitterly. "It's a time to dress up and break the routine of dull existence. But to us, to wizards, it is much, much more."

"Yeah, I remember," said Caramon. "You're supposed to offer your services free."

"Bah! That's the least of it!" Raistlin snarled impatiently. "It is, in reality, a time of great magical power. It began untold ages ago when three sorcerers of tremendous and unparalleled skill gave their lives to their crafts, ending their existence in one final, ultimate expenditure that drained their souls. They used the energy to create a force infinitely more potent than any one could ever summon on his own."

Caramon shifted uncomfortably, as he often did when his twin discussed his arcane craft.

"Certain mystical texts stated that the wizards were each dedicated to one of the three alignments," Raistlin continued. "Good, neutral, and evil—the incantations required all three members from the Great Balance of the World. Some of the books say that the wizards cast the spell to gamble on the future for their deities, hoping that their particular alignment would wrest control of the power when the time came." Raistlin shrugged. "The sorcerers chose the game, but the gods cast the dice. The wizards died, the energy remained pent up. The texts say that the energy will be released only when the Great Eye is in the heavens."

"The Great Eye?"

"Don't interrupt me, if you want to know what's going on. This year's Festival of the Eye is going to be different from most others because all three moons, including the black moon Nuitari, are moving to rare conjunction. They will form the Great Eye—an orb of red, silver, and black hovering in the night sky, looking down upon Krynn with unfathomable intent."

Raistlin paused, gazing at his brother with his own golden hourglass eyes.

"This has occurred once before in the history of the world—during the Cataclysm."

Caramon shook his head. "Look, the Festival of the Eye happens every year. You've never been sick before. Except that once."

"And on that night of the Festival—the night I was so strangely ill—my books showed the convergence of the two visible moons—Lunitari and Solinari. That is something that occurs more frequently, but still not often. Now, this year, according to my reading, that convergence will happen again. My calculations further confirm that the third—the black moon of the ancient, forgotten goddess Takhisis, Queen of Darkness—will cross over them, forming the Great Eye. What I felt so many years ago was the early gathering of mystic power that is going to be freed during the upcoming festival. Much is explained," he added, thinking of the white line, understanding now why he could see it.

"Maybe to you, but not to me," Caramon grunted, yawning. He glanced at his brother uneasily. "Is this sickness likely to happen again?"

But Raistlin was lost in thought and didn't answer.

* * * * *

Earwig walked back up Southgate Street, past the rows and blocks of houses. "Everyone sure likes this necklace," he said to himself proudly. "I'm really glad I found it. Gosh, I'm tired, though. Being a great warrior and getting kissed by beautiful women really takes a lot out of a guy."

The kender made his way back to Barnstoke Hall, where he was delighted to find the street littered with dice and game pieces. He picked them all up and stuffed them into his pants pockets, wondering where they had come from.

The large and unfriendly servant was still guarding the door to the inn. The kender kindly let the man rest and went around to the back of the inn, where he crawled up the trellis and climbed into a window.

"I'll just stop by and tell Caramon about my adventure," he said, going up to the twins' door and knocking on it loudly.

A bleary-eyed Caramon threw open the door. "You!" He glowered at the kender. "Do you know what time it is?"

"No," said Earwig cheerfully. "But I can find out if you want. There's a clock in the hall. I—" The kender's mouth flew open. He stared.

"Raistlin's staff!"

"Yeah, so what?"

"But it was . . . I mean I tried to . . . It just disa—!"

"See you in the morning, Earwig!" growled Caramon as he slammed the door, nearly taking off the kender's inquisitive nose.

"How wonderful! It must have come back all by itself! Still," Earwig added, miffed, "you'd think it would have said something before it let me go to all that trouble looking for it."

Yawning, he started to go to his room, but couldn't remember where it was. He sneaked down into the dark dining hall, undid his pack, rolled out his sleeping mats, and fell asleep under the main table.

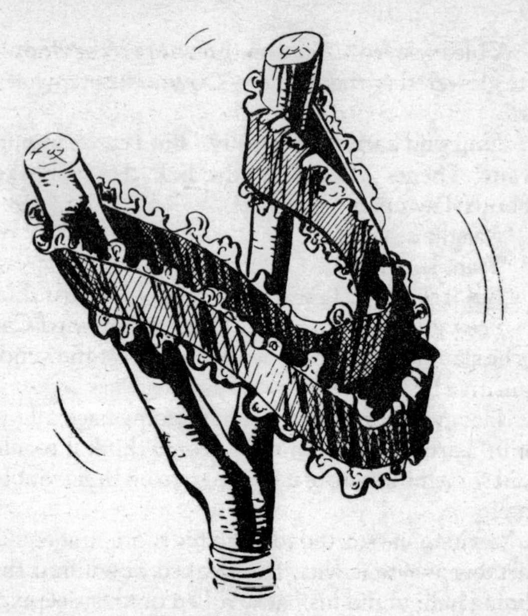

Chapter 10

"You little MONSTER!"

The woman's scream echoed through the inn, awakening Caramon. The next instant, footsteps pounded up the stair and fists banged on the door.

The fighter turned quickly to observe Raistlin, hoping the mage wouldn't wake from his slumber. A muscle in his brother's face twitched, and he stirred restlessly in his sleep.

Caramon leaped to his feet, fatigue leaving his muscles as he stormed toward the door. Flinging it open, he faced the proprietor he had met briefly last night.

"Stop that racket!" whispered Caramon loudly. "My brother is sick!"

"Please, kind sir! I know you are important people—friends of the councillor's—but you must help me!" The proprietor pointed down the stairs. "Your friend is assaulting my patrons!"

"My friend?" The warrior looked around the room to see if he'd forgotten somebody. Realization glimmered. "Earwig!" he groaned.

"Please, sir, please!" The innkeeper pulled on Caramon's arm, attempting to tug him out the door.

The fighter came to a dead standstill and looked the proprietor directly in the eye. "Don't let anything disturb my brother, understand?" He held a thick finger in front of the proprietor's face for emphasis.

"Of course not," the innkeeper said, swallowing hard. "Now would you please come reason with your friend, sir?"

"Reason? With a kender? That'll be a first!" the warrior muttered under his breath, closing the door softly behind him.

Caramon walked into the room, and his eyes widened in disbelief. Earwig stood on a small oaken table in the corner of the dining hall, hoopak in his hand, threatening the staff of the inn. Something white and frilly was on his head.

One of the cooks, a large portly man, brandished a huge butcher knife. "I'll chop off your ears!" he threatened, advancing on the kender.

"Cut out my eyes, too," taunted the kender. "Then I won't have to look at your ugly face!" *Thwop!* The hoopak flew out and slapped the man on the nose.

"Come on! Who's next? I'm the mighty warrior, Earwig Lockpicker!" He waved his staff in a wide arc as others attempted to approach. "Admired by men! Beloved by women!"

Heaving a sigh, Caramon moved forward. Seeing his friend, Earwig warned, "Stay away from me, sir. I'm in the throes of the famous Kender Berzerkergang, which has not been seen on Krynn for hundreds of years!"

Caramon grabbed the staff as it arced toward his head, the wood making a loud slap on his palm that caused many in the room to wince in sympathetic pain.

"That's enough, Earwig." The warrior wrenched the hoopak from the kender's hand.

"Draw your sword, Caramon! Cut them down!" Earwig shrieked, jumping from the table. "They attacked me!"

"Attacked you?" Caramon stared at the kender. "What in the name of the Abyss is that on your head?"

Earwig's face went from righteous anger to bland innocence in less time than it takes to tell it. "It's my hair, Caramon."

The warrior eyed the lacy headpiece wrapped around the kender's topknot. The headpiece looked familiar. It was—

"A garter!" the fighter said suddenly. Caramon's face flushed deep crimson. Reaching out, he snatched the piece of feminine underclothing from the kender's head. "I've heard of kender swiping lots of things!" he hissed into Earwig's ear, shaking the kender until his teeth rattled. "But how did you manage to steal this?"

"The problem, sir," the innkeeper spoke, stepping from the doorway where he had waited until the battle was over, "is that this . . . person . . . attempted to . . . to steal—"

"Steal!" Earwig's eyes widened in indignation. "A kender . . . steal?" He could barely speak for the injustice of the accusation.

"Sir," the proprietor continued. "A young lady was sitting down to breakfast when this person . . . uh . . ."

Ignoring the flustered innkeeper, Caramon gazed sternly at Earwig. "What happened?" he asked with a sigh, knowing that he was in for a long and convoluted explanation.

"Well, last night I went to pick up Raistlin's staff that he left in the street, only when I reached out to grab it, the staff disappeared. I thought I'd better go look for it—you know, Caramon, how much your brother thinks of that staff. Well, anyway, I went back out—"

"I locked you in your room!" thundered the innkeeper. "Councillor Shavas wouldn't want him walking around town after dark," he added hastily, for Caramon's benefit. "The little fellow might get hurt."

"Hunh," grunted Caramon, frowning.

"Well, anyway," continued Earwig, deciding magnanimously to overlook being called "little fellow," "I walked around the town, and I saw a lot of cats, and I found this bar that looked like fun. And it was! A man there tried to kill me, Caramon! With a knife! What do you think of that? I fought him off. Thwack! Over the head with my hoopak. Then the most beautiful girl I ever saw in my life kissed me on the cheek. Just as if I'd been you, Caramon! By then I was getting kind of tired, so I came back here and found all these game pieces lying on the ground, so I picked them up and climbed back up the trellis and in through the window—"

"What?" the proprietor yelled.

"Shh!" Caramon insisted, feeling that they must be nearing the important part.

"I went to your room, and Raistlin's staff had come back by itself! Which is truly remarkable, except that I did go to a lot of trouble and it might have had more consideration. Then I couldn't remember my room number, so I went to sleep under the table and when I woke up, that woman was sitting down right on top of me and I saw that this part of her clothing was sliding down her leg. And if this"—the kender pointed at the garter—"had slid down and wrapped around her ankle, she would have tripped and maybe hurt herself so I just took it off her. I guess you heard her scream, huh? After that she fainted. Then all these people jumped on me. For no reason!" Earwig added indignantly.

His face burning, still holding the garter, Caramon glanced around uncertainly, wondering what to do.

"I'll take it, sir," offered one of the female servants.

"Yeah! Thanks!" Caramon handed it over in relief. "He didn't really mean to cause any trouble, Master Innkeeper. He just sort of found himself in the wrong place at the wrong time. I'll keep an eye on him after this. It won't happen again."

"I surely hope not," said the proprietor, somewhat mollified.

"Please give our apologies to the young lady," Caramon added, marching Earwig up the stairs.

"I thought maybe I'd get another kiss, Caramon," said the kender cheerfully. "Boy! That was fun!"

* * * * *

Raistlin stood at the window, staring down into the street below. There were hardly any more people out by day than by night. Those who were moving about on some business of their own walked with heads down, casting furtive looks this way and that. Raistlin had seen cities in the grip of plague. He could smell fear in the air. Now, he thought he could detect the same odor.

And there, shining against the white stone pavement, was the line.

Caramon walked into the room just behind Earwig, pushing the kender forward so that there would be no chance for him to escape. Raistlin slowly turned around from the window.

"How are you feeling?" Caramon asked.

"How do I ever feel?" Raistlin snapped. Seeing Caramon's hurt look, the mage shook his head. "I'm sorry, my brother. I feel as if a crushing weight were on me. As if I'd been sent here to do something important, yet I haven't any idea what! And we don't have much time to do it!"

"What do you mean? We've got all the time in the world," said Caramon practically. "I've ordered breakfast. It'll be up in a moment."

"Time!" Raistlin turned back to the window, staring down at the white line. " '. . . To find the gate, to be there when the time arrives.' We have no time, my brother. We have only until the Festival of the Eye. Three days."

"Huh?" Caramon frowned.

"That's the poem you quoted, isn't it, Raistlin?" Earwig piped up. "I remember it, you see. 'Darkness sends its agents, stealthy and black, to find the gate, to be there when the time arrives.' I love stories, and that's as good as a story. Did I ever tell you the one about Dizzy Longtongue and the minotaur—?"

"I think you dropped something," said Caramon, jostling one of the kender's pouches and spilling its contents on the floor.

Glass and ivory game pieces rolled across the wood, one of the pieces coming to rest at Raistlin's feet. Reaching down, he picked it up. It was a small, yellowing statue carved into the likeness of a beautiful woman—beautiful, regal, evil, domineering. The mage held it up to his eyes, inspecting it, observing every tiny detail cut into the bone. Turning it over to look at the pedestal on which the woman stood, he saw an "X" on the bottom, a sign designating the piece as the Dark Queen in one of the mage's favorite games, *Wizards and Warriors*.

"It can't be coincidence," he murmured. "The 'cats decide the fate,' and they are vanishing. The time of the Great Eye comes once again, when untold power awaits those who can use it. If I were the Dark Queen and I wanted to choose a time to come back into the world . . ." Raistlin's voice died.

Caramon scoffed. "Hey, don't talk like that, Raist! You said it yourself. Coincidence. We'll find the cats, and there'll be a perfectly logical explanation for their disappearance. Maybe it'll be like that story about the guy with the flute who came into a town and played, and all of the rats followed him past the city limits."

"But you forget the end of the story, my brother. In the end, the piper came back and stole away the children."

Caramon kept silent. He didn't think he'd helped matters any.

Looking at the game piece carefully one more time, Raistlin handed it back to the kender. Earwig looked at the piece as carefully as the mage had, but he didn't find anything of interest. It was just another game piece.

" 'Fate moves the free,' " Caramon said under his breath, repeating one of his current, favorite proverbs. "What do we do now?"

"It's time we explored the city of Mereklar."

"How about seeing this Councillor Shavas? Shouldn't we go meet her?"

"I think, my brother, that I will let her come to me," said Raistlin coolly.

* * * * *

"You're strangers, so you don't see it like we do."

"I guess not, ma'am," Caramon said. "To me, this place looks overrun."

"No, sir, no. Where once there were thousands, there are now few. Too few," said the old woman.

"That's true," added a man who was seated at another

table. "From morning to evening, the cats would roam the streets. White, gray, brown, striped, spotted, mottled. All sorts."

"Except black," the old woman interposed. "We never knew why, but there wasn't a black cat among the lot of 'em."

"Some think mages came and took the black ones," said the man, glowering darkly at Raistlin.

Raistlin lifted an eyebrow and glanced at his brother. Caramon, looking uncomfortable, buried his head in a mug of ale. The three companions were wandering through the city, supposedly seeing the sights. But every time they came to any sort of a tavern, Raistlin insisted on going inside. He left most of the conversing to his brother. The handsome, good-natured fighter took to people easily, and they likewise warmed to him.

Caramon wondered, at first, how they were going to pay for what they drank, but all Raistlin had to do was to produce the scrollcase and, at the sight of it, no one ever asked them for money.

Raistlin listened and kept an eye on the kender, watching to note if anyone took an unusual interest in the skull necklace Earwig wore.

"We always left plates of food and small bowls of milk outside our house for the cats to eat and drink," a middle-aged man told the warrior, "though sometimes we simply left the doors open and waited for the cats to come inside, where they could join us for breakfast."

"They would always roam about on the street or in the parks, waiting to be petted," a young barmaid explained, her eyes on Caramon. "No one would dream of harming them. After all, they'll one day save the world!" The others in the tavern nodded in agreement.

"You haven't seen a guy around here, playing a flute,

have you?" Caramon began, but his brother gave him such a vicious look that the big warrior lapsed into silence. They stood up to go.

"Damn all wizards to the Abyss," one of the guests said as the magician left.

"Well, how rude!" exclaimed Earwig.

Caramon turned, fist clenched, but Raistlin put his hand on his brother's knotted arm.

"Peace, Caramon."

"How can you just let them say things like that?" the warrior demanded.

"Because I understand them," said Raistlin in his whispering voice. "These people are in the grip of fear," he added as they stepped out into the street. "They've lived in this city all of their lives, and now the one thing that they hold sacred is disappearing, without reason, without a clue. I'm an easy target because I'm someone to blame."

He looked down at the street. The white line was there, leading him on. They had not deviated from its path since leaving the inn, although neither Caramon nor Earwig could see it.

* * * * *

"The councillor's home? Just keep walking straight up the street," said a man to Caramon in response to his question.

"Thank you," the warrior replied, returning to his brother and the kender, who were seated at an outdoor table at another tavern.

They had seen a few cats since their arrival in Mereklar. Occasionally one would stroll past the companions as they were walking. Caramon had the strangest feeling that he was being scrutinized, examined by unblinking green eyes. Then, more and more started coming around, and now Earwig was surrounded by cats. The felines jumped on his shoulders, batted at his topknot of brown hair, and rubbed themselves around his neck. The kender was overjoyed at the attention and more than willing to play with his new friends.

Raistlin, on the other hand, sat silent and alone. None of the cats would come near him.

"Look at that," Caramon heard a woman whisper, and saw her pointing at the mage.

"I know," said her companion. "I've never seen our cats act so unfriendly to anybody."

"Maybe they know something we don't!"

A third woman hissed, "I bet the wizard has something to do with the missing cats! After all, there were no problems until he got here!"

"Your problems started before we arrived," Caramon began hotly, but, once again, his brother flashed him a warning look and the fighter swallowed his words.

"I've heard some people say that their kind are responsible for everything bad in the world!"

The mage ignored the words. He sat at his ease in a chair, sipping occasionally at a tiny porcelain cup containing a local speciality called *hyava*. The heat from the drink filled his body with welcome warmth, though the day was not particularly cold and he wore the red robes that covered him from head to foot.

Caramon sat down and tried to talk to his brother over Earwig's giggling. "Like the guard told us, all we have to do is follow Southgate Street to the center of the city, where we'll find the councillor's house. 'All roads lead there,' the man said. 'You can't get lost.' "

"Don't you think that's a little unusual?" Raistlin asked. "A house in the exact center of the city?"

"Yeah, I thought it was odd, but then again, this whole

damn place is pretty odd," the fighter muttered.

"I think I would like to see this house." Raistlin reached over to touch Earwig's shoulder. The cats ceased playing with the kender and turned to stare at the mage, freezing in place as if they were statues. "Earwig," said Raistlin, staring back at the cats, "it's time to leave."

"All right," said the kender, always glad to be going somewhere other than where he was. "Come on, cats," he said, shoving at those perched on his lap. "I've got to go. Move."

When the cats didn't budge, he stood up slowly from the wicker chair. The cats leaped off him but kept their eyes on Raistlin.

The mage drew the hood up over his face, covering his thin, golden features from the light of day, finding refuge in the shadows of the robes. Taking the Staff of Magius in hand, he started walking up the street, Caramon and Earwig following back.

The cats stood for a moment, then they, too, began to walk slowly after the companions, staying about ten feet back.

"Look at that!" said Earwig in delight.

Raistlin paused, glanced around. The felines came to a halt. Raistlin moved again, and the animals started after him again. More cats came to join their fellows and soon the companions were being followed by a pack of fur and tails and shining eyes that moved without the slightest sound.

"Why are they acting like that?" somebody asked.

"Don't know. Maybe he's got them under a spell or something!"

"I doubt it. He knows what we'd do to him if he used any magic on our cats."

Suddenly Raistlin turned around and jerked the hood from his head. The cats scattered, fleeing, leaving the streets to the mage.

* * * * *

Caramon had been to many cities and towns in his life, but none like Mereklar. There were more places to eat and drink on the little stretch of Southgate Street than the fighter could remember seeing in most villages, and there were actually places that specialized in one type of meal instead of serving the same thing night after night.

"And windows," the warrior said to himself in near disbelief. "Where do people get the money for glass?"

There was every type of shop imaginable, selling wondrous things. They passed by a book shop that had the name "Oxford" painted in the window. Displayed in front on a wooden pedestal was a huge dictionary, open in the middle. Raistlin looked at the tome and sighed in longing. The price displayed was an almost unbelievable amount, more than Raistlin imagine earning in a lifetime.

As the mage walked down the avenue, more and more people began to stop what they were doing and stare at the red robes that hid the man of power. Some of the children ran up to Raistlin, reaching out to touch the strange black wood staff with the golden claw and pale blue orb of crystal. The mage did not move the staff from their reach. It seemed, when they drew too near, as if the black rod itself warded them away.

Caramon attracted attention as well. Men gazed at him, envying his youth and strength. Women watched him from out the corners of their eyes, admiring his strong arms and broad chest, his curly brown hair and handsome face.

"Hey, Caramon, why do all the girls stare at you?" Earwig asked wistfully.

When the warrior looked their direction, the women turned red and buried their faces in their hands, giggling at Caramon's leer and his broad grin.

"Probably never seen a sword this big," said the fighter, winking.

Raistlin snorted in contempt.

Another hour passed, and the travelers could see Shavas's house. Earwig, with his sharper eyes, could make out some detail. "It looks like it's covered with plants. And its windows are made of colored glass!"

Raistlin listened to the kender's description of the councillor's house with interest, though he didn't say anything. If what the kender said was accurate, the house was vastly different from every other house in the city. The mage stared ahead, leaning on his staff for comfort rather than any actual need. He felt unusually refreshed, even invigorated since his trial of the night before. The white line gleamed at his feet, shining brighter and more clearly with every step he took.

Soon all the companions could clearly see the house, raised up on a hill of dirt—a perfect circle of earth that ended where the white stone of the streets and sidewalks began. The mound rose above the level of the city, and a stone path wound up to the councillor's house and around to the small groves that covered the hill of dirt. The top of the hill was large enough and flat enough to support a small pond, and streams ran out from it to water the colorful gardens along the sides of the estate.

Raistlin came to a halt, his gaze studying the stained-glass windows. Fascinated, he watched the sunlight glance off the tinted panes, reflecting a variety of colors that shone in his eyes—red, blue, green, white, and black. Five colors. It reminded him of his dream. Five colors . . .

The mage blinked his eyes and saw that the glass was nothing more than glass, held together by lead strips, bent into odd shapes that seemed somehow familiar. When he attempted to grasp where he had seen them before, his mind refused.

Raistlin suddenly felt weak and was unable to continue walking. "Caramon!" he called out, his voice reaching the ears of his brother, who was a slight distance ahead. "I must rest."

The mage slumped down in a chair that belonged to another hyava shop. He leaned against the staff. His breath shortened, and he turned around with his back to the estate, lifting the cowl up over his head as Caramon hurried to his side.

A nervous serving-girl came out of the shop, bringing out two cups of the strong, dark brew. "No," the fighter said, "he needs hot water."

"This will be fine, my brother." Raistlin snatched the drinks from the girl's hands. When his brother gave a questioning glance, the mage said, "I'm just a little tired from the walk."

Raistlin took his time, holding the ridiculously small handle between two fingers, swallowing slowly. Earwig sat down happily and began rummaging through his pouches.

"See this?" the kender said, pulling out a crystal quill shot through with veins of gold. "I found it lying in the street. I figured, 'If it's in the street, nobody wants it.' And I found this." Earwig held up a sequined ball with a piece of yellow ribbon sewn on it.

"Give that back!" Caramon yelled, leaning across the table, his fingers groping for the kender.

"It's mine! I found it!"

"It was mine first! That girl at the inn gave it to me, and it means a lot."

"Then you shouldn't have dropped it," the kender

scolded, handing the ball back to its rightful owner. It spun around, catching the sunlight, reflecting a myriad colors. "I swear, Caramon! You are *so* careless. Besides, it's a really good cat toy. They love it! See, look at that black cat watching it."

Raistlin bent forward in his chair. "What black cat?"

"That black cat," Earwig replied, pointing behind the mage.

Raistlin turned around to face the animal. The cat, not particularly large and very, very black, sat calmly, regarding the mage with wide, staring blue eyes.

"Here, puss, puss, puss." Caramon bobbed the toy on its string.

The cat stood a moment longer, staring at the mage in a contest of wills—azure orbs against black hourglasses. Then the feline rose up from its place on the white stone street and calmly walked past Raistlin. The animal batted the ball three times and sat down again, watching Caramon as it had watched his brother.

Earwig, unwilling to be left out of the cat's attentions, reached down and petted its black fur. The cat showed no sign of pleasure or annoyance. It glanced at the kender briefly before resuming its observation of the fighter.

Caramon coaxed it to play with the ball. Raistlin, watching, rubbed his fingers against the staff's wood. This was the first black cat he had seen in the entire city of Mereklar, and he was about to cast a spell that would tell him if the animal was possessed by a spirit—making it a magician's familiar—when an open carriage, drawn by two white horses, turned a corner and rumbled up the street. The coat of arms on the carriage door was the same as that on the scrollcase.

"The councillor," said Raistlin, nudging his brother.

Caramon glanced around. Earwig leaped to his feet in excitement. The black cat crouched behind the kender's legs, hidden from view.

"Stop here," came a clear voice. The carriage rolled to a halt in front of the hyava shop. A woman stood from her seat. She was dressed in rippling white silk, her skin nearly as pale as the cloth she wore. Dark brown hair was bound tightly around her head in a thick braid. Around her neck, suspended by a golden chain, hung a red fire opal.

The woman gazed at the three imperiously. "I am Councillor Shavas. Please join me for dinner." Then she was gone, her horses bearing the carriage forward to the estate on the hill, her deep, sensual voice echoing in the companions' thoughts.

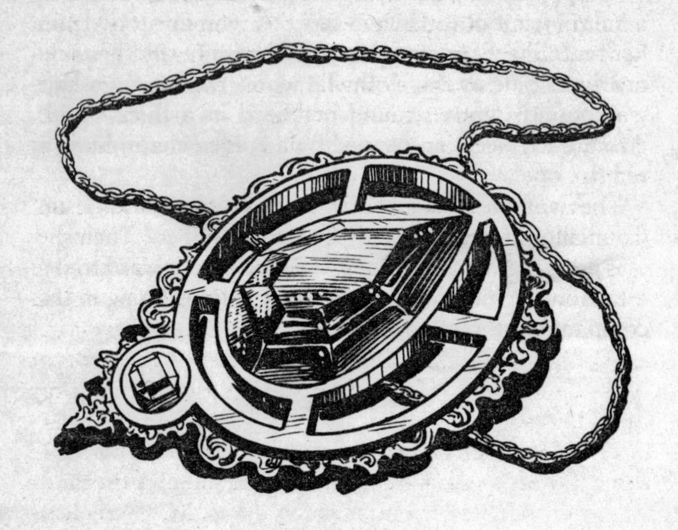

Chapter 11

"My family has lived in Mereklar for hundreds of years," Councillor Shavas said, sitting in front of the fire in the main library of her estate after a sumptuous dinner, a large, untouched glass of brandy in her fine hands.

The flames played behind her, casting flickering lights and shadows, framing her poised, fluid form. She talked comfortably with the brothers, as if she had known them all their lives. Her beauty was matchless. Her voice was like sweet flowing amber.

Small wonder, then, that neither Caramon nor Raistlin noticed the absence of the kender.

"And you say your ancestors lived in the surrounding countryside?" Raistlin huddled near the fire. He held a glass of brandy in his golden hand, and it also remained untouched, the mage unwilling to sacrifice his self-control for physical pleasures. His hood was cast back, and the fire flared in his eyes, filling their darkness with flame.

"Yes, that is correct. I am, however, unsure of the exact location," the councillor replied.

Raistlin saw that although the woman spoke to both him and his brother, she kept her gaze fixed on him. And he did not see in her eyes the loathing or fear he was accustomed to seeing in the eyes of women. In the eyes of this woman he saw fascination, admiration. It made his blood tingle.

"Perhaps their origin could be found in this library?" Raistlin suggested, sweeping an arm to indicate the thousands of volumes of books lining the walls. He remembered what he'd been told, that some of them were magical. "If you would like, I could help you search."

"Yes, I think I would like that very much," the councillor said. A slight flush suffused her pale skin. She glanced into her drink, then lifted her large eyes to stare again at the mage.

Raistlin studied the woman in front of him. Something was wrong, something was bothering him, nagging at him, demanding his attention. But, dazzled by her beauty, he couldn't think what. Perhaps it was Shavas herself. She had told them much . . . and nothing. He'd learned more talking with people in the street. He felt she was hiding something, something she would reveal to him alone. The mage cast a sharp, meaningful glance at his brother.

Caramon pretended not to notice. He had witnessed

his brother's dealings with others before. He knew of Raistlin's constant manipulations and maneuverings, the way he let a subtle hint fall on interested ears, alluding to things he only guessed at, coercing his prey into letting slip information that was best kept from the knowledge of others. The fighter was always ashamed by the mage's need to display cognitive superiority over others. Besides, Caramon didn't want to leave the presence of this beautiful woman. Caramon had noted that, though she talked to Raistlin, she seemed to be constantly looking at the big warrior.

"Well, Master Wizard," said Shavas, breaking what had become an uncomfortable silence, "will you and your brother help our city in its hour of grave need?"

"It says here," the mage stated, pulling a rolled piece of parchment from under his robes, "that the fee for the job is 'negotiable.' Exactly how much room for negotiation exists?"

"The fee quoted by the Minister of Finance is ten thousand steel pieces," Shavas said.

Caramon's mouth dropped open. Ten thousand steel was more money than he had made in his life, let alone at once. Thoughts of what such a large sum of money could buy raced through his head: An inn! No, a huge tavern, with a fireplace in the middle and a dozen rooms and stables out in back. He imagined a house perched high in the vallenwoods of Solace and grew so excited that he stood up and began to roam around the room, bumping into things, overturning a small chair.

"Caramon," said Raistlin irritably. "Where is Earwig?"

"I don't know," Caramon answered. "It's not my day to watch him."

The councillor looked alarmed, her face filling with sudden apprehension.

"I don't want him wandering around my house! There are too many precious things that shouldn't be touched!

Would you go and search for him, sir?"

Caramon, looking into the woman's eyes, felt that if she had asked him to go to the Abyss and find a five-headed dragon, he would have left immediately.

"Sure. Glad to, my lady," he said. He walked out of the room by the side door, closing it loudly behind him.

Raistlin stood from his chair, using the Staff of Magius for support, though he felt no more tired than he had earlier that afternoon. Walking to a bookshelf, he leaned against it, stealing surreptitious glances at the texts. Perhaps whatever was troubling him emanated from the books.

"There is something I need to ask you, my lady."

"Call me Shavas, please," she said, moving nearer to him.

The mage ran a golden hand along the spines of several books. Dust collected on his fingers, and he regarded the fine gray powder with a frown, disliking the treatment the texts received. He rubbed his fingers together, letting the dust fall onto the carpet. "What is our success worth to you?"

"I'm afraid I don't understand the question," Shavas replied, shaking her head slightly and furrowing her arched brows.

"It is very simple, Councillor," Raistlin said, moving, unconsciously, nearer to her. "What value do you place on our success?"

"It would mean saving the city and the entire world, of course. It means everything to me, because unless you succeed, there will be nothing left but darkness and despair." Shavas said this casually, without undue excitement. She even smiled slightly, as if darkness and despair weren't anything she couldn't handle. "What do you expect me to say? That your success is worth the wealth of the entire city? That you could take anything you wanted, Master Wizard?" She glanced at Raistlin alluringly.

He felt his body react to her presence and immediately angrily raised his defenses. "I am not a Master Wizard. I have not attained that high level," he said with mocking humility. "Forgive me, I was only asking on principle. I am sorry if you feel offended," he added, pulling the cowl of his red robes over his head.

The councillor stepped away from him. "Then you agree to our terms?"

"Oh, no, I didn't say that at all. I will have to take time to consider," the mage said from the depths of his robes.

"You will tell me tomorrow?" Shavas inquired, with a touch of impatience.

"Perhaps." Raistlin turned back to the fire and was startled to feel Shavas moving again to stand near him. Gold mask in place, he asked harshly, "Is there something wrong, Councillor?"

"No," she said, pulling back slightly and placing a hand over the necklace she wore at her throat. "It's just that I've never been this close to a mage before."

"You have no mystics in Mereklar?" Raistlin asked with a rise in his voice.

"Yes, that is correct. No mage has entered the city for a very long time."

"And why is that, I wonder?"

"I don't know." Shavas shrugged white shoulders. After a moment's consideration, she added, "There was a wizard who lived in the mountains. But I hear he was killed long ago by some . . . evil force."

"Spooks," said Raistlin, half-smiling.

"What?" The woman looked startled.

"Nothing, just some inanity of my brother's. What kind of force killed him?"

"I'm not sure. It's only a legend which began long before I was born. What you said about 'spooks,' though. I have heard that he was killed by ghosts. Is that common among wizards?"

"That type of magic is not in the realm of my studies, Councillor. I am no necromancer."

Shavas leaned forward slightly. "Have you ever considered becoming one?"

She was almost touching him. Raistlin stared at her. "Why, Councillor?" he asked softly. "Are you offering to teach me?"

The woman laughed merrily. "How droll you are! As if I could teach you anything! I know nothing of magic and magicians."

Yes, my lady, that is what you claim, but why do you ask a question like that? And why do you keep a library filled with magical books if you can't read them? the mage wondered, but he said nothing.

A moment of silence passed between councillor and magician. Raistlin looked slowly around the library. Shavas stood motionless, her head angled slightly back to observe the mage's movements. The braid of her hair shone a rich reddish brown. No light from the fire reached her deep green eyes, but they glittered like emeralds.

"Where were you going before you decided to come to Mereklar?" she asked.

Raistlin ran his fingers along the volumes, reading some of their titles and the names of the authors who wrote them.

"You have an excellent collection of books, Councillor," he said, finding a particularly interesting manuscript, *History of Modern Philosophies*.

"Thank you, but you still haven't answered my question."

Raistlin turned to face his hostess, letting the book fall back into place. "My companions and I were on our way across New Sea on personal business." His voice was cold, almost insulting.

"Now it is my turn to say that I am sorry if I have offended," the councillor said, gliding back to her seat.

Raistlin took advantage of the opportunity to dip his finger slightly into the glass he had set on a nearby table. When he was sure the councillor was not looking at him, he drew his finger across his eyes, causing them to tear from the alcohol. The mage scanned the room quickly, staring up at the ceiling and to the walls.

The line—the stream of age and untold power—did not appear. Where is it? It must lead here from Southgate Street and cut through the house!

Raistlin moved to look out a window to the road that led from the gate, hoping he would find the line there, but the pane of glass was opaque.

"Are you looking for something, Raistlin?" Shavas asked in concern.

"I have a cinder in my eyes," he said, rubbing them. Then the knowledge struck him. He knew what had been bothering him.

His hourglass eyes saw the effects of time on everything upon which his gaze fell. The Masters of the Tower had cast this curse upon him, hoping to teach him compassion for others, hoping to remind him that all men were alike, all men dying. He saw the books on the shelves rotting away, their leather bindings cracking and fading. He saw the tables lose their lacquered sheens and grow old, their timbers and slats fall in scattered stacks. But when he looked at Shavas, he saw her young, beautiful, unchanging.

This can't be! he railed, massaging his eyes with his hand. When he opened his eyes again, he felt his body grow cold. The councillor's form was now nothing but a rotting corpse, struck down by the passage of untold eons, an abomination to life, something unspeakable and unnatural, a travesty that must be destroyed.

What new joke have the masters played on me now? Raistlin demanded silently. He dug the heels of his hands into his eyes, attempting to shut out the horrible sight he had just witnessed.

"What is wrong?" Shavas asked, rising to her feet. She moved closer, and Raistlin felt her hands touch his golden flesh. He felt the touch of a woman, the fatal touch of something he never expected to feel.

"As I have said, I am fine," Raistlin replied tersely. He snatched his arm away from the woman's grasp.

She gazed at him, hurt, reminding him of Caramon.

Raistlin sighed. His hand reached for the staff, but he had left it standing beside the bookshelves.

"Please forgive me, Councillor. I'm not used to anyone . . . touching me. I apologize if I seem rude."

"No apologies are necessary, Raistlin. I think I understand. You have been misused, ill-treated. You raise your defenses swiftly." The councillor lifted her hand and placed it on the mage's arm. "I assure you, sir," she murmured, drawing nearer until he could smell the fragrance of her hair, "that you need no defenses around me!"

Raistlin caught his breath, feeling as if he were smothering. But the sensation, unlike his illness, was a pleasant one. She was beautiful to his eyes, the only thing of beauty he'd seen in a long, long time. His arm glided around the woman's slender body, and he pulled her near.

Chapter 12

CARAMON WALKED THE CORRIDORS OF THE COUNCILlor's house, becoming increasingly nervous with each step, though he could not imagine why. Nothing in the estate had been any more menacing than an inanimate suit of armor in the library. He rubbed at the muscles in his right leg, a very slight bruise rising blue on his flesh.

"How did that happen?" he asked himself. "I don't remember bumping into anything."

The hall led him from the library to the middle of the house. Here the corridor was dimly lit with a strange color, vaguely purple or lavender. Brass oil lamps, spaced at regular intervals and mounted directly to the wall, gave only a faint glow, the frosted glass covering the wicks and diffusing the yellow-white flames into almost nothing.

"Why the devil does she keep it so dark in here?" Caramon said to himself, wondering which of the many doors the kender might be behind. "Earwig! Earwig! Where are you?"

He wandered the house calling, waiting for an answer and finally, after what seemed like hours, heard one.

"Caramon? Is that you?"

"Of course, it's me! Where are you?"

"In here!"

Caramon walked a few paces to a door in the middle of the hall. He twisted the knob, walked in, and stopped dead. "Shavas's bedroom," he said.

He knew he should leave, he knew what he was doing was highly improper. But he couldn't help himself. The beauty and alluring mystery of the room seemed to beckon him forward. Besides, he told himself, he'd heard the kender's voice and the last thing the lady would want would be the kender in amid her personal belongings.

"I'll just slip in and take a quick look around for Earwig," Caramon said softly, entering the room. Without quite knowing what he was doing or why, he shut the door behind him.

The councillor's bedroom was comfortably lit, much brighter than the hallway. An abundance of candles burned in holders, each a different shape from the other, each some type of animal or creature: griffons, dragons, and other wondrous or grotesque creatures. The melting wax gave off a faint perfume that reminded Caramon of the woman herself. Desire made him tingle, and he found himself standing next to her bed.

The bed frame was made of brass, decorated with the

same bizarre creatures who held the candles. It dominated the back of the room. Curtains and drapes of gray silk hung from the ceiling and metal supports. Dressers and drawers were scattered about, lacquered black and red and orange, with pictures of odd birds and twisted trees and weird flowers. There were six chairs of the same design. Small boxes of gold and silver and other precious metals, their intricate detail and textures belaying a hint of great age, covered three tables. Though he was no expert in metalworking, the fighter could tell that the boxes were built by a master craftsmen.

The floors were embellished by a rich carpet, filled with swirls and ribbons and circles, the same colors as everything else in the room. Several mirrors were mounted to the walls, and a full-size mirror, held by a frame of gold, stood in one corner, reflecting Caramon's image. The warrior noticed that his reflection in the mirror seemed to be coming from farther away than he actually was.

"How long have I been standing here?" he asked out loud, blinking, the sound of his voice lifting the fascinating, lascivious spell of the room. "And where's Earwig?" Glancing about nervously, the fighter searched the room. He found nothing, no sign of a kender.

"I should leave," he said, leaning on a smooth, black-stained table painted with orange flowers and green leaves. The wood felt surprisingly warm under his palms. Without thinking, he took hold of a piece of cloth that had been thrown casually on the table, his fingers caressing it. Moving to sit on the bed, he held the cloth without noticing what he was doing, working his hands over the cool, smooth fabric.

"The councillor is the most magnificent woman I've ever seen," he murmured. The cloth was growing warm beneath his fingers. "I wonder what she's like?" Caramon said very softly.

Rising to his feet, he walked over to the full mirror again, studying his face—a face many considered handsome. His body was scarred from numerous battles, his muscles held unmatched strength. Drawing a deep breath, the fighter watched his huge chest expand, his arms grow firm.

Then he saw what he held in his hand.

"What am I doing?" Face burning in embarrassment, he moved swiftly back to the table, starting to replace the black-silk shawl he had been fondling, when a high-pitched voice shrilled behind him.

"What have you got in your hand, Caramon?"

"Nothing!" he yelled, spinning to face the kender, who was gazing up and smiling at the fighter.

"What's that?" Earwig asked, reaching around Caramon to the table.

"Don't touch it!" the warrior said quickly. "Just something of . . . of the councillor's."

"Oh," the kender said, shrugging.

"Come on, Earwig! We shouldn't be in here," said Caramon severely, feeling guilty and taking it out on the kender.

The warrior headed hurriedly for the door. Earwig started to follow when he noticed a small box sitting on one of the tables.

Pick me up! Pick me up!

"What?" said Earwig, pausing, staring at the box in delight.

"I didn't say anything!" snapped Caramon. Bumbling into a large, hand-painted screen, he almost knocked it over and was grappling with it, trying to keep it from falling.

Pick me up! Pick me up!

"You bet!" cried the kender. Grabbing the box, he thrust it quickly into one his pouches.

"Earwig!"

Caramon, having righted the screen, was standing near the door. He was using That Voice again. Earwig caught up with him and they left the room, the warrior carefully shutting the door behind them.

"What's the matter, Caramon?" the kender asked, noting that the big man's face was red and he appeared to be breathing more rapidly than normal.

"Nothing! Just leave me alone!" Caramon ordered, tromping down the hall.

Open me! Open me!

"This is truly remarkable," said Earwig happily as he reached into his pouch for the box. There was really no reason why he shouldn't open it in front of Caramon, but the kender felt a sudden need to keep the marvelous box hidden from his friend. Letting the warrior get ahead of him, Earwig flicked the catch with his finger. The lid of the box flew open. Inside was a single ring—a plain, gold band without stone or engraving, nestled in red velvet. Earwig frowned in disappointment, having hoped to find something more interesting. After all, the box had talked to him.

"So, where were you?" Caramon demanded, stopping dead in his tracks to confront the kender. "Hiding behind a curtain?"

Earwig thrust the box beneath his tunic. "Curtain? I wasn't behind any curtain!"

"I heard you call my name from that room! You must have been somewhere? One of the dressers?"

Earwig shook his head. "I don't know what you're talking about, Caramon. I came into that room looking for you!"

The warrior glared at the kender skeptically. Then, shrugging, he shook his head and sighed. "It's this weird house. It's got me hearing things. So, where have you been?"

"Well, I've been to Solace and Thelgaard and Southern Ergoth and—"

"I mean where in the house!" Caramon shouted, exasperated.

"Oh. Why didn't you say so?" Earwig said, slapping himself in the forehead with the palm of his hand, raising his eyes to heaven. "There's a really fantastic room that's filled with plants, and they're all growing indoors."

"Plants?" Caramon repeated. "Are you sure there's a room with plants in it?"

"Yeah. It's all hot and steamy in there, too."

"Uh-huh. Next you'll tell me there's a secret chamber somewhere."

"Wow! How did you kn—"

"Name of the Abyss, Earwig! Quit making up these wild tales of yours!" Caramon stalked off down the hall. "Come on. I think we should be getting back to Raist."

"Sure, Caramon," Earwig said cheerfully. He slipped the ring onto his finger.

* * * * *

"You and Caramon are twins?" Shavas asked from across the small table.

Raistlin glanced up from the game board before him, startled by the observation. He had made no mention of it before. "I didn't think it was that obvious," he said dryly.

"Granted, you don't resemble each other, but you and your brother are more alike than perhaps either of you realize."

"I doubt that, Lady Shavas. The same informant who told you of our plans to come to Mereklar must have given you this information, as well."

"Don't be angry, Raistlin," the lady said, looking at him with her splendid eyes, the eyes that did not age. "With such terrible trouble coming to our city, it is my duty as councillor to divine the intent and motives of all who visit Mereklar."

She was right, of course. Raistlin grudgingly admitted and sneered at himself. This cursed nature of his that must gain dominion of everything, everyone . . . despite the fact that he could still taste the sweetness of her lips on his.

The game board was a block of unidentifiable grayish metal the length of a forearm and many inches thick, checkered on top with alternating squares of silver and ebony. The mage reached over and moved the carved figure of a man on a horse two spaces left and one forward.

"An excellent move, but one with which I am familiar." The councillor smiled.

Taking a piece of gold—a small rectangle with a raised square at one end—from a scale set to the side of the players, she placed it among a small pile she was accumulating. The scales tipped toward the mage. Shavas moved one of her own pieces—a man with a large shield and spear—from in front of Raistlin's knight, next to two other knights on the same row. She placed a thick metal bar under her men, creating a barrier Raistlin's horseman could not cross.

The mage deployed one of his own pieces—a tower—behind his cavalrymen and took a larger bar from his own side of the scales, causing them to tilt slightly, though still in his favor. He removed the barrier and the three men from the board, pushing his knight forward one square.

"I am familiar with *that* move as well," Raistlin said, leaning back in his chair, regarding the board with calculating eyes.

His tactic had forced Shavas to expend important

magic—represented by the ingots—and move a piece from the side of the board where the mage's real concentration of forces was waiting. He had caused her to sacrifice three yeomen, a fortification, and position in the game through his diversion.

Shavas also leaned back in her chair, measuring the amount of magic she had available, reading the gauge at the top of the scales, a pointer leaning to her opponent's advantage.

"You play an excellent game, Master Mage."

"Thank you. I have been playing a long time."

The door opened with a bang, slamming back against the wall. Caramon and Earwig clomped into the room.

"I found him," said Caramon.

"Found who? Me? I wasn't lost, was I? Was I lost, Raistlin?" asked Earwig.

The mage, watching Shavas, saw the woman's gaze fasten on Earwig. Her eyes glinted, the lids narrowed. Raistlin glanced swiftly at Earwig and saw that the kender's collar was askew, the cat's skull necklace shone brightly in the firelight. He looked swiftly back to the councillor, but her face was expressionless.

Surely I was mistaken, he thought, a cold chill convulsing him. "It took you long enough. What have you been doing?" he demanded, speaking tersely to cover his emotion.

"Just . . . walking around," Caramon mumbled. He looked down at the game they were playing. "Wizards and Warriors. Never could get the hang of that."

"Many people have difficulty mastering it, Caramon," the woman said soothingly.

"I guess I just don't have a head for long-term strategies," the fighter confessed.

The councillor's eyes met his. She seemed to say that

she admired men who were above playing silly games. The warrior felt the blood rush to his face.

"Hey!" Earwig cried excitedly. "Those pieces are just like the pieces in my pouch. Do you want to see?"

The kender, plopping himself down on a couch, bumped into Caramon, causing the big man to lose his balance and jostle the game board. Pieces rolled everywhere.

"You clumsy oaf! We've been playing this game for hours!" Raistlin snarled in anger.

"I . . . I'm sorry, Raist," the warrior said in confusion. He started to add something, but a look from the councillor made him forget what it was.

"No harm done," Shavas said, smiling up into Caramon's eyes. "We should return to discussing business anyway. Your brother and I were only passing the time until you came back."

Her look told Caramon that she'd been counting the moments. The warrior had never met a woman so fascinating, so alluring. He couldn't understand how he'd stayed away from her for so long. It was the house . . . this strange house.

"What kept you anyway?" Raistlin asked. "Surely it didn't take that long to find the kender!"

"I wasn't lost," said Earwig sternly. "I knew where I was the whole time. If anyone was lost, it was Caramon. I found him in—ouch! Hey!"

"What? Oh, sorry, Earwig. I didn't mean to sit on you." Extricating the kender from beneath him, Caramon moved to the other side of the couch, near his brother.

"As you already know," the councillor began, waiting for all her guests to settle themselves, "Mereklar's welfare depends on the cats that live here. They protect us from evil in the world. The prophecy—"

"We've read the prophecies," interrupted Raistlin

shortly. "But perhaps you can tell us who gave them?"

"I'm sorry. I can't. May I continue? Recently, the cats have started to disappear. Nobody knows why. Nobody knows where they have gone. The citizens are beginning to fear for their lives. They believe the prophecies, you see. They fear the end of the world is coming.

"Do you know the origins of the city?" she asked of all three companions.

"We have heard some things about Mereklar," the mage replied, "but perhaps you could fill in the missing details?"

Shavas smiled slightly, nodded her head. "Nobody is certain of the origins of city, except that it apparently survived the Cataclysm untouched. Unfortunately, its inhabitants did not. When the people living in the surrounding lands fled to the city, they discovered that all of the buildings were empty. Mereklar's citizens—if there were any—had disappeared."

"What do you mean, 'if there were any'?"

"There are those who believe that the city dates only from the Cataclysm. That it wasn't here before then. Absurd, I know, but I thought I would mention it to you.

"Where was I? Ah, yes. In time, some of the families took over key positions of state, helping everyone live together in this new place."

"And your family was among them?" Raistlin asked.

"That is correct. My family have always been councillors, those who direct and guide all aspects of the city. Lord Brunswick is the Minister of Agriculture and keeps track of the lands that produce our food. Lord Alvin is Minister of Property. The others are lords and ladies of their respective spheres, such as the Sergeant at Arms, Master of the Libraries, and similar functions. There are ten in all."

Shavas shifted languidly in her chair. Her hand gracefully drew the folds of her clinging gown away from her throat, revealing her long, arched neck and marble-white skin. The brothers stared, transfixed.

"When I say that there were no signs of the former inhabitants, I am not wholly correct," Shavas murmured, her fingers toying with her opal necklace. "We found the prophecies, which were discovered in every home, without exception. These books were here, in the library. And then there were the—"

"—cats!" Earwig cried.

Raistlin and Caramon both started, the kender's voice causing them to awaken from dreams of desire.

"Yes, that's right, Earwig." The councillor smiled at the kender. "The cats. Thousands roamed the streets freely. They were always friendly, and they seemed glad to have people around. The new citizens of Mereklar took the felines to be a sign from the gods."

"When did you start noticing the disappearance of the cats?" Caramon asked, clearing his throat.

"A little more than a month ago."

"How did you know they were gone? I mean, there's still a lot of them wandering around. . . ."

"It was, of course, difficult to tell, since there were so many cats already in the city. But people had made pets of the cats—or perhaps the cats had made pets of the people, it's difficult to tell sometimes. They noticed that the cats were disappearing, and then we saw that the total number of cats in the city had decreased alarmingly."

"And you're sure that they are not hiding somewhere? Or just walking outside the city walls?"

Shavas's brows came together slightly. "We are not fools."

Caramon flushed bright red. "I didn't mean—"

"I'm sorry, sir." The councillor sighed. "Forgive me. I—This has been a very trying time. Yes, we are sure. We would not have offered the reward otherwise."

"Just what, exactly, do you want us to do?" Raistlin asked.

"Why, we want you to discover what's happening to the cats and stop it," Shavas said, looking surprised.

"You say 'we.' Am I to assume that the other members of the city council want our aid as well?" Raistlin regarded the woman carefully and thought he saw her grow slightly paler. Her eyes fell before his.

"Some are reluctant . . . to hire outside . . . ." Shavas hesitated completing the sentence.

Raistlin's lips twisted in a grim smile. "What you mean to say, lady, is that the other members of the council do not want a sorcerer in their town because they think their problem is the fault of the magical community!"

"Don't be angry, Raistlin!" Shavas gazed at him with pleading eyes. "The other members of the council do blame wizards for the cats' disappearance. For the moment. I have convinced them, however, that your help is needed, that not all magicians are evil. Won't you help us? Please?"

Caramon could almost feel the satisfaction flowing from his brother—the satisfaction at having made this beautiful, desirable woman crawl. The fighter was furious at his twin. He moved to reach out and comfort his hostess. Just then he saw Earwig stuffing all the councillor's knights and yeomen into his pouch. Sighing, Caramon changed the direction of his reach and nabbed the kender. "Put those back!"

"Put what back?"

"Those game pieces!"

"Why? They're mine."

"No, they're not."

"Yes, they are. Ask Raistlin. He was looking at them in

the room this morning. Here's the Dark Queen and here's the other Dark Queen . . . Why! I have two now! Isn't that wonderful . . ."

Caramon snatched the kender's pouch—ignoring Earwig's wail of protest—and dumped its contents out on the game board. "Do you see anything else that belongs to you, my lady?"

Shavas's gaze flicked over the kender and rested a moment on the ring on his finger. "No," she said to Caramon. "Thank you."

"It is past time for us to leave." Raistlin, leaning on the staff, pulled himself up. "I am tired and have much to think about."

"I will have my carriage drop you at the inn. You will tell me if you have decided to take the job tomorrow, Raistlin?" Shavas asked, rising gracefully to her feet.

"Perhaps, my lady," the mage replied, bowed and left the room.

Chapter 13

"Why do you treat people like that, Raist?" Caramon demanded, sitting forward on the comfortable leather seats of the councillor's private carriage. This vehicle was enclosed, to protect against the chill of the evening.

Raistlin glanced at his twin, amused at his brother's unusually antagonistic tone. "Treat people like what?"

"You know." Caramon couldn't exactly put his ire into words. "She's done nothing to hurt you."

"Hasn't she?" Raistlin murmured, but the words were muffled in the cowl of his red robes. He stirred slightly. "Don't be naive, Caramon. She wants our help only so long as it suits her needs. You heard her confess that the other council members hate us and are going to hire our services only because they have to."

"They only hate you," Caramon said, then snapped his mouth shut. He couldn't imagine why he'd said that, except that suddenly he wasn't feeling well. His insides were twisting like snakes.

Raistlin regarded his brother with a steadfast gaze.

"Well," said Earwig, "are we going to take the job or aren't we?"

"What difference does it make to you, kender?" Raistlin asked irritably. "Since when did you ever care about work?"

Earwig blinked, rubbing his hand. The skin around one of his fingers itched. "I care about a lot of things! You never take me seriously, that's all. And you should!" he stated, glaring at his companions. "If you don't, someday you'll be sorry!"

"Calm down," muttered Caramon, rubbing his hand over his churning stomach.

"We'll take the job. There was never any doubt of that," Raistlin remarked.

"Then when do we start? What do we do first? I've got to know!" Earwig cried loudly.

Caramon looked at his friend, face wrinkling in confusion and pain. "Why?"

"I just do, that's all!" Earwig said defiantly, flinging himself back into the seat and crossing his arms over his small chest.

"What's wrong with you tonight?" Caramon stared at him.

"What's wrong with any of us?" Raistlin snapped.

No one said anything. Each of the twins could have found his own answer, though neither spoke it aloud.

The ride back to the tavern was quiet, the night very still. Raistlin saw decorations hanging from many of the houses, in preparation for the upcoming Festival of the Eye. He shook his head slowly, tapping the Staff of Magius on the floor. These people. They're so foolish. They celebrate, they dance. They don't know why. They don't understand the terrible sacrifice that brought about this holiday, he said inwardly.

Raistlin thought back to his time with the councillor. The intimacy they'd shared had been exciting and over too soon. She'd slipped from his embrace as swiftly as she'd entered it, whispering something about the servants. Raistlin, to distract himself, to focus his mind back on what was important, had inspected the books on the shelves. He'd found texts on thaumaturgy, sorcery, summoning. He thought he'd glimpsed rare volumes on naming magics, illusions, invocations. Wonders from the ages lined the shelves, wonders that had been missing for hundreds of years.

I heard of some of these books while I was apprenticed. Why are they here? Why does she have them? he asked himself. Raistlin seemed to recall her saying something about the books being there when her family arrived after the Cataclysm. That was a credible answer, of course, but . . .

The mage tried to recall everything he had seen in the room—every decoration, statuette, picture. On a table were five stones of unusual hues and colors, each the length of a finger and very smooth, shining in the firelight. They might match the description of the lost Sending Stones. There was a model of the universe—a contraption of brass, a construction of moving parts, spheres and gauges, springs for winding, coils that released their energy when tightened—

Raistlin felt a hand on his. He jumped, then relaxed quickly when he saw that it was only Caramon's. "Don't touch me! You know how I hate it!" the mage snarled.

"I'm sorry, Raist, but I . . . I don't feel very good."

"Really? *Shirak*," he whispered.

The staff's light gleamed in the carriage. Raistlin stared into his brother's face. The warrior's features were sunken and his eyes had dark rings under them, as if he had been awake for many days. His back was bent, and his shoulders sagged.

"It must have been the brandy," Caramon concluded, groaning and leaning against the side of the carriage.

"Just how much did you have to drink?" Raistlin asked.

"Not much," Caramon mumbled defensively.

Raistlin regarded his brother silently. Caramon could generally drink most men under the table. Reaching out his hand, the mage closed his fingers over his brother's wrist, felt his pulse, rapid and thready. Beads of sweat began to pop out on the warrior's forehead and upper lip.

Raistlin knew the symptoms, knew them well. But he denied it to himself. "You should learn to control your appetites, my brother," said the mage.

The carriage dropped them off in front of the inn. This time it was Raistlin who assisted his twin inside the door of Barnstoke Hall.

"I'm all right, Raist. Honest," said Caramon, ashamed of his weakness. He stood up straight, refusing his brother's arm.

Raistlin looked at him, then shrugged and, leaning on his staff, walked toward the stairs. Earwig trudged along behind. The kender's head was bowed. He looked neither to the right nor the left, but kept his eyes straight ahead on the floor in front of him. Caramon followed, staggering slightly, wondering if the ceiling was actually going to cave in on him, as it seemed.

The proprietor stood behind the desk at the side of the main room, looking through a stack of books, making notes with a black quill. He looked up when he heard his guests arrive.

"You're returning late. It's way past the middle of the night. I assume your meeting with the councillor went well, then, sirs?"

"I don't see that it's any business of yours," Raistlin said softly as he passed by the desk, ascending the stairs, heading up to their room. The proprietor, affronted, went back to his work.

Caramon stumbled over to the stairway, falling to his knees. Raistlin looked back, pausing in concern.

"Go ahead," Caramon waved his brother on. "I . . . just need to rest. I'll . . . meet you in the room." The fighter heaved himself off the floor, leaning against the stairwell. Earwig, not looking around, kept climbing the stairs.

Raistlin stared after the kender, who was acting every bit as strangely as Caramon. The mage wasn't certain whom to assist.

"I will wait for you here, on the landing, my brother," he said, keeping one eye on Caramon and one on Earwig.

The warrior, nodding, made it up the stairs. Raistlin took the big man's arm and helped him to the room.

"Earwig, open the door."

The kender nodded and did as he was told without comment, acting as if he were walking in his sleep. Caramon stumbled headlong into the room. Lifting his head, he caught, by the light of the staff, a quick glimpse of movement in a dark corner.

"Raist—" he began, but before he could say anything more, his brother had shoved him to one side. A dart, its point glittering in the staff's light, sped from the darkness straight at the fighter. Raistlin threw himself into the path of the missile, opening his cloak to create a shield of cloth. Two more darts followed, burying themselves in the cloth of the red robes before they reached their target.

The assassin dashed forward—a figure in black, dodging around the mage with the agility of an acrobat. He leaped over the dumbfounded kender, took the stairs to the first floor in one jump, and disappeared into the street.

Raistlin ran to the window, pulling a shard of glass from a pouch to use in a spell, but the assassin was already gone. Turning, he hurried back to his brother, who was lying on the floor.

"Caramon? Are you hurt?" he asked, kneeling at his brother's side.

"No, I . . . don't think so."

Looking up into his twin's face, Caramon saw true concern, true worry. Warmth spread through his body, banishing the sickness for a moment. Somewhere deep inside, Raistlin cared for him. The knowledge was worth facing all the assassins in the world. "Thanks, Raist," he said weakly.

Raistlin inspected his robes and pulled the three darts from the cloth. Two were lodged in the folds, the third had struck a metal disk—the charm of good fortune he had received from the woman at the Black Cat. He looked at the amulet with a touch of amusement.

Earwig, aimlessly roaming the room, found another dart that the assassin had dropped. Without saying anything to the brothers, the kender slipped it into his pocket.

"Do you need anything, Caramon?" Raistlin asked.

"No, nothing. I just need to rest." The warrior collapsed on the bed. His brother sat by his side. "Raist, I thought you said nobody'd hurt us now. Too many people knew we were here."

"It wasn't 'us' they were after, Caramon," said Raistlin thoughtfully, studying the darts. "It was you."

"Huh?" The warrior propped himself up on his elbow.

"Why would anyone want to kill Caramon?" Earwig yawned.

"The darts were aimed directly at you. None at me or the kender. And this strange illness. If I hadn't been there, you wouldn't have been able to react, to get out of the way. You would have been easy prey, my brother."

Raistlin held one of the darts up to a lamp. The mage sniffed at the tip and drew his face back, wrinkling his nose in obvious repugnance. "Thorodrone," he said, pursing his lips and sniffing again. "Definitely. An extremely deadly poison. You were fortunate he didn't hit you, Caramon. You would have been dead in an instant."

He held the dart over the flame of a nearby lamp, causing the tip to glow green. Spitting on his fingers, then rubbing them together lightly, Raistlin flaked off the poison, now turned ash gray on the black metal. He did the same to the other two darts, then deposited them carefully in one of his pouches.

Rising from the bed, the sorcerer extinguished the lamp and the light of his staff and walked to the window. "What did you see of the man?" he said, eyes scanning the streets for signs of intruders.

"Nothing. He was dressed in black, and he was fast."

"And he was really good with a blowgun," Earwig added, removing the top of his hoopak to reveal the exit hole for his own weapon.

Unseen in the darkness, the kender took out the poisoned dart and tried to insert it into the blowgun. It wouldn't fit; it was too big. He stared at it, disappointed, until he realized that if he plucked away some of the feathers, the dart would fit quite nicely. He commensed plucking.

"I didn't see anything of him either," said Raistlin.

Earwig slid the defeathered dart into a small, hidden pocket on his sleeve, and capped his hoopak. Yawning again, he unrolled his bedclothes, lay down, and was soon fast asleep.

"Did you notice anything unusual when you were walking around inside of her house tonight?" Raistlin asked suddenly.

"Unusual?" Caramon was sick and dizzy and wanted only to go to sleep.

"Unusual. Bizarre. Out of the ordinary. Did you see or hear anything you didn't understand?"

Caramon thought back to Shavas's room, remembering the touch of silk, the feel between his fingers, cold satin turning warm. A wave of heat stole over his body. He thought about hearing Earwig's voice when the kender swore he hadn't been in the room. He thought about the fact that he had wandered through the house for hours, yet it seemed to him as if it had been only a few moments.

"No. Nothing," was his short reply. "Leave the lady out of this, Raist. She didn't have anything to do with it. I drank too much, that's all. It was my fault."

"Perhaps," murmured Raistlin. "I must get into that house again . . . alone."

"What?" asked Caramon drowsily.

"Nothing, my brother."

The mage went to his bed. When he heard Caramon snoring, his breathing deep and regular, Raistlin allowed himself to drift into sleep.

* * * * *

Earwig. What are you doing?

"I'm sleeping. What does it look like I'm doing?" the kender retorted.

Huge claws, black claws, the claws of a gigantic cat,

made a swipe at him. Earwig just barely managed to dodge out of the way.

What are your friends doing?

"They're sleeping, too."

Both of them? Safe? Unharmed?

"Yes! Now leave me alone. I have to get out of the way of this monster!" The kender jumped over something that resembled a metal box with teeth.

I'll be back, Earwig . . . I'll be back . . . I'll be back . . .

* * * * *

The next day, Caramon, after the night's sleep, felt as invigorated as ever. No trace of yesterday's sickness remained. Earwig, however, was cross and out-of-sorts.

"What's the matter with you?" Caramon asked over breakfast.

"Nothing," said the kender. "I didn't sleep well, all right?"

"Sure," said the astonished Caramon. "I was just asking. What are we going to do today, Raist?"

Two more days until the Festival of the Eye. There isn't much time. I wish I knew for what, thought Raistlin. Aloud he said, "I think we should explore the rest of the city."

"What? Why? What are you looking for?" Earwig asked sharply.

The mage stared at the kender. "Nothing in particular."

"Well, I'm coming, too," Earwig announced. "Where are we going?"

"To the other two city gates, and then we'll work our way back into the center."

"The innkeeper says those black carriages are 'public conveyances,' " said Caramon, repeating the unfamiliar words carefully. "You pay to ride in 'em."

"Councillor Shavas will pay for us to ride in them," said Raistlin. "Go find one."

* * * * *

The companions took the carriage around the outer road to Eastgate. Three major thoroughfares in Mereklar led from the gates to the center of town. The road they traveled cut across the lines of the city, making access to other neighborhoods fast and efficient. The trip took a little more than an hour on the warm day.

Cats were everywhere—lying on sidewalks or sitting in the laps of people. Some of the more adventurous felines padded into the shops to browse with the few customers out in the streets, or climbed to rooftops to gaze down at the world below.

It was Earwig who first noticed that some of the cats were following their carriage, maintaining a distance of ten feet. When the coach slowed to move around people or a cart crossing the street, the felines slowed as well.

"Look!" said the kender, entranced.

When Raistlin turned to investigate, the cats fled. All except one.

"That's the black cat. The one we found near the councillor's house."

"I don't know how you can tell, Raist," Caramon said. "All black cats look alike to me."

"Except that there are no other black cats in the city." The carriage rolled off. "It's following us."

Caramon, his face unusually serious, leaned forward on the carriage seat. "Raist, I don't like this. Any of this. I don't like the way that cat looks at us. I don't like people trying to murder us. I don't like the way the kender's acting—"

"I'm not acting any sort of way!" protested Earwig.

Caramon ignored him. "It's not worth ten thousand steel pieces, Raist. Let's leave—go find some nice, safe war."

Raistlin didn't answer at first, but stared out the back of the carriage at the cat who was following behind. Then, nodding, he said, "You're right, my brother. It isn't worth ten thousand steel pieces." He said nothing more. Caramon, heaving a sigh, sat back in the carriage.

Eventually they reached the gate. Like the portcullis in the southern wall, it was also made from metal decorated with strange plates and sheets, each inscribed with the head of a cat.

"What do you call this street?" the mage asked the driver.

"This, sir? This is called Eastgate Street, sir."

"Councillor Shavas will pay your fare," Raistlin said, climbing down out of the carriage. "No need to wait."

"Yes, sir. Thank you, sir." The driver whipped up his horses and left as quickly as he could, nearly running over Caramon and Earwig.

"Now that we're here, what do we do?" Caramon asked.

"We get a drink," Raistlin said, heading toward the first hyava house he found.

"Huh? This time of morning? Since when—"

"Hush, my brother. I'm thirsty."

The fighter stared after his twin, wondering what had come over him. Shrugging, he grabbed the kender and followed.

The hyava shop was similar to all of the other shops the companions had passed, offering tiny cups of the liquor with equally tiny saucers, and chairs and tables for sitting outside. Earwig and Caramon both ordered straight hyava with scones. Raistlin bought a small glass of brandy. The three relaxed in the warm sun.

"Why did you get that?" Caramon asked. "I thought you wanted hyava."

Raistlin sipped at his brandy. Caramon sat, brooding. Earwig ate his scone in one bite. Seeing that his large friend was not going to eat his scone, the kender snatched the pastry off the plate, lifting it to his mouth.

"Hey! What are you doing?" Caramon yelled, batting at the kender's hand.

"Watch it!" Earwig yelled in return, trying to hang on to the scone. It broke apart in his hands and fell to the ground. "Now see what you've done. You've ruined my snack!"

"Your snack?" the warrior said in disbelief. "What do you mean, *your* snack?"

"You weren't going to eat it, so I assumed you wanted to give it to me."

"How do you know I wasn't going to eat it? I— Oh, never mind. At least it won't go to waste."

Several cats had wandered by and, assuming that neither the kender nor the fighter wanted the scone, took it upon themselves to resolve the argument. The warrior cheered at the sight, bent down to pet one of the animals. Out of the corner of his eye, he caught a glimpse of a figure, dressed in black, crouched in the shadows.

"Earwig!" Caramon whispered. "Do you see someone standing in that alley? No, don't look up!"

"What?" the kender said loudly, looking up. "Where?"

Caramon gritted his teeth. There were times, he realized, when a kender's companionship was not worth the effort. "I said not to look!"

"Well, how am I supposed to see if I don't look?"

"Never mind. It's too late, now. Do you see somebody standing in that alley across the street?"

"No, not anymore," Earwig said.

Caramon sat up and turned around, staring directly

into the alley. No one was there. In fact, looking closer, the fighter saw that he must have been mistaken. What he had taken for a figure in black was a water barrel.

"Well?" demanded Raistlin.

"Nothing. I guess I'm just spooked from last night," Caramon muttered. Raising up from petting the cat, he saw—in astonishment—tears streaming down his twin's golden-skinned face.

"Raistlin! What's the mat—"

"Nothing, Caramon," the mage interrupted. "In fact, quite the opposite. I'm beginning to understand something about this city." Raistlin clenched his hand around his wooden staff to control his mounting excitement.

There are two lines, the mage concluded. They both cut through the center of the two main streets. This one must also lead directly to the councillor's house! And I'll wager my staff that a third line runs down the west street. Lines of power, stretching across the world, perhaps; shining more brightly every moment. Lines that end here! In this city. "The city that stands before the first gods."

"Caramon," said Raistlin aloud. "I must have a sextant."

* * * * *

The companions walked to the third section of the city, looking into several shops for the navigational tool. When they finally found one—a small brass sextant with an extremely accurate lens and even more accurate gradations—it was far too expensive.

"A bargain," the shopkeeper assured them, but the mage handed it back.

"Can't you use Lady Shavas's scroll to get it?" Caramon asked.

"No. It only allows for 'minor expenses.' I doubt if a sextant counts as that."

The brothers walked up the street, never noticing that the kender was missing until he rejoined them.

"Raistlin," Earwig said, tugging at the mage's robes.

A look of anger flared in the strange, black pupils. "Don't you dare touch me! Ever!" The mage shoved the kender back.

"But I've got something for you!" Earwig said. Reaching into his pouch, he pulled out the sextant.

The mage brought his hand up over his mouth quickly, putting his fingers over his twitching lips.

"Earwig. Where did you get that?" Caramon tried to sound severe.

"From the shop, of course," the kender said, nodding his head. "The owner said you could have it if you promised to return it when you were done."

"Really? And the owner actually said this to you?"

"Well, he didn't actually say it, but I'm sure he would have if he had been in the room."

Raistlin averted his head. His thin shoulders shook, and Caramon could have sworn that his brother was laughing.

"Uh, Raist, don't you think we should return it?"

"What, and spoil Earwig's gift? Never!" Raistlin said. He took the tool from the kender's hand and tucked it under his flowing robes to hide it from sight. "Thank you, Earwig," he said solemnly. "That was very thoughtful of you."

"You're welcome," the kender said, beaming, and looking much more like the old Earwig.

The travelers found another carriage. Raistlin directed the driver to take them to Westgate Street. By the time they reached their destination, the day was rapidly fading. The last portcullis was the same as the others, metal untouched by the elements, with the same indecipherable network of plates and shields on the bars.

Next, they went to another hyava house, ordered the same drinks and food that they had ordered at the last one, with exactly the same results. Earwig tried to take Caramon's scone, and when the fighter slapped the kender's hand, the pastry broke and fell to the ground, only to be eaten by several cats sitting in front of the shop.

"I have to get my own table next time, or I'll starve," the warrior muttered.

Caramon glanced into a shop across the way—a store displaying a variety of marvelous swords—and saw a dark-skinned man staring out the window, directly at them.

Boldly meeting the gaze of the mysterious watcher, Caramon shivered with cold, though the sun shone gently on his shoulders. There was something very strange about the man. Strange, yet familiar.

The fighter turned to his brother, who was attempting to feed one of the cats a piece of his own scone. Caramon had never seen Raistlin show any affection toward animals. One of the cats nibbled at the offered crumb and bumped up against the golden, outstretched hand, but soon backed away.

The mage sighed, leaning on the Staff of Magius, gripping it tightly, an expression of enraged bafflement on his face.

Caramon hated to disrupt his brother's thoughts, but this was important. "Raistlin, we're being watched."

The mage barely glanced at him. "The man across the street in the weapons shop? Yes, I know. He's been there the past ten minutes."

Caramon half-rose. "You knew? He might be the one who tried to kill us—"

"Sit, brother. Assassins do not watch their prey so openly. This man wants us to know that he is watching us."

Caramon, confused, reluctantly sat back down.

Earwig turned to look. "Hey! That's the man who wanted my necklace!"

"What? When?" Raistlin pounced on the startled kender.

"Wh-why . . ." Earwig stammered, "it was . . . let me see . . . I remember. Back at the Black Cat Inn."

"Why didn't you say anything to me then?" Raistlin practically frothed at the mouth. He began to cough, clutching at his chest.

"Hey, Raist. Calm down," said Caramon.

"Gosh, I forgot, I guess," Earwig said, shrugging. "It wasn't anything important. He just asked me where I got the necklace, and I said it had been in my family. He seemed to want it pretty badly, and I didn't need it so I tried to give it to him, but it wouldn't come off. Then a man who was with him said something about 'dragging out my guts,' but they decided not to." Earwig sounded slightly disappointed. "Then they left.

"I kind of like this necklace," the kender added, looking at it proudly. "I meet lots of entertaining people because of it. Another man at a tavern here in town tried to kill me to get it."

"I may kill you!" gasped Raistlin when he could breathe again.

"When did *this* happen?" Caramon asked.

"Let's see. It was the night before the morning that I got in trouble with the woman in the inn. I was walking around the town when I heard men laughing. I looked into a window to see what was so funny, and I saw this man hit one of the barmaids. They threw him out, and he stood in the doorway and saw my necklace and said it was his, and he came at me with a knife. So I popped him with my hoopak, and the barmaid kissed me."

"Was it the same man who wanted your necklace the first time?"

"Of course not! That man was nice. This man wasn't."

"A name?" Raistlin mouthed. "Did you hear a name?"

"No." The kender frowned, looking back in time. "But I think the girl called him 'my lord.' "

Raistlin drew a deep breath. Caramon started to go fetch hot water, but the mage shook his head. The spasm was over. Deep in thought, he stared at his gold-skinned hands. Caramon turned his head to see if they were still under observation.

"He's gone," Raistlin said.

Caramon shivered. "It was like he could see right through me. Maybe he's a mage?"

"I don't think so." Raistlin shook his head. "There are certain . . . feelings . . . shared among wizards. It's a feeling of"—he searched for a word—"power. Our watcher did not give me that feeling."

"But he did give you some sort of feeling," Caramon said, hearing doubt in his brother's voice.

"Yes, that's true. But whatever it was, I don't *think* it was the feeling I would get if I met another wizard."

Caramon would have liked to ask why Raistlin emphasized 'think,' but the mage's cold expression cut off further conversation. The warrior was about to suggest that they get a full meal they all could enjoy.

"It is time to go back to Southgate Street." Raistlin forestalled him. "I want to meet again with Councillor Shavas."

Chapter 14

"We have decided to take the assignment," Raistlin said.

The councillor looked at each of the companions with an expression of extreme pleasure. "Thank you," she said. "Somehow, I knew you would."

With a graceful movement, she seated herself in a chair in front of a suit of armor; one of its gauntleted hands held a flamberge that was taller than the kender. Gesturing, Shavas invited the others to join her. It seemed to Caramon that the woman gazed at him with a knowing expression.

She knows that I was in her room, he said to himself,

flushing in embarrassment. She knows I . . . handled her shawl. To conceal his confusion, he turned to the bookshelves and grabbed up the first volume he found.

Raistlin was talking with the councillor, discussing the terms of their arrangement, asking questions about the carvings on the walls. Caramon didn't pay any attention. He was thinking about the beautiful woman. Rich, educated, well-born—she was far above him, out of his reach, like the moon and the stars.

I'm making a fool of myself, Caramon thought. A woman like that could never love me. I'll stick to women like Maggie . . . But he couldn't keep his hungry gaze from her face.

"When the city was found," Shavas was saying, "most of the walls were blank. We believe that the stone was sent by the first gods to the architects who built the city. It is unbreakable, though many tried. Some people noticed, however, that as time went on, carvings began to appear, as if somebody were engraving them into the stone by magic." She glanced at the still form of the mage. "The engravings were of stories of some of the greatest events on Krynn, such as the fall of the Kingpriest of Istar; the Legend of Huma; the story of Lord Soth, Knight of the Black Rose. Apparently, some unknown force carves the tales of the world into the walls."

Lord Soth. What a dumb name. Caramon tore his gaze away. Opening the book, he glanced through it. And what a dumb book, he decided, leafing from one sheet to the next till he reached the back cover. There were no pictures or writing or anything.

Shrugging, he put the book back on the shelf where he had found it. Looking around, he saw Shavas staring at him. The warrior flushed beneath her penetrating gaze.

"Did you find anything interesting?" she asked.

"I doubt it," Raistlin answered for his brother. "Caramon is not particularly fond of reading. I, on the other, would be quite pleased if I could spend some time in your library."

"Of course, you may have free reign of my house and all its facilities. You all may," she added, looking at Caramon.

The big warrior grinned at her, feeling more at ease. She might be rich and educated but when it came right down to it, she was a woman, after all. And he was a man.

"We'll need to meet with the other city council members, as well," Raistlin said sharply.

Caramon glanced at his brother. If it hadn't seemed too impossible, he would have sworn his twin was jealous!

"I have already planned a meeting for tonight." Shavas smiled coyly. "As I said, I knew you'd accept."

* * * * *

The meeting was held on Lord Brunswick's estate near the northern tip of the triangular walls of Mereklar. The lord had sent his family out for the evening for the sake of privacy.

The city's officials met in the library, where the lord kept the model of the city. Chairs and tables filled the already crowded room, making it seem much smaller than it really was. Caramon felt slightly claustrophobic and more than a little nervous at the prospect of being questioned by people as important as the Ministers of Mereklar.

"Don't worry, brother," Raistlin said from the dark, engulfing cowl, "you need not become involved. I will do the talking."

The warrior relaxed. "Sure, Raist. Whatever you say."

Earwig seemed to have shaken off his fit of grouchiness, for he kept Caramon half-distracted by poking into everything. The kender nearly upset the model. He was caught trying to stuff a large book into his pouch. Eventually Caramon collared him and plunked Earwig down on the couch between him and Raistlin, threatening to tie him up if he moved. The kender took the twist of metal out of his pocket and began shaking the bead, trying to make it fall out.

The first to enter the room was Shavas, who took her place opposite the companions, the model of the city between them. Her white gown clung to her full figure, a pleasing contrast to her dark, braided hair.

Next to enter was Lord Brunswick, owner of the house. He moved slowly around the room to sit near Shavas. The minister's expression was blank and officiatious. Another man entered, Lord Alvin. He sat opposite Brunswick, casting a baleful glance at Raistlin.

Other lords and ladies entered the room through the large double doors. A short man with dark hair and a moustache sat next to Lord Brunswick. To the left of Alvin sat another man, tall and lanky.

Another woman walked into the room. Her hair was drawn back tightly from her face—a skullcap of wiry strands held by a short silver spike. With her came a stolid-looking man wearing a gray vest and slightly darker pants and shirt. He had a small scar under his right eye, and his black hair was swept back to one side.

Three other officials entered the room. Two were men. One was enveloped by a flowing brown robe—a cleric of some religious sect. The other wore a ceremonial breastplate of steel and greaves of leather. The third was a woman, dressed in a full, blue robe. She wore an amulet whose symbol could not be seen.

Shavas rose from her chair. "Raistlin Majere. Caramon Majere. Earwig Lockpicker. May I present to you the Council of the City of Mereklar.

"Lord Brunswick, Minister of Agriculture, and our gracious host. Lord Alvin, Minister of Property. Lord Young, Minister of Internal Affairs. Lord Creole, Minister of Labor. Lady Masak, Director of Records. Lord Wrightwood, Minister of Finance. Lord Cal, Captain of the Guard. Lady Volia, Director of Welfare. Lord Manion—" Shavas stopped. "Where is Lord Manion?"

The other officials glanced around.

"I don't know," said Lord Alvin in a sour voice. "He knew the time. I told him myself."

"He's never late. I don't like this." Shavas bit her lower lip. A line marred the marble smoothness of her forehead. Raistlin noticed that the fingers of one hand curled in on themselves, clenching into a fist.

"Perhaps we should wait," suggested the mage, rising to his feet.

"No . . . no." Shavas's face cleared, though with an obvious effort. "He will be here shortly, I'm certain."

"Very well, Councillor."

"Excuse us a moment, Councillor," said Lord Cal. "A word with you and the other members. In private." The ministers gathered around, talking in low voices.

Raistlin, studying the people who had been studying him, decided he couldn't trust any of them. His experiences with officials in the past had taught him that alliances among rulers of state were both invisible and dangerous.

" 'The person caught in the webs of intrigue soon finds himself fed to the spider,' " he quoted to himself, recalling a proverb of the great political revolutionary, Eyavel.

He wondered what they were discussing and was considering gliding forward to overhear, when a shrill giggle made him recall something important he'd meant to do.

Leaning over Caramon's back, Raistlin grabbed Earwig by the collar and drew him near with a golden, skeletal hand.

"Earwig, do you recognize any of these men? Was one of them the one who tried to kill you?"

The kender shook his head almost immediately. "No, Raist. But I could ask if they know who he—"

Raistlin glared, gripping the kender more tightly. "If you dare say as much as one word, I'll turn you into glass and drop you from a mountaintop."

"Really? You'd do that for me?" Earwig, touched, reached over to clasp in appreciation the thin fingers that held him.

"Ouch! Ah!" The mage snatched his hand back quickly. "What did you do? You burned me!"

"Nothing! I didn't do anything, Raistlin!" Earwig protested, staring at his hand in bewilderment.

Raistlin grabbed the kender's wrist. Holding it up to observe it better in the lamplight, he saw a plain golden ring on the fourth finger.

The mage glanced around quickly to see if anyone was watching. The ministers were still involved in their private concerns. "Earwig!" he whispered. "Where did you get this ring?"

"Ring? Oh, this! I found it somewhere," the kender replied glibly. "I think someone dropped it."

Raistlin took hold of the ring finger and muttered a simple spell. The ring began to glow, as if a light were shining on it from an unseen source. "Magic." He tried to pull the ring from the kender's finger.

"Ouch! Stop that! It hurts! Hey, did you say my ring was magic?" Earwig inquired eagerly. Raistlin let go of the ring, and the kender rubbed his hand.

"No, Earwig. I said 'tragic.' It's tragic that someone

lost such a valuable ring."

"Please, no more arguments!" Shavas's voice, sharper than normal, broke in on the mage's. "Let us start." When everyone in the room had resumed their seats and quieted down, she continued. "This meeting of the Mereklar Council is different from any other gathering to date. Our city is in peril, and the fate of the world is in question. We have asked these men"—gesturing to the companions—"to aid us in our time of need. The floor is now open to questions."

"It's a strange coincidence that a mage shows up now. Who's to say that he's not the cause of our problems?" Lord Alvin sneered, pointing at Raistlin. "All know wizards have always conspired to rule the world!"

"I tell you, Councillor, that we don't need them!" Lord Cal added, "The city guard will take care of the matter. We just need more time!"

"Please, Lord Alvin, contain yourself. You have no evidence to support your accusation. And you, Lord Cal, show respect for our guests," Shavas commanded. "I'm sure that if Lord Manion were here, he would agree with the steps I have taken."

"I am sorry, Majere, if I have slighted you," Lord Alvin apologized, though he said it between clenched teeth.

Lord Cal said nothing. It seemed, for a moment, as if he might storm out of the room, but he finally subsided beneath Shavas's icy stare.

"The mage is here only because of the ten thousand pieces of steel," stated Lord Brunswick.

"On the contrary," said Shavas aloofly. "Raistlin Majere has refused to accept any payment at all."

Obviously caught by surprise, the ministers glanced at each other. Caramon, just as shocked as they were, stared at Raistlin incredulously.

"He must be after something else, then," Alvin said under his breath.

"I must remind you, Lord Alvin," Raistlin said from the depths of his cowl, "that, according to tradition, the services of all wizards are free during the Festival of the Eye."

"And may I remind you, Master Mage, that the festival is nothing more than a child's holiday, and legends or stories will never make it more than that!" Alvin snorted. "Tell us why you're really here—if you dare!"

"Lord Alvin!" Councillor Shavas cried, shocked. "Since Lord Manion is not here to keep you silent, I shall be forced to have you removed from these proceedings if you do not cease your outbursts!"

"Thank you, Councillor, for your intervention," Raistlin said, standing slowly, gripping the Staff of Magius in his right hand. "But Lord Alvin's question is a legitimate one. My reason for remaining in your city is that I find it of interest. I have never seen a place of such beauty and wonder, and I will do whatever I can to help you. We of the red robes do not practice the dark arts of our black-robed brethren. We seek only to enlighten ourselves and grow in knowledge."

"Then you want simply to profit by the experience?" Lady Volia asked, her chin propped up on a fist, staring intently at the mage.

"That is very astute, my lady. My companions and I believe that it is a virtue to help those in need without thought of worldly profit," Raistlin said modestly.

Caramon knew that his brother was lying. Raistlin had never turned down an offer of money. Why's he telling them this? What's he really after? the fighter wondered. Looking at Councillor Shavas, who was regarding his brother with admiration, Caramon thought jealously that he knew the answer.

Silence fell, the mage's remark having caught all of

them off guard. Caramon could see, however, that Lord Alvin and Lord Cal remained unconvinced, even as the other ministers were slowly changing their opinions.

"How do you intend to begin the investigation?" Lady Masak asked.

Raistlin bowed slightly. "Forgive me, my lady, but my methods are not open to discussion."

This caused an outburst, the ministers all talking—or shouting—at once. Caramon, groaning slightly from having to sit in one place too long, shifted his position restlessly.

Earwig scratched his hand; the area around the ring was turning red and raw from his constant rubbing.

Shavas beckoned to Lord Cal. "This is impossible! Go find Manion!"

The captain left the room.

* * * * *

Lord Manion threw his dress cloak over his black cloak of office, locking the clasps held at the throat, a gold chain braided like rope. Turning back to regard the front hall once more, satisfied that everything was in order, he extinguished the lamp, closed the door, and locked it with a large bronze key.

Manion's dwelling was similar to the other houses owned by the officials of Mereklar—a large rectangular building of white stone with panes of glass in every wall. It had, however, a run-down look. The Minister of Internal Affairs was not a wealthy man. Some said he squandered his money on women and in the taverns. He didn't own his own carriage, but Lord Brunswick's estate was close enough for him to walk to.

Lord Manion set off down the street toward the middle of the city. The way led him through part of the town, then into a park. As he walked, he peered up into the sky to observe the stars and moons, smiling at the nearly full circles of Solinari and Lunitari.

Soon, he thought. Very soon.

Manion's heavy black boots clicked along the white stone sidewalks. The night was silent. The city's inhabitants had shut themselves in, barring their doors against a vague and unknown terror.

The lord was smiling, shaking his head at their folly when, turning a corner, he suddenly heard a throaty growl.

Manion looked back up the street. The sidewalk was brightly lit by the magical lights. He saw nothing and continued on his way, peering back over his shoulder from time to time.

Lord Manion heard the growl again, closer, and now a soft padding of footsteps. Instead of turning around and stopping to see what it was, the lord increased his pace. His boots sounded loudly on the pavement until he reached the park. He breathed easier. The soft ground muffled his steps, the tall trees hid his form. He couldn't hear his pursuer anymore.

And then it was there again, following him, undeterred by darkness. The growl sounded closer and more menacing.

The lord began to sweat, drawing his breath in shallow, short gasps. Ducking behind a tree, pressing his back into the hard bark, he pulled a dagger from a sheath—a long jeweled blade, curved near the narrow tip—and held it, point-down, in his hand. He waited, as still as the night, for as many heartbeats as he dared, listening intently, extending his sense of sight and hearing as far as they would go.

He heard nothing, saw nothing. Lord Manion breathed a small sigh of relief.

An arm slammed his head back against the tree. A

hand grabbed his dagger and threw it into a nearby hedge, disabling and disarming the man in one, efficient action. "How did you get here?" the attacker whispered. He was dressed in black, a shadow against shadows.

Manion stared into the eyes of his assailant—eyes that were red in the lambent light of the moons. The lord spit with loathing and hatred.

"Answer me!" the man in black hissed, driving his arm farther into the minister's throat.

The lord lifted a leg and kicked his attacker in the stomach, sending the assailant flying backward. Manion leaped at the man he had just thrown, landing on top of him, grasping for his throat.

The man in black brought his right arm across in a horizontal arc, sweeping his hand against Manion's chest. Claws ripped opened a great gash of black against the white, silk shirt. The lord screamed in agony. The attacker drove his other hand into the minister's throat, lifting him off the ground, sending him sprawling.

Manion, shaking his head to clear it, renewed the battle in a frenzy, fighting with his bare hands. The claws slashed again, tearing flesh. The lord fell to his knees. The assailant brought his right leg up in a kick that snapped Manion's head backward, causing him to land with his arms and legs spread out, completely vulnerable. Bending over the minister, the man in black reached down with an arm, attempting to drag the lord to his feet.

Manion slammed his head into the attacker's chest. Grabbing the dark-clothed limbs, he rushed forward, dashing the man full-force into a tree.

Air whooshed from the attacker's lungs, and he fell to his knees and hands, as the minister had done moments before. Manion lifted the man up by the collar and struck him in the face, causing his head to rebound back against the wood. The assailant ducked the next blow sluggishly, though just quickly enough. The lord's fist slammed against the tree, cracking the bark, throwing rough chips into the air. Manion, still holding onto the attacker with his other hand, threw him to the ground and kicked him with such force that the front of his boot ripped off.

The other man collapsed, and the lord stood over him. A look of cruelty and hatred twisted his features. He lifted his leg, preparing to smash his foot down directly on the man's head. The slight hesitation was all the attacker needed. He grabbed Manion's leg, wrenching it around, breaking it at the hip. Manion collapsed with a terrifying cry.

The attacker stood. Lifting the Minister of Affairs off the ground by the throat with one arm, he snarled, exposing unusually long and pointed teeth. "What are you doing here?" he asked again.

"You will be destroyed, as will all your kind!" Manion cried hoarsely.

"Will we?" questioned the man in black. He jerked the lord's head back. The neck snapped. The minister went limp, though—for a moment—his eyes appeared remarkably alive. Remarkably malevolent.

Tossing Manion to the ground, the assassin bent down over the corpse. Sharp claws rent cloak and clothes, skin and sinew.

* * * * *

"You will have whatever you need, Raistlin," Shavas said.

The discussions had been concluded. Lord Cal had not returned, and Caramon was wondering if Shavas had sent him out on some sort of trumped-up mission in order to get rid of him.

"Thank you, Councillor . . . and officials of Mereklar," Raistlin said with a slight sneer.

"When will you start?" Lady Masak asked.

"I have already started, Lady Masak." The mage smiled. The woman appeared somewhat alarmed.

Everyone began to make preparations to leave, gathering up any notes they had taken during the talk, when the door flew open.

Lord Cal stepped in. "Councillor! I must speak with you!"

The man's voice was strained, tense. Going to Shavas, he whispered something. Color drained from the woman's face. She swallowed, opened her mouth, closed it.

"Gentlemen." Lord Cal glared at Raistlin and his companions. "I must speak with the ministers in private. Would you excuse us, please?"

It wasn't a request, but a command. Raistlin and Caramon left the room, Caramon returning in a moment to grab the kender.

"I didn't know he meant me!" Earwig said, wriggling in the warrior's grasp. "No one ever called me a gentleman before!"

The door shut behind them. Raistlin waited until he heard the lock click, then he swiftly withdrew one of the pouches hanging from his belt. Removing the cup he used to mix his drink, he placed it against one of the walls and put his ear to it, listening intently. There came a scraping sound from inside and Raistlin sprang backward, thrusting the cup beneath the folds of his robe.

The door opened, and Shavas entered the hall. "I'm sorry, but we must end the meeting now. My carriage will take you back to your lodgings." She gazed at them, as if she wanted to say something, but couldn't make up her mind. Then, shaking her head, she dispatched a servant, turned, and reentered the council room, closing the door behind her.

"What did you hear?" Caramon came over to Raistlin, who was leaning on his staff, staring after the woman thoughtfully.

"Lord Manion. He's been killed. His body was found in a park not far from here."

Caramon stared. "Killed?"

"Excuse me, sirs." The coachman entered. "Councillor Shavas has instructed me to take to your inn."

"Maybe we're not ready to g—" Caramon began.

Raistlin laid a hand on his arm. "I am feeling tired. I could use a night's rest." He took a step forward, then suddenly halted, glancing around. "My staff! I left it behind in the council room!"

"No, you didn't," said Caramon. "You had it just a moment—" The warrior stared. The staff was nowhere to be seen.

"I don't want to interrupt the meeting. If you could wait for us, sir," said Raistlin to the coachman, "we'll be right out. You can wait outside," he added pointedly.

The driver appeared dubious, but—not having any instructions to the contrary—he left the room.

Raistlin breathed a sigh of relief. "Good. Now, Caramon, we must leave this house without anyone noticing us. There must be another door . . . Ah, yes. We'll use this one."

"Where are we going?"

"To the park, to inspect the body ourselves."

"Wow!" breathed Earwig in awe.

Raistlin started down the hall, walking rapidly, with unusual energy. Caramon trailed behind. He'd seen enough dead men in his life and didn't particularly relish the sight of another.

"Hey, Raist!" he said, remembering. "What about your staff?"

The mage turned around. The Staff of Magius was in his hand. "What about it?" he asked.

* * * * *

The park where the attack had taken place was now well lit by lamps and torches, held by guardsmen wearing blue uniforms and tall helmets. They stood in a wide circle around the corpse, staring down at it, talking in low, horror-filled voices. None noticed the silent intrusion of the mage, creeping out of the shadows to stand behind them.

What was left of Lord Manion lay sprawled on the grass, his limbs twisted at odd angles. The head, it appeared, had nearly been torn from the body.

"His neck's been broken," said one of the guards. "And 'is throat ripped open. In fact, most of 'is insides has been torn out, like a giant hand reached in and yanked 'em."

Caramon, peering over his brother's shoulder, felt his stomach turn. The big man looked away. He'd seen violent death before, but that was on the battlefield. Death by stealth, by night, made him sick.

Earwig stared. He stood, twisting his ring, his usually cheerful face turning a dull leaden color. "Raistlin," he said, gulping and tugging on the mage's sleeve.

The mage silenced him with a glance.

"A hand didn't do this," said another guard. "Leastwise not a human hand. It was claws! Gigantic claws!"

"Lady Shavas," spoke a voice that Caramon recognized as Lord Cal's. "You shouldn't be here. This is a gruesome sight."

"I am Councillor. It is my duty."

Shavas stepped forward into the light. She stared at the grisly corpse on the ground, then put her hand over her mouth and turned away. The other council members, trailing along behind, pushed through the guards to view the body.

"Brunswick, take the councillor home," ordered Lord Cal.

The minister started to lead Shavas away when she suddenly looked up and saw Raistlin. "You!" she cried in a hollow voice.

"What are these men doing here? Guards, I want them removed! Now!" Lord Alvin commanded, pointing.

Shavas recovered herself. "Please, Raistlin. Leave us. This is a personal loss. . . ."

One of the guards reached forward to grab the mage's arm, but a glance from the hourglass eyes stopped him in his tracks. Caramon took a step nearer, to be ready if his brother needed assistance. Earwig, quiet and subdued, was still staring at the body.

"Everything will be fine, Councillor," said Raistlin reassuringly. "We will say nothing about this to anyone."

"But I—"

"What are you doing here, wizard? How did you know about this man's death, unless you helped commit his murder?" demanded Lord Cal. "It's obvious he died as the result of some foul magical spell!"

"Is it?" the mage inquired with bland interest. "I suppose that explains the absence of blood?"

The question caught them all by surprise. Shavas sucked in a whistling breath through her teeth. Lord Alvin pointed at the mage with a trembling hand.

"Nobody ever died by violence in this town until you entered it!"

"Don't be a fool," said Raistlin. He glanced again at the corpse. "The man obviously died while on his way to the meeting. I was with Councillor Shavas the entire time."

"Mages can get others to do their dark deeds for them, or so I've heard," said Lord Cal grimly. "Others—like their familiars! Like giant cats!"

The councillor shot Cal a look so filled with venom that Caramon took a step back to avoid being poisoned by the glare.

Raistlin turned. "Perhaps I should leave your city to its own devices—"

"I'm sure that will not be necessary, Raistlin," Shavas said. Gliding over to the mage, she put a hand on his robed shoulder, keeping her eyes averted from the horror on the ground. "Isn't that correct, Lord Cal?"

The lord tensed, as if afraid of some veiled threat. Clearing his throat, he said, "No, of course not."

Shavas slumped, letting her body sag against Raistlin's. He put his arm around her, supporting her.

"Raistlin!" said Earwig urgently.

"Not now!" The mage didn't even glance at the kender. He and Shavas whispered together softly.

Caramon watched his brother and the councillor, feeling something hot and angry stir deep inside him. Raistlin hated to be touched! And here he was, holding Shavas! How could he do this to me? the warrior demanded inwardly in frustration.

He was about to say something, he didn't know for certain what, when he saw a cat move out from under a bush to stand next to a tree. The animal was regarding him with bright eyes that shone red in the torchlight. Caramon beckoned, and the cat darted forward. Standing on its hind paws, it clawed at his leg.

"Well, at least someone loves me," said Caramon, recognizing his black-furred friend of the other afternoon. "You want to come up?"

The cat leaped onto Caramon's shoulder, balancing perfectly. His brother and Shavas were still conferring. Raistlin kept his arm around her. The warrior reached up to scratch the feline behind the ear.

"There is a test I can make," Raistlin said, moving

away from the councillor, "to tell if the man died by magical means."

He waved the Staff of Magius over the body, closing his eyes to prepare a spell. Shavas's terse voice broke his concentration.

"We cannot allow you do to that, Master Mage! We have certain . . . sacred rituals that must be performed before the body is interred in the ground."

"I would not do anything that interferes with your religious beliefs—"

"I'm afraid I must insist. Please, Raistlin." Choking back tears, Shavas put her hand to the necklace at her throat. "This is very difficult for me. He was . . . a close friend!"

Raistlin lowered the staff. "I'm sorry, Councillor. I have been thoughtless, it seems. Forgive me."

Lady Shavas beckoned to a guardsman, then leaned over to speak softly into his ear. The soldier nodded once and ran off.

"This evening has been a great strain on all of us," she said, addressing everyone in the park. "It is time for us all to return to our homes."

The soldier came back, driving a carriage that he had commandeered. It was obvious to Caramon that this time they weren't going to be able to convince the fellow to wait for them outside.

Raistlin drew his hood up over his head. Taking his brother's arm, he said softly, "Come, Caramon, Earwig . . . Let us go."

The cat dug its claws into Caramon's shoulder, drawing a very small trickle of blood.

"Ouch! Hey!" he exclaimed, attempting to dislodge the animal. The cat, however, would not be moved but clung to Caramon tenaciously. They clambered into the carriage. Once Caramon was inside and seated, the cat jumped lightly from his shoulder and curled up in his lap, its red eyes fixed on the twin opposite. The carriage, driven by the soldier, rumbled through the empty, silent streets.

"Raistlin," said Earwig in a small voice.

"What is it, kender?" the mage asked wearily.

"That man. He's the one who tried to kill me."

Caramon jerked his head up, staring. Raistlin, however, did not move.

"What do you think, Raist?" Caramon asked, feeling a chill of horror creep over his body.

"I think," said the mage, "that we have one more day, my brother. One more day."

Chapter 15

No one spoke during the carriage ride. No one made a sound except the cat, who purred loudly, rumbling like a small thunderstorm. Earwig sat in one corner of the carriage, scratching his hand. Raistlin sat huddled in another, his cowl pulled low over his head. He might have been thinking or fast asleep. Caramon sat miserably, his broad shoulders spanning two corners, wishing he was back in Solace.

"I'd ask Tanis about this mess," he said quietly to himself, a wave of homesickness sweeping over him. The half-elf was the wisest man Caramon knew. Always calm and steady-going, Tanis rarely allowed anything to shake him—with the possible exception of the twins' older sister, Kitiara. Caramon heaved a great sigh. He wouldn't see Tanis again for a long time, perhaps ever, the way the world seemed to be falling headlong into darkness. They were supposed to meet again in five—no, now make it four—years time. It seemed an eternity. Caramon sighed again. The cat licked his hand with its rough tongue.

"Barnstoke Hall, sirs," said the soldier-driver.

The carriage rolled to a halt. The companions climbed out, the soldier watching every step. It was obvious he wasn't going to leave until they were safely inside the inn. From the look of him, Caramon thought, he might be planning to spend the night.

The fighter, cat tucked under one arm, attempted to open the door of the hall, but discovered it was locked. He pounded on it loudly. Minutes passed, then the proprietor slid open a panel in the door and peered outside. Seeing the companions, he slid the panel shut. They waited another several moments, hearing bolts being drawn and chains rattling. Finally the door opened a crack, barely large enough for the warrior to squeeze through.

The proprietor slammed the door shut again immediately after the three were inside. He was trembling so hard he could barely stand.

"Forgive me, sirs, but there's been a terrible accident in town! Lord Manion—"

"We know," snapped Raistlin, moving past the man. "And it was no accident."

Caramon noticed that his brother barely needed the assistance of the staff to walk anymore. Raistlin's gait was strong, even after being up all hours of the night. He had not coughed once. The mage reminded Caramon so much of what he had been before the test that tears came to the warrior's eyes. He blinked them back and prayed to whatever gods were listening that this change would last.

The cat in his arms suddenly began to wriggle and squirm. Jumping out of Caramon's grasp, it landed on the floor and sat there, staring at him for a moment. Then, tail stuck straight up in the air, the cat wandered off, heading for the kitchen.

The proprietor began bolting the door, chained it securely. Raistlin climbed the stairs to their room. Caramon came after him, dragging Earwig, who was staring with professional interest at the numerous locks on the door.

Arriving outside their room, Raistlin held up a warning hand. Caramon kept hold of Earwig, who would have charged heedlessly ahead.

"Wait," said the warrior.

"Why?" Earwig asked, staring at Raistlin.

"*Shirak*!" The mage held the beaming orb to the floor, stared intently underneath the door.

"What's he doing, checking for dust?" asked the kender.

"Yeah, sort of," said Caramon.

"It's all right," said Raistlin, standing up. He held a rose petal in his hand. "This was where I left it. No one has passed."

"You better let me go first, just in case," said Caramon, drawing his sword.

The mage unlocked the door, and the warrior pushed it aside with his hand, both of them keeping well out of the way. Nothing happened. Carefully, Caramon entered the room. Raistlin came after him, holding the light of his staff high. Earwig bounded in, hoping the rose petal had been wrong and that there might be something interesting inside.

There wasn't.

Raistlin sank down on the bed and gave way to a sudden fit of coughing. He fumbled for his pouch of herbs. "It's gone!"

"What? What's gone?"

"My herbal mixture! My pouch must have fallen off in the park."

"I'll go—" Caramon began.

"No, don't leave me, brother!" Raistlin clutched his chest. "Besides, you'd never get out of the inn. Not the way it's locked up!"

"I'll go!" said Earwig, jumping up and down with excitement. "I can get out!"

"Yes!" Raistlin nodded, sinking down on the bed. "Send the kender." He shut his eyes.

"Hurry up!" Caramon admonished Earwig sternly. "No stops along the way!"

"Not me!"

Opening the door, the kender darted out. They could hear his light footsteps racing down the hall and clattering down the stairs. Then, silence.

Raistlin, drawing a deep breath, sat up briskly. Rising from the bed, he went to the window. Caramon stared at him.

"Raist? What—"

"Hush, my brother." The mage drew back the curtain, being careful to keep himself behind it. "Yes," he said after a moment. "There he goes. Now we may talk freely."

"You think Earwig's a spy?" Caramon didn't know whether to burst into laughter or tears.

"I don't know what to think," Raistlin answered gravely. "Except that he wears a magic ring and has no idea how he came by it. Or, at least, so he says. You've seen how strangely he's been acting."

Caramon sat down heavily in a chair. Leaning his elbows on the table, he let his head sink into his hands. "I don't like this, any of it! A man murdered—his body ripped apart. No blood. Only a kind of brown dust. The kender wearing a magic ring . . ."

"It's going to get worse, my brother, before it gets better." Reaching into his robes, Raistlin brought out the bag of herbs and regarded it thoughtfully. He was growing stronger. There was no doubt about it. Was it his cure? Or . . .

"Could you break a tree, Caramon? One of the trees in the park?" he asked abruptly.

"Wha— Why do you want to know?"

"One of the trees near the body of the murdered man had its bark shattered, as if someone had struck it."

Caramon thought. "I suppose I could, if I were wearing a gauntlet to protect my fist." He shuddered as the full implications occurred to the warrior. "Whoever did that terrible thing must be strong! Do you . . . do you think it was a . . . a big cat? There were all those claw marks—"

"It was either a cat, or we are meant to think it was a cat," said Raistlin absently, preoccupied with other thoughts. He dragged a chair over to sit directly across from Caramon. "What do you think of Lady Shavas?"

The question took Caramon by surprise.

"I think she's . . . attractive."

"You find her irresistible!"

"What do you mean?" the fighter asked defensively.

"I mean you have feelings for her."

"How would you know what my feelings are?" Caramon demanded, rising to his feet and pacing about the room.

He and his twin had never before discussed women. It had always been one part of Caramon's life in which Raistlin had taken no interest. But then, never before had any woman been attracted to the thin and sickly young man. Recalling this, Caramon began to feel a certain amount of remorse. He could have any woman he wanted. It might be good for Raistlin to . . . well . . . get to know the lady better. Perhaps that's what was working this miraculous cure. Love had been known to perform miracles.

"Look, Raist," said Caramon, sitting down again. "If you want her, I'll back off—"

"Want her!" Raistlin's golden eyes flared. He glared at his brother with such contempt that Caramon shrank away from him. "I don't 'want' her, not in the vulgar sense you mean."

Yet the mage lingered over the word. His fingers stroked the wood of the table, as if caressing smooth skin.

"Why did you bring her up, then?"

"I have been observing you. Ever since the first night we met her, you've been acting like a love-struck boy, staring at her with that stupid grin."

"The lady seems to like it," retorted Caramon.

"Yes, she does." Raistlin's voice dropped.

Caramon cast him an uneasy glance. "What do you mean?"

"Her house contains very ancient, very powerful tomes of magic. I must look at them . . . alone."

"I don't like this, Raist."

"Oh, but you will, my brother. I'm certain that you will."

"What if she won't go out with me?"

"I've seen her looking at you," said Raistlin.

Caramon heard the bitterness in his brother's voice. "I've seen her looking at you, too, Raist," he said softly.

"Yes, well . . ." Raistlin let the comment pass.

Caramon could have sworn he saw a faint flush of blood beneath the golden skin. To his surprise, his twin suddenly clenched both fists, the golden eyes glinted.

"The books! The magic! That's what's important. All else is fleeting. All else is of the flesh!" A drop of sweat trickled down the mage's brow. "You will do it?" he demanded hoarsely, not looking at his brother.

"Sure, Raist," said Caramon. It was what he answered to every request his twin made of him.

"Thank you, my brother." Raistlin's tone was cold. "You must be tired. I suggest you go to bed."

Caramon shrugged. "What about you?"

"I have work to do."

Raistlin pulled the sextant out from under his robes, along with the datebook to which he had referred earlier. Opening the text, he laid it on the table next to a quill and inkwell. The mage walked to the window and gazed at the heavens through the brass navigation tool. He began to take notes, drawing odd lines and strange curves, parallels of ink and words on parchment.

Caramon, after watching a moment, went to bed.

* * * * *

The mage was working so intently that he didn't hear the door open.

"Gosh, Raistlin, you're up late. Feeling better?"

The kender's voice startled the mage. He glanced up, irritated by the disturbance.

"That was quick," he muttered, returning to his drawing.

"Oh, the soldier gave me a ride. He didn't know he gave me a ride, but I guessed he must be going back to the park, so I just jumped on behind the carriage and off we went. It's a lot more fun than riding inside. When I got to the park there was a big meeting going on. All the ministers were still there and Councillor Shavas—"

"Shavas?" Raistlin looked up again.

"Yes." Earwig gave a yawn that nearly split his head in two. "I told her you dropped the pouch. She helped look for it, but we couldn't find it. I did find some others, in case you're interested." The kender pulled numerous purses—mostly filled with money—out of his pockets and dumped them on the table. Along with them came a tiny scroll, wrapped tightly in red ribbon.

"What is this?" Raistlin asked, lifting it.

"Oh, that's from Lady Shavas. She said I was to give it to Caramon."

Raistlin glanced at the bed where his brother lay sleeping. The mage untied the ribbon and unrolled the scroll.

Dinner. Tomorrow evening. A private place, known only to myself, where we can be alone. I will send my carriage for you at dusk.

It was signed, *Shavas*.

Raistlin dropped the note, as if it had burned him.

Earwig was unrolling his sleeping mat. "Oh, I found out something else," he said, yawning again. "The soldier was talking about it with one of his buddies. That man who was murdered. He didn't have a heart!"

Raistlin sat, staring at the note.

"How fortunate for him," said the mage.

* * * * *

Caramon awoke to find that his brother had fallen asleep at the table, his head lying on the books, his hand resting protectively over the sextant.

"Raist?" said Caramon, shaking him.

The mage started and sat up swiftly. "Not yet! Now is not the time! I must be stronger. . . ."

"Raist!" said Caramon.

The mage blinked and stared around, wondering where he was. Then, recognizing the room and his twin, he closed his eyes and sighed.

"Are you all right? Did you get any sleep last night?"

"Not much," Raistlin conceded. "But that is not important. I now know the exact time."

"Time for what?"

"For when the three moons converge." Raistlin spoke in hollow tones. Dark circles rimmed his eyes. "We have exactly one day, one night, and another day. Tomorrow night, when the darkness is deepest, it will be lit by the Great Eye."

"What do we do now?"

"Now we look for the cats. I can't believe they have simply vanished off the face of Krynn. Once we find them, we will hold the key to the mystery."

"And tonight . . ."

Caramon spoke reluctantly, hoping Raistlin had either forgotten his instructions of the previous evening or had changed his mind. The big warrior just couldn't envision himself asking that lovely, regal woman to accompany him on an evening's romantic tryst. He had no doubt she would laugh at him.

His twin pointed to a scroll rolled up and wrapped with red ribbon. "The kender brought that for you last night after you were asleep. It is from Lady Shavas."

Caramon felt the blood rush to his face. He reached for the scroll, opened it, and glanced at it. There was no need to read it to his twin. He knew Raistlin would have looked at it last night.

The warrior cleared his throat. He should feel elated, but he didn't. He felt cold all over. "It's like . . . she's reading our minds."

"Isn't it?" said Raistlin, rising to his feet. "Wake Earwig. I need him."

"You do?" Caramon stared, astonished.

"Yes." Raistlin gave his brother a shrewd look. "Or, let us say, I need to know where he is . . . and where he is not."

Caramon, not understanding, shrugged, and went to wake the kender.

* * * * *

The warrior had absolutely no idea how to begin searching for missing cats, other than by dragging a string around and shouting, "Here, puss! Here, puss!" He had other, more important worries. The streets, previously so empty, were today crowded with people, talking about last night's murder. Their voices stopped whenever the red-robed mage came into view. Soon they started up again, this time finding a focus for their fear.

"It was magic killed our lord. . . . No one ever died until a wizard came to town! . . . Likely killed our cats, too!"

Caramon stalked the streets, hand on the hilt of his sword, glaring balefully at any who might have the nerve to speak too loudly or take a step toward Raistlin. Whether it was the aura of mystery and power surrounding the magic-user or the threat of the strong arm and sharp blade of the warrior beside him, nobody came close. The people melted away, sidling into alleys or ducking into dark doorways. But Caramon heard the muttered threats and saw the hatred on the faces as he, his twin, and the kender passed.

They'd walked about half a mile from Barnstoke Hall, traveling on one of the three main thoroughfares of Mereklar, when Raistlin came to a stop.

"Now, instructions. Earwig, I have a spell that will lead us to the cats, but in order to cast it, I need a bagful of a certain herb—*nepeta cataria*. When you find it, meet us back at Barnstoke Hall."

Earwig leaped at Raistlin, clutching at him, nearly knocking him over. "No! Please don't make me leave you. I really want to stay with you! I feel . . . afraid if I'm not with you."

"Hey, let go!" Caramon said, dragging the kender off his brother. "What's got into you? Kender aren't afraid of anything!"

"Don't make me leave you, Caramon!" Earwig was clinging to the big man's arm, despite all Caramon's efforts to shake him loose. "Please! I'll behave . . ."

Raistlin's hand slipped into his pouch. He drew out a handful of rose petals and slowly sifted them over the kender's head.

"*Ast tasarak sinuralan krynawi,*" he murmured.

Earwig suddenly yawned and began to rub his eyes.

"I'll be goooo. . . ." The kender's fingers slipped off Caramon's arm. Earwig crumpled over in a heap on the sidewalk.

"What happened?" Caramon knelt down beside his little friend.

"He's all right, my brother," said Raistlin. "He's asleep."

Earwig had begun to snore softly.

"Lift him up onto that bench so that no one steps on him," Raistlin instructed. "Now, you and I can proceed with our search alone." The mage's gaze went to the ring on the kender's hand.

Caramon did as he was told. They left Earwig, blissfully snoring, in a hyava shop.

"What was that stuff you wanted him to get? Some kind of herb?"

"*Nepeta cataria.*" The mage smiled slightly. "Catnip."

The brothers continued up the street, appearing to do nothing more than look in shop and store windows. But all the stores were empty, the houses had their windows shuttered. People roamed the streets, sharing their own fear and panic.

"It's like a town under siege," Caramon remarked.

"Precisely. And for much the same reason. Fear. Terror. And notice," added Raistlin. "No cats. Anywhere."

Caramon glanced around. "You're right! I haven't seen one! Have they all disappeared?"

"I don't think so. I think they're in hiding. They, too, are afraid."

Caramon wondered at their destination. Raistlin seemed to have an exact idea of where he was going and walked without hesitation. The warrior thought he understood when he saw the park, the same park Lord Manion had been killed in the night before. No one was around, the townspeople avoiding the place as if it were infected with the plague.

"What are we doing here?" Caramon asked uncomfortably, having much the same impression himself.

His brother did not answer. The mage stopped near a bench. Leaning on his staff, he stared at the trampled grass.

Caramon, growing increasingly nervous, pulled out the yellow ball Maggie had given him and began to play with it, trying to distract his gloomy thoughts. But thinking of Maggie made him think of Shavas. He knew he should be looking forward to tonight—what man wouldn't, being alone with a beautiful, desirable woman? But there was the knowledge in the back of Caramon's mind that he was using the woman, deceiving her. He was a diversion, nothing more. He didn't like it and he had about decided to tell Raistlin he wasn't going when he felt a light tugging at his hand.

Caramon looked down. The black cat, sitting on its hind legs, was batting at the ball.

"Hello," Caramon said, bending over to pick up the cat.

The feline bounded sideways, ears and tail twitching. The warrior shrugged his shoulders and sat down on the bench, shutting his eyes against the morning glare. The cat brushed up against his legs.

"All right, I'll pet you," he said, leaning down.

The cat turned and walked away, craning its head back to regard the fighter with reflecting eyes. Caramon shook his head. "What a strange animal."

Raistlin seemed to wake from a dream. He stared at the cat intently.

"Isn't that the same cat who came with us last night, the one you had on your shoulder?"

"I guess so. It's the only black cat I've seen in town."

Raistlin watched it. "He wanted us to follow."

"How can you tell?"

The cat dashed off, then dashed up to Caramon again. The warrior took a step after it and it ran off again.

"Let's see where it takes us," said Raistlin.

The cat raced ahead of them about twenty feet, heading around the park to the western portion of the city. Just when it seemed that they would lose the animal, it stopped, waiting for them, sitting on the ground patiently. When the twins were within arm's reach, the cat darted off again, moving in the same direction.

"Where do you think he's leading us?" Caramon asked.

"If I knew that, we wouldn't be following it!" Raistlin snapped.

The brothers went up street after street, until even the mage became lost in the flow of alleys, avenues, and paths. Every time the twins came within a few feet of the black cat, it would dart off, staying always ahead, always within sight. It never uttered a sound, but gazed back with eyes that held the sunlight as brilliantly as the blue orb on Raistlin's staff.

Caramon craned his head back, staring into the sky as he walked. "It's almost noon," he said. "I hope we arrive at wherever we're going soon."

"I think we must be getting closer," Raistlin said. "The animal has increased its speed."

"Do you recognize this part of the city?"

"No. I take it you don't either."

Caramon shook his head. They were on a boulevard surrounded by buildings, shops, and houses that looked abandoned or unused. Trash filled several alleys that cut through the blocks like great wounds, darkened and dirty. Even the white stones of the city appeared gray, worn, and old.

"This is very odd." Raistlin pulled his cowl back, staring at the black windows.

"Yeah. This place feels dead." Caramon spoke softly, uneasily, though it seemed there was no one around.

"A part of the city that died and was never buried. Look, our friend has evidently found what it wanted us to see."

The black cat was scratching at a sewer cover near the sidewalk on the right. The twins walked warily up to the feline. It did not run away as it had before, but continued scratching, voicing a harsh "meow!"

"It wants us to go down there," Raistlin realized. Pointing with a long, thin finger, he commanded, "Lift the grating, Caramon."

The warrior glanced at his brother. "Into a sewer? Are you sure, Raist?"

The cat screeched loudly.

"Do as I say!" Raistlin hissed.

The huge warrior bent down, grasping the metal cover with both hands, and began to lift, his muscles straining. His face turned red with effort, and his expression distorted into one of concentration and exertion. After a few moments, the plate grated and he dragged it aside.

The cat stared at the brothers intently, cocking its head sideways, flicking its eyes toward the street and back up at them. Without warning, the animal leaped down into the hole, disappearing in the darkness.

Caramon wiped sweat from his forehead. He stared down into the impenetrable hole. It was like looking into the Abyss. He fancied he could feel icy talons reach out, grasping to drag him down to the realm of death. He shuddered, standing back.

"Do we really have to go down there?"

Raistlin nodded in confirmation. The mage's face was rigid. It seemed he was subject to the same impressions as his brother. But he started forward.

"Better let me go first," said Caramon.

The warrior forced himself to approach the lip of the pit. Kneeling, he took several deep breaths and then lowered himself into the hole. His legs were swallowed by shadow that slowly engulfed his arms and, finally, his head.

Gathering his robes around him, Raistlin prepared to descend beneath Mereklar.

* * * * *

"Hey, you! Either drink or move on."

Earwig opened his eyes to see the irate face of a tavern owner glaring down at him.

"No loitering."

"I wasn't loitering," said the kender indignantly. "I was napping. Although," he added, brushing rose petals out of his hair, "I don't remember having taken a nap since I was a very small kender. But I was up late last night, so maybe that explains it. Now, I wonder where Raistlin and Caramon have got to?"

At first Earwig was terribly worried that he couldn't find his friends, but then the uncomfortable feeling went away, leaving him more cheerful than he'd felt in days. The small, irritating voice inside of him quit nagging him to do this, do that. And there was no longer the threat that if he didn't do what the voice said, he'd be dragged off to someplace where there were no locks to pick, no pouches to find, no people to meet. Someplace eternally boring.

Now that he was away from Raistlin and Caramon, Earwig felt carefree and happy again, and he began doing what all kender do best: explore.

Earwig walked up the street, gazing about with interest. Some of the people, associating him with the mage, whispered to each other that the little man with the pointed ears might be a demon. They drew away from him, pushing their children into their houses, closing and barring doors in his face.

"How rude," said Earwig. Shrugging his shoulders, he walked on, tapping the wooden hoopak on the ground with a steady, hollow rhythm.

"I've been here before, haven't I?" he asked himself aloud. He had come to an intersection and saw a narrow alley that led to an arcade.

"I remember! This is where I went the first night I was here! That's the inn where the man tried to kill me and the girl kissed me."

Earwig walked into the market. None of the shops were open, and only a few nervous people walked through the alley, anxious to finish their business and return to the safety of their homes. "Hello, there," a bright young voice said.

Earwig glanced around.

"Do you remember me? You helped me the other night. I didn't get a chance to ask your name. Mine's Catherine. What's yours?"

"Earwig. Earwig Lockpicker," the kender said, holding out his small hand. Is this how Caramon greets a girl? he wondered, trying to remember.

"I never got a chance to thank you, either. You ran away before I could say anything. May I buy you a drink? I work right over there," Catherine said, pointing to the inn. "Our house speciality is Stonewash Surprise."

"Stonewash Surprise? I've never heard of it," Earwig replied.

"Oh, only the hardiest of adventurers have ever tried it. And lived," Catherine added, giggling.

The tavern was as large and dirty as the kender remembered; beer and other unmentionable stains darkened the floor. The walls were constructed from ill-fitting planks of wood that were knotted and rotting with age. Catherine walked behind the bar and began to pour liquors into a glass, filling the cup from decanters of red, green, and blue. The drink complete, she pushed it in front of Earwig, who sat at one of the many mismatched stools.

He took a sip, and his eyes widened. "Celebration Punch!" he exclaimed in recognition. "Kind of."

"Celebration Punch. What's that?" Catherine asked.

"It's what kender use to celebrate with, of course." Earwig looked around. "You're not doing much business today."

The bar was, in fact, empty except for the kender and the young woman.

"It's the murder," Catherine said matter-of-factly. "Everyone's scared to death. I say good riddance."

"Yes, I remember. He was the man who hit you." Earwig sipped his drink.

"You know, it's funny. Lord Manion came in here a lot and he generally got drunk, but he was always a gentleman. Many nights I've made certain he reached his home safely. But then, just the past few weeks, he changed. He turned"—the girl frowned, thinking—"ugly, cruel. It was when he started wearing that necklace, like the one you're wearing."

"What necklace? Oh, this?" said Earwig, glancing down at the silver cat's skull with the ruby eyes.

"You're not going to turn mean, are you?"

"Gee, do you think there's a chance I might?" Earwig asked eagerly.

Catherine began to laugh. "No, I'm sorry. I don't."

"I didn't think so." Earwig sighed. The kender ran through a list of things to say to women as he tugged at the gold ring on his finger. He chose one he thought appropriate and asked, "What's a nice girl like you doing in a place like this?"

Catherine giggled. "It's just my job. One of them."

"How many do you have?"

"Two or three, depending on business. I work at Hyava Tavern, on Westgate Street."

"I hope it's not as rough as this place."

"Pooh! I can take care of myself. I'll bet you've been to a lot of places," Catherine said wistfully.

"Oh, my, yes. All around Krynn. Southern Ergoth, Northern Ergoth, Solamnia—"

"I've never been anywhere but here."

Earwig looked intently at the woman across the bar from him. She stood straight and strong, her arms well-muscled. He believed that she could handle herself in almost any situation.

"You remind me a little of someone I know. Her name's Kitiara."

"Really? What's she like?"

"She's a fierce and cunning warrior," said the kender.

Catherine looked a little shocked. "Wh—why thank you, Earwig. I think. . . . "

"You sound like you want to leave this place." The kender took several gulps of his drink. "Why don't you just pick up and go?"

"I don't have the steel yet."

"You don't need money to travel! All you need is a hoopak and a good walking tune." Earwig laughed, swinging his hoopak into the air. He was feeling really good. He couldn't remember ever having felt this good before.

Catherine shrugged and frowned. She leaned back from her guest, propping her elbows against a shelf.

"I'm sorry, Catherine. I didn't mean to make you unhappy." Earwig rummaged through his pockets, pulling out the first thing he came to—the tangle of wire with the bead in it. "Here. I want you to have this."

The barmaid, smiling in spite of herself, reached over to take the gift. Holding the wire up to the light, she stared at it in fascination. "What is it?"

"I don't know. I got it when I was on some adventure with my friends. We go adventuring a lot together, my friends and I. One of them is a magic-user," the kender added importantly.

"This is really amazing, Earwig." Catherine was still staring at the wire. "If you look closely, it appears that the bead has writing on it!"

Earwig heard the door open behind him, but he didn't turn around. He was trying to remember how Caramon got girls to kiss him. Catherine glanced up and hurriedly tucked the wire away in a pocket. She nodded once, and then leaned over the bar, her face close to the kender's.

"Tell me about your friends," she said. "Tell me about the mage. I'd love to meet him."

"Raistlin and Caramon? They were born in a place called Solace, to the east of here. Caramon is a great and powerful warrior. His muscles are as big as . . . as that," Earwig said pointing to a beer barrel in the corner. "I've seen him cut twenty men in two with one stroke!"

"No! Really?" Catherine appeared nervous. She seemed to have to force her eyes to remain on the kender.

Earwig blinked. Leaning over, he said confidentially, "Don't look now, Cather . . . Cather . . . whatever. But your walls are spinning around and around."

"You need another drink. That's all. Tell me about your other friend."

"My other friend's name is . . . Raishlin. He has shkin that shines like gold, and eyes the shape of hourglasses. He sees death," the kender said solemnly, sticking his nose in his drink. "But, as frightening as that shounds, even more frightening are the spells he casts and powers he can call down to deshtroy an enemy."

"There used to be a wizard who lived in the hills to the east," Catherine said, darting a swift glance behind the kender.

"Whatsh his name?"

"Nobody knows, but it's rumored that his cave is still there. It's built around a series of stones that look like an animal's paw."

The walls were spinning more rapidly, and now the ceiling had joined in, much to Earwig's fascination. He sat on the stool, watching them revolve around and around and then the stool joined the wild dance, spinning the kender around and around until Earwig suddenly discovered that he was lying on the floor.

A man dressed in black leather armor loomed over him, knelt beside him. Strong hands lifted the kender and flung him over a massive shoulder.

"You won't hurt him?" Catherine's voice floated around the kender like a lovely cloud.

"No," said a harsh voice in reply. "Like our lord told you. The little fellow's in danger, wearing that necklace around in the open. We want to protect him, that's all. Thanks for your help."

Earwig, bobbing up and down against the man's back, started to feel incredibly dizzy. He stared, bleary-eyed, at Catherine, who seemed to be growing smaller and smaller and smaller.

"One Celebration Punch. . . for the . . . road!" cried the kender, and passed out.

* * * * *

"Ack! Ugh!"

"What is it, Caramon?"

"There's a stream running through here! It's as cold as ice. You better let me carry you."

Raistlin climbed down the stairs and plunged into the water. "Nonsense! Don't worry about me. I'm fine."

Caramon peered into the darkness, trying to locate his twin.

"Are you sure. I mean, I know how much you hate getting wet and cold."

"As I said, I am fine," the mage snapped irritably. "If the cold bothers you so much, perhaps you would like *me* to carry you?"

"No, of course not!" Caramon felt foolish.

"*Shirak*."

The soft white light of the Staff of Magius filled the tunnel. A long, dark, passage extended ahead of them, far beyond the summoned field of magical light. The walls glistened wetly.

"It smells bad," said Caramon. "But not quite what I expected from a sewer. It smells like . . . iron." He sounded disbelieving.

"Or blood," said Raistlin softly.

"Yeah."

There was no room to swing a sword. Caramon drew a dagger from its sheath. Its blade gleamed in the light of the staff.

"We must therefore assume that this is not a sewer, but a connection to a waterway," Raistlin added.

The cat meowed impatiently, and the mage walked forward, moving past his brother. Caramon started to protest—he always took the point when the two walked into danger together. But he remembered, then, that Raistlin carried the light. He kept close behind him.

The cat moved slowly, ensuring that his followers would not become lost in what Caramon soon discovered was a maze of tunnels. The feline didn't appear to like the water any better than the warrior, for it shook its paw with each step and seemed to grimace at setting a foot back into the stream.

They walked for what seemed like miles, though something in the back of Caramon's mind insisted that they had not gone any great distance at all.

"What are you saying, Caramon?"

"I said we could use a dwarf now," the warrior replied. "I wish I could see better! Anything could jump out at us."

"I don't sense any threat to ourselves down here. The only feeling I get from this place is that it is old . . . very, very old."

"Old and forgotten."

"I agree, my brother. It is most unusual."

They walked and walked. The chill water seeped through Caramon's boots. He was shivering and he worried about his twin, knowing that Raistlin's robes must be soaked through. The warrior knew better, however, than to ask. The cat made a sudden turn, darting down another passage that angled off from the first. The new passage was equally as black as the old. Caramon hesitated, but the cat meowed, urging them to come forward.

Without hesitation, Raistlin walked on, holding the staff at eye-level, able to raise it no higher because of the low roof.

"Come, Caramon. Don't fall behind!"

They came to an intersection, and the black cat skipped on, moving to the left, beginning to run, splashing through the water. The brothers increased their pace, both prompted by curiosity.

"—which killed the cat," Caramon said, but under his breath.

The tunnels became a dizzying maze, a labyrinth created for some unknown purpose. Raistlin held the Staff of Magius forward, a lance of light piercing the dark. Caramon sloshed along behind. He noticed that the walls were beginning to change, becoming drier.

"Look at that!" Raistlin breathed, holding up the staff.

The wall was covered with paintings and engravings, showing sights neither brother could identify. They moved swiftly on, left and right, straight and back, a curving tunnel leading to a crooked passage leading to a sloping floor.

The cat moved faster. The twins rounded a corner behind it and stopped suddenly, staring wide-eyed.

"Name of the Abyss!" Caramon cried aloud, steadying himself against the cavern entrance with his hand.

Raistlin said nothing, but simply stared in the staff's soft radiance. The black cat turned to face them, eyes red in the staff's light.

The chamber in which they stood was huge—hundreds of feet long. Numerous passages led in and out, black gashes in the rock. Small rivers collected in ponds that glittered with an oily reflection. And everywhere they looked they saw the cats of Mereklar. Thousands of cats lay resting on their sides without sound, without motion. Raistlin knelt down, holding the staff close.

"Look," he said, pointing.

From every mouth and nose poured a small stream of blood.

"They're all . . . dead!" Caramon gasped.

Raistlin examined one of the small bodies. Putting a thin, golden hand on tiger-striped fur, he stroked it gently. He moved to another body, then another, lifting heads and peering into shining eyes.

"I don't understand," Caramon said softly, "What could have killed them all? Poison?"

"They're not dead."

"They sure look dead to me."

"I assure you they are quite alive. However, their minds are gone."

Caramon went to the nearest cat and touched its fur. He felt warmth under his hand, a tiny heart still beating, breath barely entering and leaving.

The black cat leaped in front of him, hunching down on its forepaws. It spat at him.

"All right." Caramon rose to his feet and backed away. "I'm not going to hurt them. You're right, Raist. They are alive!"

"In answer to your first question, they were not poisoned. There is no poison I know of that could do this."

"What do you think it was?"

"The only answer I have is magic, though a spell that could cause this kind of destruction is beyond my means."

Caramon paused, considering the implications. "Then you think this is the work of a wizard?"

"A wizard of extraordinary power, perhaps greater than Par-Salian."

Caramon shivered, recalling the powerful master of

the Tower of High Sorcery.

The black cat watched and listened intently to the brothers talk, never taking its bright, reflecting eyes from them.

Raistlin raised his arms and began to speak the strange, spidery language of magic. The room glowed—a dull, purple aura that covered everything, including the corridor through which they had walked.

"There," the mage said in satisfaction. "We can return here whenever we wish." He turned to go.

"But—"

"There is nothing more we can do. I cannot save these cats. I must go back to my room and think. And you, if you will remember, have an engagement tonight." Raistlin headed down the corridor.

Caramon stood, looking back, a sadness in his heart. Removing the yellow sequined ball from his pocket, he laid it down gently on the blood-wet floor.

"I'm sorry," he started to say to the black cat, but it was gone.

Chapter 16

"I wonder where Earwig is. Maybe he got lost," Caramon said, straightening the room. His mother had always made him clean up after himself, and the fighter did not let old habits die.

"Kender never get lost, perhaps because they never truly know where they are."

Raistlin sat at the desk in front of the window in the companions' room, writing something on a roll of parchment. Caramon, when he was through with his own cleaning, did his brother's. The mage was also unwilling to let old habits die.

"What are you doing?"

The red cowl was pulled back from Raistlin's face, allowing the afternoon sun to fall on his golden features. He rested his quill, scowling at Caramon with a sideways glance before returning to his work.

"If you must know, I am asking Lady Shavas for access to her library tonight."

"That's great!" Caramon said heartily, relieved.

"Why that tone, my brother?"

"It's just . . . I thought . . . "

"You thought I was going to sneak into her house like a thief?"

"Well . . ." the fighter began uncomfortably.

"You're a dolt, Caramon."

The big man kept silent. Usually his twin was the more intuitive of the two, but this time Caramon knew precisely what his brother was feeling. The pangs of jealously were sharp and left festering wounds.

Raistlin finished his writing and sat, waiting for the ink to dry. A knock on the door startled them both.

"Were you expecting anyone, Caramon?"

"No," said the warrior, sliding his sword from its scabbard. "You?"

"No. Enter!" Raistlin called out.

The messenger, instead of opening the door, slid something under the crack between frame and floor. Footsteps retreated rapidly away from the room.

The mage retrieved the message, breaking the wax seal with a loud snapping sound. Turning to the light at the window, he held the parchment in both hands, reading.

"What is it?" the warrior asked, still holding the sword.

"It is a letter from Lady Shavas. She is waiting for you downstairs," Raistlin said in even tones.

Caramon saw that his brother's golden hands trembled. "Anything else?"

Raistlin crumpled the message into a ball. "It says that I may use the councillor's library tonight."

* * * * *

"I am so very glad you could accept my offer for this evening, Caramon," said the Councillor of Mereklar.

The two sat in Shavas's private carriage, guided by her personal driver.

"My p-pleasure," Caramon stammered, gazing at his companion across the gulf that stretched between their seats.

Shavas wore a gown similar to the one she had worn when the companions first met her, only this one left her white shoulders bare. She had wrapped around her a silk shawl—the black one, Caramon noted nervously—with a lace pattern woven into the fabric, fringe hanging from the ends. From her neck hung the opal pendant.

"Are you cold, my lady? You may have my cloak," the warrior offered, thinking his gesture gentlemanly.

Before Shavas could answer, he unclasped the black cloak from around his neck and tossed it clumsily over her body. Straightening the folds, Caramon accidentally touched the woman's neck, her skin as soft as delicate clouds. He felt her warmth, a flush of life beneath his fingers.

"Sorry," he apologized, blushing and returning to his seat.

Shavas smiled, arranging his cloak around her. The red inner lining of the fighter's cloak made the woman seem magical—as dark and glittering as the three moons of Krynn.

I am being a real dolt, just like Raistlin said, Caramon thought with chagrin. Why can't I relax when I'm with her? I've never felt this way around any woman before. It's because she's a lady—a true lady. The most beautiful

I've ever seen. Just like the royal ladies in the stories about the Knights of Solamnia. Sturm, my old friend, how would you act? How does a knight treat a lady?

Caramon didn't realize that he was staring at her until he saw Shavas lower her head, her cheeks mantling with a faint flush.

"I—I'm sorry. I know I'm acting like an idiot, but I can't help it. You are so lovely!" Caramon stammered.

"Thank you, my brave warrior," Shavas said. Reaching out to him almost shyly, she allowed her fingers to brush against his hand. He trembled at her touch. "I am so glad you could come with me tonight. You help me forget about . . . about—"

The woman shivered, her face became pale.

"Don't talk about it," said Caramon firmly.

"No, you're right. I won't." Shavas lifted her head bravely. "And I have nothing to fear, have I? Not with you by my side!"

"I would die before I let any harm come to you, Lady Shavas."

The councillor smiled again at the sincerity in the big man's voice. Her hand grasped his, tightening around his strong fingers. "Thank you," she said, "but I much prefer you alive!"

Desire flashed through Caramon. His blood burned. All thoughts of royal ladies vanished from his mind. She was a woman, and now he knew just what to do. He tried to pull Shavas near, but she suddenly snatched her hand away. Leaning back in the carriage, she glanced languidly out the window. Caramon, wrestling with his passion, thought it best to do the same.

The lights of the city shone as they always did—bright stars above the streets. The few people shuffling along the sidewalks of Mereklar tipped their hats and bowed as they passed. Caramon watched Shavas smile and nod to the citizens in turn. But he thought her smile seemed strained.

The coach turned left on another street and entered a large, open park surrounded by a fence of thick trees and hedges. At one end of the park stood a small building.

"Is this where we're going?" Caramon asked, his heart pounding. The place seemed deserted.

"If you don't like it, we can go elsewhere," the councillor said coolly.

"Oh, no. This is . . . fine," the warrior replied.

The carriage pulled alongside the building, and Caramon jumped down, holding out his hands. He lifted Shavas by her slim waist, pressing her warm body next to his as he lowered her to the ground. The black shawl fluttered like wings.

"Thank you, Caramon," she said, lingering near him for an instant.

"Good evening, Councillor Shavas. I'm so very glad you have arrived on time," someone said in a high voice.

Startled, Caramon whipped around. Behind him stood a thin man wearing a black coat. He was visibly nervous, casting his gaze up and down the street. "Are you sure you wish to have dinner here tonight, my lady? The servants refused to come after dark, and—"

"Thank you, Robere, this will be fine," Shavas interrupted smoothly.

"Shall I show you the way, madame?" Robere asked, hands clasped together.

The councillor shook her head slightly and smiled. "No. I think we can find our own way."

"Very good, madame," Robere replied. Bowing again, he turned on his heel and left the travelers.

"Don't wait," Shavas told the carriage driver.

"When shall I return for you, my lady?"

Shavas glanced at Caramon from the corner of her

eye. "Tomorrow morning," she said softly.

Caramon thought the beating of his heart might suffocate him.

The two walked around the little building that he assumed, from the smell, was a kitchen. They came to what appeared to be an entrance into a park. The fighter's eyes adjusted to the darkness. He saw a cloth spread on the ground, and he realized that they were going to dine outdoors. He glanced around uneasily. What a great place for an ambush. The memory of the corpse he had seen last night almost made him turn and run. Shavas slipped her hand through his arm, walking close beside him.

"This is one of my favorite places. It allows me to be a little more . . . relaxed . . . than I can be at home," she whispered into Caramon's ear, bringing her soft cheek next to his.

The area was prepared when they arrived. Robere added several black pillows, placing them into comfortable positions around the white spread. Two silver candlesticks stood in the middle, scented tapers burning with a warm light. Plates and trays held fresh fruits and warm meats. Two crystal glasses, filled with sparkling red wine, waited to be sipped.

Shavas led Caramon to the cloth. Letting go of his hand, she sank to the pillows opposite him, stretching her lithe body comfortably.

"Please, sit down," she said, gracefully indicating a mound of cushions.

Clumsily, the fighter sat, crossing his legs under him, his tall boots creaking.

"You look splendid, Caramon." Shavas's compliment made the fighter flush.

"Uh, thank you," he said, unsure if he should return

the compliment or merely accept gracefully. "This is a very nice spot you've picked out. It's very . . . uh—"

"Private." The woman finished for him. "As Councillor of Mereklar, I am constantly called upon to stand in the public eye. But even I have needs, and one of them is occasional privacy."

"It sounds like you lead a very busy life." Caramon gulped at his wine.

"Yes, very busy and very . . . lonely."

Shavas lowered her eyes. Her lashes cast long shadows, and a tear slid down her cheek. Caramon longed to take her in his arms, but he couldn't figure out how to get around the food on the plates.

Staring at her glass, Shavas held it up to candle's flame. The councillor suddenly blinked her eyes and frowned, shaking her head, as if awakening from a dream.

"A toast," she said clearly. "To you and your brother—"

"And the success of our mission," Caramon added loudly.

This seemed to take the woman by surprise. "Of course," she said. "To . . . success."

They sipped at the same time. Caramon would have downed his glass in one motion had he not seen his companion put her glass down, still mostly full.

"Are you hungry?" the councillor asked, reaching across the cloth to take the warrior's plate.

Without waiting for an answer, she began dishing up food, selecting meat and fruit and fish. She took some herself, though nowhere near the same amount.

Caramon searched for forks and spoons, but found nothing and grew nervous, wondering if he had missed something again. Shavas saw his worry.

"Eat with your hands, Caramon. Nobody's watching! We're completely, absolutely alone."

The woman took a berry between her fingers and

brought it slowly up to her mouth, licking a drop of juice. The fighter looked on, felt heat rise to his face. He'd been hungry before they sat down, but now he wondered if he could eat a mouthful. He'd never in his life wanted a woman as much as he wanted this one.

Neither said anything during the meal. Both seemed only to be waiting with anticipation for it to end.

When they finished, Shavas wiped her fingers on a silk napkin. Robere appeared, seemingly from out of nowhere, and began clearing away plates.

"When you are finished, you may leave," said Shavas, her gaze fixed on Caramon.

"Thank you, my lady," said Robere in obvious relief.

"Now, Caramon," said Shavas, "What shall we talk about?"

"Talk?" the fighter returned, startled and disappointed. He'd had other ideas in mind. "I don't know. What do you want to talk about?"

Shavas poured herself another glass of wine. "Tell me about yourself. Tell me about one of your adventures."

The fighter thought of the stories he usually told in taverns, of blood and guts and cold steel. "I doubt any tales I know would interest you, my lady," he mumbled, almost tipping over his wine. Grabbing it, he downed the glass at a swallow.

"You might be surprised," said Shavas. "But if you don't want to talk of battle, tell me about your brother. Tell me about Raistlin."

Ah ha! Caramon shifted restlessly, jealously. Now he'd found her true interest! "Raist? What do you want to know about him?"

"Tell me what he's like. He's very young to have such power, isn't he?"

"He is the first of his age to pass the Test at the Towers

of High Sorcery," said Caramon reluctantly, not wanting to think or talk about that terrible time.

"Truly?" Shavas prompted. "It must have been a frightening experience."

"It was. Those who don't pass the test die."

Shavas, seeing him growing uncomfortable, smiled to herself and changed the subject.

"Have you and your brother journeyed together long?"

"All of our lives," Caramon said softly, staring at the empty glass in his hands. "We're never apart."

"Except when each of you goes in search of what he truly desires."

Shavas rose gracefully to her feet. Bringing her arms up over her head, she undid the braids coiled around her head, releasing cascading waves of soft, brown hair.

Caramon watched her, his desire a physical pain. " 'I long to hear the epiphany of your woman's crown, and play upon its shining strands,' " he whispered.

The councillor bent down, kneeling in front of her guest. Bringing her cheek close to Caramon's mouth, she nestled near him. "That's beautiful. Did you make it up?"

"No," the fighter replied, clasping her in his arms, drawing her down to lie beside him in the cool grass. "It's something Raist used to say. I think he read it in a book. He's always . . . reading . . . books."

Shavas brought her hands up to caress his face, brushing the backs of her long, perfect fingernails against his rough skin.

"Say it to me again, Caramon," she whispered.

But he knew she didn't really want to hear the quote.

Which was good, because he couldn't, for the life of him, remember it.

* * * * *

Raistlin sat on the couch in Shavas's library, flipping absently through the book Caramon had glanced over two evenings ago. Noting the blank pages, he tossed it aside in contempt.

The councillor had left the door to her estate open, allowing the mage access. Her note did not say when she would return. Raistlin, knowing Caramon's prowess, decided that the lady probably wouldn't be back until morning. The mage stifled a small flame of jealous desire that threatened to engulf him in a raging fire.

"The magic," he said to himself. "Never forget what is important."

Raistlin rose to his feet, preparing to cast a spell. His chant began as a low murmuring, a song that filled the room with indescribable music. His left hand opened wide, then closed, fingers opening again in patterns of power, drawing strength from Krynn and the unseen planes. He raised the black staff high into the air, arm straight, bringing it slowly back against his robed body, curving it in an arc to his side.

In answer to his command, three books began to glow.

Knowing the spell wouldn't last long, Raistlin marked in his memory their location and sat back down on the couch. He drew a deep, shivering breath. Staring at his treasure, his body, too, ached with desire.

Gathering and calming his thoughts, he moved slowly to the bookshelf, reached up a trembling hand, and pulled down the first text. It was entitled, *Mereklar*. Below that was inscribed, *The Lord of the Cats.*

"What's this?" Raistlin studied the brown cover, frowning. It appeared that the second half of the title had been added on in haste, as if the binder had been given a last-minute instruction. He placed it on the table near the fire, sitting down in the wooden chair, opening the book to the first page. Among the illuminations of red, blue, and gold were scrawling letters, written by an unknown, unnamed scholar of ages past.

The origins of Mereklar are unknown, and will remain unknown until such time as it needs to be discovered. The purpose of the city is clear and final, and those within know its reasons. The cats must live here, for their purpose will be known when the time is come.

"What nonsense!" the mage snarled. "I expected magical spells, not a tour guide!"

He turned to another page and found a picture of a black-skinned man dressed in black clothes standing in front of a blasted cityscape. Lightning cracked against an orange sky, and three moons formed a Great Eye in the unnatural air. The street looked familiar to Raistlin, but he couldn't immediately place it. Underneath the painting was the caption: *The Lord of Cats in his realm of despair, waiting, stealthy and black, for the gate to open.*

"Interesting. Very interesting," said Raistlin, his anger gone. He began to carefully turn the ancient parchments, one by one, until he reached the end of the book. "This certainly puts matters in a different light than the prophecies would have it."

The Lord of Cats brings his demons . . . will lead the cats against the world . . . destroys the city that stands before the first gods . . . slays those who bring harm to his dominion . . . agent of evil.

Reaching the end, Raistlin brought his index fingers to his lips. It was of interest, certainly, but it wasn't in the least magical. What had caused it to respond to his spell? "I have never come across anything like this before. And what am I to believe? The legends of the city or the facts in this book?"

He replaced the text on the shelf, going to the next of the three he had discovered. Lifting his hand to the top shelf, he noticed another book on the ledge.

The title was *Tanis Half-Elven*.

"Fascinating, but, unfortunately, not important," Raistlin remarked.

Taking the text he originally wanted back to the table, he lifted the black, fraying cover and turned to the opening page.

The Accounts of the Mage Ali Azra of the Shining Planes—The City of the White Stone.

"Ah!" Raistlin breathed in excitement. The tales of the supposedly mad wizard Ali Azra of the mythical Shining Planes were among his favorites, combining magical text with entertaining stories. He had read them against the commands of his masters, who maintained that the information was too advanced and dangerous for a young mage's comprehension. But that had never stopped Raistlin, who found Azra's techniques fascinating, though his style was rather irritating.

Long have I studied the stones of Mereklar, longer even than when I studied the Pillars of Isclangaard.

Raistlin smiled at the mention of Isclangaard. The chronicle was the first he had ever read.

And like the pillars, many fantastic things have I learned, which I now lay down upon these pages for my children to know. Among my children I list— Raistlin skipped ahead. Ali Azra never failed to list every one of his pupils. The mage flipped pages until he found the first chapter heading.

The Walls: Symbols of Purity. The walls of the fantastic and wonderful city of Mereklar surround the land with three great barriers against evil. The white marble is a warning to those who would bring harm upon the inhabitants. Inscribed on the Walls of the Fantastic and Wonderful City of Mereklar are the legends and tales of the world, Krynn, and other places that even I, the Great and Powerful Mage Ali Azra, must confess I have only glimpsed briefly, hardly long enough to give full and accurate accountings, as I am sure you, gentle reader, would desire.

Raistlin scowled. "Gentle reader" was a term he detested.

When you follow in my illustrious footsteps, as I am sure you shall, wanting to become more familiar with my greatness, desiring to taste of the power which I now freely command, you will find that the Walls of the Fantastic and Wonderful the City of Mereklar cannot be scratched by any force, and no spell, of good intent or evil, can affect it. "Why is this" you ask, and ask you should, for in the knowing there is power. Let it be known that I, the Great and Powerful Mage Ali Azra, know the origins of the City of Mereklar, and they are that the Incomparable Gods of Good, among them numbered Paladine, Majere, and Mishakal, with whom I have had the pleasure of conversing, sent the city to the land, commanding that it not be harmed by element or man.

"All right, all right!" Raistlin muttered impatiently. "If the gods of good did create Mereklar, what was their purpose?" The magician read further into the book, hoping to discover an answer to his question. However, he learned nothing of interest, merely accounts of Azra's journeys and wanderings, occasionally mentioning the city, though without giving any useful information. The wizard hadn't even bothered to include a useful spell.

Slamming shut the account of the mad mage, Raistlin placed it back on the shelf. Going to the third and final text, he pulled out a volume covered in red velvet, darkened by age. The title was simple, *Arcanus*, a name found on many magical treatises. Walking back to the table, Raistlin opened to the first page, and his eyes widened as he beheld a spiral of runes, burned into the page, the sigla surrounded by the yellow discolorations of heat.

"Ah!" he whispered. "At last!"

He clutched the staff near him, golden face shining in the red heat of the fireplace. He began to read when suddenly he saw before his eyes the figures of Shavas and Caramon, bodies twined together in passionate embrace.

"I have no time for such things!" he snarled, closing his eyes, banishing the vision. Discipline. He prepared himself for the first glyph. Taking a deep breath, he aligned his mind with his goals, his will with his desires, and started down the winding path of power.

A bolt of white sent his senses reeling in pain, and his nerves caught fire. Yellow shafts rained down on him, contorting his body into impossible forms. Orange beams seared his brain, a flood of cold that broke his essence. Red coils destroyed his thoughts, spiriting them away to the infinite. Blue spears cut into his flesh.

"No! Never!" Raistlin cried.

Grabbing the black staff in both hands, standing alone in a universe of pain, he drew his will about him, gathering himself into a shining star of desire that kept his shattered form from falling to despair. The multi-colored demons wailed around him, formless creatures from nether-planes trying to ensnare his spirit and drag him into the Abyss. Though he felt his essence falling deeper and deeper, he forced his eyes to gaze still at the cursed runes. Raistlin knew that to give in, to cease reading for the slightest instant, would spell destruction for his being.

Then he knew that he did not fight alone. Someone else had a stake in this battle for Raistlin's being. He laughed, daring and defying any world to take him, any plane to claim him for its own.

The creatures ceased their tortures and fled.

Exhausted, Raistlin fell across the book. Beneath him, he heard the text disappear with the hiss of a snake. The trap was defeated. He had escaped.

CHAPTER 17

Shavas walked the path of crushed white stone that led back to her house, admiring her flowers, whose dew-heavy heads hung over the path. The morning sun glinted off the stained-glass windows. Smiling, she tossed her head, shaking the mass of disheveled hair from her face.

The estate was very quiet, and even the sound of the waterclock was muffled, as if afraid to disturb her. Shavas went to the library, opening the heavy doors, closing them softly behind her. The room was empty. She frowned, wondering. What had she expected to find? The body of a young magic-user, his soul torn from him, dragged to stand before the Dark Queen? Had he truly escaped, proving his power? Or had he simply not tried? Shavas searched the room for some sign of his presence. There was none. The books on her shelf stood undisturbed. Perhaps he hadn't read them. Perhaps he hadn't even come.

No. Shavas smiled, and lifted the one book that the mage had not thought to replace, the one book that had seemed innocuous. He'd been here. And he had been triumphant. He was, indeed, worthy.

Shavas carried the book upstairs to her room. Without disrobing, she lay down in her bed. Opening the heavy book, she settled into a comfortable position to read the pages that were no longer blank. On the spine of the text were two words, freshly inlaid with gold: *Brothers Majere*.

A painting showed two men sitting around a campfire—one a large, handsome warrior; the other thin and frail, dressed in red robes, holding a black staff with a gold dragon's claw clutching a pale blue orb. Shavas began to read.

Caramon enjoys guarding Raistlin's sleep. This is the only time that the mage seems to his brother to be at peace, though occasionally this peace, too, is shattered by disturbing dreams. Caramon has always guarded his weaker brother against the dangers of the world, whether cold, sickness, or more obvious threats. He feels personally responsible for Raistlin's well-being, though his brother does little to show his appreciation.

The responsibility Caramon feels for his brother stems from their youth. Raistlin's physical weakness, his high intelligence and naturally sly, cynical nature, made him a target for bullies. Caramon's timely intervention prevented his frail brother's injury on several occasions when some of the pranks turned serious. Incapable of understanding the need to abuse the weak and helpless,

Caramon became Raistlin's guardian. Raistlin himself developed a hatred of those who would harm the innocent, the weak. The brothers have championed several such causes in Krynn.

Shavas sighed and bit her lip. Had she misjudged Raistlin? No, how could she? She had felt his ambition burning through his skin. And she had determined correctly that his lust for magic would overcome his lust for the pleasures of the flesh.

The twins are inseparable, always together, yet always apart. Caramon has watched Raistlin grow more moody and introspective even as the warrior himself becomes more outgoing. When Raistlin left to study magic, Caramon saw him change even more. Raistlin discovered that magic could compensate for his physical weakness. Through magic he can control, manipulate, dominate—needs Caramon cannot understand, or rather, has no need to understand.

The fighter is popular. Strong and handsome, he is admired and respected by his peers, most notably the friends of his youth, a rather motley collection of vagabond wanderers. (See volumes: Tanis Half-Elven, Flint Fireforge, Sturm Brightblade, Kitiara Uth-Matar, Tasslehoff Burrfoot.) *Among them, Raistlin is tolerated.*

Raistlin possess many qualities none of his peers can see. The most prominent is his courage, his willingness to fight those who would rule with an iron fist. This attribute is hidden beneath the young magician's unfriendly demeanor and cynical attitude.

There have been many times when Raistlin, even as an apprentice mage, successfully unmasked the trickeries and glamours of the clerics of the so-called "new gods," revealing them to be charlatans of the most parasitic kind, feeding on the fears of the populace.

Raistlin believed none of them and turned their venomous trickeries upon themselves, showing the crowds of awestruck, fear-ridden people that these clerics were as false as their ideals. More than once, Caramon has been forced to pull his brother out of the way of ruined clerics bent on revenge.

Caramon knows, deep inside, that he and his brother are slowly, inevitably drifting apart. Caramon sees that each day brings new power, insights, and magics to Raistlin, though the mage's body can barely stand the strain. Caramon has watched his brother cast spells that turn the strongest warrior to ashes, only to see Raistlin collapse with convulsions that wracked his body from inside, bringing blood to his lips.

But each time Raistlin rises from his torment, struggling on arms too weak to lift himself, standing on legs limp with fatigue. And Caramon sees a very faint smile illumine his brother's face—a smile that speaks of a great spirit unwilling to die, unwilling to let go of mortal flesh until every goal is ultimately achieved.

It is because of this perseverance that Caramon knows he must admit ultimate defeat at the hands of his brother, though he rails against the thought. The vision at the Towers of High Sorcery— showing that Raistlin, in his jealous rage, was willing to kill even his twin—was the death knoll of Caramon's fond dreams.

"Ah," murmured Shavas. "Now we're getting somewhere. More detailed information please."

The book obliged, adding a new page before the woman's eyes.

No one knows for certain how Raistlin managed to pass the test, for the mysteries of the Tower are hidden even to me. Certainly the young mage was nearly defeated in a contest with a dark elf known as Dalamar. It is thought that Raistlin traded his life's essence for his life. If that is true, then on some plane of existence there is a powerful being who watches over and protects the young mage—not out of kindness, perhaps, but to protect the being's own interests.

Shavas closed the book for a moment, her fingers keeping her place. If that were true, it might hinder her plans. Or it might help them, depending on the nature of the protector. She wished she'd known this information earlier. Now there was so little time. Shavas returned to her reading.

At the end of the test, the masters arranged it so that it seemed to Raistlin that his twin, Caramon, was endowed with magic. In a jealous rage, thinking his brother had stolen the only thing in the mage's unhappy life that gave it any meaning, Raistlin killed Caramon. Actually, it was only a phantom of Caramon, created by the masters. But Par-Salian, Head of the White Robes, had also arranged for Caramon to watch his own murder at the hands of his twin. When the brothers left the Towers, their lives were forever changed. Raistlin has the power he seeks, but all Caramon has is time.

Shavas tossed the book to the floor. Leaning back among the pillows, she began to laugh.

* * * * *

That same morning, Lord Brunswick sat in his favorite chair in his estate's main living room, a spacious area covered with dark wood and filled with the accoutrements of wealth and power. The minister watched his children play with cold eyes, running his fingers along the length and width of a leather bag, shaped like an oddly formed triangle.

His youngest daughter ran over to him and grabbed the pouch. "What's that, Daddy?"

The lord slapped her across the face, pulling the bag away. "Don't touch that, brat!"

The girl wailed and ran to her mother. The lord's wife, comforting the child, stared at her husband, aghast. "Alfred! What's come over you?"

The minister refused to answer, but stalked out of the room, slamming the double-doors behind him. He heard the muffled voice of the woman consoling the child. "There, there. Tonight's the Festival of the Eye. Think of the fun you'll have!"

The lord grinned. Yes, tonight the fun would begin.

The large house was dark. None of the rooms were occupied, the servants gone for the holiday. Brunswick walked through it hurriedly and into the grassy yard, clutching the bag to his chest.

Tucking the pouch away under his belt, the lord strode through the field surrounding his home, coming upon one of the many streams that ran out the city. He followed the tributary against the flow, walking steadily, with purpose, into Mereklar.

Lord Brunswick came to a park with a small grove of trees standing in the middle—a monument to his family. He stood, staring at it, then laughed in derision.

A small mew answered his laugh. At the foot of the tree was a kitten, lost, looking, perhaps, for a mother who would never return. The lord reached down and grabbed the kitten by the neck. Frantic with fright, the kitten clawed and scratched and sank its sharp milk teeth into the lord's thumb.

Swearing, the minister hurled the kitten from him. Brunswick concentrated on the pain; the blood dried, and the wound closed and healed.

Lord Brunswick's face darkened. He took the pouch from under his belt, tore open the flap, and pulled out a short wand, bent to an odd angle at one end. He pointed the wand at the kitten.

An enraged snarl, sounding from above his head, caused the lord to glance upward in fear. Too late. A huge black cat dropped from the tree, its weight driving the man to the ground. The wand flew from Brunswick's hand. The animal bared its long fangs, preparing to tear out the man's throat.

The minister, with superhuman strength, threw the animal off his chest. Leaping to his feet, he crouched in a fighting stance.

The huge feline slowly circled to the left, the lord side-stepping in turn. Man and beast eyed each other warily, their bright, reflecting eyes shining. In a single motion, the minister shot forward, attempting to grab the cat by the neck, but the animal was too quick. It leaped aside and jumped on the man's back.

The minister fought desperately, attempting to dislodge the panther by reaching up from behind. The cat worried the lord in the back of the neck, using its hind claws to flay his flesh, tearing bleeding rents that should have killed the man in an instant.

The minister fell heavily, his hand lighting on an object on the ground. There was a blazing flash of red light. The panther, stunned, toppled off the man. Lord Brunswick, reddish liquid pouring from his wounds, rose up and narrowed his eyes, concentrating his vision on the enemy before him. Another flash of red seared the skin from the panther's back. The cat made no sound; the pain shook it back to consciousness. It leaped again, straight at its enemy, but the minister had suddenly disappeared.

The panther began to stalk the grove, casting its gaze about. It walked slowly, head sunk beneath its shoulders in fury. It made no sound until it whipped around, sinking its foreclaws into the arm of the minister as he reached out to aim the wand. The man's mangled arm went limp, and the wand fell from his nerveless fingers.

The lord, in desperation, attempted to grab the animal by the neck with his remaining good arm. The panther freed himself easily. Crouching on its hind legs, gathering strength, it sprang for the man's throat, white teeth flashing.

A scream, a ripping sound, and a blood-drenched necklace rolled on the grass—a silver cat's skull with ruby eyes.

CHAPTER 18

"Have you ever heard of Dizzy Longtongue, the kender who could throw his hoopak with such skill and accuracy that he could make it return to his hand? Well, one day a minotaur made a bet with Dizzy that he couldn't throw his staff around the girth of a forest, and Dizzy said, 'I'll bet you the gold in my pocket against the ring in your nose that I can make my hoopak come back to me from around the forest.' The minotaur accepted and said that if he didn't make it, he would have Dizzy for dessert. Dizzy naturally agreed."

Earwig paused to hear if any of his fellow prisoners had any comments, such as "Wow, isn't that interesting?" or "I can hardly wait to hear what happens!" There was, however, only silence.

Sighing, Earwig pressed on. "Dizzy took a hundred-pace running start before he let go of his hoopak with a mighty zing! Dizzy and the minotaur waited for hours, listening for the sound of the returning hoopak. After a day, the minotaur said, 'Well, my lad, it looks like I'm having you for afters,' and Dizzy said—"

A stabbing pain behind his eyes caused Earwig to lose his place in the story of Dizzy Longtongue. It was certainly an interesting sensation—his temples throbbed so that he thought his head would crack. But, after consideration, the kender decided it was one sensation he could do without.

Earwig tried to raise his hands to massage his eyes, but he couldn't move them that far, due to the chains on his wrists. That, too, was another interesting development.

"I'm a prisoner in some black, damp cell, probably hundreds of feet below the ground, guarded by thousands of warriors who are armed to the teeth. A situation I've wanted to try. " He enjoyed himself immensely for about an hour, but after that . . .

"You know," said Earwig to his cellmates, whom he could see only dimly (one of them appeared to be quite bald), "this isn't nearly as much fun as I'd expected. "

In point of fact, despite the pain in his head and the chains on his wrists, Earwig was getting bored. And, as anyone on Krynn knows, a bored kender is a most dangerous thing.

"Boy, you guys are sure quiet!" Earwig said, peering into the darkness. All he heard in answer was the steady, melodic drip of water, and even it quieted for a moment, as if wondering what the cell's latest inhabitant had to say. It soon grew loud again, uninterested in the conversation.

Earwig sighed, thrashing in his chains. He had examined the lock as best he could, but it was just too dark to see.

"I couldn't open it anyway. My tools are missing. " The kender, thinking of this, became highly indignant. "That's really not fair. I'll just mention that, on my way out."

The chains themselves were heavy and thick, and he doubted if even his mighty friend Caramon could break them in one try. The floor he sat on was cold and wet; the damp was making him sneeze. The walls were constructed from solid rock that nothing, seemingly, would penetrate. He thought of his Uncle Trapspringer, who had purportedly escaped from a prison cell by digging his way out with a spoon. That very spoon had become a sacred relic among kender.

"I wonder what Uncle Trapspringer would do if he were down here?" Earwig said out loud, half-hoping he might get an answer. One never knew when or where Uncle Trapspringer might pop up.

Apparently, however, it wasn't here.

Earwig had no idea how long he'd been down wherever here was. He only knew he had to get out soon, or his mind would leave on its own.

"Why don't one of you guys tell me a story? Something I haven't heard before," the kender prompted his silent cellmates. "Well? How about it?"

No answer. Earwig frowned. He was beginning to lose all patience with the situation. He rummaged through his pockets for the tenth time, hoping to find something that could either help him escape or provide interesting entertainment.

"Handkerchief and a bit of fluff. Empty. Empty. My spinner and nothing else." Frustrated, he dragged his chained hand over and gave the spinner a flick with his finger. Something jabbed him in the arm, coming from his right sleeve.

"The dart!" Earwig exclaimed, pulling back the inner flap that kept the missile hidden. "Don't worry, you guys. I'll have us out in a minute!" he called to his silent companions in the cell. "It's really strange, you know"—he continued talking to alleviate his cellmates' impatience—"but someone used a dart like this to try to kill Caramon, and now it's helping me to escape."

Earwig thrust the dart into the lock of the manacle around his wrist. He seemed to recall Raistlin saying that the dart was tipped with a deadly poison, but that didn't matter. Death was better than sitting here and doing nothing.

Inserting the tip of the dart into the keyhole, he ran the metal along his finger as a guide, feeling the point come to the first tumbler. Jiggling the projectile, he bypassed the second and third tumblers, jimmied past the fourth, and felt a sharp point press against his skin. "That's it!"

The last tumbler gave way to his gentle proddings. Something soft—dust, perhaps—flaked off the dart onto his skin, but in his excitement, Earwig didn't notice. He slipped the dart into a pocket, threw the chains from his body, and stood triumphantly.

"All right! You guys are next."

For just one brief, fascinating moment, the kender thought he might pass out from the sudden pain in his head. But the dizzy spell went away, and the pain in his head eased. Earwig began to stumble blindly about the room, holding his arms out in front of him. He came to a wall, his hand slapping against the moist stone. "Don't worry, Baldy. I'm coming."

He followed the wall until his foot clattered into a heap of chains on the floor. "There you are!" he said, bending down to feel the shackles. "Why didn't you tell me where you were?" His hand closed, not around flesh, but around bone, the bone of a man long dead.

"I guess that's why you weren't much interested in Dizzy," said Earwig, feeling comforted. He'd really begun to think he was losing his talent as a storyteller. "Well, Baldy, if you'll excuse me, I'll be leaving now. I don't mean to be rude, but you're not very good company."

Earwig moved blindly around the cell for a few moments more when he kicked an object, large and soft, lying on the ground near a wall. Kneeling down, he closed his hands around a long piece of wood—a piece of wood with which he was very familiar.

"My hoopak!" he cried. Reaching out with his other hand, he found his pouches. Rummaging through his gear, he discovered that everything he could remember having was still there, including the tinderbox and a small torch. Soon, bright, yellow flame lit the room.

Earwig gazed around the cell. There were four more skeletons chained to the walls in addition to the one he had found. It looked as if they'd been there a while. But what really caught his attention were the walls themselves. They were covered with paintings and decorations, gold against black.

"More stories!" sighed Earwig, enraptured. He began to study them. "A long time ago," he said, tracing the pattern with his finger, "the world was . . . whole . . . and everything was fine. Then, something happened, and there were wars. Then nothing happened and everyone thought they were happy, but they weren't, really. Then came the Cataclysm!" he surmised, seeing what could only be pictures of a great mountain of fire falling from the sky. "Then what? We go back, and a guy in a red robe builds a great city of white stone. No,' that doesn't seem right. Let's see, a guy in a black robe tricks the guy in the red robe into building the city of white stone. And then, the guy in the red robes builds the city and a guy in a white robes helps from behind."

Earwig stood back, scratching his head in confusion. The first part of the story had been easy to follow, flowing in a vertical direction down the wall, but now everything he looked at branched out in hundreds of directions, over the ceiling, across the floor, along the walls, lines of gold connecting each to a large triangle. Following the lines, he came to a great, stylized eye done in colors of red and white and black, staring at him in the wall opposite the triangle. All the gold lines in the room met at this symbol.

"Not much of a story," Earwig sniffed. "The plot goes absolutely nowhere."

The kender put his pack on his back, adjusting it for comfort, shifting his shoulders against the weight. He started to walk out of the room when he realized that something essential to his plan of escape was missing.

"A door. There's no door! How am I supposed to get out of here?" he demanded angrily. "Wait! Maybe they hid the door, just so I'd have to find it."

Cheering up, Earwig started to tap his hoopak against the walls, the wooden staff making a loud sound in the quiet of the cell. He systematically worked around from one corner to the others. "Tack, tack tack, tack, tack. Tick! That's it!"

He pushed with all his strength against the block, but couldn't move it. "Maybe this isn't it," he concluded, leaning back against the wall to rest. "Wha-oh!" The stone swung on hidden hinges, dumping the startled but highly elated kender onto the floor on the other side.

* * * * *

"Wake up, Caramon!"

Thin fingers bit into the young man's shoulders. He

was up and moving in an instant. With the instinct of a warrior, his body was functioning before his brain.

"I'm here! I'm ready!" he shouted, hands fumbling for his weapons.

"Don't be alarmed. Yet. Get dressed."

Caramon stared around sleepily, and realized he was in his comfortable room in Barnstoke Hall rather than in a war camp that had come under the attack of hordes of goblins.

"Sure, Raist." He'd only been asleep, he judged, for several hours. "Just give me a couple of minutes to wash up and shave and—"

Raistlin brought the metal-shod end of his staff to the floor with enough force to shake the lamps on the walls.

Caramon, startled, stared at his twin. Pain and outrage lined the golden face, flickering in the narrowed eyes. The warrior put his gear on quickly, as if he were about to engage in battle.

Raistlin, saying nothing, led the way from their room to the street. He seemed to have become a spirit of retribution overnight. What had happened? Caramon wondered.

The people they met walking on the avenue shied away, crossing over to the other sidewalk to avoid meeting the mage. The brothers entered a carriage. Raistlin commanded, "Westgate Street." The driver nodded confirmation, snapping the reins.

The coach moved from along Southwall Street at a steady pace. Questions burned Caramon's tongue, but he kept quiet. Raistlin had not looked at him directly since he'd wakened him. The mage stared intently into the shops along the roads, pointedly ignoring his twin.

Caramon, remembering with a rush of blood how he had spent the night, thought he knew the reason for his brother's ill-humor. Why's he blaming me? the warrior demanded silently, feeling guilty and not liking it. He made his choice. He got what he wanted, and so did I.

The coach turned right onto Westgate Street, and Caramon saw his brother tense, both hands gripping the black staff until the skin over the knuckles turned white. The fighter could see nothing, could sense no element of danger, but he drew his dagger.

Raistlin saw his action and snorted in derision. "Put your knife away, Caramon. You are in no danger."

"Are you in danger?" the warrior asked.

Raistlin glanced at his brother. Pain twisted the golden face, then the mage looked swiftly away. His hands gripped the Staff of Magius with such intensity that his fingers seemed likely to crack and bleed.

"Stop," Raistlin commanded the driver.

The carriage rolled to a halt. The mage jumped out and began walking at a rapid pace down Westgate Street. Caramon followed his brother's quick footsteps as best he could.

"Where are we going?" he asked.

"To get a cup of hyava," Raistlin replied, without turning.

Caramon stared at him in amazement. He was about to risk drawing down his brother's wrath by asking another stupid question when he saw a sight that stole the words from his mouth. The street was suddenly infested with a huge wave of cats and in the middle of the tide, in front of a tavern, sat a single figure—a black-skinned man, dressed in black.

"Raist! That's the man who—"

"Caramon, shut up," said his twin.

At the brothers' approach, the cats scattered, running up and over walls and down the street. Raistlin came to stand in front of the man. Caramon joined his brother, the warrior's hand on the hilt of his sword.

"Please, join me," the man in black said. His voice had a faint hissing quality to it that made Caramon shiver. He glanced at Raistlin, who nodded. The fighter pulled a chair out and sat. The mage did likewise.

Caramon stared at the man. He was incredibly handsome, with dark black hair that curled down the back of his neck. His eyes were blue, a startling contrast to his shining black skin, and they were slightly slanted. He stared at them intently, without blinking.

"My name is Bast," he said suddenly. Jewels sewn onto his black clothing in a band around his neck glowed softly in the sunlight. "May I offer you a drink?"

Without waiting for a reply, Bast lifted his hand, motioning for a barmaid. "Please, Catherine. Two cups of hyava for my guests." Catherine stared a moment, then spun on her heel and ran back into the restaurant. She came back almost immediately with two small cups.

"Thank you," Caramon said. The girl mumbled something and backed away, but lingered near, watching.

Raistlin sat as still and motionless as the city, his mouth set in grim, dark lines.

"Yes. Questions," the man in black said, staring at the mage with intense blue eyes.

"Who are you?" Raistlin asked.

"You know who I am."

"Why have you been following us?"

"You know why."

Raistlin flushed, growing angered. The man in black appeared amused. Caramon took a large gulp of his drink and burned the roof of his mouth. Apparently, his brother had finally met his match.

"Then what is your part in all this?" Raistlin demanded. "Why are you here?"

"You know why," answered Bast, sharp white teeth

flashing in a slow smile.

Caramon cringed, waiting for the outburst. His brother seemed to literally swell with suppressed rage and frustration. The man in black watched him calmly, and the anger seeped from Raistlin like blood from a wound.

"Do I? How do I know what to believe?"

"Believe what you want. It makes little difference to me."

"No, I don't believe that!" Raistlin said softly. "If so, why are you here, meeting with me?"

"I came here not to prove myself to you, but to prove you to myself."

The man in black, who called himself Bast, rose slowly and lazily to his feet. Stretching luxuriously, muscles rippling in his slender arms, he gave them a graceful nod of his head and moved off down the street.

"Do you want me to stop him?" Caramon half rose.

"No!" said his brother sharply, gripping the warrior's wrist. "He's a foe beyond your strength, beyond your comprehension. You would be dead within moments."

Caramon sat back down, somewhat relieved. He felt the truth of his brother's statement, though he couldn't quite say why. The big warrior only knew that, for one of the few times in his life, he'd actually been afraid.

Raistlin was regarding his brother coldly, his eyes narrowing to thin lines. "One night with a woman makes you very bold this morning, brother. She must have been something . . . special."

"I don't want to talk about it," said Caramon quietly.

"Why not? You've never minded flaunting your conquests before!"

"Maybe I did, but that's because I can still have those kind of feelings! I can know what it is to love someone!"

Caramon tossed his barbed words without aim, goaded into fighting by his brother's bitter sarcasm. But when he saw them hit their target, he would have given his soul to take them back.

Raistlin's shoulders jerked, as if pierced to the heart. The thin frame seemed to collapse in on itself. His head bent, his body trembled. He gathered his robes around him.

"I'm sorry, Raist—" Caramon began.

"No, Caramon." His twin raised a feeble hand. "I am the one who should apologize. Your comments were most . . . perceptive."

"What happened to you last night?" asked Caramon, with the intuitive knowledge of a twin.

The mage said nothing for a minute. He stared down into his hyava, watching the brew swirl in the cup. "I was nearly destroyed last night. "

"An ambush?" Caramon started to stand again. "It was that man, wasn't it? That Bast fellow! I'll—"

"No, my brother. It was a trap—a magical trap. It was set for me in one of the books."

"Trap? Where? In Lady Shavas's house?" Caramon stared, incredulous.

"Yes, in Lady Shavas's house."

"You think she set it, don't you?" Caramon demanded, growing angry.

"I found three books of magic in her library, my brother, and one of them contained a rune-spiral that nearly captured my soul and dragged me into the Abyss! What would you think?"

"It was an accident. She couldn't know she had something like that in her house!"

"How could she not know? Ah, I remember now. 'There are no magicians in Mereklar' " The mage mimicked the woman's voice. "A perfect excuse."

"You don't suspect . . . You *do* think she did it on purpose!"

His twin's silence spurred Caramon further.

"Why would she want to do that?" he yelled. "She's the one who hired us! She defended us to the ministers!"

"Exactly. Why would she want me . . . ?" Raistlin paused, eyes narrowing.

"Look, Raist!" said Caramon, breathing heavily, trying to control his anger. "You're smarter than I am. I admit that. You seem to know a lot more about what's going on here than I do. Someone tried to kill both of us in the woods. Then someone tried to kill me. Someone's tried to trap you. Earwig's disappeared. Now you come here on purpose to meet that man who's been following us. How did you know he'd be here? Who is he? I think you should me tell what's going on."

Raistlin shook his head. "So much to do. And so little time. Tonight, Caramon. The Great Eye shines tonight. And I'm not ready. . . ." He sighed, then said, "If you must know, in one of the books, I saw a picture of that man standing in a place that looked familiar to me. I realized this morning that the place was here—Westgate Street."

"You saw him in a book? What did it say about him?"

"That he was a creature of great evil. But, after meeting him, I'm no longer sure what to believe."

"I know." Caramon shuddered. "He'd just as soon rip out your heart as look at you."

"Perhaps. But—"

"Excuse me, gentlemen." It was the barmaid. Caramon vaguely remembered that her name was Catherine. "I couldn't help overhearing you mention Earwig. Do you mean Earwig Lockpicker, the kender?"

"You've seen Earwig? Where is he?" Raistlin asked with interest.

"I don't know. That's what I've come to tell you. I think he's been abducted."

"Abducted?" Caramon snorted. "Who in his right mind would run off with a kender?"

"Well, we were talking in the tavern where I work, and I went into the back to get some ale, and when I returned, he was gone!" Catherine stared down at her shoes.

Raistlin's shrewd eyes watched the girl from the shadows of his hood. "He probably just wandered off."

"No, he didn't." Catherine began to twist and tug at her apron.

Raistlin eyed the girl speculatively, then suddenly the golden skinned hand shot out and grabbed hold of her wrist. "Where have they taken him?"

"Ouch!" Catherine gave a little scream and began to squirm. "Please, sir. I— You're hurting me!"

"Where have they taken him?" Raistlin tightened his grip. The girl's face grew deathly pale. She tried to pull away.

"Raist—" Caramon began.

"Come, come, girl!" Raistlin ignored his twin. "You were in on it, weren't you? You lured him into the trap."

Catherine snatched her arm away. "It was him who told me to do it."

"Who?"

"That man. Bast. He said your friend was in danger, because he wore that strange necklace. He said he and his men would protect him. All I had to do was see to it that the kender went with them peacefully. Not make any trouble." She twisted her apron into a knot. "I never meant any harm! I only wanted to help!"

Tears slid down her cheeks. Lifting her arm, she wiped it across her nose.

"Where did they take him?" Raistlin persisted.

"The . . . the dead wizard's cave, I think."

"Where is it?"

"In the mountains, a half day's journey from here," Catherine said, jerking her thumb in a southeasterly direction. "There's an old path that leads there, marked by black flowers."

"Black flowers!" Raistlin stared at her. "Don't lie to me!"

"I'm not!" Catherine rubbed her hands across her eyes. "I'm sorry for what I did. He was nice to me. Just go and find him, will you?"

"Black flowers," muttered the mage.

"What is it, Raist?"

"Black flowers have a certain meaning among us, my brother. They denote the spot of an evil wizard's death." Raistlin rose to his feet. "We must search for Earwig."

"I didn't think you cared that much about the kender," said Caramon, pleased.

"Not him! The magic ring he's wearing!" Raistlin began moving at a rapid pace down the street.

Caramon, shaking his head, was starting after his brother when he felt a gentle touch on his arm. He turned to see the girl. "Well, what is it now?" he asked gruffly. "Haven't you done enough?"

Catherine flushed, her eyes lowered. "I just wanted you to . . . If you see Earwig, tell him"—she shrugged—"tell him that I'm sorry."

"Yeah, sure!" muttered Caramon and stalked off.

CHAPTER 19

Earwig entered a long tunnel. The kender sighed. It was the fifth tunnel he'd encountered in his escape, and he was beginning to get tired of them. Even the pictures on the walls, interlaced with the gold, black, and white lines—pictures that had formerly been so fascinating—were starting to lose their charm. His stomach growled.

"I'm hungry, too," said Earwig, patting his belly sympathetically.

The little torch he held in his hand continued to burn with a soft, yellow glow, the amber at the end of the wood sputtering occasionally. Such torches were the favorite of kender, and no respectable adventurer left home without a few in his pack. Earwig had started with five, and though each would stay lit for a couple of hours, he had already used up one in his wanderings.

"This isn't fun anymore!" he shouted. "I want out of here, and I want out of here right now. I mean it! No nonsense!"

The sound of his thin voice echoed in the walkways, but not for very long or very far or else the kender would have done little more than stand and yell, listening for his voice repeated hundreds of times against the ancient stones. He heard no answer, however, and was disappointed. He walked off to his right and stepped in a warm puddle of amber.

"I've been here before! I'm walking in circles." He remembered then, what his great-grandfather had always told him. Whenever you're in a boring situation, turn left and keep turning left. Earwig thought this good advice, and so he decided to follow it now.

He came to more tunnels, with more pictures filling the walls, more gold and black and white lines. The kender ignored them. He went through several more hallways and suddenly noticed that the pictures began to fade. The lines ran together to form a single, great band of gold, black, and white.

"I don't blame you," the kender told the unknown artist. "I was getting tired of that other stuff, too."

Earwig stopped short, dropping his torch and clutching a wall to keep himself from falling forward. He had stumbled into a room—a dome underneath the ground. Set in the bare walls at regular intervals were burning torches whose light did not fully penetrate the gray fog drifting through the air.

"Well, at least this is different from tunnels!" said the kender, feeling cheered.

He walked inside, staring about curiously. The floor

was smooth and hard, and in the middle of the chamber sat a huge circular stone dais, taller than the kender.

"And that's big!" he exclaimed, moving up to the stone, running his hands along its smooth, unmarked surface. "What's it for? I know! It must be the way out."

It wasn't. Earwig moved around the circumference of the disk, using his hoopak as he did in the cell, searching for a secret door or hidden opening. Finding nothing, he looked over the rest of the room.

The torches were held in sconces set into the wall at regular intervals, ten in all. He tried to remove one, but didn't have the strength to lift the pole out of its holder. The light they cast was yellow, like the sun on a hazy day. They gave off no heat and no smoke.

"Magic," said the kender knowingly, and was bitterly disappointed that he couldn't take one with him.

The chamber was small, and there was very little to see and no way out except the way he'd come, and that led to tunnels. His stomach growled more insistently.

"I'm trying to get us out of here, darn it!" said the kender to that unhappy portion of his anatomy. "And I could concentrate a lot better if you'd leave me alone!"

Earwig leaned against the dais, irritably tapping on it with the golden ring on his finger.

"Now what do I do?" he asked aloud.

Who calls? A voice rang in his head, hissing the words as a snake spits venom.

"Wow!" said the kender, awed.

The room began to grow dark. The torches dimmed in their holders. The gray mist turned black.

Who calls? the voice asked again.

"Me!" Earwig yelled in excitement. "My name's Earwig Lockpicker." He paused, then asked politely, "What's yours?"

The space above him filled with points of light, nodes and motes swirling in a pool of darkness. The kender suddenly realized that he was seeing the stars in Krynn's night sky, and the foremost constellation shown was—

What do you want of me, Wearer of the Ring?

"You don't sound very friendly," Earwig pointed out, in case the voice was interested. The stars kept swirling around him, he was starting to feel dizzy. "And after I've come all this way—"

What do you want of me? the voice thundered.

"Uh," said Earwig, growing more and more confused. He thought it was a marvelous experience, watching the stars spin, but his stomach didn't seem at all impressed. "Uh, I think I want to leave. . . . "

We leave through the gate!

"Good, now we're getting somewhere. Where's the gate?"

You know I cannot reveal its location! That would bring them to our door!

"First a gate, now a door. " The kender was growing dizzier and dizzier. He wondered if he might have consumed more Celebration Punch than he thought.

You must wait and take no part! Do not interfere with our agents lest you bring them to our door! They will find— They will find— They will— They—"

The voice faded away to a whisper, then disappeared completely. The dark closed in on the kender. He couldn't see anything. He couldn't hear anything.

His stomach rumbled loudly. "Oh, shut up," said Earwig miserably. The ring burned his hand. He scratched at it violently, fingers clawing his flesh until he felt something warm and sticky run down his wrist.

"Stop it!" he cried frantically. "Stop it! Stop it!"

* * * * *

A carriage took the twins to the edge of the city, where they exited through Southgate.

"Good riddance," said one of the guards.

"Don't bother coming back," added another.

"How are we going to get in the gate again?" Caramon asked.

Raistlin glanced behind him. "There are only four of them, my brother."

"Oh, yeah," said Caramon, flexing his sword arm.

The twins turned their steps in the direction the barmaid had indicated and soon left the city behind them.

" 'A journey by day, the map of a friend, and fair weather is all I crave,' " said a voice.

Caramon turned, his sword rattling in its sheath.

"Peace, my brother," said Raistlin.

Bast was leaning up against a tree, his arms crossed in front of his chest. The shadow from his curling hair fell over his features, making his countenance appear even darker.

"You are well read," Raistlin said, planting the Staff of Magius into the soft ground.

"Willians is a favorite of mine." Bast moved over to the twins. He seemed to flow rather than walk. His footsteps were as silent as night stealing over the world.

"What do you want? And don't tell me that I already know what you want," Raistlin added dryly.

"But you do. I want to accompany you to the wizard's cave."

Caramon tensed. He could still feel the mysterious power emanating from the man. "We don't need any com—" the big man began.

"Come along then," Raistlin interrupted as though Caramon had not spoken. The mage pulled the hood of his red robes over his face.

The lands surrounding Mereklar were rich with crops and food-bearing trees, planted there since the first people inhabited the city. Wheat, corn, and various grains lay in measured patterns, interspersed between regular groves of bushes and other plants. But there were no farmers in the fields, and tools lay scattered about, as if they had been discarded hurriedly. The travelers ignored these sights, moving on the main road leading from the great south gate until they came to a lake.

"We turn east here," said Bast.

"If my friend has come to any harm," began Caramon hotly, "I'll—"

The man in black turned, fixed him with his blue eyes. "No," he said. "You won't."

Caramon didn't argue.

It was midday when they reached the end of the planted lands, coming to a forest. They paused to observe the path that ran through the trees, the tracks of animals, and the leaves of previous winters scattered about. The smell of sap and flowers wafted among the scattered sunshine like a light perfume.

Raistlin walked forward, crushing branches under his heel. His brother followed, making more noise. Bast, however, padded after the twins without disturbing a blade of grass or leaf on the ground.

Suddenly the mage stopped and moved over to a tree. He bent down, studying the grass.

"What is it?" Caramon asked.

Raistlin pulled a flower from the roots of the tree. He held it up for the others to see. "A black lily."

Caramon sniffed at it and wrinkled his nose. "It smells like . . . death."

The sorcerer nodded, holding the flower up for Bast to inspect. The man in black did not appear interested. Shrugging, Raistlin, holding the lily carefully in his hand, stepped off the path into the woods.

"This way," he said. He glanced at Bast. "Right?"

"The decision is yours," said Bast. "I do not make use of this entrance. But you should, mage. You will find it . . . interesting."

Raistlin's eyes flickered. "What do you want of me?"

"Nothing. Everything. It all depends now, doesn't it?"

The mage swept past the man in black and headed deeper into the forest. Following his brother, Caramon saw a carpet of darkness spread on the green floor, a path of black lilies. The mouth of a cave was visible in the distance—a circle of stones set in the shape of an animal's paw.

"Well, what are we waiting for?" the fighter asked, starting forward.

The Staff of Magius swept out, rapping him lightly on the chest. "We will proceed with caution, my brother," Raistlin said softly. "This is the tomb of a wizard!"

The three moved up the path slowly—the mage in front, then the fighter, then Bast. Though it was midday, the sun's rays were blocked by the thick trees and the ancient stones and rocks. Chill air flowed from the cave's entrance.

Caramon rubbed his arms. "Trust that dratted kender to get himself in a place like this. It would serve him right if he had to get himself out. I suppose we go inside?"

"Of course!" Raistlin held the black staff over his head with one hand and whispered, "*Shirak*." The pale blue orb in the golden dragon's claw burst with light. The illumination did not reach far into the cavern, however.

Caramon started to draw his sword, but Raistlin shook his head. "Steel will do you no good here, my brother. Other skills are called for now."

Raistlin bent to enter the cave's mouth, motioning for the others to follow. The cave was not very large or very high, and Caramon had some difficulty standing. Despite what his brother had told him, he removed the bastard sword from his back and carried the weapon in both hands. He saw, by the staff's light, curved walls and ceiling, extending back ten paces before smoothing out into the dirt floor.

In the middle of the cavern stood a replica of Mereklar. "Another model?" he asked, bending over to get a closer look. "It's exactly the same as the model at Lord Brunswick's."

"Not exactly," said Raistlin.

Caramon stared at it, and his eyes widened. "Where's Shavas's house?" The warrior's head jerked up, and he grew suddenly cold and scared. "Where is it?"

"Where is the house of the Lady Shavas?" Raistlin asked, glancing at Bast. "Perhaps you could tell us."

The man in black shook his head slowly. "No. I cannot tell you. But he can," he said, pointing.

A sudden gust of wind made Caramon shudder. The cave grew dark, the light from the Staff of Magius covered by a hidden hand that blocked its illumination. A shadowy form at the rear of the cave coalesced into a man shrouded in black robes. His hands were bone, covered with rotting flesh. There were no eyes in the hollow sockets, yet Caramon knew the dead wizard could see them.

The warrior's throat constricted as if the skeletal hands had clutched his windpipe. He tried to move, to keep near his brother to protect him, but he felt invisible ropes and coils wrap around his limbs.

Raistlin walked toward the wizard, holding the black staff in front of him. Reaching out, the wizard touched Raistlin's forehead with a spectral finger. The mage went flying violently backward, his body crashing into the model of Mereklar.

Caramon strained against his prison, using all his

strength and will to break free. But his legs were held by great chains, his arms pinioned to his sides by heavy weights. The warrior looked to Bast, pleading with him to help, but the black-skinned man stood motionless—a seemingly disinterested spectator.

Raistlin struggled to his feet from the wreckage of the model. Leaning on his staff, gazing at the wraith with narrowed eyes, he gritted his teeth and started again to walk toward him.

"You are brave, Red Robes. I admire that. We could have understood one another, I think. Look. Look behind you."

Raistlin turned. The model was perfectly whole again. Three glowing white lines stretched from each gate to the center of the city, where a domed building stood, also glowing with power. Lines extended along the walls of the city, creating a triangle divided into three sections.

A loud moaning sound rose in the cave, writhing in the air as if it were something alive, dying down to a voice filled with wrath.

"Hear my words! You wear the mask of gold, but another wears a mask of flesh. Do not be deceived, for you have seen its true complexion. It was my downfall. If you falter, it will be yours."

The wraith vanished. Raistlin collapsed, falling unconscious. Caramon saw Bast bending over his brother, and the warrior—freed from enchantment—lurched forward.

Something small and furry leaped at him from out of the shadows. Startled, Caramon staggered backward and hit his head on a rock. Pain shot through his head. He fell and lay, stunned, unable to move. Dimly, he heard voices. . . .

"Do I get rid of them, my lord?"

"No, they may yet be of some use. We can always destroy them later. The kender?"

"We lost him, my lord."

"I told you to guard him carefully!"

"He appeared harmless. . . ."

"He is. The ring is not."

"Your orders, my lord?"

"Let these two go. I have business elsewhere. Time runs short, and there are still seven left. Keep your eyes on these two."

"Yes, my lord."

Caramon shook his head to clear it. Putting a hand up, he tried to rub away the pain. "Raist?" he called, sitting.

His brother lay unconscious on the ground. Near him, curled up by his side, purring loudly, was a large tabby cat.

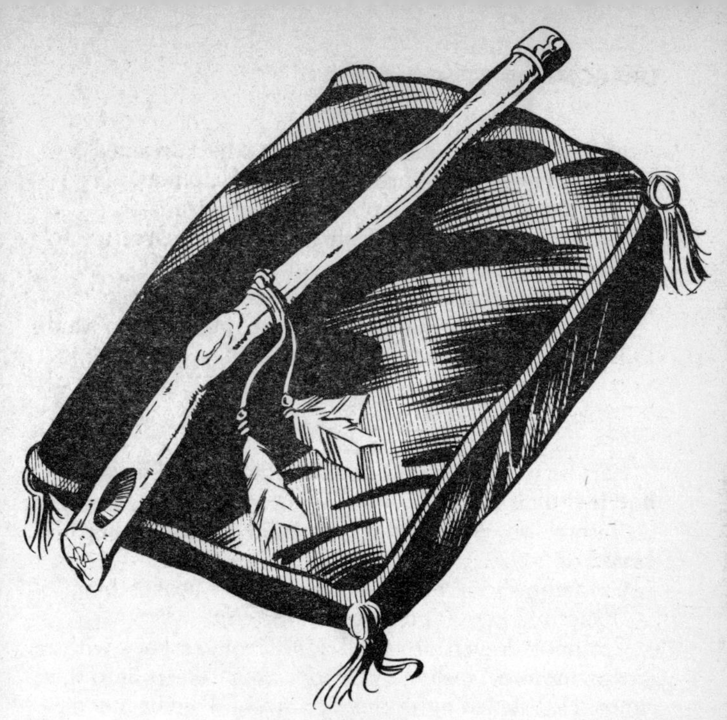

CHAPTER 20

"Raist!" Caramon, glancing askance at the tabby cat, bent over his brother. "Raist, are you all right?" he asked helplessly. If his twin was suffering from some sort of magical affliction, Caramon had no idea what he would do.

Raistlin's eyelids fluttered. He opened them and gazed around as if trying to recall where he was. Suddenly remembering, he sat bolt upright.

"How long was I unconscious?"

"Not long. Only a few moments."

The mage looked sharply around. "Where's Bast?"

"Gone, I guess," said Caramon uneasily, remembering the

dimly heard conversation, wondering if he'd dreamed it.

Raistlin gripped his brother's arm. "Help me up."

"Should you? What happened? That wizard—"

"No time for questions! Help me up! We must return to the city!"

"The city? How? They won't let us in the gate!"

"It may be easier than you suppose, my brother," said Raistlin grimly. "It may be far too easy."

* * * * *

Raistlin was right. The gate was deserted. The guards had fled their posts.

"Listen, do you hear it?" Raistlin asked, tilting his head.

Caramon shook his head. "No, I don't hear a thing."

"Exactly. There is no sound in the city."

Caramon drew the bastard sword from his back with a single motion, feeling 'warrior's fear' creep into his limbs. He listened more closely now, and did hear something, something that was moving closer to their present location with great speed.

"Raist, come on!" he yelled, grabbing his brother and pulling him through the gate, into an alley, ducking behind old barrels and boxes. He recognized the sound now, the sound of terror and hatred, the need to destroy the misunderstood.

"We'll find 'em! First Lord Manion. Now Lord Brunswick!"

"The wizard wears long red robes!"

"The big one's got more muscles than a horse!"

The mob surged past them. Raistlin frowned in irritation. "I don't have time for this. I must see Councillor Shavas."

Caramon stared at him. "But— You think she tried to kill you!"

"No, my brother. Not kill me. You see, Caramon," Raistlin said, with a soft sigh, "I think that I am at last beginning to understand."

"I'm glad *you* are. I don't understand a damn thing! Well, we better get started, before they come back."

"No, my brother. Not *we*. I must go alone."

"But—"

"Return to Barnstoke Hall. There may be news of the kender. If what you say you overheard is true, he has probably escaped. Caramon"—Raistlin looked at him intently—"beware the ring he wears!"

And then, before Caramon could say a word, the mage was gone, slipping into the shadows of late afternoon, gliding down the street like a wraith.

* * * * *

Lady Masak closed the record book, shuddering slightly at what she'd read. With an unsteady hand, she placed the text back on the shelf among the others of its kind, the rows and rows of gold-inlaid dates shining brightly in the afternoon sunlight. She sat down in her white chair, sipping at a cup of steaming tea.

The room was very long, colored gray by stains and paints, and dominated by a single table that stretched its expanse. The only chair was the one the Director of Records occupied. Over a thousand books filled the hall—the legacy of the citizens and council members of Mereklar since the city was discovered.

The woman cocked her head suddenly and turned her gaze out the window to the city below. She'd heard something, or thought she had. It sounded like a scream.

Lady Masak placed the cup of tea onto its saucer and reached under the table, pulling out a triangular roll of cloth, black and worn with age. Unfolding the wrap, she lifted a wand from its coverings, balancing the object with a finger. One end of it bent down from the line of its construction and was covered with sigla burned into the dark wood. The other end was surrounded by a band of metal, seamless and perfect—a ring that left the tip exposed, revealing a deep, circular gouge. The lady looked down the object's length and smiled.

A loud noise came from downstairs. She pushed the chair back from the table, then crossed in silence to the door. Lady Masak put her ear to the wood.

A hand smashed through, reaching for her throat. The woman brought the end of the wand down onto the clutching black fingers, cracking bone and ripping tendons. The hand withdrew, seemingly injured from the blow, pulling out of the hole it had created.

Lady Masak backed up, behind the chair. No sound came from the other side of the door. The woman raised the wand, pointed the metal-shod tip toward the portal, and concentrated. A bright red beam flashed out from the gouge, struck the door, and disintegrated the wood, sending smoke and dust through the air in a choking cloud.

Lady Masak remained standing where she was, listening intently for the intruder. Glass shattered behind her. Too late, she tried to turn. A blow sent her sprawling against the table, her back rent open by tearing claws. She twisted around, bringing the wand up. Another bolt of crimson arced out from the gouge, but the panther had leaped lightly to one side. The red flame hit the city's records, setting them ablaze.

The lady concentrated, sweeping the beam across the library, the wand transforming her lust to kill into reality.

Another strike to her back sent her sprawling across the floor. The wand flew from her grasp. She reached out blindly for the weapon, hidden by a cloak of smoke and fire that filled the room. A booted foot smashed down on her arm, snapping it at the elbow.

Lady Masak grasped her assailant by the ankle and dragged his leg out from beneath him, sending him crashing to the floor. She groped frantically for the wand.

An open palm came up and under her chin, snapped her head back, causing her to smash up against the bookshelves. She tried to stand. A black-skinned hand, its fingers bleeding, reached down and lifted the woman by the neck. Claws slashed out and tore open the woman's throat.

Lady Masak rose on shaking legs and staggered to the window, feebly clutching her neck, around which hung a necklace bearing a silver cat's skull, ruby eyes gleaming in the flames. Blood ran between her grasping fingers. She shook her head once and smiled—a hideous smile that remained on her face as she sank to the floor.

The fire consumed the room. A hand reached from the roiling clouds of smoke to pick up the wand from the floor. Clawed fingers snapped the rod in two, discarding the splintered wooden halves, leaving it to be destroyed by the blaze.

CHAPTER 21

*The door to the estate was unlocked, and Raist*lin turned the handle without a sound, walking through the foyer and front room to the library. The councillor, wearing a white silk gown that clung about her flawless shoulders as if it possessed a life of its own, sat in a chair in front of the fire, arranging the varied pieces on the black and white gameboard on top of a small table.

"Very fitting," said Raistlin softly, the door closing behind him.

"Welcome, Master Mage. Have you been successful in your mission?"

"It appears that you were expecting me," he said.

"Please." Shavas gestured to the chair opposite her. "Yes, I have."

The mage nodded, taking the offered seat. His face was flushed with red light from the fireplace, giving his skin a sheen of bronze.

"A game?"

"We are much alike, Councillor," Raistlin said.

"How do you mean?" Shavas asked, her graceful hands arranging her pieces for the first move.

"We both have the same desires."

"Ah!" Shavas lifted her head. Her word held a volume of meaning, of promise. Her gaze was warm, her voice and body alluring. Her face was incomparably beautiful.

Raistlin, swallowing, began setting up his own pieces. He watched Shavas's hands carefully, saw her fingers shake. She accidentally knocked over a foot soldier.

"Is there something wrong, my lady?"

She shook her head briskly, tightening her lips, her pale skin flushing in the heat of the fire. "Who shall go first?" she asked.

"I will," Raistlin replied, pushing a yeoman forward. "I must admit that I am surprised to find you so calm, with your city in such chaos. What has happened?"

Shavas glanced up. "Don't you know? Where have you been?" She pushed her own yeoman to counter her opponent's. "Lord Brunswick was murdered last night. Lady Masak was killed just . . . just this afternoon."

"You can't move that piece yet."

"I'm sorry. I wasn't . . . thinking."

"How did they die?" Raistlin brought out another yeoman.

"The same as Lord Manion. They were killed by a giant cat."

The mage lifted one of his knights from the board, replacing it in front of his lines.

The councillor removed a small bar from the scales at the side of the table, shifting the balance very slightly in Raistlin's favor. She placed a metal barrier, carved to resemble a hedgerow, in front of the knight.

"It is now my turn to ask questions. You have found the reason for the cats' disappearances?"

Raistlin sent the knight around the hedge, pressing forward, evening the scales by removing one of his own ingots and placing it next to the figure.

"No, I have not. Do you have any information to add to the investigation?"

Shavas paused before answering, placing her fingers against her mouth in thought. She opened a drawer in the board and took out a footman, clad in heaviest armor, placing it two squares in front of Raistlin's champion.

"It seems late to further a lost cause."

Raistlin detected a note of relief in her voice.

"How, then, have you spent your time?" she questioned.

The mage left his knight where it was, placing another marker next to it. "In strange company."

"Whose?"

Raistlin moved the piece forward, in front of Shavas's footman. "You know him, I think. You keep his picture . . . there." He pointed.

"Really? In a book?"

"Allow me to show you."

The mage rose from his seat, aided by his staff, and went to the shelf where he had replaced the volume entitled, *Mereklar and the Lord of Cats.*

It was gone.

Raistlin glanced back at Shavas. "Ah, I see you've found it for yourself."

The woman appeared uneasy. "I have no idea what

you mean. But perhaps I have seen the man. What does he look like?"

"Tall, with dark skin and hair. Many would consider him handsome," the mage replied, with a slight touch of bitterness. He returned to his seat, scanning the board with expert ability.

"And his eyes, are they . . . unusual in any way?"

"Unusual? How do you mean?"

"Did they . . . shine, reflect, in the light?"

"Perhaps. I didn't notice. I didn't spend time gazing into his eyes," said Raistlin. He removed the opposing footman from the board and the yeoman behind it, setting it into its square.

The councillor bit her lower lip and scraped her tapered fingernails against the varnished table, leaving a slight mark of their passage in the wood. Reaching to the scales, she removed another ingot, this one larger than the others.

Raistlin frowned, wondering at her strategy. The spell she was about to cast was powerful. In defense, he took a marker of his own.

Shavas lifted her knight, dropped it nervously.

"He is here!" she said in a hollow voice. "He has come to kill us all!"

"Who?"

"You know very well who I'm talking about! The Lord of the Cats! He has come to punish the Council of Mereklar." Shavas reached out a lovely, trembling hand to Raistlin. "I desperately need your protection!"

"The Cat Lord? If is it truly he, then he is a demi-god. How can I stand against one so powerful?" Raistlin asked.

"I didn't tell you this before," Shavas began, taking a deep breath, "but my ancestors collected several items of magic in their journeys. One of them is this broach of good fortune I wear"—she touched the golden necklace with the fire opal—"and the other is this." Opening the drawer to the table, Shavas removed a triangular leather pouch that bulged in the center. "It is a weapon."

Raistlin was not looking at the bag. He was staring at the necklace, thinking that it looked incomplete, unfinished. Why didn't I notice that before? he asked himself.

Because you weren't looking at the necklace, a mocking, inner voice answered.

Shavas opened the pouch, taking out a short wand. Raistlin glanced at it, saw that it was bent at one end, and fitted with a metal ring at the other. It was covered with runes and sigla. He did not touch it.

"How does it work?"

"I'm not certain. I've never used it. I've never had any need. But, I was told by my father that it takes our feelings and amplifies them a hundredfold. If you want to destroy an enemy, you have only to feel his destruction and point the wand at him, like this."

She held the weapon by the bent end, pointing the tip at Raistlin.

The mage made no comment. He did not move.

Shavas, smiling and lowering her eyes, turned the wand around and handed it to him. Raistlin replaced it in the bag, then tucked the bag into his robes.

"Now, you can protect me," Shavas said. "It is a powerful weapon. It can destroy even a demi-god."

She leaned forward and her gown slipped, revealing her white bosom. The opal hung glittering from her soft neck. "And when this terrible nightdream is over, we will have time to ourselves."

"You mean you and my brother will have time," Raistlin said, sneering. Why did I say that? What is she doing to me? He snarled at himself inwardly. Remember! Remember what you have seen!

"I admit it," said Shavas, her fingers caressing the mage's hand. "I . . . met with Caramon"—she blushed like a schoolgirl—"but it was only to make you jealous. You're the one I want!"

Her voice was low and husky. There was a ring of truth to her last statement that startled Raistlin. He stared at her, entranced.

"I am wealthy, powerful! I could give you . . . so much! Do this one thing for me! Destroy the Lord of the Cats!"

Raistlin slowly removed his arm from the woman's grasp. She let him go, sitting back in her chair. The mage stared down at the board, at the warrior of the dead who stood before his champion.

"From the way you speak, you sound as if you know where he is."

"Not where he is, where he might be. Lord Cal is very efficient. We think the Cat Lord may be trapped in Leman Square, east of the center of Southgate Street."

"I have seen it," the mage said, standing. "Shall I go there now, lady?"

"Yes!" she cried. "And if you succeed, come back to me . . . tonight."

"Yes," said Raistlin, gazing at her intently. "I will be back. Tonight."

CHAPTER 22

Caramon made excellent time, running at a steady pace up Southgate Street. The road was, for the most part, empty. Lord Cal and his guards were busy dispersing the people, attempting to restore order. Still, the warrior thought it best to keep to the shadows of twilight. He didn't have time to beat off an enraged mob.

When he reached Barnstoke Hall, the place appeared deserted. He put his hand on the doorknob. It wouldn't turn. The door was locked. He started to bang on it, demanding entrance, then realized the proprietor might not be exactly delighted to see him.

Well, I opened it once, he thought. I can do it again.

Taking a deep breath, Caramon stepped back, then threw his weight into the door. It gave a little. Gathering himself together, rubbing his shoulder, he started to try again when a voice shrilled behind him.

"Hey, Caramon. Can I help you?"

"Earwig!" the warrior exclaimed, whirling around. "Where have you been? We've looked all over! Are you sick or something?"

The kender seemed unusually pale, his face drawn and pinched. He stood with a slight stoop, leaning as heavily on his hoopak as Raistlin did on the Staff of Magius.

"I haven't eaten in a few days, I think," he said vaguely. "I was captured by . . . by that man."

"Yeah, we went looking for you. In the cave . . . the cave of the dead wizard?"

Earwig appeared thoughtful, then shrugged. "I don't remember. I've been through quite a lot recently, you know."

"Where have you been? How did you escape? Wait till I bust this door down, and we'll have a bite to eat and then talk."

"No!" cried Earwig, clinging to Caramon. "There's something I need to show you. We have to go now."

"But what about you? You don't look like you're in any condition to—"

"Do not worry about me, Caramon. We have more pressing matters to attend to!"

The warrior's eyes opened in surprise. "You're sure talking funny. You sound kind of like Raist."

"Don't be a fool, Caramon!" the kender said sharply. "Come on!"

Caramon didn't like this, and he wished his brother were around to advise him. Thinking of Raistlin made him recall the mage's warning. Caramon looked at the kender's ring finger. The flesh around the ring was swollen and fiery red. Blood trickled from beneath it.

Seeing the warrior's stare, Earwig shoved his hand into his pocket. "Are you coming? Or do I have to go by myself?"

"All right, Earwig," said Caramon, not wanting the kender to run around loose. "Lead the way."

The kender headed at a run back toward the center of the city. Caramon had to work to catch up with him.

"Where are we going?" the warrior asked, searching the streets for signs of the mob.

"Uh, back to where I was, when I was captured, that is," Earwig replied, apparently distracted by having to walk and think at the same time. "I mean, to the tunnels underneath the city."

"Tunnels? What tunnels?"

"The tunnels where my jail cell was, dolt!" Earwig muttered beneath his breath.

"Did the tunnels have paintings all over them, like somebody was trying to tell a story or something?"

"Uh, yeah, I think so. It's kind of hard to remember. I have this terrible headache," the kender mumbled, rubbing his head with his right hand.

"Here, stop. Wait a minute. Let me see. Maybe you were—" The warrior reached out.

"Hey! What are you doing?!" the kender yelled. Spinning around, he clobbered the fighter on the hand with his hoopak.

"Ouch! Hey, yourself!" Caramon said in dismay, clutching his hand, staring at his friend. "I was only trying to help."

Earwig glared at him, then a look of confusion crossed his face. "I—I'm sorry. I'm . . . nervous, that's all." The kender turned, moving back up the street.

"A nervous kender!" Caramon marveled. "Maybe I should have him stuffed for posterity." Shrugging, massaging his bruise, the fighter followed.

After a few blocks, the street began to curve inward toward the center of the city, running parallel to several other boulevards going in the same direction. At the corner of a small park, empty of all life except for the grass and brush, Earwig went to the left, cutting across an open market till he reached a mansion, belonging to one of Mereklar's ten councillors.

"Whose house is this?" Caramon asked, peering up to the second floor, then back down at the grounds.

"Lord Manion's. But he's dead now," Earwig said sullenly. "Come on, will you! Don't worry. Nobody's home."

"How do you know that?"

"Simple. Nobody lived in the house except for the lord, and he's dead." Earwig disappeared, starting to whistle in a weird, unnatural tone.

The warrior brought his parrying dagger up to his face, tapping himself lightly in the forehead with the pommel. "I can't believe I'm actually listening to a kender," he muttered. "Much less following one."

A large pond surrounded by short hedgerows and dotted with flowerbeds reflected the light of the two visible moons, just beginning to rise.

Caramon, glancing at them, saw that they were very close together. "The Great Eye!" he recalled aloud. The deepest part of the night, his brother had said. That is when all three will converge. . . and great magical power will be unleashed!

Earwig was searching around in the bushes when Caramon found him. "What are you looking for?" the warrior asked, bending down to help.

"A door."

"A door? In a bush? Boy, your head must have really gotten cracked hard!"

"There it is!" the kender exclaimed, pulling up on a clump of grass that was growing over a wooden cover. The kender scooted down. Caramon peered inside. The door led to a staircase carved into the stone walls.

"Well, aren't you coming?" Earwig asked, staring up at Caramon from out of the hole.

Heaving a great sigh, Caramon followed, sheathing his main-gauche but leaving his broadsword out, ready for action.

Earwig lit a small torch, throwing flickering yellow light against the walls. The passage was similar to those in the sewer, except these contained different pictures, and strange lines of gold, white, and black ran as far as his eye could see. Caramon reached out and touched a white line. He snatched his hand back in astonishment, shaking it vigorously.

"Hey! That burned me!"

"Cut it out, Caramon! We don't have time for your nonsense!"

The kender tugged at the leather harness the fighter wore, attempting to drag his huge friend down the tunnel.

"All right, I'm coming! What's the big hurry?"

"We have to get somewhere quickly. We . . . uh . . . we have to save the city! That's it!"

"What do you mean, 'save the city'? What's going on?" the fighter demanded.

"Help me look for my amber meltings. On the floor," Earwig said, dropping to his hands and knees, patting the ground with his palms. "Here they are! We go this way!" The kender ran down a corridor.

Caramon dashed after him, his concern over Earwig's strange behavior now laced with fear. The kender's little torch brought unnatural shadows to life, but the only sounds were the rapping of boot and shoe against the stone. Earwig outpaced his larger friend, running with ease through the maze of tunnels. The fighter, stumbling every once in a while when he caught his foot in a crack in the floor, was hard pressed to keep up. Suddenly, the kender's light vanished altogether, and the warrior stopped, perplexed.

"Earwig! Where are you?"

"Over here, Caramon!" came the kender's voice, strangely muffled, as if he were talking into his hand.

"Where?" The fighter turned in the darkness, trying to locate the other's yell. "Is this one of your stupid games? Because—"

"Here I am!"

Using his sword's hilt as a prod, Caramon walked with careful steps toward the direction of his companion's voice. He bumped into walls several times, the metal of the blade clashing with loud, insensitive vibrations that made the warrior shudder nervously. He was completely blind. The darkness was impenetrable. Then, ahead, he saw a dim light. Torn between relief and the sincere desire to throttle the kender, Caramon stumbled forward and entered a room.

"Earwig. Are you in here?" the fighter called, staring with wonder at the dimly flickering torches.

He heard a puff of breath, then a metal dart struck him in the finger. Caramon fell forward, losing his grip on his sword.

He could see Earwig now, and he stared up at his friend, who was standing on a large stone dais, hoopak in hand. The top had been removed, turning it into a blowgun.

"That's one of those poisoned darts, Caramon," said the kender. "I found it on the floor the night the assassin came. You'll be dead pretty soon."

"Why?" Caramon managed weakly, feeling himself

begin to grow lightheaded. Heat rushed up from his arm to engulf his face and neck.

"You must die, Majere!" the kender hissed, his face twisted into an expression of cruel triumph. "Our plans cannot be stopped!"

Caramon fell to his knees, leaning back against the smooth, unmarked wall. His head bent to one side, black and silver stars flickered before his eyes. His mouth was dry, and his lips could barely shape the words.

"Whose plans?"

"Whose plans?" Earwig mocked.

He raised his arm above his head, pulling down the sleeve on his brown tunic to reveal his hand. The gold band flashed in the torchlight.

Beware the ring! Raistlin's voice echoed in Caramon's mind.

The ceiling had darkened. Motes of light appeared, forming pictures and patterns the warrior found vaguely familiar. The poison dulled his mind like a stone against the edge of a sword.

Earwig laughed. "Yes! Look! Look up into your doom! Worship our Queen! Our Queen of Darkness! Takhisis! Takhisis! We celebrate your return to the world!"

Caramon didn't understand. "Earwig," he whispered, shivering. "Help me!"

The kender stared down at his friend, and his features softened. Suddenly, he cried, "Help *me*, Caramon! I can't stop!"

Pulling a dagger from his belt, Earwig leaped off the stone and ran at the warrior.

* * * * *

The Lord of the Cats slid through the streets of the city, a blur of dark shadow in the moonlit night. He bypassed most of the town's guard, avoiding Lord Cal's command troops by traveling up side streets and over buildings, climbing with incredible agility, using nothing more than his hands and long, perfect nails.

At the edge of the city limits, he ascended to the rooftops to get a better view. He could see that most of the people were safely locked behind their doors, windows shut and barred. There were still a few roaming about the town, set on spilling the mage's blood. But most of the mobs had dispersed, their members hurrying home to their wives and family before the coming of the Festival of the Eye. No children in Mereklar would be going out this night to beg for cookies.

Reaching the last building on Southgate Street, Bast leaped the great distance between the dwelling and the wall, jumping gracefully through the air to land without sound. He came to his feet instantly, prepared for danger. He paused, listening intently, then turned to face the lands outside the white barriers of Mereklar. Standing straight, he raised his arms above his head and called to his dominion, summoning them to the world's end.

* * * * *

Waving the knife wildly, Earwig ran straight at Caramon. The big warrior managed to catch the kender and ward off the knife, both of them falling to the floor. Earwig struggled to free himself, the small body flailing on top of the fighter's huge frame. Caramon, weakened by the poison, rolled over and pinioned the kender with a wrestling hold, his arm jammed under the small, pointed chin.

"What in the name of the Abyss are you doing?" Caramon grunted.

"You're not dead yet!" Earwig shrieked.

"No thanks to you! Oof—"

The kender had slipped his leg underneath the fighter and kicked upward, landing his attack just below the abdomen.

Caramon fell back with a groan. Earwig slashed with the knife, ripping open the warrior's shoulder before the blade came up against the leather harness and flipped out of the kender's hands.

Finding himself defenseless, Earwig fell back, taking refuge behind the stone dais.

Caramon leaned against the wall. The wound in his shoulder wasn't deep, and he managed to stop the bleeding by pressing part of his shirt against it. He reached under his belt and pulled out his cestus, slipping it over his fingers, driving the metal into his flesh to help retain his failing consciousness. He, too, wondered why he wasn't dead.

As awful as I feel, I sort of wish I were, he thought briefly, pain twisting his insides.

Earwig was staring at him hopefully, perhaps waiting for him to keel over. Using the smooth stone as a prop, Caramon slid back up the wall, pushing with his powerful legs. Three throwing spikes clattered beside his head, bouncing off the smooth stone and falling to his feet. The fighter was late to duck, then realized that the weapons had already missed. Three more projectiles flew out from behind the dais, and two struck him in the arm and chest, bouncing off his armor.

If I don't stop the kender soon, Caramon thought, it'll be a race to see if I die from the poison or loss of blood! Taking a deep breath, he dropped to his knees and began to crawl around the giant disk, hoping to take the kender by surprise. The chamber was very quiet, and he knew he sounded as loud as a dwarf on a drinking binge, but he couldn't help it.

Caramon saw movement and sprang, attempting to

grab his friend. But the kender dodged backward and threw an egg at the ground, breaking it open, creating billowing clouds of foul-smelling smoke.

Beware the ring!

If I can get hold of him, maybe I can get the cursed thing off his finger, Caramon thought desperately. The warrior peered through the smoke, blinking back tears that streamed down his cheeks.

"Earwig, are you here?"

"Of course, I'm here. I'm waiting to kill you!" The voice came from the opposite side of the chamber.

"No, I don't want to talk to *you*!" Caramon shouted, having the strangest impression that there were two different kender in the room. "I want to talk to Earwig! I'm his friend."

"Caramon, help—" came a muffled voice, but it was cut off.

Good, if I can just keep him off-balance. . . . Caramon began to babble, talking about the first thing that came into his head. "Hey, Earwig, the cats really miss you, especially that black one that kept following you around. Remember him?"

"All the cats will die! I'll kill them, too!"

"Why do you want to kill the cats, Earwig?"

"I don't, Caramon," came the kender's voice. "You've got to believe—" he faltered, then shouted, "The prophecy speaks. Hear its words. 'The cats alive are the turning stone, they decide the fate, darkness or light.' Darkness will triumph!"

The kender had moved, and Caramon was no longer sure where, though the smoke was beginning to dissipate. He sat still, gathering his strength, hoping soon to be able to see.

"Oh, by the way, Earwig. Catherine says to tell you

she's sorry. She feels real bad about what she did."

"Catherine? Catherine who?" It was Earwig who answered, sounding lost and frightened.

"Catherine. The girl at the tavern. The one who kissed you."

"I remember! I . . . I . . . I need your help, Caramon. *She's* trying to control me, and I can't stop her!" Earwig cried.

"I'll help you, Earwig, just tell me where you are," the fighter called.

"I'm right here!"

The kender leaped on Caramon's shoulders. Grabbing Caramon by the hair, the kender pulled the warrior's head back and tried to slash his neck with a knife.

Caramon, roaring like a wounded bull, reached back over his head, caught Earwig, and jerked him forward. The kender slammed against the wall and lay motionless.

The warrior eyed him warily a moment to see if he was shamming. The kender was obviously out cold.

Caramon lifted the kender's left arm and held it up to the dim light in the chamber. Grasping the gold ring, he tugged. As Raistlin had discovered, the band would not come off.

"This is gonna hurt real bad, Earwig," Caramon whispered.

He saw blood seeping from under the gold, as if the finger were being bitten. Shuddering, he tried again, but the flow of blood increased and the ring stayed where it was. Earwig moaned and thrashed about in pain.

"What am I going to do?" Caramon wracked his brain for an answer. The realm of magic was far beyond his comprehension. "What would you do, Raist?" he muttered. He could almost hear his brother's voice: "Cut off the finger."

Caramon slowly drew out his knife. "Well, if that's

what I have to do . . . " He took hold of the ring, now wet with blood, and gave it one last try. He thought he felt it wiggle slightly.

Wet with blood. Wet. Rub soap around a ring and it will slip off. No soap, but if I could get it slick enough . . . "That's it!"

Caramon turned the dagger on himself, slashing a large cut in his thumb. He dripped his blood over the ring, pouring more and more of his life's essence onto the gold until the kender's hand was stained crimson.

"It's not soap, but let's see if this works!"

Caramon pinched the band between his thumb and forefinger and pulled. The ring slipped off easily—too easily. It almost seemed as if was growing and expanding, pulsing in his grip. Caramon stared at it in fascination.

Put me on! Put me on!

It is a beautiful ring and it will fit me now, Caramon thought.

Earwig screamed in pain, a sound that echoed in the chamber for many minutes. He writhed in throes of incredible agony, moaning like a child.

"She was in my head—she was in my head—she was in my head!"

Caramon threw the ring aside. Catching his friend up in his huge arms, the warrior held Earwig close to his chest, rocking the sobbing kender gently.

CHAPTER 23

Mereklar remained silent and foreboding, awaiting the forming of the Great Eye. The three moons, Solinari, Lunitari, and dark Nuitari, forging the same arcs they had crossed for thousands of years, would once more meet again. White over red over black—an eye to gaze upon the world, a focus to release the power of wizards dead since the Age of Might.

Who would use it?

Walking, his head bent into a wind only he could feel, Raistlin searched the paths and portents of his life, from his childhood to his indoctrination into the ranks of the adept, to where he stood now on the flawless street. He sought to discover the key to the mystery of the festival that had remained locked since the Cataclysm.

His right hand gripped the Staff of Magius, using it both as support and reference. Its black wood, golden claw, and pale blue orb were the pinnacles of magical knowledge—an artifact containing runes and glyphs to spells he could not yet comprehend. It held the wisdom of the one who had created it, potent rituals and sacrifices lost to the past, available to those who could hear its silent tales. It was to these venerable voices that the mage listened, ignoring all else around him.

Pictures and images floated across his consciousness, sensation more than substance. He let his spirit flow into the lines of the staff. Paths of power took him, scattered parts of his mind to other roads. But the mage did not have the experience to clutch through the veil of time and penetrate to the past. His will was forced from the rune-paths again and again, until he finally admitted defeat.

"The Eye forms tonight, and I still don't know what is happening! Who will use its power? How can I use its power!"

He gripped the black staff harder than before, feeling strength in his hand, arm, and limbs. The sickness had drained from his body since his first encounter with the growing force of the Great Eye, his frame infused by magics. The idea of having his shattered health restored permanently stirred him to action, bringing hope he once thought impossible to have. Could I truly break free of *him*?

Yes, whispered Shavas's rich and sensuous voice in his mind. *Ally yourself with me, and together we will fight him. Powerful forces will soon be mine to command. After this night's work, I will be richly rewarded and you shall share!*

Raistlin heard an answering echo in his mind, the echo of a dream.

Where is my reward?

Forthcoming.

With that word Raistlin understood where to find the knowledge he sought. But only at great cost. Snap the golden thread, and magic would be lost to him forever. But he would have Shavas. He would have wealth, power. Would it matter so much that he didn't have the magic? Raistlin pressed his hand against his head. The blood throbbed in his brain.

The Staff of Magius rapped in frustration against the ground, the metal tip ringing, its vibrations bringing the mage back to the present. The moons were rising higher, the two he could see casting imperfect shadows onto the streets as mystic lights began to collect in their eternal parade—stars of illumination that leaped to their positions above the sidewalk and atop the highest buildings. Raistlin stopped and watched their creation, staring as a pool of white collected at his feet then shot away, speeding to a nearby park. It was as if Mereklar itself were coming alive.

The scream of a wounded animal cut through the quiet, causing Raistlin to start from his meditative observations. The noise had come from a few blocks away, forward and to the left, from an area where he was already headed.

It appears I will have to make my decision much sooner than I expected, he thought, and felt a pang of fear.

The mage increased his pace, searching the alleys and sidestreets. Another block farther and Raistlin was forced to duck into a doorway. An organized unit of men came around a corner, marching in regular lines, holding short spears or swords. Another group followed, carrying the same equipment, moving with a listless gait.

Raistlin wondered where they were going. The town seemed deserted.

The sound came again—another scream of pain and rage. The mage removed the leather bag from his belt and opened the flap to reveal the wand Shavas had given him, the wand covered in strange, angled runes. Slowly, he drew it out and bolted from the alley, running as swiftly as he dared up Southgate Street, heading for Leman Square.

There he knew he would find him—Bast, the Lord of Cats.

Raistlin turned left down a dark sidestreet, going to the right when he reached the end of the block. He noticed that the lights hovering above the sidewalk appeared to be growing dim, as if their fuel were slowly running out. He went left again, down the main street. Reaching the open area leading to the square, he rounded the final corner and came to a sudden halt.

Wounded and panting, the man in black stood at bay beneath a tree, surrounded by the remaining ministers of Mereklar. Lord Cal advanced on him, a red-glowing wand in his hand.

"Hear me, Lord of the Cats. Our Lady does not want you for her enemy. She bids you and those you rule to join us and find power in the darkness you know so well."

"Your 'lady' cares nothing for us!" Bast spat the words. "She wants only to use us as she uses all who come under her sway." The Lord of the Cats lifted his head proudly. "We are free. We serve ourselves. So it has been, and so shall it be."

"Die free, then!" snarled Lord Cal, and raised the wand.

We are free. We serve ourselves.

"*Shirak*," called Raistlin, his voice clear and strong.

The Staff of Magius burst into light, shining more brightly than the two converging moons. Bast's eyes, staring at the mage, shone with red flame. The ministers half-turned, blinking against the brilliance.

"Who—"

"The mage," said Lord Cal, his lip curling.

"I'll handle this," said Lord Alvin in an undertone. "Raistlin Majere, we accused you falsely and we apologize. As you can see, we have the murderous beast cornered. Serve us in our fight, and you will be richly rewarded! Lady Shavas will see to that!"

Raistlin thought of the sickness, the pain, the terrifying moments when he feared he would never be able to draw the next breath. He thought of being always dependent on his brother. He thought of women, gazing at him with expressions of horror or pity. Never expressions of love.

Raistlin thought of the magic, burning in his blood.

"The choice is made," he murmured.

Yes, said the other. *Long ago. Here, then, is your reward.*

Raistlin stood before great falls of light, the bands of magic traveling inside the Staff of Magius in the infinite spaces between the runes of the cantrips, a place where ancient knowledge waited for the touch of his summoning gold fingers. He embraced a silver strand with his will, a pass to the past that showed him surmounting a mountain with three other wizards—pictures of another time that he felt with all his senses.

White robe, red robe, and black walked slowly, braving storm and gale and lightning, moving up a path cut into the rock by natural forces to a high plateau. They looked over the whole of the world standing at the edge.

"It is time," the white robe said.

"To lose our lives for a greater cause," the red robe said.

"To give our gods greater power than any one of us could command," the black robe said.

They cast their spell and died, wrenched apart by the powers they summoned, trapped in the three heavenly spheres.

Raistlin watched their actions, the motions they made with their hands, the words uttered above the winds that whipped their clothes with violence, and knew that the might of the Great Eye could be his to command.

He lifted the wand. It began to glow red in his hand.

"He's ours!" said Lord Cal, laughing, and turned back to face the Lord of the Cats.

A bolt of red shot from Raistlin's wand and struck Lord Cal in the back. The man screamed in rage and pain, the searing beam melting clothes and flesh. He whirled to face his enemy, but his strength gave out. Writhing in agony, he crumpled to the ground.

Bast lashed out with his right hand, stabbing his fingers into Lord Alvin's throat, tearing a great wound that severed the man's head. Alvin fell, dead.

The other minsters, yelling in rage, attacked the Lord of Cats. Raistlin dared not help, fearing that any spell he would cast would harm the man in black.

Bast needed no help, it seemed. He took one of his enemies by the chest with a sweeping kick and killed the other with an open-palmed strike to the forehead, snapping the head back, skull crushed and neck broken.

The night was silent once again.

Raistlin came forward, leaning on the staff.

The bodies of the ministers lay on the ground, reddish liquid appeared black in the moonlight. Around each neck he could see, shining, silver cats' skulls.

"What are they?" asked the mage.

"See them in their true form," answered Bast.

The corpses began to undergo a horrible change. Their bodies twisted and contorted, black fur grew from their skin, hands and feet changed to paws—an evil, demented dream of cats.

"Demons," said Raistlin.

"Agents from the Abyss," replied Bast.

"The 'lady' of whom they spoke—"

"Takhisis, Queen of Darkness." The Lord of the Cats answered quietly, in awe and reverence.

Raistlin felt a shudder run through his body, a shivering premonition. "Not yet!" he whispered. "Not yet! I am not strong enough." He drew a deep breath. "And now?"

"That is your decision, mage. Krynn is in peril. 'The land will know five ages, but the last shall not come if darkness succeeds, coming through the gate.' The Queen is trying to enter the world. Her way must be stopped."

Raistlin looked at the Lord of Cats—a demi-god—torn by the demons' claws. "If you could not withstand them, how can I?"

"The nine sent were the most powerful among their kind. They murdered the true lords and ladies of Mereklar and took their places on the council. They would have opened the gate without hindrance, but for you."

"But there are ten on the council."

"Shavas is something you must discover for yourself. Now I must leave." As Raistlin watched, the Cat Lord's wounds began to heal. "However, I am compelled to ask you this directly, though I think I know your answer. Will you help us stop the Dark Queen?"

Raistlin looked down at the councillor's wand, faintly glowing red in his hand.

The choice is made.

He tossed the wand to the ground, brought the metal-shod tip of the staff down hard upon it. The wand splintered, and its red glow faded and died.

* * * * *

"Keep near," said Bast, and Raistlin found himself in a large chamber. Flickering torches filled the room with a stifling gray light. Men wearing black leather armor stood near a huge stone dais.

Caramon, injured and bleeding, sat on the floor, cradling Earwig in his arms.

Raistlin knelt down swiftly beside his twin.

"Caramon," he said softly.

The big man lifted his head, too dazed and grief-stricken to be surprised at the sight of his brother.

"It's Earwig, Raist! You were right about the ring. He was possessed. When I took the ring off, he began to scream. He shot me with that poisoned dart there, but it didn't kill me."

Raistlin listened to Caramon's slightly incoherent account, then reached down on the floor to examine both the poisoned dart and the ring.

Looking at the dart closely, he saw scratch marks on the metal tip. "Much of the poison was worn off before the dart hit you. It appears"—Raistlin glanced at the kender and almost smiled—"that it has been used to pick a lock."

Caramon wasn't paying attention. The big man was vainly trying to sooth the babbling kender.

Raistlin lifted the ring warily, holding it in the palm of his hand. Almost immediately, he heard the silken whisper: *Put me on. Put me on.*

He stared at it, thinking he had seen the ring somewhere before.

No, he realized. I haven't seen it! I've seen where it is supposed to be!

Shavas's necklace—the opal she wore around her neck. Closing his eyes, he pictured the golden band fitting around the top of the jewel where it attached to the chain. Swiftly, he thrust the ring into one of his pouches.

The kender began to writhe and thrash about, screaming, "In my head! In my head! In my head!"

"I can't help him, Raistlin!" said Caramon, looking up at his brother with pleading eyes. "Can't you do something?"

"No, my brother," said Raistlin softly. "But there is one here who can."

Bast bent down, touched Earwig's forehead. The kender blinked and rubbed his eyes.

"Hi, Caramon! Why are you holding me— Hey! You've been in a fight!" Earwig cried accusingly, pointing at the blood on the warrior's sleeve. He sprang to his feet. "You've been in a fight, and you let me sleep through it again!"

"Earwig," said the confused warrior. "I— Wait!"

The kender lashed out with his small foot and kicked Caramon in the shins.

"Ouch! Drat it, Earwig. Let me explain—"

"What must we do?" Raistlin asked the Cat Lord.

Bast's long, white teeth flashed. "You must decide. I cannot intervene."

"It seems to me, my lord," said Raistlin dryly, "that you have already intervened!"

"I have done nothing. The choices have always been yours."

Yes, thought Raistlin. You are right. The choices have always been mine. Now it is up to me to put together what I have learned.

"Mereklar itself is the gate spoken of in the prophecy. Tonight, when the Great Eye forms, the Dark Queen will try to use its magic to open the gate."

"How do you know that?" Caramon asked, looking at his brother dubiously.

"From the model in the dead wizard's cave. You saw the lines glowing then. I have seen the lines glowing ever since I was in the Black Cat Inn. I didn't know what they were until the wizard touched me. He gave me his knowledge, to avenge himself on the one who had destroyed him."

Caramon struggled to his feet. His shoulder wound had reopened. A trickle of blood poured down his arm. "So how do we keep the gate from opening?"

"When the gate opens, it will act as a door for any to enter or leave. However, only one side of the door allows access *to* a place, and the other only allows access *from* a place."

"That is correct," the Lord of Cats said. "The manner in which this gate is created allows only one person to enter at a given point."

"And that point would be the corners of the city walls, where the portal will be formed, giving us three from which to enter," said Raistlin. "I need to know how the portal was formed, my lord. You said you cannot choose for us, but apparently you can aid us in some way. Tell me what I need to know."

"There is an altar that will be used by the Dark Queen when the Great Eye forms. Destroy it, and the gate closes."

Caramon shook his head. "But how do we destroy this thing? I mean, we don't even know what it looks like!"

"Yes, you do," said Bast. "I will enter by the southeast corner."

"Enter where?" Caramon demanded. "Would someone tell me what's going on!"

"Enter the city of Mereklar that lies beneath the city of Mereklar, my brother," said Raistlin. "The city shown in the wizard's model. The city where Lady Shavas's house does not stand."

"What's in its place?" Caramon asked, almost positive he didn't want to know.

"A temple to the Dark Queen," answered the Cat Lord. "We must hurry. Time grows short."

"What about them?" Caramon demanded, pointing at the men standing around the dais.

Bast made a motion with his hand. Caramon, watching, caught his breath. He was no longer staring at men but at cats—all shapes and sizes. They curled around the legs of the Cat Lord, rubbing against him, awaiting his orders.

"They will fulfill the prophecy. The Great Eye begins to form." Bast started to leave. At the entrance to the chamber, he turned. "Use only that sword, Caramon Majere." The Cat Lord pointed to the hand-and-a-half sword strapped to the warrior's broad back. "I have enchanted it to slay the demons."

"I thought you couldn't aid us," said Raistlin with some asperity.

Bast raised dark eyebrows. "A gift, in return for one he gave the fallen." The Cat Lord held a ball in his hand. Round and yellow, its sequins sparkled in the light.

"What about me?" Earwig cried, disappointed. "Don't I get an enchanted weapon?"

"You are a kender," said the Lord of the Cats. "That is enchantment enough." With that, Bast disappeared into the darkness, the cats following him.

"Wow!" said Earwig, eyes wide. "Did you hear that?"

Caramon drew his sword, staring at it suspiciously. He tested the balance with a rotating swing.

"I don't like anyone messing with my weapons," he muttered. "Not even gods."

"Oh, boy! A fight! And this time no one's going to cheat me out of being in it!" Earwig spun his hoopak in the air.

"Do you know what you have to do, my brother?" Raistlin asked.

"No," said Caramon bluntly. "I don't understand a damn thing!"

"You must each find a place atop the city walls, over the gates. Caramon, you go over Eastgate. Earwig . . ." Raistlin paused to consider entrusting the fate of the world to a kender. He sighed. There was no help for it. "Earwig, you go above Westgate. When you're inside, head for the center of the city, to the place in which we're standing."

Caramon's face wrinkled in perplexity. "But, Raist! We're already in the gates! We're already standing in the center of the city."

"You are standing in this city," Raistlin corrected. "You must enter the one below. The one that resides in the Abyss!"

Earwig's eyes opened wide in joy.

Caramon's eyes opened wide.

"Once you are in this room, you must destroy whatever you find on top of that." Raistlin pointed at the stone dais.

"How?"

"That you must discover for yourself, my brother!" the mage answered testily, turning. "Time grows short, and I have much to do."

"But . . . you're not coming with us?" Caramon reached to stop him. "I can't let you go off by yourself!"

"You must, my brother," said Raistlin.

"Where are you going?"

"Into an abyss of my own."

* * * * *

The night sky was filled with stars, constellations of great powers watching in anticipation. The three moons moved slowly together. Solinari and Lunitari embraced each other first. The black sphere of Nuitari began to slide over their combined light, heading for the center of their unity, three flawless orbs starting to form the most wonderful and fearsome sight in the world: the Great Eye.

The power from three wizards long dead began to flood the land—water released to drown the world with magic. A canopy formed over the white walls of the city of Mereklar, a pointed cover whose apex rose in the middle, held above the hill in the center of Mereklar where a temple lay beneath earth and stone, buried for hundreds of years. Darkness choked the light from the stars, and even the sight of the Eye was dimmed, as if it were closing.

Recognizing what was happening, the gods of good acted as they had foreseen they must. The three gates of the city slammed closed and sealed shut, trapping everything within. When next they opened to the world—if they opened—they would do so at the command of the Dark Queen.

CHAPTER 24

Earwig stood atop Mereklar's wall at the Westgate. All around him it was dark but directly above him, the sky was clear and bright. He stood fascinated, watching the Great Eye glare down upon the land, casting shadows that flickered and moved like red and silver phantoms.

Finally growing bored with watching the Eye, however, Earwig glanced down below. That was boring, too. Mereklar had completely disappeared. Darkness engulfed the towers and buildings and streets, removing it from the ground as if it had never been. But the darkness wasn't doing anything. It was just sitting there, and the kender yawned.

He thrust the tip of his hoopak down into the darkness, bringing it back out, checking it hopefully for a coating of horrible ooze or slime.

Nothing.

"I really don't think this is being handled properly. I mean, if this is supposed to lead to the Abyss, it could at least look more . . . more . . . awful!"

Earwig paced the corner, searching for something entertaining, when a shimmer caught his eye—a shining staircase was slowly forming, sparkling motes of light spinning and coalescing into a solid object.

"Now that's more like it!" he exclaimed and was about to hop down it when he heard a shout.

"Earwig! . . . Earwig!"

"Drat," said the kender.

Caramon was yelling from his position on the other gate. The big man was jumping up and down to catch his friend's attention, his distant figure distorted by the three moons.

"Hi!" Earwig yelled back, whirling his hoopak in the air, causing the leather thong to whistle loudly.

"Meet in the center!"

"What?"

"I said, meet me in the center!"

"The center of what?"

"The center of the city, you—" The last words were, fortunately, swallowed up in the darkness.

"That's where I was going, before you interrupted me!" The kender said indignantly. Turning, he headed again for the magical stairs. "Boy, this is the last time I take him on any of my adventures!"

Holding his breath and pinching his nose between thumb and forefinger, the kender skipped down the stairway; the last sight of him on Krynn—his topknot of hair.

* * * * *

Glowering, not liking this in the least, Caramon stood at the top of the magical staircase that had appeared before him. He hesitated, gripping his sword tightly. He didn't want to go down into the darkness. He knew that, if he did, he would meet his own death, and it would be a terrible one.

"But maybe Raist is down there. He's alone. He needs me."

Caramon put a foot on the stair. Then, deciding that—like bad-tasting medicine—it was best to drink it quickly and get it over with, the warrior ran full speed down the staircase.

Reaching the bottom, he stepped off and instantly red beams flared around him. One glanced off his arm, searing his flesh painfully. Caramon rolled on the ground and ducked into a nearby building, shutting the door behind him. Looking out a window, he could see three creatures, aiming red-glowing wands at him.

The creatures were bent and twisted, their bodies covered with fur. Their heads looked like the skulls of dead cats, teeth gleaming in a rictus grin. One of the demons, wearing a harness of some strange, glossy material with a silver medallion in the middle, shouted something in a strange language, pointing at the building where Caramon was hiding.

The demon's voice, rough and hissing, reminded Caramon of a cat that could talk like a human. Moving slowly and as quietly as he could, the big man crept up the stairs.

Down below, he heard the door crash and saw a bolt of crimson flare in the room, scoring the back wall and setting furniture aflame.

Footsteps, claws scraping against the floor, padded through the room, searching. Then they began to ascend the stairs. A head appeared in Caramon's view. It saw him the same time he saw it.

"*Das—*" it began to shout the alarm.

Caramon's sword bit into its neck, the keen metal driving so far into the flesh that the blade plunged through the demon into the wall. The warrior yanked his blade free and pounded up the stairs that led to the third floor.

The hallway exploded with red light, shattering chairs and tables, sending splinters flying through the air. Caramon kept running. Another demon, growling in anger at missing its target, dashed up the stairs in pursuit.

Caramon waited in ambush at the head of the stairs, drew his throwing dagger, and tossed. The knife struck the demon point-blank in the chest.

Reaching up, irritated, the demon plucked it out of its black pelt.

"Huh? I guess that's why Bast said to use the sword," Caramon muttered.

He saw the wand aiming at him and threw himself to the floor. Red light burned through the room, over his head. Looking about wildly, the fighter discovered a portal in the ceiling, just low enough for him to reach. He pushed the wood-slatted cover off with his bastard sword, throwing the blade through it to land on the roof. Leaping up, he grabbed the edges of the portal and started to pull himself up.

Powerful hands grabbed hold of his ankles and jerked him to the floor. The demon's paws smashed down onto his ears, stunning him. The creature extended its claws and cut down under the warrior's armor, digging forward, dragging dirty talons through his flesh.

The pain brought Caramon to his senses, and he kicked up with his legs, knocking the demon over. Leaping after it, he tried to pin it to the floor. The demon slipped out of his hold, and Caramon scrambled backward.

His sword was high above him, and he cursed himself for his carelessness. Then he put his hand on something on the floor and, thinking he recognized it by its feel, he closed his fingers over it.

The demon reached for its wand, snarling in dismay when its clawed fingers closed on air.

"This what you lost?" Caramon said, holding up the weapon.

The demon leaped for it. The warrior brought his knee up straight at its stomach. The creature doubled over and Caramon clasped both arms around the demon in a bear hug, muscles straining against its dark fur, crushing until he felt bones snap beneath his grip. The body went limp. Dropping the corpse to the floor, the warrior leaned against the wall, gasping for breath. After a short time, he moved back up to the hole in the ceiling, lifting himself easily through the portal and onto the empty rooftop. Picking up his blade, he crawled to the edge and stared down to see if the other demon had returned with—

A powerful fist slammed across the side of his head, nearly sending him reeling over the edge of the roof. The demon, apparently uninjured, bared its fangs, biting deep into the human's shoulder.

Caramon stifled his cry of pain for fear of alerting any others of its kind, and brought the hilt of his sword up into the demon's chin, knocking it backward. The warrior slashed the bastard sword across in a horizontal arc, cleaving the head from furred shoulders.

White and silver spots danced before Caramon's vision. His legs weakened and gave out under his weight, forcing him to sit down roughly on the smooth stone.

Stretching himself out on the roof, closing his eyes to the image of the Great Eye, he swallowed, breathing hard.

"And there's an army of these things!" he said with a groan.

* * * * *

In his room in Barnstoke Hall, Raistlin removed several black bags from his pack—flat pouches heavily lined with fur and other soft materials. He opened one of them to reveal an array of bottles and tubes, capped with cork and stoppered with rubber blocks, containing a variety of colored liquids and crystals and powders. Unfolding a brass frame used to store chemicals while working, he took the containers out from their holding straps and placed them into their proper locations—solids in front, liquids at the back.

Another pouch produced a shallow mixing dish with matching pestle and a glass bottle of clear liquid with a wick jutting from the top. From another he drew a melting pan and stand, and a smaller pan with a handle covered in wound leather. A third contained holding stands, tiny metal chains, and various silvered tools.

The mage erected the apparatus on top of the table. Reaching into his voluminous robes, he pulled out a hollow gold tube, as long as one of his gold fingers, unadorned by symbol or rune, and placed it next to the pan.

Raistlin sat in a chair, placing his hands on his knees, fists clenched in concentration. He began to search through his memories for the proper potion—an elixir that would suit his purpose. Ingredients began to filter through his mind as he allowed the discipline of alchemy to take control of his consciousness, his knowledge of the world and familiarity with the art drawing out an answer.

A pinch of white powder as the base, another of black to equalize, blood from all parties, the symbols of sympathetic magic, dust taken at great risk to spirit and body, clear crystals to bend, green to expand, red to destroy, heat to forge, a cylinder of gold to cool.

"And alcohol," Raistlin concluded, coming out of his near-trance.

He stood and set to work, putting the bottles he was not going to use back into their holding straps, closing the pouch and setting it aside for safety. With a long fingernail, he drew a measured amount of rough, white powder, most of which had clung together into small clumps, from a bottle and tapped it out onto the melting pan.

He lit the wick on the squat clear bottle, summoning up a dancing yellow flame. Taking a dark bottle from the rack, Raistlin carefully removed the rubber stopper, revealing a small spoon pushed into the bottom. Removing an amount equal to the white powder, he mixed them together with a wooden rod—a thin stick no wider than a leaf of grass—and spread the now gray mixture into a thin ring with an open center.

Throwing the stick far across the room with a flick of his wrist, the mage wiped a small bead of sweat that had formed on his brow. He tried to keep his thoughts and purpose straight, clear and free from influence, but—looking at the materials before him—he caught his breath, hands trembling. His eyes closed tight for a moment.

His will held. He opened his eyes.

The mage removed three more bottles from the rack, each containing crystal shards of varying sizes and shapes—one was clear, another green, and the third red. He removed a piece of the clear crystal and placed it on the shallow dish, crushing it against the metal with the marble hammer. He wiped the debris from the tool on his sleeve. Doing the same with the other crystals, he began to measure the amounts he thought he would need with the edge of his little finger—a bit of red gone, add a little more green, too much clear, then, not enough.

Raistlin was conscious of time passing and fought down the impulse to hurry, crushing additional rock and taking it away until the balance was finally correct. He took all the clear powder and combined it with uneven parts of the others—more green than red—rubbing it against his thumb and forefinger until their individual colors became part of the whole, inseparable. He added the new mixture into the confines of the gray-powder ring on the melting pan.

Wiping his hands on his red robes, Raistlin rubbed his eyes, which were beginning to ache from the strain. Then, with a silver knife, he scraped the blood off the gold ring Earwig had worn. The mage worked quickly, dropping the dried flakes into the small pan with the leather handle.

He reached for another stoppered bottle. This one was coated with black patches, as if it were diseased. Raistlin opened it with more care than any previous bottle, drawing back at the stench that rose out from it like a wraith. Holding the container in his fist, leaving only the mouth and end exposed, he tapped its back.

A cloud of darkness reached forward and engulfed the blood, discoloring the dried fluid to a darker shade. The mage tilted the bottle back up and placed the top on it again just as the rest of the contents began to writhe out, grasping for the promise of another's life.

Raistlin let out a long sigh, relieved to be free of the deadly dust. Setting the pan down, he took the remaining crystals and dumped them into a crucible, holding the vessel with a pair of metal tongs over the flame, watching as they melted together.

When they began to glow from the heat, he dropped the dried blood in, the flakes instantly disappearing with a puff of dirty smoke.

"Wait! There's something missing," he whispered, catching his error. Searching through his materials, he grew increasingly frustrated. "I cannot find it! And without the stone, this won't work!"

Raistlin clutched a hand to his chest in frustration, tearing at the cloth, when he suddenly noticed something hard and round in one of his inner pockets—a disk on a chain. Hastily, he removed the object.

"The charm of good fortune the woman gave me," he murmured. "I must definitely reconsider my position on the superstitious beliefs of peasants."

Grasping the pestle, he smashed the amulet to pieces and picked out the stones he needed, throwing them into the crucible where they melted almost instantly. He poured the new substance onto a shallow plate, spreading it thin and letting it cool. Cracking noises filled the air. The substance shattered into fine dust as red as rubies, black at the center.

The sorcerer arched his back, feeling the vertebrae crack from stiffness. He had finally come to a point where he could relax for a moment. But even as he did so, he felt time running from between his fingers. He raised the melting pan onto its stand and chains, moving carefully so as not to disturb the powder ring. Scraping the red powder into a curved half-tube with a tapering tip, he slowly formed symbols of power against the white circle in the pan, one atop the other. When it was completed, he let the tube drop to the floor.

"The final stage," Raistlin whispered.

He erected another stand around the melting pan, two

wire legs with a connecting bar at the top. He pulled two metal link chains—covered in some black, slippery substance from an opaque bottle—and hung them from the legs, placing the gold tube into the curve at the lowest point, and stoppered the top with a golden cap.

Lifting a small silver bell and hammer from the third pouch, he struck the bell with the hammer, listening carefully as its clear sound eventually died out. He struck again, nodding when there was silence.

The bell rang a third time—the clear, scintillating sound penetrating through the night. The mage listened as the echo slowly grew fainter and fainter, fading and disappearing until nothing was left.

Raistlin removed the cap and blew cool air through the tube. The symbols on the melting pan boiled and faded, melding and mixing into one another until their forms intertwined into a single sigil of power. Created through the destruction of its elements, the sigil settled against its white background and then rose upward in a flash as the gray ring flared alive with flame. Its essence coated the tube.

The mage replaced the cap, doused the flame, and leaned on the Staff of Magius for support. He breathed heavily, and lowered his head in fatigue. The ritual was complete.

Raistlin peered into the tube, saw that opaque brown crystals had formed on its inner surface—the proper result. No expression of satisfaction crossed his features, however. He raised the cowl up over his head, hiding the golden mask of his face in the darkness of his robes.

CHAPTER 25

Earwig stared in wonder into the Great Eye, which seemed to be reversed down here—it was black, glimmering with red and a small white dot in the center. Bolts of power arced through the cloudless heavens, reaching out with forked fingers to touch unknown spaces. He thought he might watch that wonderful sight forever—or least the next ten minutes—but an irritating voice inside him kept nagging at him to do something.

"But what, that's the question? Oh, I remember! I'm supposed to meet Caramon in the center of town."

Earwig was starting to turn the corner when he almost ran headlong into a group of twisted, demented-looking cats.

The creatures certainly looked interesting. Earwig was considering going up and introducing himself when he remembered that he was on another Very Important Mission. He backed up hurriedly, therefore, sliding with kender agility into a shadow so that the cats wouldn't be tempted to stop and chat.

A loud noise made him look around curiously. It was a carriage, rumbling past, drawn by nothing at all that the kender could see.

"Gee," he sighed, watching, "that looks like fun. And it's heading in the direction I want to go. I guess they wouldn't mind if I tagged along."

Earwig dashed out, ran in back of the coach, caught hold, and perched himself on the rear. Kicking his feet, he gazed around happily.

The conveyance raced on, metal-banded wheels clashing noisily against the white stone of the city. He recognized the road they were approaching as Southgate Street. Here the carriage came to a halt. Earwig hopped off and looked around at the front. Three creatures jumped out, stretching lazily, arching their long backs in the manner of cats. Two drank from bottles they wore strapped to shining harnesses. When they were done, they shook their heads violently and grimaced.

"Celebration Punch," Earwig remarked in sympathetic understanding.

He was about to step forward and inquire the way to the center of the city, or perhaps ask if any of these guys had seen Caramon, when the demented-looking cats jumped back into the carriage. Before the kender could get back on, it careened off down the street.

"Hey!" yelled Earwig, waving his arms. "You forgot me!"

* * * * *

Caramon jumped from rooftop to rooftop, stopping occasionally to catch his breath and rest. He still felt slightly nauseated from the poison and weak from loss of blood. He leaned out over the edge of the roof and saw that he was on Eastgate Street. He had only about another block to go.

"Time to move again. I hope Earwig and Bast are already there so that we can destroy that thing and get the hell out of here."

Caramon gripped his sword, lowering himself as quickly and quietly as he could manage to the next house. He heard a scraping sound, then silence, then snuffling, as if an animal was following a track. His heart began to beat so hard that he could feel it in his ears.

Caramon forced himself to stay hidden, to wait. He longed to leap up, swinging his sword, and take the demon by surprise. But, considering its speed and incredible senses, he wasn't sure if that were possible.

A scarlet beam pierced the warrior's left shoulder, leaving an exit hole out the front of his armor. Wisps of smoke rose from his smoldering shirt. Another bolt seared across his arm as he tried to dodge out of the line of fire. Hoping to distract the creature, he drew a dagger from his belt and threw.

The demon ducked, giving Caramon time to lunge forward, driving his blade into its chest. The demon fell dead.

Fight over, Caramon felt the pain of his wound. The sound of rushing water filled his ears, and the black sky disappeared, lost before the darkness that was covering his eyes. Locking his knees, fearing he might faint, he attempted to keep himself from falling over.

The attempt failed.

He was lying prone, legs stretched out. The temptation to close his eyes and rest until the pain and fear went away was almost overpowering.

"Raist . . . must find Raist," Caramon mumbled. Groaning, he forced himself to sit up and examine the wound. The burned shirt and armor had fallen away, revealing the hole, which was sealed by heat.

"At least it won't get infected," the fighter giggled and began to laugh. Recognizing that he was nearing hysteria, Caramon choked back his laughter. He staggered to his feet. There was no way he could leap over rooftops. Finding a stair, he stumbled to the street below.

* * * * *

Raistlin stood before Shavas's estate. The stained-glass windows were more vibrant and alive than ever, casting lines and arcs of color that shot and darted against the ground. The sight no longer fascinated the mage, and he knocked on the entrance door loudly, rapping his knuckles against the wood.

No answer came to his hail, but the door opened before him, closing and locking when he had entered the hallway. The mage walked to the library. It was empty.

Just as well. That made it easier.

Moving to the sideboard, he lifted the bottle of brandywine and removed the stopper. Glancing back at the door, checking to see that he was alone and unobserved, he withdrew the tube from his robes. He took the cap off and started to pour the brown crystals into the bottle. His hand shook.

"If I make a mistake," he said to himself coolly, "then it will be my last." He dumped the contents of the tube into the bottle.

Replacing the stopper, he turned and regarded the game board, remembering where he had left off before leaving on his mission for the lady of the house.

Shavas had made a move after he had gone. His champion had been transformed into one of the undead.

"How very fitting," Raistlin murmured.

Heavy double-doors opened on silent hinges, and perfume wafted into the room. Shavas entered. She was wearing a loose, enfolding gown of purest silk, as white as the curve of her shoulders. The cloth flowed with the graceful movement of her body like wandering wisps of cloud. She smiled at Raistlin. Her face glowed with an inner radiance. She looked as if she had just completed some great triumph and now sought relaxing entertainment.

"I am pleased that you returned, Raistlin," she said, taking the chair across from the mage. "At last I see we understand each other."

"Is that the reason for your apparent happiness, Councillor?"

"Councillor? Don't insult me! I am no longer Councillor. There is, after all, nothing left to counsel." She laughed at her joke.

"You seem very sure of yourself, my lady," the mage corrected with emphasis. "The city has not yet fallen." He moved a priest from its confines behind the lines of his knights and yeomen.

Shavas placed her fingertips on her own priest, deciding on a move. "There is no one to stop us. The people of Mereklar will soon be dead." She slid the priest forward.

Her move put the mage in a precarious position. Raistlin leaned back, considering. "How long have you lived in this city?" he asked without looking up from the board.

"Oh, many years, many years—in one form or another. I was the first councillor. I will be the last," the woman replied.

Raistlin looked up at her. The woman's beautiful eyes gazed directly into the mage's face.

Rising to his feet, Raistlin walked to the sideboard and picked up the brandy bottle. He poured himself a glass.

"Pour one for me, my love," said Shavas.

Raistlin shivered at the sound of the word that slid so glibly from tempting lips. He poured a glass of brandy and handed it to her.

"A toast," he said. "To the Lord of the Cats."

Shavas gave a small, silvery laugh. "How droll you are!"

Raistlin lifted the glass of brandy to his lips and drank the burning liquid. Shavas drank deeply, her eyes gleaming above the rim of the goblet.

She moved to stand near the mage. Flames from the fire shone through the gossamer of her robes, exposing the curvature of her figure. Languidly, she reached above her head and released the cascading flow of her long brown hair, letting it fall about her face and shoulders.

"What do you want of me?" Raistlin asked. "I am not like my brother. I am not . . . attractive."

"You are powerful, Raistlin. I always find power attractive. And you could become more powerful over time."

"Time? . . ."

"Yes. We will have all the time in the world."

"And how would we do that?" he asked, taking another drink from his glass.

"My magic is vast, stronger than almost any you have encountered before. I would be willing to . . . share it with you."

"To what end?"

Shavas drank the brandy. Emptying her glass, she filled it again from the decanter and wandered about the library, running her fingers across the suits of armor standing guard in the room. Going to a bookcase, she lifted out a volume. The title, *Brothers Majere,* was stamped in gold on the back.

"You wear the red robes, mage, but you will not wear them forever. You do not have the patience to stand in the middle. You must make a choice, or your passions will tear you asunder."

"That may be, but all in my own time. I repeat, what do you want of me?"

"It is, rather, what you want of me," said Shavas, coming close and putting her soft hand on his arm. "I am offering you the chance to control your own destiny. I am offering you an alliance with the Dark Queen!"

CHAPTER 26

"The carriage is gone. Now, I'll have to walk," said the kender, disgruntled.

He started down the street, thinking just between himself and the fish market that it would have been a lot more fun if he and Caramon had come down here together when one of the ugly, twisted creatures popped out of a side street and came to stand in front of him.

"Hullo," said the kender brightly, extending a hand. "My name's Earwig—"

The creature raised its hand. It was holding a most fascinating-looking device, a wand of some sort. It began to glow bright red. Thinking the creature was offering the wand to him—since it was pointing it at him—the kender reached out and took it.

"Thank you," he said.

The creature, with a snarl, tried to snatch the wand back.

"Hey!" said Earwig. "You gave it to me! Gully dwarf-giver!" he taunted.

The creature flew into a rage and came at Earwig, teeth bared, slavering.

"No! You're not getting this back!"

The kender swung the hoopak. Thwack! It caught the creature on the side of its head. It tumbled to the street and lay there, unmoving.

"Gosh, I'm sorry," said Earwig, nudging it with the toe of his boot. "Well, let that be a lesson to you," he added.

"Now, let's see you turn red and glow!" He looked at the wand expectantly. Nothing happened. The kender shook it. Still nothing.

"Broken!" he said in disgust. "Here, you can have it back after all," he said and tossed the wand onto the body of the creature, who was just beginning to stir and sit up groggily.

Thinking that Caramon might be wanting him, the kender continued on his way.

Arriving in the center of the city, Earwig discovered an army of the ugly creatures marching about in the street, shouting and singing in terrible-sounding voices. The kender was feeling disgruntled and out-of-sorts and didn't particularly want to talk to anybody, so he ducked into a doorway to take a look around. Across from where he was standing was a tall, domed building.

"Say!" exclaimed Earwig. "That's where Lady Shavas is supposed to have her house. Drat! Maybe I've come the wrong way."

But he looked at the streets and recognized them. Yes, he was definitely in the center of town.

"I should go tell her," said the thoughtful kender, completely forgetting what Raistlin had told him about the Dark Queen's temple. "Lady Shavas might not know her house is gone."

Earwig stepped out from the doorway and was about to cross the street (eyeing with interest some of the pouches the creatures were carrying), when he heard a smothered cry, almost right behind him.

"Earwig. Over here!"

"Caramon?" The kender squinted into the shadows and saw a glint of metal.

"Caramon?" he called loudly. "Is that you?"

An arm reached out, grabbed him by the collar, and dragged him into an alleyway.

"Hey! Don't! You'll wrinkle my—"

"Shut up!" Caramon clapped his hand over the kender's mouth.

The warrior, holding the wriggling kender tightly, peered out into the street. The marching demons were making a great deal of noise and didn't appear to have heard anything.

"Shhhh!" he whispered, letting go of Earwig slowly.

The kender stared at him, face flushing in anger. "You've been fighting again!" Earwig cried, stamping his foot. "Without me!"

"I'm sorry," Caramon growled. "Keep your voice down! Have you seen the Cat Lord?"

"Sure," said Earwig.

Caramon brightened. "You have? Where?"

"Right there." The kender pointed.

Caramon turned, hand on his sword. Bast stood in the shadows, a graceful form, his skin a deeper shade of black against the darkness.

Leaning back against the wall, Caramon drew a deep

breath. His shoulder burned, but his fear was stronger than the pain, driving it somewhere deep inside of him. He hated this place. He would have traded this army of demons for six armies of goblins, with a regiment of hobgoblins thrown in.

"Where is the whatever-it-is that we're supposed to break? In that building?"

"No. The temple is used as a tunnel between the worlds. The Dark Queen's altar is beneath the city."

"In the same place that big stone disk was in," Earwig stated helpfully.

"Correct," said the Cat Lord. "I will show you how to go there, but I cannot assist you in more than that."

Seeing Caramon scowl, Bast added, "My forces and I will be fighting in the city above. Already, the demon army marches down the streets of Mereklar, headed for the gates that, if they should open, would let them out onto an unsuspecting world. Time grows short, the Great Eye burns in the heavens. Follow me!"

Caramon, groaning, heaved himself from the wall on which he'd been leaning.

"You really look bad, Caramon," said Earwig in concern. "Are you sure you can make it? Here, you can lean on my hoopak."

Caramon glanced at the frail wooden stick and, smiling, shook his head. "I'll make it. I have to."

"Now! This way," urged Bast.

He slid around the corner and the companions followed, keeping to the shadows. The Cat Lord moved like part of the night, and even the kender's light footfalls sounded loud compared to Bast's. Caramon rattled and jangled, his breath came in grunting gasps, and he gritted his teeth against the pain that every move jarred through his body. After traversing several blocks, they either left the creatures behind or the demons were moving up into the city of Mereklar.

"I know this street," said Caramon suddenly.

"You should." The man in black bent down. Lifting a metal grating from the stone, he pointed down into a black hole. Caramon could hear the sound of running water.

"This tunnel will lead you where you must go," said the Cat Lord. "You must destroy the altar as quickly as possible. It will detect any tampering and alert its mistress."

"You mean it's alive?" the kender questioned with interest.

"In a manner of speaking. Good-bye, warrior and kender. I will not see you again. Your own gods be with you."

"Wait!" Caramon yelled, reaching out his hand. But he grasped hold of air. The Lord of Cats was gone, vanishing as silently as the night into day.

"What did you want with him?" asked Earwig, preparing to jump into the sewer.

"I wanted to ask him how to get back home," said Caramon softly.

* * * * *

Demons dropped from their world through the gate to the real city of Mereklar, landing on their feet with perfect agility. They gazed about with yellow eyes, finally freed from their other-world prison. Mereklar was theirs. They would soon take the rest of Krynn.

They moved forward in small packs, heading toward the city gates, prepared to break out and flood the world with darkness. They had no fear. Their enemy, the cats that once guarded the city, were now dead.

But the gates were closed and would not open, guarded by magic built into them by the gods of good.

Forming into ranks, demon attack groups knelt and

pointed their wands at the heavy portcullises enclosing the city, firing red streams at the thick metal plates in an attempt to burn them down. Their power, however, had no effect, though they tried for a long time. Sheathing their weapons, they attempted to force the gates with their great strength, but the might of the city's builders kept them safe.

At Westgate, a commander recalled its troops from their work and sent for reinforcements. The demons retreated at the order, some snarling and baring their teeth in anger.

The commander sniffed at the air, turning its head, checking the air for a scent it recognized, a scent it feared and hated. Moving up to the gate, it glared into the darkness outside the city wall—darkness lit by the Great Eye. Its muzzle twitched in alarm.

"Weapons out—"

The sweep of a claw cut through its back, rending the flesh from the bone in a spray of watery blood. The demon fell to the ground, lifeless. A huge tiger stood over its body, the demon's fur hanging from its paw. The enemy fired its deadly bolts at the beast, but it had vanished.

"Find it!" a demon yelled, pointing up the street.

Five of the troops obeyed the command, running after the tiger with the speed of darkness, rounding corners and searching through hidden alleys and side streets.

Within minutes, their bodies were thrown into the avenue, dismembered, rent and torn by giant claws.

The demons were furious. Red explosions concussed the air, scattering boxes, wood, and metal. The invisible enemy did not appear to have been hit. More demons were struck down, and the creatures began to mill about in frustration.

"Reinforcements!" cried one, waving up the street.

Another contingent of demons moved cautiously toward their position, searching the darkness with keen yellow eyes, sniffing at the air in distaste. They surged over a carriage, surrounding it, using it as a point of cover. Eventually they reached the first group, and a demon wearing a harness with a gold medallion in the center asked what had happened.

In reply, some of the demons pointed to their dead leader. "We were told the cats were dead," it said, snarling.

"I guess someone made a mistake," said another.

"Yeah, I wonder what other mistakes they've made this night. You stay here and wait for additional troops. When they arrive, work on opening that gate." It turned, directing the forces into position. "Form into squads and find the enemy. I want them dead!"

Twisted bodies gathered together into groups of five with a quickness and efficiency the Knights of Solamnia would have envied. They appeared to need no further guidance than a single order, cooperating perfectly with one another. After a moment they moved out, lithe forms, shadow in shadows.

None of them came back.

Several demons began to edge forward of their own volition, unwilling to wait when the promise of battle called to them, but the commander told them to stay, hissing the words between clenched fangs. "Hold your position!"

Fifteen men and women stepped out from the alleys and boulevards. They held no weapons. Blood dripped from their hands. Their eyes glistened with triumph. They made no sound of running, their movements smooth and fluid.

"Hah! Humans!" spat one demon.

It and its fellows released a barrage of red beams that

surged through the air—deadly bolts reaching out for their targets, striking ground and building, sending up clouds of dust and dirt. But the attackers were upon them in an instant, closing the distance with incredible speed.

"These are not humans!" the leader yelled. "They are the enemy!"

Lions leaped toward their victims, bringing five down immediately under their great weight, killing five more within seconds. The demons fell back, battling with claw and fang and red-glowing wand, yellow eyes flaring. The demons lost half their number within the first minute; the lions, five.

Rallying his forces, the commander ordered, "Pull back and regroup! They cannot win!"

The demon troops immediately obeyed, fighting back-to-back until they reached their rapidly forming lines. They pushed forward again, the shock of impact sending the giant cats back to the gate. There were few left. They knew they could not hold.

"Destroy them! Now!"

But the demons hesitated. The city stood silent, waiting. Both sides ceased their battle, listening.

A sound of distant thunder filled the fields outside the great walls, thunder that moved closer and closer until it was upon the gates themselves. Suddenly, a thousand cats burst through the portcullis, their small bodies sliding easily between the great plates mounted on the bars, the barriers spaced together so closely that only their slim forms would fit. They ran past their larger brethren and attacked the demons, tiny claws and fangs digging into the twisted bodies, inflicting wounds that dark magic could not heal.

The demons at the gate were destroyed, their bodies lying torn on the perfect white stone, and more cats ran over and past them, advancing on silent paws to fulfill the prophecy.

* * * * *

"There it is, Caramon," Earwig said, pointing his hoopak toward the stone dais. "The altar!"

"Yes, I think you're right," the fighter replied, standing in the cavern's entrance, his eyes attempting to pierce the dimness ahead.

The kender started to dart forward, but Caramon laid a restraining hand on the small shoulder. "Wait a minute. There might be guards. Can you see anything?"

Earwig stared with all his might. "No, nothing."

"I don't either. But I think I hear something."

"Caramon," said Earwig after a moment. "I can't hear anything because your heart's beating too loudly. Do you think you could make it stop?"

"What do you want me to do? Drop dead? Besides, that's not my heartbeat! It's the same noise I'm hearing, and it sounds like cogs grinding together."

"Are you sure?" said Earwig skeptically. "It sounds just like a heartbeat to me."

"Yes, I'm sure!" Caramon snapped. "Well, come on. We can't stand here all night."

The two moved forward. The cavern was much the same as the one Earwig had discovered in the city above. There were the same flickering torches, the same stone dais. But, reaching the entrance, they saw something on top of the dais—the altar used to create the gate between the Abyss and Krynn.

It appeared to be a large box, uneven on all sides, adorned with gold and silver and bronze. Strange, evil-looking figures had been engraved on its shining surface.

"Wow!" Earwig cried and, before Caramon could stop him, the kender dashed into the room.

"No! Wait!" the fighter yelled.

"What? What is it?" Earwig cried in excitement, spinning around. "What's wrong?"

Caramon's heart was in his throat. He had to cough to get it back down. "Just . . . don't ever . . . run into a . . . place like this . . . without looking first!"

"All right, Caramon."

The fighter winced, anticipating the next question.

"Why?" asked Earwig.

"I just thought you might like to live a little longer!" Caramon growled. The warrior stared into the room, blinking his eyes, raising his sword. "Earwig, behind you!" he shouted.

"Whu—?" The kender swung his hoopak around in a great arc. "What is it, Caramon?" he shouted, batting at nothing. "I can't see anything!"

"That—thing," Caramon cried, pointing. "It looks like a . . . a . . . hand!"

"Oh, yeah! Wow!"

A slender, sinuous, extraordinarily beautiful arm appeared out of the air, hand waving aimlessly, seemingly grasping for something it could not see.

Earwig reached up his own hand. "Hullo. My name's—"

"No!" shrieked Caramon, but the arm passed straight through Earwig's fingers.

Earwig stared. "Well, how rude!"

The kender tried to catch the hand again, but it always passed right through him. Growing bored, he skipped over to inspect the box.

Caramon held his bastard sword, ready to swing. He stepped slowly into the room, turning to regard the entrance, then turned back to the box.

"Don't touch it!" he reprimanded the kender sharply.

Earwig snatched his hand back.

"What are we supposed to do with it?" he asked.

"Destroy it," the fighter replied, involuntarily ducking as a shadowy arm passed above him. Several more arms appeared, hands reaching down out of the darkness. "That's what Raistlin told us to do."

"How?" Earwig eyed the sealed box with a professional air. "I don't suppose you could hack it to bits?"

Caramon gave the box a troubled glance. "I don't think so."

"Well, what are we doing down here, then?" demanded Earwig in exasperation.

"Don't ask me! I just . . . always figured that Raist'd be here to help us."

"Well, if we can't destroy it, then let's open it and see what's inside."

Rubbing his hands in anticipation, Earwig jumped up on the dais. He inspected the box, running his hands along the artifact's sides, attempting to find a keyhole or a crack.

"Earwig, I'm not sure about this—" Caramon began, his attention divided between the kender and the flailing arms.

"Ah, ha!"

A loud click came from the box, and a crack opened in its center, running around it horizontally.

"Oops," said Earwig.

Caramon, having been with other kender on adventures, knew that dreaded word all too well. He immediately assumed a fighting stance.

"What is it? What did you do, Earwig?"

"Nothing!" said the kender with an air of offended innocence. "But I think you could pry this open now."

Caramon edged his way toward the dais, noticing, as he moved, that the weaving arms were becoming more real. There were now too many to duck, and the warrior braced himself when the first touched him. But it passed right through his body as if he were as insubstantial as they.

"Hurry, Caramon!" said Earwig in excitement. "I can't wait to see what's inside."

"I can," muttered the warrior.

He stepped up to the box. Glancing around him one last time, he propped his sword on the side of the box, spat on his hands, and rubbed them together. He braced himself, grasped the top, and heaved.

There was a hissing sound. The lid opened so easily that he nearly fell on top of it. Gingerly, holding the heavy top open with both hands, he gazed into the box.

"Let me see! Let me see!" shouted Earwig, shoving his head beneath Caramon's big arm.

Jewels sparkled in the flickering torchlight. Earwig's small hand darted forward.

"Hey!" said Caramon, panting beneath the weight of the lid. "We're here to destroy those . . . not steal them."

"I've never stolen anything in my life!" Earwig cried indignantly. He lifted a glass tube filled with glowing blue sapphires from the box.

"Look at this!" he said in awe. "Did you ever see anything more beautiful?" A line of blue light trailed from the jewels back into the box.

"I don't think you should do that," Caramon said nervously. "Put it—"

Without warning, one of the hands reached out, grabbed the tube, and replaced it in the box. Caramon braced himself for an attack, but the hand returned to its incomprehensible wavings.

"Wasn't that great, Caramon? Let's see if it'll do it again!"

Earwig reached in and took hold of a glass tube lined

with black obsidian. Rubies and emeralds and sapphires gleamed in the center. The kender pulled, but he couldn't budge it.

The hands seemed to pause in their wavings. Caramon had the uneasy impression he was being watched by unseen eyes.

"Earwig," he said in a low undertone. "I think you've found something there."

"I know, but"—the kender tugged, his face turning red—"it won't come out!"

Caramon risked a glance. "Give it a twist." His arms were beginning to give beneath the lid's weight. "Hurry! I don't think I can hold this open much longer!"

Earwig put both hands around the tube and tried to rotate it, but his fingers slipped on the smooth container.

"Try the other way," Caramon suggested.

He was watching the hands closely and could have sworn that he saw the fingers twitch in alarm. We're doing something that somebody doesn't like, Caramon thought grimly. He only wished he knew what.

The kender turned the tube to his left.

"I've got it!" he shouted. "It's giving way!" He twisted it harder.

"Great! Keep going and—"

A shadowy hand suddenly gripped Caramon around the neck. Two others caught him beneath his shoulders and began to tug at him. He exerted his strength against them, keeping a tight grip on the lid.

"I don't know . . . how long . . . I can keep this . . . raised!" he gasped. "Hurry!"

"Hurry? Hurry and do what?" Earwig cried frantically, twisting faster.

The tube was slowly coming out of its hole. Hands reached for him, but seemed unwilling to touch him, perhaps because he held the tube.

"What am I supposed to do after I get it?"

Caramon could only grunt in answer. His face was twisted in pain, turning red with the strain of trying to hang on to the lid and pulling against the hands.

"I've got it!" Earwig yanked out the tube.

He stared into it, shook it, and held it against his ear, listening for a sound. Fingers on the hands near him curled and twitched, as if in an agony of frustration.

Caramon issued a smothered scream. More hands were descending, gripping him, endeavoring to haul him up into the air. He clung to the lid with all his strength.

"Do something!"

"I'm trying!" Earwig gasped.

He turned the tube over and over. "Argh!" he finally cried in frustration and smashed the tube against the side of the box.

A high-pitched keening noise cut through the air, piercing the head. Caramon had never heard anything so horrible, felt anything more painful. He dropped the lid, and it closed with a slam. Hands wrapped around his throat and began choking out his life.

Shoulders hunched to try to block out the noise, Earwig bashed the dark cylinder against the side of the box again.

Caramon felt himself losing consciousness. His neck was thick, but the hands were strong and were slowly cutting off his air.

Earwig, looking at his friend, saw the warrior's mouth gaping open, his eyes bulging from his head.

"Break!" the kender commanded frantically, and hit the tube against the box once again. The bottom of the tube gave way, and a smaller tube slid out. Inside it was a band of gold.

"Oh, no!" Earwig groaned.

Kender aren't afraid anything, but this one had definitely had his fill of rings.

I have to do something, though. They're killing Caramon. He shook the tube and the ring rolled out into his palm.

What do you want of me? boomed a voice.

"You again!" Earwig muttered.

The hands near him curled into fists. One swung at him. Earwig ducked. The air whistling past from the force of the blow nearly knocked him down. He looked at Caramon. His friend had lost consciousness and was hanging limply in the grip of the hands that were slowly hauling the big man up into the air.

Earwig looked back at the ring.

"I want out of here!" he cried.

Put the ring on your thumb, Your Dark Majesty, and the gate will open.

"Well, I'm not a Dark Majesty, but there's certainly no time to go and find someone who is. Here goes!" said Earwig and shoved the ring onto his thumb.

"No!" shrieked a terrible-sounding voice, and it seemed to the kender that five voices were actually screaming at once. "It is not the time! I do not have the power of the Eye!"

A blast of air hit the kender, knocking him flat on top of Caramon. The darkness rushed past him, and then the street rushed past him and then buildings and ugly creatures rushed past him, all seeming to be going somewhere in a tremendous hurry. Oddly enough, however, they all seemed to be going backward.

And then the rushing ceased.

Earwig, feeling tumbled and upsidedown, didn't know for a minute if he was on his head or his feet. In actuality, he was on Caramon. And Caramon was lying on a white stone street.

Earwig knelt down and put his small hand over Caramon's heart. It was beating strongly. He could feel the warrior's chest rise and fall, breathing in air. But the big man was unconscious. Earwig could hear sounds of fighting quite near him—horrible screams and shrieks.

"Like a bunch of cats in barrel," said the kender. Looking around, he saw the magical lights—dim but shining. He saw the arcade and the inn where Catherine had kissed him.

"We're back!" he said, slightly disappointed. "Oh, well. It was fun while it lasted."

Settling down beside Caramon, waiting for the warrior to regain consciousness, Earwig admired his new ring.

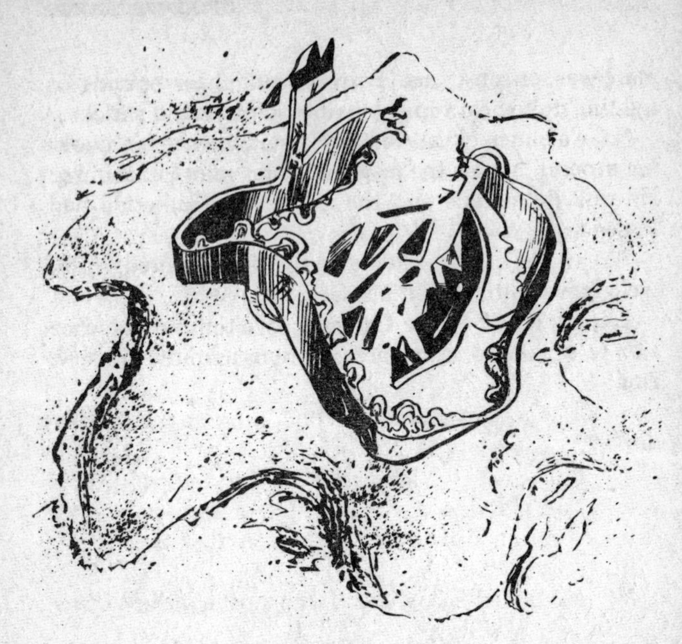

CHAPTER 27

"AND what if I were to tell you that I am not interested in an alliance with the Dark Queen?" Raistlin asked softly.

Shavas raised her eyebrows in disbelief. "You think you will gain that much power without Her Dark Majesty making some attempt to stop you?" The woman began to laugh. "This is one of the reasons you are so incredibly attractive to me, Raistlin. You fear nothing."

" 'Those who live in fear fall prey to their own disquiet.' "

"Yes. Eyavel would be one of your favorite authors. 'And you, gentle reader, must follow in my path, for I am the way you must know.' Ali Azra, another of your favorites." Shavas set her half-emptied brandy glass down on the sideboard. "The wizard knew where to turn, who to worship. Like him, you could find great power. And great pleasure."

The woman removed her gown, twisting open the buttons one at a time, twenty-three in all. She shrugged her shoulders with a slow, graceful movement. The silk gown fell to the floor. Firelight gleamed on her white skin, casting a ruddy glow that emphasized the shadowy curves of her body.

She moved near him. Reaching up, Shavas touched Raistlin's face with the tips of her fingers.

The mage clasped her hands, feeling the coolness of her flesh against the burning warmth of his own. A shudder ran through his body, a shudder that the woman could sense.

Shavas pulled away from him, staring at him uncertainly, suspiciously.

Raistlin lifted his brandy glass, but his shaking hand nearly dropped it. He set it back down and turned abruptly to look at the game board, staring at the piece of his champion. As he watched, he saw it twist into a hideous, undead warrior. The mage sat down, afraid that his legs would not support him.

"Your offer is tempting . . ."

"Then you accept?"

Shavas knelt beside the mage's chair. Placing her hands on his, she gazed, smiling, up into the hourglass eyes. She seemed certain of victory.

Raistlin shook his head. "I cannot."

"Why? I've offered you everything! The chance to rule with me. Power to forge your own destiny. Myself!"

The mage said nothing. He did not look at her, but

gazed at the board and his destroyed game piece.

Shavas slowly and with dignity rose to her feet. "You desire me. You can't deny it!"

Without looking up, the mage replied, "That I desire you, lady, I cannot deny. But I can deny my desire."

"Then you are a fool!"

"Perhaps," Raistlin said in a subdued voice. "Perhaps. But I've won the game."

Reaching out his hand, he removed the Dark Queen from the board and tossed it contemptuously into the fire.

He could feel the woman's anger rise up around him, more scorching than the flames.

"You? You've won nothing!" Shavas cried. "Nothing but your own destruction!"

She raised her arms into the air. Dark bolts of lightning formed at her fingertips, surrounding her naked body with a cold, enervating halo. Her long hair rose around her head like writhing snakes. Her eyes vanished, sinking into deep pools of blackness.

Raistlin rose to his feet, leaning on the Staff of Magius.

"That puny toy will not save you! You will die by—" The woman's voice cracked, then rose in a terrified scream. "What is happening?"

"The magics you summoned are growing beyond the confines of your ability to control them," Raistlin answered.

"Help me!" Shavas screamed. Black lightning streaked down from the sky, engulfing the woman's naked body. She reached for Raistlin, but her hands were beginning to wither, the flesh melting from the bones.

"I cannot," said the mage. "I am the cause of your destruction!"

Shavas writhed in agony. "One day you will fall! One day the Dark Queen will have you!"

"No," answered Raistlin. "No matter what happens, I will always be my own."

The woman's body slowly disintegrated until all that was left was a pile of dust on the carpet of the library. In its center lay a necklace; the fire opal glistened with a mockery of life.

Raistlin stood unmoving, watching the dust of Shavas stir, clutching for life. Walking over, he lifted the Staff of Magius and brought it down with crushing force on the necklace. The fire opal exploded.

Reaching around, grabbing a book, Raistlin soaked it in brandy and hurled it into the fire. The binding began to blacken and curl as the flames consumed the golden words, *Brothers Majere.*

Raistlin thrust the tip of his staff into the fire, holding it in the coals until the end burned brightly. Bringing out the flaming staff, the mage touched it to the curtains, the furniture, and, finally, the game board. Flames crackled. The air filled with smoke.

Raistlin tapped the staff on the floor and its fire died, leaving the black wood smooth, cold, and unscarred.

The mage turned and walked out of the burning house.

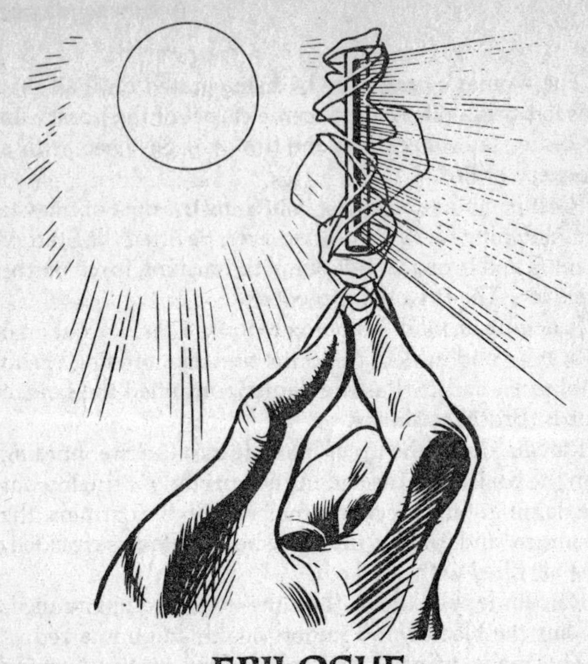

EPILOGUE

Raistlin and Caramon stood outside the south gate of Mereklar, beyond the city's white confines.

"—and the woman rushed back to her home, screaming and waving her arms." Earwig waved his own arms to illustrate. "The next day, there was a knock at the door. Know who it was?"

Catherine shook her head, "No. Who?"

"Dizzy's hoopak!" Earwig tumbled to the ground and rolled around in uncontrolled mirth.

Catherine stood there, lips twitching.

"Don't you get it?" Earwig asked after a moment, sitting up.

Catherine raised her eyes to the heavens, a gesture she would come to repeat often. The young woman was dressed in leather pants and a long, buckskin tunic. Soft, supple boots hugged her legs, and she carried a pack on her back. In her hand she held a small tangle of wire—the gift Earwig had given her. She tossed it in the air. The bead inside caught the sun, flashing brightly. Catching the wire as it fell, Catherine winked at the kender.

Earwig, grinning, winked back. The two shared a wonderful secret, a secret that was about to lead them on what the kender hoped would be another wonderful adventure.

Caramon shuffled his feet. "I wish you'd change your mind and travel with us. At least as far as the Black Cat."

"Can't," said Earwig, almost ready to explode with excitement. "We have a Very Important Mission. You see, it's this wire—"

Catherine prodded him in the back. "Hush up," she said. "It's also a Very Secret Mission."

"That's right," said Earwig, rubbing the ring on his thumb. "Well, good-bye, Caramon. Good-bye, Raistlin. It sure was fun!"

Raistlin started to say something, then began to cough violently. Clutching his chest, he leaned on the staff to maintain his balance. Caramon looked at him in concern.

"Are you sure *you* can make it?"

"Are you sure you can?" Raistlin cast a scathing glance at his brother, who was bandaged and walking stiffly and painfully.

Drawing a white cloth from his robes, the mage dabbed his lips. The cloth came away stained red with blood. "If you must know," he whispered, "I have no desire to spend another night in this city."

Caramon glanced around. The gate was empty, unguarded. The streets were filled with people hurrying from door to door, each relating to another his own version of the terrifying wonders that had occurred during the night. The city was in chaos, its leaders dead. Rumor had it that they had perished, fighting alongside the Lord of the Cats to protect the city from some great evil. The walls of Mereklar knew better, but few in the city paid any attention to the new carvings.

A cat carrying a newborn kitten in her mouth hurried past on light feet, moving her family from the wilderness into the city that was said to welcome felines. Several townsfolk, spotting the cat, knelt down to make overtures.

"I still think we should say good-bye to Lady Shavas," Caramon said.

Raistlin glanced back to the center of Mereklar where a thin column of black smoke still lingered in the air.

"No." The mage spoke from the depths of his hood. When it seemed Caramon was going to persist, he gently laid a hand on his brother's arm. "Come. We must go."

"Oh, here, Raist." Earwig drew the mage's cure—the bag of pungent herbs—from his pouch. "You dropped it. You really did!" said the kender, eyes wide.

"I didn't drop it, Earwig," said Raistlin. "I threw it a—" He paused, then said, "That is . . . you may keep it, if you want."

"I may! Gosh, thanks!"

"Thank you, Earwig, for your help," Raistlin said. He lifted his eyes and fixed them on the girl.

Take care of him.

The words formed in Catherine's mind. Startled, she nodded her head. "I will," she promised.

"Well, be seein' you, Earwig," said Caramon. "Good luck with your adventuring."

The twins started down the road in one direction,

Catherine and Earwig turned the other. They were walking past what had once been the blank walls of Mereklar when Earwig suddenly stopped and stared.

"Wow!" he said in awe.

Tears filled his eyes, and he ran his hand across the stone on which was carved a kender perched bravely on the back of a carriage in the Abyss. And there was another carving, of a kender hero slaying a demon. And a third, of a kender gallantly thrusting his hand into a deadly box. . . .

"Hey, Caramon! Raistlin!" Earwig shouted in wild excitement.

The twins—small figures in the distance—turned. The mage was leaning on his brother's arm. Both looked sad and weary and in pain.

"Never mind," said Earwig softly.

" 'Bye!" shouted the kender, waving the pouch. "Say 'hi' to Cousin Tas for me!"

* * * * *

The journey back to the Black Cat was long and tiring for both brothers. They had to stop often to rest. Near midday, Raistlin turned off the path and entered the forest. Caramon, as usual, stopped to wait for him, but this time Raistlin glanced back and gestured.

"Come, Caramon."

"Sure. Is something wrong?" the warrior asked in concern.

"We must speak."

Caramon felt himself grow cold. The warrior had awakened from a deep, nightmare-ridden sleep to find himself lying in a bed in Barnstoke Hall, his brother watching over him, guarding his rest. Raistlin had treated his brother's wounds and told him that it was all over, it was time to leave Mereklar.

"Then the city's safe?" Caramon had asked.

"I'll tell you all later, my brother!" Raistlin had said. "When I feel the time is right."

That time, seemingly, was now.

The twins left the road. Walking into a sparse forest, they picked their way carefully through the undergrowth. Raistlin moved slowly, his strength waning. Caramon grimaced with every step.

"Does your shoulder hurt?" Raistlin asked.

"Like fire," Caramon admitted.

"I will change the dressings."

The mage's slender hands, which could be gentle when he wanted them to be, ministered to Caramon's wound, washing it with cool water from the stream. Raistlin spread a salve of his own invention over the inflamed area. Caramon grunted, sighing in relief as the balm eased his pain.

Raistlin settled himself on the bank of the stream and stared for long moments into the rippling water. Caramon waited in trepidation. He had never seen his brother so withdrawn, so silent and preoccupied.

"Shavas is dead," said Raistlin suddenly.

"What?" Caramon gasped. "Dead! How—"

"I killed her."

Caramon made a strangled sound. Raistlin glanced up at him. His twin was gazing at him in horror. The expression on his brother's face was familiar. Raistlin had seen it once before—in the Tower of High Sorcery. The mage's thin lips twisted in bitterness.

"Perhaps I should explain—"

"Yes, perhaps you should!" Caramon's voice grated harshly.

"I will start at the beginning. Since her banishment from the world, the Dark Queen has always sought a way to reenter. She lacks the strength to do so on her own, and so she decided to attempt to take advantage of the power unleashed by the Great Eye.

"To this end, she sent her agents into Mereklar. The gods of neutrality were tricked by Takhisis and her cohorts into building the city, not knowing, at the time, that they were forging an entrance from the Abyss into the world.

"The gods of good discovered the plot, however, and constructed the city's three gates in such a way that they would close if the forces of evil tried to escape. In addition, to make amends for the part he played in the trickery, the Cat Lord offered his services and those of his kind to guard the city. But that, my brother, is another story and one which I have neither the breath nor the inclination to relate."

"Agents?" said Caramon, regarding his brother skeptically. "Who were the Dark Queen's agents in Mereklar?"

"The nine members of the council—"

"But there were ten members," interrupted Caramon.

"And Lady Shavas," Raistlin concluded softly.

The warrior rose to his feet, glaring at his brother in anger.

"Sit still, Caramon, and listen!"

Pierced by Raistlin's golden-eyed stare, Caramon subsided and reluctantly sat back down.

"The council members were, in fact, demons from the Abyss who murdered the original members and took their form and features. Lady Shavas was . . . " Raistlin hesitated.

"Was what?" Caramon demanded.

"An . . . evil wizardess," the mage lied, his gaze leaving his brother, moving to gaze at the water. "This is the chain of events as I have been able to reconstruct it.

"The demons arrived in Mereklar and, aware of the prophecy, immediately began to get rid of the city's cats. They reduced the feline population slowly, in hopes that they would not arouse suspicion, but it didn't work. The townspeople became upset and demanded action. To keep up the pretense, the Dark Queen's agents were forced to appear to be interested in hiring someone to solve the mystery. That was why they posted that reward announcement."

"And that was why Lord Manion tried to kill us!" Caramon said, his suspicion starting to crumble beneath the weight of his brother's words.

"Yes. When that attempt failed, we made it to the Black Cat Inn and revealed our intent to go to Mereklar. The demons feared then to kill us outright, afraid it would start a panic—perhaps even a revolt—in the city. Councillor Shavas had to pretend to be thankful to see us. She had to make a show of offering us the job. I don't believe she was ever much afraid of us," Raistlin added dryly. "She knew she had a hold on us both."

Caramon's face burned. He lowered his head and moodily began to toss bits of bark into the stream. "Go on."

"Shavas even managed to gain control of the kender, trapping Earwig with the gold ring. It turned him into a spy and eventually put him under the sway of the Dark Queen.

"When we were at the Black Cat, I had seen a magical line of power flowing into Mereklar. I discovered three of them, forming a triangle that ended at the councillor's house. I didn't understand their meaning until we visited the cave of the dead wizard. Our doing so, by the way, was all arranged by the Cat Lord. As a demi-god, he could not interfere directly, but he managed, nonetheless, to guide us toward the truth. I have the feeling"—Raistlin smiled slightly—"that Bast does not always play by the rules, even those laid down by heaven.

"The dead wizard showed me what I needed to know—both about Mereklar and about Shavas."

"He didn't say anything about her!" Caramon protested.

"He did. To me."

"Why would he?"

"To avenge himself, avenge his death. Shavas killed him, you see, my brother. He was a threat to her. He knew the truth. 'A mask of flesh.'" Raistlin sighed. "I saw her truly for what she was the first time I met her. I saw—" He paused, shuddering.

"What?"

Raistlin looked at his twin intently, then sighed and glanced away. "It doesn't matter what I saw. You wouldn't understand. At any rate, I knew the truth. I knew what she was. I knew why she had tried to have you assassinated—"

"I don't believe it!" Caramon shook his head stubbornly.

"Don't persist in being a fool! She was the only one who knew we would be returning to the inn at that time that night. She sent her assassin ahead of us, to wait for us in our room."

"But it was me he tried to kill!"

"So that you would no longer be around to protect me."

"Oh, you're saying she wanted you?" Caramon sneered.

"Yes, but not the way you imagine. She wanted . . . my soul."

Raistlin whispered the word. Caramon, seeing his brother's strained face, could not repress a shiver. Against his will, he was beginning to believe.

"When the attempt to kill you failed," the mage continued, "Shavas seduced you, rendering you helpless to harm her. She sought to catch me in a magical trap. That, however, failed. She was not too concerned, believing that I, too, would fall under her spell as had you. Then, disaster struck.

"The Lord of the Cats, enraged by the murder of his people, appeared. He knew the demons for what they were, but not why they were here. He tried to get information from them. When that failed, he started killing them, one by one, hoping to scare the others and rouse the townspeople to a knowledge of their danger.

"The rest of what happened after that—about the gate, the demons' entry into the world, and their failure—you know, my brother, for you were part of the reason they failed." Raistlin fell silent.

"Shavas?" Caramon persisted, softly.

"Yes, Shavas. I knew she had to be stopped. She was supremely powerful. If she were free to act, she would have insured her Queen's entry. You and the kender and perhaps even the Cat Lord would have fallen. And so, I prepared a poison. I took it with me to her house and I put it in the brandy. To allay her suspicions, I drank the poison along with her."

Caramon sucked in his breath, clenched his hands to stop them from trembling. He couldn't believe his twin's terrible calm. He stared at Raistlin wildly.

"But you're not—you won't—"

"Die? No, the poison did not affect me. You see, my brother, I was able, at last, to command the power of the Great Eye. I developed a poison that would channel the Eye's power and destroy Shavas."

"I don't understand!" Caramon let his head fall into his hands.

"It's simple." Raistlin spoke like a teacher to a dullard pupil. "When induced into a user of magic, the poison I made causes all magical energy suffusing an area to flow into the wizard. After I refused her offer to align myself with the Dark Queen, Shavas cast a spell to destroy me. She destroyed herself, instead."

"But, since you drank the poison—" Caramon hesitated, staring in disbelief.

"Yes." Raistlin nodded. "If I had tried to cast a spell, it would have destroyed me instantly. I left myself defenseless. But it was the only way . . . the only way."

"I can't believe it," said Caramon, but he spoke in a tone that admitted his belief. "She was so beautiful! So young!"

Raistlin began to cough. Hiding his face behind the white cloth he held to his mouth, he gazed at his brother from the shadows of his cowl.

I could tell you the truth. I could tell you that she was a lich. I could tell you she had been alive since before the Cataclysm. I could tell you that she had been Councillor of Mereklar since its beginning, taking the guise of one person, then another. I could tell you her life was bound in that opal necklace, giving her the semblance of youth, of beauty. I could tell you, my brother, that the lips you kissed were, in reality, rotting and decaying flesh. . . .

"Yes, my brother," said Raistlin, reaching out his hand to touch Caramon's arm. "She was very beautiful."

The big man lifted his head and gazed at his twin in astonishment. Gingerly, fearing rebuff, he laid his hand on his brother's.

"I'm sorry," he said.

Raistlin curled his thin fingers around his brother's hand and held it tightly. The twins sat quietly together for a long time beside the stream, watching the water flow.

ACKNOWLEDGEMENTS

I would like to thank the following people for their indispensable aid:

Margaret Weis, the Queen of Darkness, whose teachings and advice are like a much-needed chocolate-covered cattle prod.

Barbara Peekner, my agent, a mysterious voice at the end of the phone.

My friends and other strangers, for encouragement and support.